THROUGH THE BARRIER

Larry, holding Celia close to him, pressed the activating stud.

Suddenly the light changed, became brighter: mottled sunlight, fractured by myriad leaves overhead, had replaced the artificial light of the laboratory.

Celia looked in wonder at the surrounding forest. "No Evanston . . . no Chicago."

She was entranced as they explored the virgin woodland that, in this new world, replaced the teeming metropolis . . .

. . . until a coarse blanket engulfed her head and remorseless, unseen hands bound her tightly. . . .

SHADOW OF EARTH

PHYLLIS EISENSTEIN

A DELL BOOK

Published by
Dell Publishing Co., Inc.
1 Dag Hammarskjold Plaza
New York, New York 10017

Dell ® TM 681510, Dell Publishing Co., Inc.

ISBN: 0-440-18032-5

Printed in the United States of America
First printing—September 1979

*To my brother Merv,
because it's all his fault . . .*

*. . . and for Robin Shuster,
who will understand
when she reads Chapter Two*

SHADOW
OF EARTH

CHAPTER ONE

Celia discovered the guns while searching for her sweater in the walk-in closet. As she rummaged among the crowded racks, the heel of her sandal caught on a tenpenny nail near the baseboard; she lost her balance, pulling down a heap of flashy ski togs in a wild attempt to catch herself. Growling softly, she rehung the garments, then bent to investigate the offending nail. It was coated with paint like the woodwork, and several clear, black scratches now betrayed its camouflage. She plucked angrily at the thing, mentally castigating both carpenter and painter for their careless conspiracy. At her third and fiercest tug, a large section of flooring came up with the nail.

The trap opened into a four-foot crawl space beneath the house. Light from the naked bulb overhead spilled across two crates lying side by side in the hole. Celia stretched out on her stomach and reached down toward the nearest one. The lid was fastened so lightly that her prying fingers lifted it with little effort. Nestled inside, under a cover of slick oilcloth, were a dozen gleaming rifles.

She broke a fingernail on the second crate before deciding it was sealed too tightly for anything short of a crowbar. After lowering the lid of the first, Celia eased the trapdoor back into place; it settled with a faint *whump* that blew dust in her face. She emerged from the closet to hear Larry's footsteps fast approaching the bedroom door. When he entered, she was casually swabbing her fingers with a tissue.

"Celia, what are you doing?" he inquired in a tone of mild exasperation.

"Looking for the sweater I left here last week. That closet could use a good cleaning." She dropped the dirty tissue on the nightstand.

"Why didn't you ask me for it? I usually know where things are around here . . . until you rearrange them." He crossed the room to his dresser, opened the second drawer, and pulled out a fuzzy, peach-colored cardigan. He tossed it onto the bed.

"I didn't want to bother you, *querido*," she said in Spanish, stepping so close that her breasts grazed his arm. She reached up and stroked his chin with a forefinger. "I thought you were busy in the living room, conjugating verbs."

"Terminé," he replied, also switching tongues. He continued with carefully measured phrases: "I thought if I finished quickly, you would not have enough time to wash all the windows and scrub the floors."

She laughed and kissed his chin. "Your subjunctive-conditional construction is excellent, dearest. But I wouldn't scrub your floors for you, not even if I were planning to move in."

"It would save a lot of carfare."

She laid her head on his shoulder and sighed. "Oh, my darling, if only I *could*. My parents disapprove of *this* situation, but at least they don't forbid it. If I moved out of my baby-doll bedroom, they might disown me; I'm too close to my degree to take any chance like that."

"Maybe it is better this way," he murmured, nuzzling her ear. His hands traced the curve of her spine and came to rest on her fleshy rump. "You are already too much of a distraction. How could I finish my Project if I spent all my time with you?" He molded her slender body to his own.

"Amor mio," she whispered, guiding his hand to the zipper of her skirt.

The unmade bed received them and was soon responding to their easy rhythms.

They had known each other for three months. Larry Meyers was in his sixth year of graduate study at Northwestern University, approaching his Ph.D. with infinite patience. His family had long since given up on his scholastic career—except for an uncle, who lent him, rent free, a shabby frame cottage near the Evanston campus. There he lived on a tight budget, augmenting his slim stipend with modest poker winnings. He ate frugally and seldom dated. When he approached the Romance Languages Department for a Spanish tutor, he was appalled at the fees quoted. But he wanted a basic proficiency in Spanish as soon as possible, so he agreed to hire the first available instructor.

Celia Ward was only twenty and lived with her parents on the far north side of Chicago. She had a flair for languages and a ready fluency in Spanish, French, and Italian; recently she had started toying with Portuguese, simply as a summer diversion. Spanish, however, was her first love; to the annoyance of several professors, she spoke it with a distinct Argentine accent, acquired through friendship with a young man from Buenos Aires. She felt the easy, slurring Argentine mode lent an individuality to her speech that other students in the department lacked. She enjoyed tutoring freshmen, and during her third year at the university, she earned almost a thousand dollars that way. By June, however, her students had trickled away, leaving her with more free time than money; when Larry Meyers called, she quickly agreed to devote her summer to his instruction.

His house was a short bus-ride from her home, and at first she gave him three two-hour sessions a week, at ten dollars each. But she often stayed longer. Soon she began to check on his studies over the weekends, and even on days between lessons. At last she waived her regular charge, to settle for coffee and his company. She was smitten by his pale gray eyes and unruly waves of sandy hair, but mostly by the engaging smile which lit up his whole face at the smallest provocation. She would croon to him in Spanish as they lay entwined, sprawling in the slick, cooling sweat of exhausted passion. And thus she also taught him the many words not listed in *Langenscheidt's*.

Her long blonde hair lay in a golden flow across the pillow as he cradled her head in his arm. Absently, he twirled a few strands between his fingers as he gazed at the ceiling. "You start a new semester next week, don't you?" he asked, reverting to English.

She nodded, rubbing her cheek against his shoulder.

"Your last year. The most important one."

Again she nodded.

"You'll be busy. We won't see each other much." His arm tightened on her.

Celia laughed softly. "Wishful thinking, *querido*. Some things are more important than homework." She rolled over and sat up, stretching. "Besides," she added, grinning impishly over a pale shoulder, "you still owe me a look at the Project."

"Celia, I've told you a thousand times, there's really nothing to see. Not yet, anyway; maybe never. I'm having some trouble with it."

She gathered up her garments and began to dress, facing the mirror. "Are you strapped for cash, darling?"

He shrugged. "No, not really."

"You've been buying a lot of new clothes lately."

"I've been very lucky at poker lately."

"The university's going to clamp down on campus gambling."

"Oh? That's too bad. The exposure will hurt their image."

Fully clothed, Celia gazed at the reflection of Larry's reclining body. "Do you love me, *querido?*"

He raised himself on his elbows and smiled. "Come on; you know I do."

"Then . . . will you tell me what the guns are for?"

Slowly, the smile drained from his face. "You found the guns," he said in an even voice.

She nodded, her eyes meeting his in the mirror.

"How—no, never mind; that doesn't matter now." He looked pensive. "It's not what you think."

She shrugged. "What do I think?"

"I mean, I'm not part of a radical plot or anything; I'm not stockpiling for an assault on the university. You see, the guns—well . . ." He frowned, unwilling to finish the sentence, and the silence stretched thin and cold as Celia waited, motionless, for the rest. At last, he cleared his throat and admitted, "They do have a certain relationship to my Project."

She turned to face him. "Don't you think you should show me what your Project is all about now?"

He sat up and swung his feet over the side of the bed. He motioned her toward him. "I'll tell you." He pulled her down on his lap, grasped her chin firmly, and stared straight into her blue eyes. "I'll tell you, but you must promise me you'll never let anyone know about either the guns or the Project. Promise me!" His eyes were like gray agates, without the familiar warmth that Celia knew; a bold rim of white around each iris underscored his intensity.

"It isn't . . . illegal, is it?" She didn't want to say that, not quite so baldly, but she didn't know how else to broach the question.

He blinked and smiled, metamorphosing back into the affectionate Larry she knew. "No, it isn't illegal; but I can't let anyone else know about it. At least, not yet. I've got to know you'll keep quiet. Believe me, this isn't a frivolous request."

"Okay," she replied, leaning in close to immerse herself in the firm comfort of his arms.

He hugged her tight. "Celia, if you weren't so damned curious, you'd be perfect."

When he finally released her, Celia went to the bathroom to wash her face and comb her tousled hair. Opening the medicine cabinet, she withdrew the bottle of Morning-After Pills and shook one into her hand. She swallowed it dry, savoring the bitter aftertaste as emblematic of the power of medical science. She had started on the old steroid Pill during her first year of college but had suffered extreme nausea at the beginning of each month; she gladly switched to the new contraceptive when it first came on the market. Her parents were vaguely aware of her sexual habits and disapproved in various nonverbal ways, though they had been rather less negative in the days of the young Argentine, who came of a wealthy upper-class family.

She straightened her skirt one last time and returned to the bedroom. Larry was again fully dressed; when she pronounced herself ready, he produced an antique iron key from the top drawer of his bureau. "Let us now dispel the mystery," he said.

The door to the second bedroom had always been closed while Celia was in the house. "It's full of junk for my Project," Larry had told her. "It's a mess." She had believed him, but that did not keep her from glancing at it every time she passed through the dining room, nor from testing the knob when Larry wasn't present. Once she even brought an old key from home to try in the lock; it slipped in easily and turned halfway, but then it stuck, and she was almost unable to remove it before his return.

Larry opened the door.

Celia had expected a musty clutter of paraphernalia, like an old attic. Instead the bright overhead light revealed a large, clean room, furnished only with a wooden workbench, a steel filing cabinet, and two boxlike consoles that might have been ham-radio sets. A large metallic pole stood oddly alone in the middle of the room, and a circular section of the floor around it was sunken a couple feet below the rest. The well was about ten feet across, its border painted orange, and the ceiling above was likewise marked with an orange circle. The pole, etched overall with an intricate silver pattern, stood as the common axis of the two circles, and a small red light bulb sprouted from a socket near its midpoint. The two consoles sat on the normal floor level, on opposite edges of the large round depression.

After a moment, Celia noticed something else: an outdoor freshness pervaded the air—not aerosol-can outdoor, but real tree-leaf-green outdoor. On the back wall of the room, however, was the only window, coated with grime, its frosted pane admitting a mere ghost of late-afternoon sunlight.

"Behold the laboratory of the mad scientist," said Larry. He swept a pile of rumpled canvas bags off the workbench and seated himself there.

Celia stepped forward hesitantly, stopping when her toes were within an inch of the orange line.

"It's safe," Larry said. "The power's off."

She circled the well, staring in turn at each of the consoles, trying to make some sense out of the array of dials, switches, and telltales clustered on their faces.

"What is it?" she asked at last.

"A portal to another world."

Her eyebrows raised skeptically. "Mars? Or Venus?"

Larry chuckled. "Not that kind of other world. Not at all." He held out his hand to her. "Come here, and I'll tell you all about it. I've wanted to tell someone for a long time, but I could never bring myself to trust anyone else with the secret."

She pulled herself up on the workbench, and he wrapped an arm about her shoulders.

"I was working on the development of a limited locus projection of repellant field ambience—in plainer language, a shell or shield of force, impervious to penetration by any form of matter or energy. I had some new ideas on the propagation of discontinuous fields, and I thought I'd make a big splash in the scientific community, not to mention the history books. But when it came to building the prototype, I had one difficulty: the first time I established a localized field with a certain gradient, the field generator disappeared."

"Destroyed?" asked Celia.

He shook his head. "Hurled away into some other space, some other dimension of existence. The field protected what was inside it, all right—by removing it from our universe.

"The most important part of my apparatus was lost; I thought my Project was *kaput*. Who would believe what had happened? Anyway, I didn't want anyone to know—not until *I* knew exactly what it meant.

"I told Professor Carlson, my research adviser, that a freakish circuit overload had fused the generator beyond any hope of repair. I actually had to dummy up an artifact that would pass as the remains of the generator, as well as a cookbook explanation of what caused the overload. I got a rather strong reprimand for not following the authorized schedule of procedures, but even so he gave me a free hand to requisition materials for another generator.

"It wasn't that simple to rebuild, of course. I had to redesign it from bottom up, resolving the field into two separately generated components, to prevent any future loss of the entire apparatus.

"The setup you see here is the end product. The pole projects a cylindrical field, an 'enabling' field, to any desired distance, depending on the available power. In this case, there's a radio-isotope battery under the floor that can maintain a field of roughly five-foot radius for several lifetimes. The enabling field alone, however, does nothing but use up current. To initiate the transfer, a low-power activating field must intersect it." Leaning over to the file cabinet, he opened the top drawer and fished out a wide black leather belt with a massive square buckle of solid-plate brass. "This is the activator I use now. Laminated circuits are sewn between two strips of leather; the power cell and starting switch are embedded in the buckle." He passed it to Celia. "Of course, on my first jump, I used a bulkier harness rig."

Celia turned the belt over in her hands. Its only evident peculiarity was a small burr or stud at one corner of the buckle's underside, like a casting flaw that had not been filed smooth. Celia pressed it with her thumb, and it sank into the metal surface, popping back up when the pressure was released: a spring-loaded button. "Surely you didn't test it out on yourself?"

"Oh, no; I sent a mouse through in an activator cage, with a timer set to trigger his return trip. Of course, I had no guarantee the phase-relationship between the two fields would be preserved in the other continuum, but the cage didn't cost much, and mice are pretty cheap, too. For Marmaduke's first hop, I set the timer for ten seconds. I flicked the remote switch and he was off. Ten seconds later I heard a muffled thump, followed by a squeal, but no Marmaduke in sight; then silence." Larry grinned. "It took me a while to realize where he was; the damned cage had reappeared in the crawl space underneath the floorboards. Perhaps I wouldn't have guessed at all if I hadn't heard him squeak.

"You see, the ground level in the other world is a couple feet lower than this floor. Fortunately, the enabling field actually extended into the crawl space, where the base of the pole is anchored. If Marmaduke had fallen another six inches, he would have landed beyond the effective range of the field, forever lost.

But he came back intact and chipper, so I cut a hole in the floor and sent him back again. This time I set up a camera to photograph his return and thus determine the proper level for the floor of the pit."

"And then *you* went?"

"Oh. I sent him on a dozen more jumps, the last an hour long. He never showed any signs of damage, so I decided it was safe enough for a quick bit of sightseeing."

Celia glanced from the belt in her hands to his face. "Well, you *look* okay."

He hugged her. "I *am* okay. There's no hazard involved, and no unpleasant sensations. One second you're here, and an eyeblink later, you're there. And what a place it is! It's another Earth, very much like our own. Only everyone there speaks Spanish."

"So *that's* why you were so eager to learn!"

"That was later. At first I tried to isolate the input variables that made the field couple with this particular world; I thought there might be others that I could tune in. No such luck, though. Manipulating the various parameters only changes the size and orientation of the field, or distorts it beyond utility. I wasted months on that effort. Finally I decided to explore what I had; I made contact with the natives, communicating rather poorly with gestures . . . and that's when I realized I had to learn Spanish."

Celia took his hands in her own. "I don't mean to disparage your achievement, Larry—but are you sure you haven't just invented a fantastic new way to travel to South America?"

"Oh, I thought of that. But I've been there a dozen times now, and I'm sure it isn't South America. Or Spain. Believe me, Celia, it isn't anyplace on this Earth. And yet, it's Evanston—or rather, the space that Evanston occupies, with the same sort of rivers, the same lake, and the same kind of forest that was here before

Evanston was a gleam in a speculator's eye. Or Chicago, for that matter."

Celia frowned, perplexed. "No Chicago? But . . . how?"

Larry got down off the bench and walked slowly about the room. His eyes flickered from Celia to the glittering pole, and back again. "Think about history. It's full of turning points, forks in the road. Take the Second World War as an example: One avenue was victory for our side, and that's the one we took. The other led to victory for the Axis, which would have resulted in a very different world from the one we know. For every turning point in history, perhaps for every instant, there's a road that wasn't taken but *might* have been—an alternative to our reality. Somewhere, somehow, all of those alternatives may actually exist. I think so. At least, I believe I've stumbled on one such—one in which the Spanish settled North America instead of the English. What turning point do you suppose could have caused that? Columbus landing in Florida? I'm not a history buff; I don't know. But *something*.

"It's a very undeveloped world, Celia. Backward—a culture barely beyond the Seventeenth Century, even though their year is the same as ours. This whole area is mainly virgin forest; the nearest town has a population of three hundred. I haven't been able to find out much more than that; most of the inhabitants are illiterate trappers or farmers."

Celia slid off her perch, took a few steps, and hopped into the pit; she touched the filigreed pole with hesitant fingers. "You know," she said, not looking at Larry, "this is all kind of difficult to believe."

He shrugged. "So were flying machines, once upon a time."

"But . . . assuming it's all true, where do the guns fit in?"

"I sell them over there."

"You *sell* them?"

"It's a primitive place, Celia; mostly wilderness. Bears and cougars and even Indians are a constant threat. And the locals hunt deer and such to supplement their diet. Those guns you found in the closet are more accurate, easier to load, more reliable than their weapons. Celia, they still use muzzle-loading flintlocks over there! I grant you I'm making some money: they pay me in silver and jewelry. But they also pay in information. That's the important thing. Believe me, when I wandered around as a nosey stranger I didn't get many answers—but when I became a peddler of useful merchandise, everyone talked to me."

"But *guns.* Couldn't you have found something else they needed?"

"I learned quickly that an efficient firearm was the only real commodity I could offer them. There's nothing else they need so desperately."

She sat down on the rim of the pit, her back to him. "Well, I suppose if I can accept your gambling I shouldn't balk at gun-running."

"Don't call it that, Celia," he said in an injured tone. He kneeled close behind her, put his hands on her shoulders. "I'm not selling them in carload lots. It's not like they're machine guns, after all; they're just vintage Enfields—long obsolete by U.S. Army standards."

"Guns are guns," she replied. She cast him a sidelong glance. "What's wrong with something peaceful, like sewing machines?"

He raised an eyebrow. "Sewing machines? What made you think of that?"

Celia smiled faintly. "According to literary tradition, guns sold to Latin American *juntas* are always shipped as 'sewing machine parts.' "

"Might not be a bad idea at that, if I could find some old treadle machines."

"Maybe I should take a commission on that idea. Is it nice jewelry?"

"Several hock-shops think so."

She relaxed against his chest and sighed. "When the G-men put you away for tax-evasion, I'll bring you homemade fudge every Saturday."

"What are you talking about? I'm not making *that* kind of money!"

She looked up at him and laid a finger against his lips. "But you *will*. I know you, darling. I know those little poker games were never enough for you. You *like* money, and that's going to get you into a lot of trouble some day."

"Don't worry about it."

"But I do." Her arms slid upward and locked around his neck. "I love you very much, and I can't help worrying." She pulled him down for a kiss. When he responded satisfactorily, she ventured another question. "Why haven't you told Dr. Carlson about any of this?"

"I'm—not ready yet."

"But couldn't you get a much larger grant if you showed him what you found? Surely hordes of eminent scientists would flock to your lab, begging for a chance to work on such a spectacular project."

"I'm sure of that. So would the government, only it wouldn't exactly beg." His lips twitched in a grim smile. "I have a pretty fair notion of what our government would do with my invention. The alternate Earth never went through a full-scale Industrial Revolution—it has a planetful of raw materials just waiting to be exploited. If I revealed its existence, I might be responsible for the greatest mass plunder in the histories of *two* worlds."

"Do you really think so?"

"There's another reason, too. It would be so simple to plant an H-bomb in the alternate-world Moscow or Peking or *anywhere*, transfer it back to our world, and detonate it. No bombers necessary, no missiles to detect coming over the Pole. Just the bomb, appearing magically in Red Square."

Celia looked horror-stricken. "No! No one would order such a thing!"

"It would be tempting. I'm cynical enough to believe it could be too tempting. Can I take the chance? Would I sleep nights knowing what kind of weapon I gave my government? God, Celia, we were searching for the ideal passive *defense!*"

"What will you do then?" she asked in a small voice. "Scrap the whole thing?"

He looked at the pole pensively. "I don't know. It's my brainchild; I don't want to suppress it, but I don't want it misused, either. I just don't know."

"Before you make a final decision . . . will you give me a peek at this alternate world?"

A thin smile crept over his face. "Will I ever hear the end of it if I don't?"

"No; never."

He glanced at his watch. "Not today, though; it's getting late. You better head for home before Mama throws out your dinner."

"She won't; she thinks cold suppers will punish me for wasting my life over here with you."

"It's almost sundown. There are no streetlights on the other side, so it has to be tomorrow. Also no streets right here; I recommend you wear slacks."

"All right." Preparing to rise, Celia lifted her feet and swung back from the edge of the circle. "Tomorrow, then," she said as she stood up.

Larry nodded. "After lunch. I have a few errands to run in the morning."

"So late? I'll hardly be able to sleep tonight." She stretched and yawned nevertheless.

He reached up to brush away a lock of blonde hair that had fallen in her face. "You'll manage okay." He walked her to the front door.

On the steps, she paused and looked back at him. "Larry—you never showed me Marmaduke."

"Oh . . . I set him free when I had no further use for him. Long before I met you."

"Oh."

"See you tomorrow." He closed the door.

At exactly 1 P.M., Celia appeared on Larry's doorstep. She wore corduroy jeans and a loose, lightweight blouse that partly masked her gentle contours. "Ready?" she asked, marching straight for the back room.

Larry already wore the special belt. "I've been working on a second activator for several weeks," he said, and indeed, the workbench was now littered with tools and ribbonlike components, some of which were already joined to a leather strap. "I thought I might finish it today, but I was wrong."

"You mean I'll have to wait some more?"

"No, I can still get you there. The activating field is a cylinder about two feet in diameter; just hold me close and you'll transfer when I do."

"Is that how you take the guns along?"

"Nope. I have special canvas bags synchronized with the belt, but I don't suppose you'd care to make the transit in one of them."

"You bet; I'd much rather cling to you."

"Good. In just a minute, we'll be on our way." Larry went to the file cabinet, opened the bottom drawer, and drew out a snub-nosed .38 revolver, which he slipped into the right pocket of his slacks. A fistful of extra rounds went into the other pocket. He turned to find Celia watching him, her head cocked to one side.

"I told you there were bears and cougars in the area. Imagine you're in a Gene Autry film come to life."

"What happens if a cougar jumps us just as we arrive?"

"We probably die. Don't talk like that; you'll just make us both nervous." He made a few adjustments at each console, then hopped into the pit and flipped a single small toggle on the silver-etched pole. The little red bulb above his head blinked on. He motioned to Celia. "Stand as close to me as you can."

Celia stepped down into the circle and quickly closed the gap between them. Hooking her thumbs in his belt, she arched upward on tiptoe to reach his lips. She kissed them lingeringly, flicking her tongue against his palate. "You know, your belt vibrates," she whispered. "I can feel it with my hands."

"Yes, that shows we're within the target area. Ready?"

"Ready, darling."

He spanned her waist with his left arm, drawing her snugly against him; with his right hand, he probed behind the buckle for the stud.

Suddenly, the light changed, became brighter: mottled sunlight, fractured by myriad leaves overhead, had replaced the artificial light of the laboratory. Tall trees rose on every side—oak and elm and hickory; underfoot were loosely matted leaves and herbs, strewn in a mossy carpet over the forest floor. The scent of damp earth permeated the air, and a lazy breeze rustled the spreading boughs. Birds twittered and cackled as they skipped from branch to branch or swooped through dappled greenery, while insects softly hummed and creaked their ancient, mindless chorus.

"You're really a genius," said Celia, stepping away from Larry's arms.

"I see you weren't wholly convinced."

"I didn't know what to think." She scanned the surrounding greenery in wonder. "No Evanston," she muttered. "No Evanston at all."

"And no Lincolnwood and no Skokie, or Glencoe, or Wilmette . . . the whole Chicagoland area entirely replaced by a tiny frontier hamlet. Come on . . . I'll show you the booming metropolis of Verdura." Clasping her hand, he proceeded to thread a casual path between the trees and brush.

"Hey, are you sure you know the way back?"

"Don't fret. By this time, I could find the place blindfolded. Anyway, the belt is a perfect guide: it maintains a directional oscillation up to a hundred yards from ground zero."

With linked hands, they hiked a steady pace through the woods, ducking low branches and leaping rotten logs. Larry spied a patch of poison ivy, which they gave a wide berth. Celia startled a gray squirrel on a low limb; it chattered peevishly at them until they passed its domain. After tramping for some distance along a narrow game trail, they emerged from the trees into a small clearing, where unfiltered sunlight had parched the thickest clumps of grass to brittle straw. At first, Celia faltered in the glare, but Larry continued without a pause, leading her forward quickly; she squinted and raised a hand to shield her eyes.

As she did so, a sudden black shadow engulfed her head and shoulders, blotting out the sun and open air. She screamed and fell, half smothered by a coarse, heavy blanket. She clawed in a frenzy at the enveloping folds, kicked frantically at abrasive coils of rope that unseen captors wound about her ankles. Remorseless hands yanked her, pummeled her, held her fast while sandpaper fingers tightened the bonds unmercifully. Far away, Larry was shouting, but his words were muffled by the dense fabric; someone much closer growled a curse in Spanish, and two deafening gunshots exploded in quick succession, followed by an ominous silence.

Celia felt them bind her body with a dozen more turns of rope, the last of which nearly throttled her as it was looped about her neck. Thus bundled and trussed, she was half-carried, half-dragged through bushes and brambles. She cried out in Spanish, begging to be released—demanding it—but her abductors merely grumbled among themselves, never breaking their steady strides. Celia shouted herself hoarse before they came to a halt. Abruptly she was heaved into the air, and an instant later, a hard jolt to the midriff knocked her breath away.

She lay jacknifed over something barrel-shaped, something that snorted and jittered while anonymous hands roughly secured her to it.

With a lurch, the skittish animal began to jounce along in quick time, trotting off through the woods, taking Celia farther and farther away from the invisible portal between the worlds. "Larry!" she croaked weakly. But there was, as expected, no answer. Gasping and choking, she wept in an agony of frustration and fear.

INTERMEDIO
I

On Twelfth April, the Year of Our Lord 1587, Sir Francis Drake's privateer squadron sailed on orders from the Queen of England, its mission to hinder, by any and all means, the assembly of the Spanish Armada at Lisbon. After harrying the Iberian coast for some weeks, Drake seized Cape St. Vincent, the strategic southwestern corner of the peninsula; there he cleaned and scraped his ships, grown foul at sea, and thus effectively barred Lisbon from its major sources of supply in the Mediterranean. Of the ships that rounded the point, none escaped him, neither cargo vessels nor fishing boats; he caught and burned them all. He was especially pleased to destroy those laden with coopers' stores, for he knew the importance of hoops and barrel staves to this kind of war.

Early in June he learned of a fabulous Spanish treasure ship, bound from India and due to stop at the Azores en route to Lisbon. Its hoard, intended to pay Armada expenses, was too rich a target for Drake to resist; eagerly he sailed for the islands, intercepting the prize. He then returned directly to England, to distribute the bounty among himself and his backers. Queen Elizabeth received the largest share, which she invested in expanding the English Navy.

Because of Drake's depredations, barrels of seasoned wood were virtually unavailable to Spain for the next three years. The Armada's provisions had to be packed instead in casks of fresh-cut wood, and in such poor storage, both food and water spoiled quickly. Admiral Santa Cruz, one of the ablest commanders of his day, obtained new provisions, but he could do nothing to stop the rotting—and the resulting scurvy, dysentery, and typhus. Inevitably, the launching date of the Invincible Armada was pushed further and further ahead.

After eight months of frustration and despair, Santa Cruz took ill and died. His replacement, the Duke of Medina Sidonia, was well-meaning but no seaman, nor even a real military officer. From the beginning of his association with the enterprise, he anticipated defeat. He saw his men ravaged by disease and demoralized by delay, and his stores decomposing almost as fast as they were loaded. He saw the very elements conspiring against him: 1588 was a year of freakish storms, of wild wind and rain and hail. For three weeks, bad weather sealed the fleet into Lisbon harbor. At last Medina Sidonia lost patience and gave the order to sail, but *La Armada Invencible* was so battered by two weeks at sea that it put into Coruña, on the northern coast, for major repairs. By this time, so many sailors were sick that a hospital had to be set up on shore.

Medina Sidonia petitioned his king with a tactful request to postpone the mission. Philip the Second denied this and instructed him to sail onward as soon as possible.

By the time the Armada sighted England, the men who had recovered at Coruña were once more haggard and shaking. Medina Sidonia himself suffered, though not from the various ills of his crew: constant seasickness had killed his appetite, and he gave all commands from his bed. Weak and dispirited, the Armada made its slow way up the English Channel.

Philip's plan called for rendezvous at Flanders with an army of twenty thousand headed by the Duke of Parma. Parma had been lately waging a successful war against the rebellious Netherlands. He held the city of Sluys at the mouth of the Scheldt River—just across the Channel from the Thames Estuary, gateway to London. The Invincible Armada was intended to convoy his troop barges across the Channel.

On its second day in the Channel, the Armada met the English Navy, but the battle was indecisive; neither side had accurate firepower at any distance, and neither dared approach the other too closely. The stalemated opponents moved northward toward Sluys. There the Dutch were blockading the Scheldt, bottling up Parma's troops.

The shallow mouth of the river was guarded by flat-bottomed Dutch boats. The Armada included a number of shallow-draft vessels which could have engaged the Dutch, but Medina Sidonia was loath to divide his forces with the English at his back. Instead, he anchored off Calais and sent desperate notes to Parma.

On the night of August 7, the English seized upon a good wind to send unmanned fireships into the Spanish formation. The blazing hulks posed little danger to wary seamen, but the Spanish captains panicked, thinking these were "hellburners" loaded with gunpowder. Ship after ship cut anchor and fled into the treacherous North Sea, many to destruction in storms and along the rocky coasts of Scotland and Ireland.

The failure of the Invincible Armada marked the beginning of Spain's decline as a world power—a decline that was long and slow but inexorable. The Spanish domain was an unwieldy one; Philip dubbed it "the empire on which the sun never sets," and no one better understood how difficult its supervision for one lonely man. After his death, it dwindled away through war and revolution . . . and almost always, England was involved: the backer of the Dutch and the Portuguese, the enemy in the New World, the enemy in the continental wars of the Spanish and Austrian Succession and the Seven Years War. As Spain's fortunes waned, those of England increased, bringing forth a new Empire on which the sun never set.

But the failure of the Armada was more than just the failure of Spain; it was the beginning of the end of Roman Catholic hegemony over Europe. As self-styled Defender of the Faith, Philip had suppressed heresy throughout his realm; his persecution of the Protestant Dutch was in fact what prompted their bid for independence. The failure of the Armada left the Protestants free to flourish in northern Europe, and thereafter in the New World. Their worldly philosophy fostered the Industrial Revolution, which began in England and then spread to other Protestant countries long before it touched the Catholic world. The steam engine, invented in Scotland by a Protestant, became the key to the Industrial Age, the key to a pyramiding technology that produced the automobile, the airplane, the atomic bomb. In the last half of the Twentieth Century, the only significant frontiers left on the planet were those of human knowledge.

INTERMEDIO
II

On Twelfth April, the Year of Our Lord 1587, Sir Francis Drake's privateer squadron sailed on orders from the Queen of England, its mission to hinder, by any and all means, the assembly of the Spanish Armada at Lisbon. Late in the month, while harrying the Iberian coast, Drake learned of a fabulous Spanish treasure ship, bound from India and due to stop at the Azores en route to Lisbon. Its hoard, intended to pay Armada expenses, was a tempting target; eagerly, he sailed for the islands, where he lay in wait, cleaning and scraping his ships until the prize hove into view. . . .

Off Cape St. Vincent, cargo vessels carried seventeen hundred tons of seasoned barrel staves safely toward Lisbon. . . .

Admiral Santa Cruz personally supervised the packing and stowing of provisions, and on the tenth of August, 1587, his flagship led the Armada out of Lisbon harbor. The summer weather was beautiful, and the Spanish fleet made the run to England in good time. It met the small English Navy on its second day in the Channel; after some exchange of gunfire, Santa Cruz boldly ordered his ships to approach the English, grapple and board. The superior Spanish numbers overwhelmed the English fleet, and before dusk the Channel was clear of defenders.

Two mornings later, the blockading Dutch were scattered before the Spanish might, and Parma's troops made an easy crossing from Sluys. Untrained militiamen armed only with pikes and pitchforks attempted to oppose the invasion; they were mowed down by hardened Spanish regulars. In two weeks, London was occupied. In two months, all but a few isolated pockets of resistance had been pacified.

Philip the Second arrived in autumn for his wedding to Elizabeth, who had been absolved of her sins and admitted to the One True Church. Immediately after the nuptial mass, the Pope himself crowned Philip King of England. His first official act as monarch was to declare Protestantism illegal. Thousands of recalcitrant "heretics" were burned at his orders; thousands more fled penniless to the continent, to the remaining enclaves of dissent, mainly in the Germanies. Eventually Philip's armies followed them. After a time, the Pope crowned him again, with a new and greater title.

By the end of his life, Philip ruled the vastest empire the world had ever seen. But it was an unwieldy domain, too much for any one man to supervise, and in the centuries following his death, it decayed gradually into myriad separate fiefdoms. As the Twentieth Century dawned, the mother country was bereft of most of her European realms, and of many others in all but name.

Though Spain's hegemony was transitory, the reign of Catholicism was not. Eclipsed as a great power, England could no longer be the wealthy, wily ally of all Protestantism. Forced underground, the Protestant faiths virtually disappeared in a century. Holy Mother Church, stifler of innovation, persecutor of Copernicus, Bruno, and Galileo, bred a world of limited horizons and scant technological progress. The horse-drawn wagon and the sailing ship were its best means of transport, the black-powder siege cannon its ultimate weapon.

In the last half of the Twentieth Century, large portions of the globe were still Terra Incognita to civilized Europe, and a broad frontier stretched from Atlantic to Pacific, across the virgin forests of North America.

CHAPTER TWO

Eventually, the horse clattered to a stop. When Celia was dragged off the beast's back, her head uppermost once more, she saw spinning, sparkling, golden lights and felt her eyes trying to pop out of their sockets. Her stomach heaved and her head pounded. Sweat ran into her eyes. She panted inside the enveloping blanket, sucking frantically at the hot, close air. *"Aire!"* she screamed, but her captors paid no attention. She was lugged between two sets of hands for a few minutes and then dumped on top of something scratchy and yielding. The ropes were whisked off, and the blanket followed; Celia found herself lying in a pile of hay. She gulped relatively cool air tainted strongly with the scent of horse manure, and shut her eyes tightly against stomach-churning dizziness.

"I just hope she's worth it," a masculine voice said in Spanish.

"Cállate!" said someone else. "Your nose isn't broken. You've had worse from the girls at the inn. Go get Rodríguez. I'll watch her."

"I want my turn first."

"And let her do worse than a bloody nose? Go get Rodríguez. With the money from her, we can buy a couple of nights at the inn with girls who won't fight back so much."

"I never had a girl with yellow hair."

"You've never even *seen* a girl with yellow hair."

"Yes, I have. Last year in Concepción."

"Go to another dog with that bone. It wasn't yellow but white; the whore was old enough to be scrub-woman to Ysabel de Inglaterra. Now do as I say."

Celia opened her eyes, but the world still spun sick-eningly about her, and she closed them once more. In a while the nausea passed and she tried again. Dim sunlight slanted through half a dozen narrow, glassless windows, revealing a large, rough-hewn gallery partly divided into stalls. Celia herself lay in an open space in the center of the room.

One of her captors had left already; the other stood before her. He was a very small, dark man whose skin was deeply pitted by smallpox. He wore a patched and faded blue shirt, mud-spotted pants, and shabby brown boots with thick, high heels. A low-crowned, sweat-stained sombrero of indeterminate color hung at his back, and on his belt were a sheathed dagger and an age-crusted pistol. When he noticed that Celia's eyes were open, he smiled, showing crooked yellow teeth, and his hands lifted to rest on the hilts of his weapons.

"Buenos días," he said. "Welcome to Verdura."

"Why have you brought me here?" Celia croaked in Spanish. Her throat ached from screaming, and speech was an effort.

"You will find out," he replied. He came close to her, so close that the toe of his left boot touched her arm. "You are very pretty." He squatted and reached out to stroke her hair; at that distance, some of the darkness of his face resolved into a thick, streaky layer of dirt. Celia shuddered and sat up, squirming away from him.

"Don't go. I'm your friend." He caught her arm, his fingers digging into her flesh like pincers.

"Please let go. You're hurting me. Where is Larry, the man I was with?"

"Forget about Larry. José is here." He pulled her to

him. His thin body was wiry and solid, and his breath stank of garlic and rotten teeth.

Celia raised a hand to slap him, but he caught her wrist and pinned her to the hay, his body half atop hers, trapping her other hand beneath her hip. She went limp and acquiescent then, but when he paused to rip open her slacks, she jammed her left knee into his groin. José curled into a fetal position, swearing and clutching himself, and Celia rolled to her knees, with José's pistol.

She held the unwieldy, double-barreled weapon in her right hand and cocked the two hammers with her left. As José snarled and sprang at her, she jerked both triggers at once. The hammers thudded home, showering her hand with sparks, but the gun did not fire. José laughed, and Celia slammed the pistol across the side of his head—metal barrel and carved wooden stock parted with a dull crack, and half of the gun fell to the floor.

"Enough!" came a loud, bass voice from Celia's left.

She looked up and saw two men, one thin, the other husky. They stood just inside the wide double doors of the stable entrance; the midday sunlight behind their backs spilled through the open doorway, dazzling Celia's gloom-adapted eyes. She saw the figures as black shadows until the doors swung shut, and then she realized that the husky man held a long-barreled pistol in his hand. Its muzzle was pointed directly at her. She dropped the useless handle.

"I told you he would try to get her while I was gone, Rodríguez," said the thin man. His voice identified him as José's partner. A slim trail of blood leaked from his nose and mingled with his sparse mustache; he dabbed at it occasionally with a piece of dark cloth but only succeeded in smearing it over his upper lip. "José, you bastard, you deserve everything you got!"

"I'm a busy man, Tomás," said the husky one referred to as Rodríguez. His complexion was swarthy, but he was cleaner than either Tomás or José, and he was obviously better fed. His dark clothes were similar in cut to theirs, but comparatively spotless, unpatched, and unfaded. "This is the woman?"

Tomás bobbed his head.

José glared at Celia, his fingers gingerly probing his scalp for blood. "Take her," he said. "Take her before I kill her." He knelt to retrieve the wreckage of his pistol. "She's ruined my *miquelet* that cost me twenty *reales!*"

"Ten," said Tomás, "and it was not new at the time, you liar. I told you it was so rusty that it would fall apart one of these days."

"Shut up, *hijo 'e puta!*" He swung around to look at Rodríguez. "Well?"

"Perhaps I will take her and perhaps I will not," said Rodríguez, holstering his gun and rocking back on his heels. "She doesn't look strong." He stepped close to her and took her hands in his, examining them speculatively. "She hasn't done much work with these fingers; not a callus on them, except for this strange bump on the second finger." He grasped her shoulder with one scarred paw. "She's thin and bony, with no muscles to speak of."

"She looks like she'd be good enough for *some* things," ventured Tomás.

Rodríguez shook his head and folded his arms. "A man who buys a woman wants her to work for him. She's soft. I don't know." He put a hand under her jaw, lifting her chin. "Open your mouth, woman."

"I don't belong to these men," Celia said quietly. "They have no right to sell me."

"Do you have a man to protect you?"

"Ask them. They captured him at the same time they captured me."

Rodríguez glanced at Tomás and José, who stood together now, Tomás supporting his partner. "What about the man?"

"There is no man," José growled.

"What did you do with him?" Celia screamed, her voice cracking on the last word. She started toward her captors with raised fists, but Rodríguez restrained her with a brusque hand.

"There is no man," José repeated.

"Come on, *chica*," said Rodríguez. "The sooner you're sold, the sooner you'll belong to someone again. Open your mouth."

Celia obeyed, her mind in a turmoil. *There is no man.* It couldn't be true. Larry must have gotten loose. He must have escaped. He was bigger than they were and better armed, judging from José's *miquelet*. Yet they implied he was dead; every time Celia thought of those four ominous words, she felt faint. Larry—sweet, strong Larry, whose touch made her pulse hammer and her knees melt—was dead. And her way home was gone.

"You have good teeth," Rodríguez remarked. "How long have those metal fillings been there?"

"They're lying," Celia snapped. "They couldn't have killed him. He'll be back for me; don't believe them!"

"I asked how long those metal fillings had been in your teeth."

Celia focused her eyes on the husky man's expressionless face and saw no help there. Larry might be alive or dead or waiting for sale into slavery like herself, and this man didn't care. "Seven or eight years," she said sullenly.

"A very good job. Now take off your clothes."

Indignation sent angry blood to Celia's cheeks. "I will not!"

Rodríguez sighed. "I would hate to rip them; they look good enough to bring a fair price. Take them off or Tomás, José and I will remove them without your help. I refuse to buy merchandise sight unseen!"

She shrank back and glanced at their faces. José's

was hard; he would like nothing better than to get his grimy hands on her again—she could almost feel his merciless fingers slyly torturing her tender skin as he pretended merely to strip her. Tomás's expression was avid; he, too, hoped that she would balk and give him a taste of the opportunity he had been denied. Rodríguez was blankly patient; he looked upon her with much the same indifference a butcher gave to a steer carcass on a hook at the stockyards. Celia turned her back to them and began to unbutton her blouse.

"Amazing workmanship," Rodríguez said, taking the pieces of clothing from her and examining them one by one before folding them over his arm. "These buttons—are they mother of pearl?"

"Plastic," Celia muttered under her breath in English. She unhooked her bra and passed it to him, then she slipped off her nylon tricot underpants and tossed them over her shoulder in his direction. She turned, wanting to cover herself with her hands but grimly determined not to betray her embarrassment.

Rodríguez paid her no attention but turned her clothes over and over in his hands, inspecting every detail of their workmanship. "What is this sliding thing that causes these tiny bits of metal to interlock? What is this material that stretches like India rubber yet snaps back to its original shape? Where did you get these things? Who made them?"

"They're quite common where I come from."

"The South? I know they have luxuries in México that we've never dreamed of . . ." He turned sharply toward Tomás and José. "If she's nobility, I won't have any part of selling her. Who knows what army might come after her someday—and after my head!"

"Listen to her accent," said José, "and ask me again if she's nobility."

Rodríguez nodded. "True enough. Woman, where do you come from?"

She swallowed with difficulty, trying to ignore

José's and Tomás's eyes tracking over her naked flesh. "A long way from here," she said finally. "You wouldn't be able to find the place."

"She can't be an Indian," Rodríguez mused, surveying her body with a clinical eye. "Although, on second thought, I have heard of fair-haired Indians in the East."

"They say a group of heretics once settled beyond the Eastern Mountains," offered Tomás.

"Is that where you're from—near the Atlantic Sea?"

Celia shook her head, then shrugged, staring at the floor.

"What can you expect from a woman?" José jeered. "She doesn't know. She doesn't even know where she is!"

"I am somewhere near the southernmost shore of Lake Michigan," Celia said coldly, rendering the name of the lake in English.

"The Indians may call it that," said Tomás, "but *we* call it El Lago de Nuestra Señora Reina del Cielo." He mouthed the word "Indians" contemptuously, and Celia wondered why; he was obviously part Indian himself. Whom did he include in that proud, disdainful "we"? Was the social hierarchy of this world the traditional Latin American one, where pure-blooded Spaniards ranked highest in status, followed by half-breeds and then Indians? If so, where would a slave fit? Celia grimaced—at the bottom, of course, lower even than an Indian. Visions of whips and chains and back-breaking dawn-to-dusk labor flitted across her mind. How had Latin American masters treated their slaves? She couldn't remember and prayed silently that an opportunity to escape would materialize soon and preclude her having any kind of master at all.

"I wouldn't lie to you, Señor Rodríguez," José insisted. "She's a lone woman. Will you take her?"

"It will be your head, too, if something should hap-

SHADOW OF EARTH 43

pen," Rodríguez replied. "My commission will be one half."

"*One half?*" barked José. "It is always a quarter! And what about my *miquelet?*"

"The pistol is your problem, not mine. As for the woman—she is a special case, *amigo.* In the first place, there is the danger we have just spoken of."

"There is no danger!"

"In the second place, I shall have to feed her until auction day, which is two weeks away. Am I right in thinking that you have no money, *amigos?*"

José spat on the floor.

"In the third place, she is obviously useless and will bring a low price unless some trapper fancies her beauty." He eyed her once more, perfunctorily. "She is too thin. Her breasts are too small. Her hips are too narrow for easy childbearing. And her skin is pale as a corpse's. She is not to *my* taste, *amigos,* except perhaps as a temporary diversion. I don't expect to make much money from her. But as a favor to you, I will also give you half the price of her clothes, which I will sell privately a little later this year; they will probably bring more than she will."

José and Tomás grumbled quietly to each other for a moment. "We thought you were a fair man," José said. "We will sell her ourselves when auction day comes."

Rodríguez shook his head. "You will not sell her in Verdura without my help. I don't allow it." His bland expression slipped into a frown for an instant. "My *men* don't allow it." His lips curled upward amiably. "I'm surprised that you think of such a thing, José. The people who come to Verdura trust my merchandise and give me a good price for it; I have a reputation. Now I am willing to risk that reputation to auction off this"—he waved toward Celia—"and get you a better price than you could get yourselves. I'm doing you a favor, *amigos.* Shall we say no more?"

José pursed his lips until they showed white. His right hand hovered indecisively over the hilt of his knife, then dropped to his side. "All right. We will see you at the auction." He turned on his heel and limped toward the door, dragging Tomás by the arm.

Rodríguez threw Celia's blouse and slacks to her and kicked her shoes in her general direction. "Put these back on for now. You'll wear something else later." He stroked the smooth fabric of her panties and stretched the elastic of her bra once more. When she was dressed, he gripped her arm and guided her out the stable entrance.

Verdura could have been any American frontier community except that instead of having a stockade of sharpened wooden stakes, it was surrounded by a high stone wall. The streets were narrow and crooked and deeply rutted, harboring neither trees nor weeds. Rodríguez led a tortuous route, stopping here and there to exchange a few words with a shopkeeper at a small general store, a blacksmith at his forge, or a farmer on his way home from the fields adjacent to the town. Always, he kept a tight hold on Celia's left wrist. At a house that looked like any other—two unadorned stories of wooden planking—he stopped. He drew a massive key from his pocket and inserted it into the great lock of the ponderous oaken door; it turned with a loud click. He grasped the horizontal door-handle and pushed it down through an arc of ninety degrees; when he put his shoulder to the wood, the door groaned and slowly gave inward.

"This is my home," he informed her, "and yours, for a short while."

To their left was a sitting room furnished with wooden tables and chairs. To their right, a door slightly ajar half concealed a bedroom. Directly in front of them were stairs to the second floor. Rodríguez began to climb.

"These are the slave quarters," he said when they

reached the upper story. "The room on the left is for men, the other for women. At the moment, you are my only slave, but it won't be long before my regular suppliers begin to deliver others."

It was a dark room with two windows, both shuttered from the inside. Rodríguez opened one to reveal heavy wooden slats nailed like bars across the glassless frame; sunlight sliced in skinny shafts through the gaps between them.

Celia saw a straw pallet occupying each of three corners of the room. The fourth corner was curtained off by a length of faded cotton nailed to the ceiling and one wall. To one side of the curtain stood a table bearing a chipped, white ceramic pitcher and matching bowl.

"Sleep wherever you like," said Rodríguez, indicating the pallets. "The chamber pot is behind the curtain; you will empty it in the mornings, when Lázaro can watch you. Have you eaten recently?"

Celia shrugged.

"Lázaro will bring your supper a little later." He went out the door, closing it loudly behind himself.

When Rodríguez's heavy footsteps on the stairs had faded away, Celia cautiously tried the door. It was locked. She went to the shuttered window and flung it open; it, too, was barred. She pushed at the slats with her palms, with her shoulders, even kicked them, but they held like iron. Pressing her face against one of the narrow gaps, she gazed downward: the outside wall seemed to be sheer and without handholds. Five feet away, the next building offered only a blank wall. Even if she could get past the barricade of timbers, she would still face a fifteen-foot drop to the hard, stony ground.

The sound of the door opening ripped her away from the window. Rodríguez was back, carrying a shapeless, brown cotton dress and a worn gray blanket. He tossed them to her.

"You will give your clothing back to me now."

Silently, she stripped off her blouse and slacks and slipped into the coarse smock. It covered her from neck to knee, leaving her arms bare, and it was five or six sizes too large. She handed over her shoes and stood barefoot in the center of the room.

"As long as you're here," Rodríguez said, "you can scrub the floor. Lázaro will bring the soap and water with your supper." He exited as before.

Celia patted a pile of straw into a semblance of neatness, shook the blanket out, and smoothed it over the crude bedding. She lay down, staring at the ceiling, watching dust motes dance in the beams from the westering sun. She thought about the new semester that would start in a week—she was registered for Seventeenth Century Spanish Literature, Linguistics 332, and Modern French Poetry. She had purchased most of the books already—they were sitting on the third shelf from the bottom in her apricot bedroom. Her last year of college . . . would begin without her.

She refused to believe that Larry was dead. He *must* be alive. He would realize what had happened to her and come after her with more than just a pistol; he'd wipe out this town if he had to. It was only a matter of time. She ached for the feel of his soothing arms around her; tears welled up and flowed freely, uncontrollably, down her cheeks when she thought of him. She clenched her teeth against the fear that settled in her bones; Larry would find her. Larry *had to* find her.

By the time the door opened to admit Lázaro with her supper, Celia had discovered that her pallet had other inhabitants much smaller than herself— inhabitants that bit unmercifully.

Lázaro was a middle-aged Indian with a sunburnt complexion and a large, sharply hooked nose. He wore the same kind of clothes as all the other men, but his shoes were soft moccasins, and his hair hung in two long, greasy braids. A crude wooden cross dangled from a leather thong about his neck. He handed her supper, saying, "Bread. Cheese. Water."

Celia ate without relish, watching Lázaro warily. He stood patiently at the door, observing her in much the same manner as Rodríguez had.

"You will wash the floor," he said slowly. Stepping just outside the doorway, he bent to pick up a pail, a stiff brush, and a mop that were sitting there.

The bucket was full of harsh, soapy water, and it had no wringer, so Celia had to squeeze the suds out of the mop by hand. Soon her hands were red, raw, and aching, but she continued to slosh suds on the floor, scrub, and mop up the dirty water until a discernible degree of grime had been removed from the wood. By the time she finished, her braided hair was soaked and filthy, her hands were lacerated and bleeding, and her back was ablaze with pain. She whimpered softly, but Lázaro's impassive face warned her not to waste any breath on complaints. He gathered up the cleaning implements and made an exit punctuated by the sound of his key in the lock.

Celia stumbled to the table and slumped there momentarily. Lázaro had filled the pitcher with water, and now she poured some into the bowl to clean her smarting fingers. After that, she found the chamber pot and used it awkwardly, finding her distaste for the unsanitary conditions tempered by exhaustion. The newly cleaned floor proved a more satisfactory bed than the vermin-infested straw, and Celia wrapped the blanket around herself and sank into sleep as the sun slipped below the horizon.

Morning found her almost too stiff to move, but Lázaro came with breakfast and a few floors to scrub, and she dragged herself through the day. She went outside once—to empty the chamber pot—and she saw only a fleeting glimpse of Rodríguez. During the days that followed, she viewed the whole house from the vantage point of a charwoman—the male slaves' quarters, which were identical to her own; the kitchen, which stank perpetually of stale grease; Lázaro's spartan cubicle; and Rodríguez's comparatively sumptuous bedroom, with its beaver bed coverlet and mink throw rug.

"Rodríguez must be a very rich man to own such furs," was the first and only of Celia's conversational gambits that Lázaro took up.

"We sell things in summer, trap mink, beaver, and fox in winter," he replied. "Winter is better. *Trabaja,* woman. When you talk, you forget work."

She would have liked very much to forget work. Her hands hadn't toughened up; the scabs kept rubbing off and bleeding again. Her knees were raw now, too. Her back, however, had begun to limber up through constant exercise.

On her tenth day in Verdura, two more slaves came to the house of Rodríguez. They were young Indian girls who didn't speak a word of Spanish. Lázaro was able to communicate with them, however, and he set them to work washing walls while he allowed Celia to rest. The three women slept in that one room, and all three shunned the straw.

Auction day drew near, and more slaves came—a nine- or ten-year-old Indian boy, three middle-aged squaws whose half-breed owners no longer wanted them, an old man who had outlived his master's entire family, and a little two-year-old girl saved from a massacred settlement somewhere to the north. The women's section was particularly crowded, and Celia found herself looking forward to auction day as a way out of the teeming room even as she dreaded the thought of being sold to some trapper as his helpmate. She wracked her brain for a way out, but there was none; if Lázaro was not on guard, then Rodríguez himself was. And as auction day drew closer, the town began to wake up. The streets were filled with people at all hours; she could never leave unnoticed, even if some miracle provided a means of escape. And where would she go? She felt utterly helpless.

During the early morning of the big day, Rodríguez set a tub of fresh water in the center of the women's room and supervised a community bath. Because Celia had been the first arrival and was presumably the dirtiest, he gave her the brown cake of alkaline soap and let her begin. She reveled in the feel of clean water all over her body, for the first time in two weeks. Her pubic hair was still disgustingly matted with dried blood from her menstrual period the previous week— Rodríguez, on one of his infrequent visits, had allowed her a rag for soaking up the blood, and Lázaro had supplied a little extra water for rinsing the cloth, but true bathing had been impossible. She scrubbed and rinsed quickly but thoroughly, then escaped to a window to let the warm summer air dry her skin and hair. When everyone else was finished, one of the older women mopped up the spills, and they all dipped buckets into the tub and trooped downstairs to pour the scummy water into the street.

Rodríguez inspected his charges. He passed a comb around, and all the women took down their hair, combed it, and rebraided it more neatly. His Indian assistant then bound the slaves together, neck to neck, with a tough boat line. Each noose was secured by a simple, overhand knot, to minimize the difficulty of releasing individuals from the group; nevertheless, the bristly rope held fast to Celia's tender neck once tied in place. With Lázaro in front and Rodríguez at the rear, they filed down the street to the center of town.

Auction day was market day, and since early that morning, wagons had been moving on the road that led to Verdura. Booths and tables had been set up in the square, and people hawked vegetables, milk, meat, and cloth in strident tones. The auction block was set up at one end of the square, and as Rodríguez and his train of slaves approached it, an audience gathered and the other transactions quieted down. The block was a wooden stage that resembled nothing so much as a gallows platform. Rodríguez climbed to the top, where he could look out over a sea of dark-haired, dark-eyed faces. The audience was composed mostly of men, wearing rude, homespun garments and carrying long-barreled flintlock rifles; here and there a woman stood by her husband, a swarthy baby riding her hip. Scores of shuffling feet raised clouds of dust into the air, and the sound of much coughing and sneezing joined murmured gossip to fill the square with a sea of bubbling noise.

"*Mis amigos!*" shouted Rodríguez, raising his hands for silence. The hubbub diminished somewhat. "*Mis amigos,* the monthly auction will now begin!"

One of the Indian girls was led up the stairs to the front of the block. She looked out over the heads of the crowd, her face expressionless. Rodríguez stripped the doeskin mantle from her back, exposing her deeply tanned arms, her full breasts and rounded thighs, to the eager leers of the audience. Bidding was lively, and she sold for a hundred and fifty *reales* to a grizzled trapper near the front of the crowd.

The little girl went next, for a handful of coins, to a middle-aged couple.

Then Celia was brought forward. When the auctioneer pulled her dress off, she closed her eyes and focused on other sensations—the sun burning on her shoulders; the hot, grainy platform beneath her bare feet; the small insistent insects buzzing round her face. The audience was strangely quiet. No one offered a bid.

"Come, come," Rodríguez was saying. "Who'll start with, say, a couple of dozen *reales* for this fine-looking woman? Who'll toss three *duros,* if only to bed her for a night and pass her on?"

"Scrawny wench!" someone in the middle of the crowd shouted.

"She's been starved and mistreated," Rodríguez replied. "A few good meals will fatten her up and round her out. She's a strong, willing worker."

"Two rabbit skins!" volunteered someone.

"*Amigos*, you know I'll take barter if you haven't any money. She's strong; Lázaro will vouch for her ability at floor-washing!"

"What other abilities will he vouch for?" came a call from the crowd.

"Do I hear any bids?"

"Ten *reales!*"

"I am bid ten *reales*. Do I hear twenty?"

Silence.

"I can't sell this one for ten pieces of silver," said Rodríguez. "She has cost me more in food and clothing than that." He looked down at the crowd, staring earnestly into a face here, a face there. "*Amigos*, I tell you the truth: this poor woman was badly treated by her former master. She was beaten almost daily, and she was starved; she will be eternally grateful for good treatment. She will love you as a faithful dog, or in any other manner you might wish. Do I hear fifteen?"

"Ten *reales*, Rodríguez, and not one *cuartillo* more!"

Rodríguez spread his hands in humility. "Is she not worth more than ten measly pieces of silver? For twelve *reales*, *amigos*—"

"Ten only, and you won't get more from anyone here."

The crowd was getting restless, raising fresh dust. Rodríguez himself sneezed and decided it was time to go on to the next Indian girl. "Ten, then, and the deal is done. Let the fellow in the gray shirt pick up his merchandise." He tossed Celia her dress and handed her over to Lázaro, who made the actual financial transaction with her buyer while Celia struggled to clothe herself.

Tall. That was her first impression. Most of the people standing in the square were short—shorter even than her five-foot-six. But her buyer was tall, a bit over six feet. She looked up into lively dark eyes set in an olive-toned face.

"What is your name?" he asked.

"Celia."

"Celia." He took her arm in a firm grip. "Come with me, Celia."

He pushed through the crowd, hauling her after.

CHAPTER THREE

Celia's new master set an easy pace, and she trailed a few steps behind him as they paralleled the river her own world knew as the Des Plaines. Cultivated fields gave way to forest a few miles outside Verdura, and forest thinned to prairie shortly after that. The late-afternoon sun was hot, and the infrequent clumps of cottonwood and beech trees afforded scant shelter. Celia's new master had bought her a sombrero and a pair of moccasins at the inn where they had stopped to pick up his belongings before setting out on this journey. He had made her a pack, too, of odds and ends of clothing rolled into his blanket and secured to her shoulders with rope. His own bulging pack contained utensils and provisions; in addition to that, he was burdened with his bow, a buckskin quiver of arrows, a canteen, and a lute. He walked as if he carried nothing at all.

"You will follow me," he had said. "Don't try to run away, because you won't be able to."

His back was turned, and escape looked easy, but every time Celia tried to creep away, she felt a strong hand on her arm. Once she stopped dead in her tracks to let the distance between them widen. After two more paces, he stopped, too, and waited for her to catch up. Even when one of them had to step behind a bush to answer a call of nature, he retained a clear view of at least the top of Celia's head.

"Where are we going? What are you going to do with me?" Celia wanted to know.

"Save your breath, *chica*. We have a long way to go."

So they walked in silence, splashed through the river to the west bank in silence, and tramped through the tall, coarse prairie grass all afternoon.

"At least tell me your name . . . *señor*," Celia ventured finally.

He glanced back at her then, for the first time in a couple of hours. "Señor . . . Juan Francisco Manuel Rincón y Carvajal." He smiled at the uncertain expression on her face, and crows'-feet showed at the corners of his eyes. "My father called me Paco, but my mother called me Río because I was born on the Río Pato, that runs into the great Lodísimo. Choose whichever you like."

She looked at him carefully, judged his age at about thirty-five, and made her decision. "Señor Rincón."

He shrugged. "That sounds good, until we know each other better."

Celia followed docilely. Some things about Rincón were reassuring: he smiled disarmingly with his eyes as well as his mouth. And the lute seemed to indicate a somewhat delicate turn of mind. Or so Celia hoped as she watched his lean, tireless legs eat up the miles while her own legs changed slowly to leaden weights. Her perception narrowed to the swish of grass about his brown leather boots and the sway of the lute slung over his knapsack.

The prairie ended abruptly at a small creek; the densely wooded opposite bank rose at a steep angle to a height of forty or fifty feet. Celia's new master crossed the stream and scrambled easily up the slope; when he turned to gauge Celia's progress, he saw her still at the bottom, one foot in the water. He descended then, gripped her wrist, led her across, and proceeded to drag her up the hillside. She scrabbled at bushes and large roots for additional support, badly abrading her free hand. A few yards inside the forest, she slumped to the ground, panting, and refused to get up.

"Are we going to walk all *night*, too, Señor Rincón?" she gasped, shaking her stinging palm. Unaccustomed to hiking in pliable shoes, she had continually bruised her soles and stubbed her toes on rocks and roots along the way.

"We'll stop at the first clearing that looks like a good campsite," he promised, glancing at the low sun. "Come, Celia." His strong hands lifted her to her feet, and a slap across the rump gave her the impetus to trudge onward.

The campsite materialized before sunset but after the air had begun to chill. Celia sank gratefully to a clump of coarse grass while Rincón dropped his burdens. He fished a tinderbox out of his knapsack and soon had a small pile of dry grass and dead twigs blazing. At this time of summer, dry wood was plentiful within easy reach of the clearing; he gathered an armload in a few moments and gradually built up the fire to useful proportions.

"You're not accustomed to so much walking," he said.

She pulled herself closer to the source of heat. "No, *señor*. Not at all."

He set a forked, green branch upright in the earth at either side of the fire and laid a third across them, to form a support for his small stewpot. Then he filled the pot carefully from his brimming canteen. "Well, we have a lot of walking to do in the next couple of weeks."

"*Weeks?*" Celia squawked. "Where are we walking to? California?"

Her master laughed. "We go to San Felipe Emperador."

"Where's that?"

"South. Here, you'd better eat before you fall asleep." He held out a loaf of bread and a piece of beef jerky. Celia, who had grown quite weary of cheese while imprisoned in Verdura, took the jerky gratefully. She was less grateful when she tasted it, but forced it down anyway.

Rincón tossed a strip of reddish bark into the pot when the water boiled, and while Celia struggled earnestly with her bit of parched meat, he sipped the resulting brew from a dented tin cup, munching easily on his own share of dinner. After drinking his fill, he passed the remainder of the cup to Celia, who tasted with trepidation; she recognized the weedy flavor of sassafras tea and returned it quickly to her master.

"You'll have to get used to these things, too," he said. "We've no cow for milk, and Verdura is not famous for her wine. Herb tea and jerky are not such bad stuff, if you're hungry and thirsty enough."

"Sugar would improve the tea, I think."

"You amaze me, *chica*. One would suppose you had lived in a palace, judging from your tastes. Perhaps I should have spent my silver on sugar instead of you."

Celia looked across the fire into his dark eyes. "What are you going to do with me, Señor Rincón? Please tell me."

He put the cup on the ground beside his left thigh. "They were all wrong: Rodríguez, the people at the auction today. You're not too thin; *they* are too fat."

"*Please.*"

"Celia, do not worry so much about tomorrow. It will come soon enough." He reached for the lute and cradled its almond-shaped body in his lap. He tuned it carefully and began to pluck the strings, humming to himself. His slim, strong fingers moved with practiced facility, weaving a sad, minor-key air. When he finally sang, his rich baritone produced a song of melancholy love that made Celia shiver.

She studied his face; firelight rendered the clean-shaven planes in stark chiaroscuro: an aquiline nose dominated, and the other features seemed delicate by comparison. He was handsome, though not in the usual movie-star sense, and his face reflected his song with great sensitivity.

By the fifth or sixth chorus, Celia picked up the words and melody and blended her sweet soprano with his baritone. Her voice was raspy and soft at first, but it mellowed and strengthened with use and soon acquired the plaintive quality of Rincón's.

"You never sang for Rodríguez, did you?" he said when the song was finished.

"No."

"I wonder what difference it would have made. . . . Do you play?" He held the lute out toward her.

She shook her head. "I never had much time for musical instruments."

"If you're willing to learn, I will teach you on the way to San Felipe. Yes, I think it would be a very fine idea."

"What's in San Felipe?"

Rincón pushed the lute aside and leaned back on his elbows. "This is how I earn my silver, Celia—with my songs and my lute. There are not so many *trovadores,* and we are very welcome in many parts of the world. As one of us, you would be much more valuable than the floor-washer Rodríguez claimed you were."

"What's in San Felipe?" Celia demanded.

He settled back, arms under his head. "In San Felipe Emperador is a castle which will welcome a pair of minstrels and give them much honor and silver. Is that clear, Celia?"

"That isn't why you bought me."

"You are too curious, *chica.* Let the days pass, and your questions will be answered. Now, since you are shivering, I suggest that you unroll the blanket."

Her fingers were numb and clumsy, but the knots

Rincón had tied came loose eventually, and Celia shook the blanket out. "Won't you be cold?" she said, trying to keep her teeth from chattering as she spoke.

"No." He rose and circled the fire. "Since there is only one blanket, we will use it together." He gathered a pile of leafy twigs and dry grass, draped the coverlet over it, and lay down facing the flames, leaving a space in front of himself for her. He motioned to her impatiently. "You don't think I'm going to allow you such a beautiful chance to escape, do you? It'll be warmer this way, too. Come. I know you're tired."

Celia shrank back, remembering the bottle of Morning-After Pills on the shelf in Larry's bathroom. Her new master was temptingly handsome, and she found herself breathing a little more quickly when she thought of lying in his arms, but she felt too vulnerable to be pleased by the prospect. The thought of pregnancy made her mouth go dry.

"I said come *here,* Celia." His right hand reached out for her shoulder and pulled her toward him. She half fell across his body and fought to break free as his arms encircled her tightly, driving the breath from her lungs. With a hand at the back of her neck, he forced her mouth down to his for a long moment. His lips were firm but mobile and tasted of sassafras tea.

When his embrace loosened, she lifted her head. "Please. Don't do this, please."

"You aren't a slut," Rincón said. "I didn't think you were, because you closed your eyes up on the auction block. How many men have had your favors?"

"Not many."

"*How* many?"

She counted silently. "Six."

"Children? Or with child now?"

She shook her head to both questions.

"A bad sign. Perhaps you can't have children."

"In my world . . . where I come from, we have medicine to prevent conception."

"Really? Permanently?"

"Not permanently. We have children only when we want them. The rest of the time, we use the medicine."

"Amazing. Where is this strange place you come from?"

Celia swallowed with difficulty. "Very far away. To the north." She gripped his shoulder, her fingers curling into the fabric of his roughly woven shirt. "If you take me back to Verdura, Señor Rincón, and help me find a man named Larry Meyers, I can get you a lot of silver. My parents are very rich."

"This Larry Meyers . . . who is he?"

"He brought me here, and he is the only person who knows the way back to my country. The men who gave me to Rodríguez said they killed him, but I don't believe it. He was too strong for them. He must be looking for me even now. If you'll take me back—"

He pulled her close and cut her words off with a kiss that made her tremble. "No, *chiquita*. You go south with me. Forget your home and your parents and this man. If he were alive, he would have gone to the slave auction for you."

She bent her head into the curve of his neck and let her body go limp. Sobs welled up in her throat, and she couldn't choke them off.

"Do not weep, Celia," Rincón said, suddenly tender. He stroked her back gently. "One must leave one's parents sometime. This life can be good if you stop thinking about the past."

She looked up, snuffling, and saw the firelight reflected in his dark eyes. "Yes, my master," she whispered.

"Call me Río." His fingers wiped her tears away. "You weep because you are tired and lonely and because a stranger lies beside you. Go to sleep, Celia. In the morning you will be refreshed and we will be friends." He pulled the blanket around them and shifted Celia into a more comfortable position, her back resting against his chest. His right arm curved around her body, and his hand cupped her breast. In a few minutes his breathing became deep and regular.

Celia, too, soon fell asleep, and in her sleep she snuggled closer to Río's warmth.

She woke as the first pale glow of morning filtered through the trees. She did not open her eyes but concentrated, rather, on kinesthetic awareness: her body lay on its left side, legs bent, knees drawn up in fetal posture; her arms were crossed, covering her breasts, and her right hand clutched a corner of the blanket. She could feel the close fit of Río against her back—his knees were flexed behind hers, and one of his hands rested upon her hip. His low, even breathing sounded loud in her ear.

She wanted to move gradually, sliding his hand gently off her body and imperceptibly drawing her hair from under his cheek, but she couldn't chance waking him that way—he would grab her in an instant. Instead, she rolled away suddenly and sprang to her feet, losing a few hairs in the process and skinning one knee. But his hands no longer touched her. She broke into a run without a single backward glance. Low branches tore at her face and shoulders; gnarled roots and tangled brush tripped her, but she stumbled on without falling. Adrenalin coursed through her system, erasing the stiffness of sore muscles.

She came out of the forest abruptly and tumbled down a sharp incline, sprawling in the shallow creek they had crossed the day before. Shakily, she heaved herself up. To the north stretched the flat, bare prairie, and beyond that, the unmarked river road back to Verdura. North. North to Larry and home.

Río tackled her before she reached the far bank. They thrashed in the shallow water, rolling over and over. Stones set in the creek bed bit into Celia's back and shoulders as she fought, scratching and kicking. She reached for his eyes, his belly, his crotch, and met skillful opposition everywhere—a bent leg here, an elbow there. He couldn't hold her still, though—her arms jerked away from his grasping fingers too quickly; he held her waist fast, but not her fists. A vicious jab at his throat made him flinch, and Celia used the opportunity to wrench the knife from his belt. Instantly, she stuck the point against his left kidney.

"Go ahead," he panted.

She couldn't do it, couldn't draw blood from the man whose arms had sheltered her from the cold all night. In the moment of her hesitation, he had her wrist in his iron grip and forced her to drop the blade. It splashed in the water beside him.

"I never guessed you had so much spirit," he said, getting up and pulling her to her feet. He wiped water out of his eyes with the heel of one hand, then stooped to fish the knife out of the creek.

"I just wanted to get away," she replied, rubbing her aching wrist. "I didn't want to kill you."

"You'd go back to Verdura alone?"

"If I had to."

Río led her back up the steep bank. "If my lute has been stolen while we were gone, I'll take it out in lashings, Celia. There are Indians in this area. They won't attack a man, but they'll steal from a deserted camp, and a lone woman would be just to their cowardly taste. Even if you could evade them all the way back to Verdura, you'd still be a slave—someone would catch you, or Rodríguez would claim you. Possibly he would save you for me until I came back, but possibly not, and your next master might not be as kind as I am. Without a protector, you couldn't hope for anything else. A lone woman can't roam wherever she pleases, or didn't your mother teach you that?"

"Things are different where I come from. Women are just as free as men, and there's no slavery."

"A very interesting idea, but it doesn't sound practical. Women and their children must be cared for." He looked sideways at her. "Unless a woman chooses never to conceive. That would be possible, wouldn't it?"

Celia nodded.

"Well, then she could behave like a man, claim a piece of land to farm, fight for it . . . is that what you planned, *chica?* You've had some training already, I see."

"I had a brother. We used to play together. He taught me how to fight."

"That is where you get such strange ideas—your parents treated you like another son. A mistake; women are women. You will have to learn more about being a woman before we reach San Felipe."

"Yes, Señor Rincón."

"My name is Río, *chica.*" They stopped in the shade of a tall oak tree. He lifted her chin till her eyes met his. "I do not ask you for happiness or pleasantness, Celia, but you will make yourself doubly miserable if you continue to behave this way. I ask for obedience only, and if I do not get it, I will beat you. Till now, you have found me a lenient master. I will remain lenient as long as you do what I say. Now smile."

Celia looked down and forced a smile.

He tilted her head up once more and held her glance in his. His dark brows were knitted and his forehead furrowed as he gazed at her sternly. "What is my name?"

"Río."

"Now we are friends again."

"Yes, Río."

"And I will forget that you ran away." His forehead smoothed out, and his hand moved gently along her cheek. He bent and touched her lips lightly with his. "I will take care of you, Celia, and we will go to San Felipe together."

Before he drew back, she closed her eyes for just a moment, trying to shut away the world so different from her own. But she could still see the warm red sunlight through her lids, and the shadows of wavering branches. There was no escaping this world. She knew then that she would go to San Felipe with this man, because she had no other choice.

Obediently clinging to his hand, she followed him back to their campsite. Everything was as they had left it. First Río shaved with a bright straight razor; afterward, they breakfasted briefly on bread and cheese, then tied up their packs and started south again.

When they stopped to eat at midday, he showed her how to finger the lute and made her practice a simple series of notes. He then taught her the nursery rhyme that accompanied those notes, and they sang it over and over in a round as they resumed their march that afternoon. In the evening, she played and sang until her fingers grew sore with pressing and plucking the gut strings.

"You can make the fire this time," he said, and he was astonished when she admitted that she didn't know how to use the tinderbox. He demonstrated, striking the flint and steel over a fragment of scorched cloth till the fabric caught in a tiny yellow flame. He lit a long blade of dry grass from it and transferred the fire to a pile of twigs as he had done the previous day.

"You never made a fire?" he said. "I can't believe it."

"Never."

"I'm beginning to wonder where Rodríguez found you. Did you have a lot of servants in your home?"

"You wouldn't understand." She sighed. "Yes, you might say I had a lot of servants," she said, thinking of the furnace thermostat and the air conditioner as well as the woman her mother paid to clean the house once a week.

"Chicago," he repeated when she told him the name of her home. He carefully pronounced it exactly as she had, without a trace of Spanish accent. "An Indian name, true? Yet you look . . . European."

"I am European. At least, my ancestors were English and Dutch."

His eyebrows rose. "Heretics?"

Celia stared at him blankly for a moment, then bit her lip as she thought of Lázaro's wooden cross. She stammered, "No, no. I'm a good Catholic." In reality, she was nothing—although her parents were Presbyterian and Methodist—and had never given religion much thought. But the word "heretic" conjured up visions of the Inquisition, and she suddenly feared that her safety in this alternate Spanish America depended entirely upon her embracing—or pretending to embrace—a religion that she knew very little about.

Río was shaking his head. "I think you'd better be an Indian. If you call yourself a Catholic in that tone of voice, no one will believe you. Heathen is safer than heretic . . . and is easily converted to the true faith. Remember that."

"But I'm *not* an Indian."

He toyed with a burning splint from the edge of the fire. "*I* don't care *what* you are, Celia, but some people will. For your own sake, be an Indian."

Celia's lips quirked, and she raised her right hand, palm outward. "Ugh," she said. "I hope no one asks me to speak Indian."

"No one will ask," Río assured her.

They slept huddled close together again that night. He kissed her once, deeply and passionately; she felt his prominent erection stab her belly. For a moment, she responded warmly to his embrace, then she stiffened resolutely and drew back. She didn't want to encourage him, she told herself. He was her master and she was, however unwilling, his slave; she tried to work up a hatred and a loathing for him but couldn't.

His muscles were too smooth, his arms too strong, his lips too sweet. When he released her, she wanted to cling to him but forced herself to turn away and curl up for sleep.

The days passed, and Celia's fingers toughened slowly from lute playing as her feet toughened from walking. She learned the nursery rhyme to perfection and started doggedly on a second and a third. In the evenings, when her fingers were too sore to play any more, Río taught her the words and melodies of longer songs, including the first one he had sung for her.

On the seventh morning, they passed into cultivated fields.

"We're going to San Pedro," he told her, "and Río Pato. I've been avoiding the river because the pirates are very bad to the north, but from here on the towns are fairly thick, and the Marqués's soldiers sometimes even come this way. I think we can pick up a few *cuartillos* here, and some fresh bread."

This town was walled, like Verdura. Two sentries with rifles sat on top of the twenty-foot stone wall, scanning the fields of corn spread out before them. A meandering dirt road snaked up to the entrance and became San Pedro's main street. Río sauntered through the open gate, playing his lute and singing merrily, while Celia carried everything else and followed obediently behind. After a few minutes, they had attracted an audience of men and women who trailed after them with bundles, baskets, and babes in arms. They came upon the local church, which was a small stone structure surmounted by a gabled roof, a bell tower, and several elaborate crosses. Río halted there and signaled Celia to drop her burdens at his feet, where he could keep an eye on all his possessions and face the audience at the same time. Then he nodded for her to join in singing harmony to his songs as she passed her hat around the semicircle of listeners.

She collected a fistful of small silver coins by the time Río finished his little program.

"Why wouldn't you let me play the lute?" she asked later, as they climbed the wooden steps of a bake shop to purchase bread.

"You need more practice. I was sure of myself; you might have gotten nervous and made too many mistakes. The crowd pays only for real entertainment."

When they left town, she carried the lute, practicing diligently.

"You know, I feel like eating fresh meat tonight," Río remarked, unslinging his five-and-a-half-foot bow as they entered the woods again.

"I've felt like eating fresh meat for two or three weeks."

"Well, be quiet and I'll catch us a rabbit or a squirrel." He nocked a gray-feathered arrow and half-raised the bow. The broad-bladed steel arrowhead glinted in the sun. Río moved forward slowly, stopping now and then to scan the underbrush ahead for small, betraying movements. Fifteen or twenty minutes later, he bagged a brown rabbit.

"We'll camp early today. While I build a fire, you skin and clean the rabbit." He thrust the bloody carcass into Celia's hands and gave her his knife.

She held the rabbit gingerly. "I never skinned anything in my life."

"You'll do it now." He drew and nocked another arrow and turned in a slow circle, looking at the trees that surrounded them. "There's a cord in the knapsack," he said. "Loop it around the legs and hang the carcass from a tree limb. Slit the skin at the hips and peel it down like a stocking."

"Are you going to get another one?"

"Another *something*." He shrugged off the straps of his pack and let it slide to the ground. Kneeling, holding the ready bow and arrow in his left hand, he opened the knapsack with his right and rummaged inside.

The first gunshot made Celia's head jerk up. Two men with rifles were about twenty yards away, moving from tree to tree and getting closer every second.

Río knocked Celia to the ground and rolled with her to the shelter of a fallen log. Two more rounds hit the forest floor near them, knocking clods of earth into the air. Celia hid her face in a welter of decaying leaves and spiderwebs, afraid to look up. She heard a loud click to her left; straining her eyes sideways, she could see that Río held a pistol with its hammer cocked. He aimed and fired two deafening shots.

"Too bad, *trovador!*" came a derisive shout from the direction of the strangers.

Seconds dragged by. The ringing in her ears subsided, and Celia was able to hear leaves rustle beneath the strangers' feet as they approached.

"Will they kill us?" she whispered.

"Not you, *chiquita*," Río replied.

She had to look up then, and she saw the two men so close that there were no trees in the way. Their teeth were brilliant white as they smiled and slowly raised their weapons.

Río fired first—three rapid shots into their surprised faces at a range of ten feet. They crumpled like unstrung marionettes.

Celia started to get up, but Río held her back. He approached the bodies cautiously, kicked them a couple of times, and, when they didn't move, felt for a pulse at the top of each neck.

"I think we'd better find another campsite," he remarked.

"Río, your side!" Celia exclaimed. "It's drenched with blood!"

He swabbed at the stain with his sleeve. "My arm, too."

Celia ripped his shirt away from the two wounds. "*Dios,* what a gash! The one in your arm is a scratch compared to the one in your side." She fought down nausea at the sight of his freely flowing blood. "The bullet seems to be gone, though."

"It's all right, then, unless he rubbed his ammunition in manure . . . in which case I'll die fairly soon."

She gasped. "We've got to stop the bleeding, Río."

"Pressure. Make a bandage from my spare shirt; it's rolled in the blanket."

She made him lie down and covered him with the blanket, in spite of his protests, while she ripped the shirt into pieces.

"We should move on," he told her a short time later. "The corpses will attract hungry cats."

"How *can* we?" Every time she lifted the bandage, fresh blood welled up from the wound. "The bullet may have broken a rib, and the rib might have punctured your lung. You could be bleeding inside!" She bit her lip to stifle a sob, and her hands shook as they held the wad of cloth tight against his side.

"We have to move. Celia, those bodies will stink by tomorrow in this hot weather; we've got to travel now, when I know I can do it."

"I can't let you bleed to death!"

"Tie some cloth around my chest to hold the bandage in place, then take the lute and the knapsack. I'll carry the rest." He rose to steady feet and took a slow, deep breath. "Do as I say *now.*"

Celia complied, tearing one shirt arm laterally to obtain an adequate length of cloth.

"And dig the ammunition pouch out of my pack in case we have more visitors."

As Celia searched in the knapsack, Río walked over to the corpses and picked up the strangers' flintlocks. He opened their stocks to sniff at the magazines. "Smells like plain powder and ball. I guess I'm in luck."

Celia spread the mouth of the small leather pouch and spilled a heap of brass cartridges into her palm.

"It takes six of these things," he said, swinging the cylinder out of his revolver. "I'll always remember the expressions on their faces when I fired more than twice."

For the first time, Celia looked carefully at Río's pistol. "Why were they so sure they had us?"

"They knew I carried no rifle; they were certain that I would have to reload after the second shot, since the best weapon I could conceal in the pack would be a double-barreled *miquelet*. But *this* . . . this fires *six* bullets instead of one or two, without priming and from a single barrel. A very useful invention."

"Where . . . where did you get it?" Celia bustled with the knapsack and lute to avoid betraying her desperate interest in the gun.

"From a peddler in Verdura, about a month ago."

Celia's heart sank and she let out the breath she had been holding. She knew the gun was from her own world. She had hoped it was a more recent acquisition and would indicate that Larry was alive, safe, and still near Verdura. Before the kidnapping, he had told her he was only peddling a few rifles; apparently, he had lied. She wasn't too surprised—Larry's clothes indicated that he had access to more than a little money— nor particularly angry, but she regretted allowing herself to hope. Her shoulders slumped as she stood up.

"Let's go," Río said, tossing the blanket and the sling of one flintlock over his good shoulder; he let the pistol swing casually from his right hand as he walked.

Celia followed, bent slightly under her load. She kept her eyes on the revolver, and she thought wistfully of Larry and of a life that seemed years behind her. She felt as though she had been walking through this forest forever, and when she tried to remember the comforting touch of Larry's hands on her flesh, she could only think of Río's warm, muscular body pressing close to hers.

After two or three hundred paces, Río leaned against a tree, breathing heavily. "This is it, Celia. Build a fire." He slid to his knees.

Once more, Celia insisted on covering him, but this time she averted her eyes from his wound; blood was beginning to leak through the improvised bandage. She threw the fire together and salvaged the rabbit from the bottom of the knapsack, where it had bled over a chunk of bread. She stripped off the skin as he had directed, hacked at the carcass till it split open, tossed away the entrails, and dumped the meat and soggy bread into the pot to stew. While dinner bubbled, she sat close to Río, pillowing his head on her lap.

"He was aiming for my heart, but I moved," he said.

"Do you think anything is broken?"

He started to shrug and winced slightly at the pain it caused. "Five more days to San Felipe."

"You can't be serious!"

"I wasn't shot in the leg."

"It's a bad wound, Río. You won't feel so well in the morning."

"I've had worse, *chiquita*. This will heal, but we may have to spend an extra day or two traveling."

She stroked his dark hair, unable to say anything, unable to share his optimism. The makeshift bandage was soaked through, and she had no choice but to remove it and substitute a fresh one, made from a spare kerchief she found in the pack. She curled her lip at the bloody, used cloth as she set it aside to be boiled later on. She thought about the very real chance of infection out here, where the wound couldn't even be cleaned properly. Without antibiotics—which were lacking, she was sure, in this primitive world—Río might die.

"This is your chance, Celia," he murmured. "If you run now, I won't be able to go after you."

She shook her head. "You talked about Indians and river pirates and slavery. Even without all that, there isn't enough food in the pack to last me all the way back to Verdura, and I don't know anything about hunting." She touched his forehead: it was cool and dry. She wracked her brains for the symptoms of internal bleeding; shock was the only one she would remember—paleness, clammy skin, ragged pulse. Río exhibited none but the paleness. Yet. She tucked the knapsack under his feet to elevate them.

"Very practical, *chiquita*. Now, while we wait for dinner, will you sing for me? I would sing myself, but I have a slight difficulty with my voice."

She started to reach for the lute.

"No, don't move." He caught her hand. "Just stay here and sing."

She held his fingers in both her hands as she sang the first song she had heard from his lips. She watched his face for signs of pain and saw none; nevertheless, she felt a sympathetic agony in her own left side. She knew he suffered, and she hadn't even an aspirin to offer. Long before she finished that song of sorrow, she was weeping.

"What is wrong, Celia?" Río whispered.

"Oh, I'm so afraid," she told him brokenly, moving his hand to her cheek. "I'm so afraid you'll die and leave me alone."

He laughed softly, then clenched his teeth to cut the laugh short. "I won't die. At least, not till after we arrive in San Felipe."

"And when we arrive in San Felipe . . . ?"

"We will live happily ever after. Isn't that rabbit done yet?"

CHAPTER FOUR

Celia woke, trembling, as a puma screamed petulantly into the darkness. She groped frantically for the revolver, thinking for the hundredth time of how vulnerable she and Río were. She had followed him passively and then blindly run off in that single serious attempt at escape, naively believing all the while that he was the sole danger in acres of open countryside. Until the instant of that first shot, despite everything he had said, she still subconsciously expected this world to be as tame as the forest preserves of home. No more, though. Suddenly the woods were full of stealthy menace, and she was astonished that she and Río could have slept so peacefully these last six nights.

The cat yowled again—or perhaps a second one answered the first—and Celia sat bolt upright, clutching the gun in both her shaking hands. After the sudden noises, the forest seemed preternaturally quiet; gradually, she became aware of the small, common sounds of crickets and katydids. A few fireflies glowed fitfully among the nearby trees.

"Lie down, Celia," Río murmured. "The fire will keep us safe from animals, and few men venture out at night."

She lay down obediently, placing the gun near her head. "How do you feel?"

"Ask me in the morning." He shifted position to lean against her arm and slept once more.

The night passed too slowly. Celia would drift off

to sleep, only to be awakened again and again by some unidentifiable noise. The revolver reassured her, even though she had never fired one in her life, did not know whether the safety was on or off, and had no idea of how to break it open for reloading, in case that was necessary. Long before morning light pierced the forest mantle, myriad birds woke her permanently with their early declarations. Wearily, Celia lurched to her feet and replenished the fire for breakfast—warmed-over stew on bread. Mist rose about her as sunlight dispelled the chill of night; by the time Río woke, the air was already balmy, promising a day of excessive heat.

"Mother of God," Río muttered. "Now I know how Christ felt with the wound in His side." He rolled over and sat up stiffly.

"How is it this morning?"

"Lend me your arm first."

She helped him up as she had last night, when he insisted on moving some distance from the campsite to unburden his bladder. She leaned him against a tree now and stepped a few paces away for the sake of whatever shreds of modesty she had left. He merely laughed, but the laugh turned into a deep, half-stifled groan.

Back at the fire, he let her peel the crusty bandage from his side. She tried to be gentle, but it stuck and required quite a bit of tugging to pull it free. A very small amount of blood welled up from the gash; it was fairly well clotted over. A swollen purple bruise spread out in all directions from the wound, covering Río's entire left side.

"You see, it wasn't so bad," he said, leaning toward the stewpot to fill his mug with the steaming mess.

"Not so bad," Celia repeated, "if you don't do anything to open it up."

"We can't stay here. When our two friends are missed, someone may come after them."

"But we *can't* keep walking!"

"The next town is no more than half a day away. It is possible that we may find a boat there and not have to walk all the way to San Felipe."

"And a doctor . . . ?"

Río shrugged and immediately winced. "A barber, perhaps, no better. I doubt that he will know any more than we. Do you know how to use the very expensive rifle that our bandit friends surely stole from some rich merchant?"

"No."

He opened the stock to expose two magazines, one holding black powder, the other paper wads and spherical lead bullets. Movement of a lever behind the trigger forced a wad, a single ball, and a measured charge of powder into the breech; at the same time it pulled back the cock, which held a piece of flint. Priming the pan with very fine powder from a small horn took a few seconds more, and then the trigger could be pulled, causing the flint to strike the steel pan lid and shower sparks over the powder; the measured charge then ignited in its turn and fired the bullet. Usually. Río noted that this complex and costly weapon unfortunately tended to jam rather often.

After going through the motions once or twice, Celia well understood how valuable Enfield rifles would be in this world; priming the pan was an inescapable bottleneck in the smooth operation of a repeating flintlock (or *miquelet*, as Río called all flintlocks), and reloading under tense conditions would be a nightmare. Yet it was the best weapon of this whole world and better than no weapon at all.

When they continued on their trek, Celia carried the rifle under her arm. In spite of her encumbrances, she insisted that Río lean on her. But after walking for a little while, he pushed her away, contending that her presence hampered his movement. Though she didn't believe him, she was grateful for the release—

the knapsack, lute, bedroll, and rifle weighed her down and kept her best pace equal to Río's shortened stride.

"Back to my river," he said, as they came out of the forest onto a high ridge that paralleled the meandering Río Pato. "It won't be long now." He paused to draw a few easy breaths before setting out along the ridge.

Low-lying brambles became a problem beyond the trees; Celia tried to skirt the worst of them, but the hem of her smock was soon in tatters and her limbs fared little better. She muttered irritably under her breath, mostly in English, but said nothing loud enough for Río to hear. She was determined not to complain of minor discomfort while he marched on relentlessly, betraying his pain only in the hard set of his jaw and his labored respiration. If this route were easiest for him, she would endure it stoically.

At last the town came into view, nestled in a bend of the river. San Esteban, as Río called it, appeared from a distance to be very much like Verdura or San Pedro. A low stone wall enclosed a jumbled cluster of wooden buildings—some of them newly whitewashed, but most weatherbeaten and drab. Winding streets of rutted yellow clay ran like worm-trails through the settlement.

Celia and Río descended the gently sloping hillside and entered the village by its main gate.

"Where will I find the barber?" Río called to the constable guarding the gate.

"Felipe Gómez y Cortado is the barber," the man replied, spitting casually and pointing his rifle steadily in their direction. "Also the blacksmith and the miller. He lives across from the church. Just walk straight ahead."

They walked, and Celia felt the gun at her back long after the guard was out of sight. "Friendly bastard, isn't he?" she commented in an undertone.

"No one is very friendly in these parts," Río replied. "Here is the church, and I see the smithy—and the smith himself, resting in the sun."

Naked from the waist up, Gómez was a short, powerfully built man with deeply sun-bronzed skin. He sat on a bench made of a split tree trunk and smoked a long-stemmed pipe. "Strangers," he called out loudly as Río and Celia approached.

A pimply-faced teen, slimmer than Gómez but with corded muscles in his bare arms and shoulders, emerged from the darkness inside the smithy and squinted through the sunshine at the newcomers.

"I was told you are the barber," Río said.

"I am, and many other things as well. What do you want?"

"I have some trouble with my side . . . perhaps indoors, where it is cooler—"

Gómez jerked one hand toward the wooden door of the house beside the smithy. The boy ran to it and stepped inside, holding it open for the others. Celia and Río entered, followed closely by the husky blacksmith. Within, a dark-haired, middle-aged woman and a little girl of seven or eight stood by a stone hearth; for a moment they watched the strangers warily, but then their hard shells dissolved and they ran to help Celia unload her various burdens. They made her sit in a high-back wooden chair by the dinner table and brought her a drink of water, demanding all the while to know her life story, with only minor emphasis on current details such as where she came from and where she was going.

"Enough! You chatter like squirrels!" barked Gómez. "What is this trouble now, and do you have money?"

"A little money," Río replied. "As you can see, I'm a *trovador*, and I earned a couple of *reales* in San Pedro a few days since. The trouble . . ." Gingerly, he rolled up his shirt.

Exhausted as she was, Celia sprang forward to help him remove the bandage.

"*Sangre de Dios!*" sputtered Gómez. "Did a tree fall on you? When did this happen?"

"Yesterday."

"What kind of pain is there? Dull or sharp?"

"Dull. I can walk."

"You are crazy. Woman! Cloths and water. Soap, too."

Her dun-colored skirts sweeping the floor, the woman disappeared into the next room, to return in a moment with the required items.

The barber's spatulate fingers probed the wound. "This was done by a bullet, yes? You were very lucky. A rib is cracked, I think. Worse than that and you would still be lying where it happened." He cleaned the gash carefully, but the bleeding increased. At Celia's inadvertent groan, he said, "Sometimes it is better to bleed a little—it cleanses the wound." He secured a fresh bandage in place. "More than this I cannot do. Now you must rest and put yourself in God's hands."

"How much do I owe you?"

Gómez tapped his front teeth with one forefinger. "I have not done much. But if you rest at our house and share our dinner, I might say three *reales* for both of you."

"One," countered Río.

"You haggle with the man who saves your life?"

"You said yourself that you have done little."

"Six *cuartillos,* then, and I promise you a good dinner."

"Six," agreed Río.

"My wife will make you a pallet on the floor. You need rest, *trovador;* you are almost asleep already. Woman, come!"

The barber's spouse went out and returned with a great armload of straw, which she heaped on the wooden floor near the hearth. Over that she spread Río's bedroll, augmented by a blanket of her own.

Celia helped Río to the pallet, then collapsed beside him. She was already half asleep when he nudged her.

"Watch the dinner pot," he whispered in her ear. "If anything goes into our share that doesn't go in theirs, let me know."

Celia's eyes flew open. "You think they'll try to poison us?"

Río shrugged and closed his eyes.

After that, she couldn't sleep; her eyes were riveted on her host's family, watching for a suspicious movement, a single glance, even, that might betoken some sort of duplicity. She saw nothing of the kind. The mother bustled quietly with dinner, aided by the little girl, who would occasionally look at Celia and smile. The youth and Gómez himself stayed outside until called for supper.

The family and Celia ate plentiful servings of meaty stew at the table; Río was served where he lay and went to sleep again as soon as he finished. After dinner, as the sun lowered, Celia was prodded with a thousand questions, each one followed so quickly by another that answers were impossible.

"You are so fair; where were you born?"

"Have you been among the savage Indians?"

"Is he your man—or has he kidnapped you from someone else?"

"Do you play the lute and sing?"

"Where did you get the lute, and how do you make new strings for it when the old ones break?"

"How are the people in San Pedro, and while you were there did you see—"

Celia raised her hand to call a halt to it all. "I'm really very tired and would just like to sleep."

"Oh, sing us a song, sing us a song!" cried the little girl.

"I'm just an apprentice," Celia replied. "I only know a few simple ones."

"We'll listen to a simple one," said Gómez.

Celia fetched the lute, which seemed to be in proper tune, and sang one of the nursery rhymes Río had taught her. She felt oddly nervous, performing solo, and she made a few mistakes, skipping one chord entirely in her desire to be done. But no one seemed to notice. The little girl, in particular, was fascinated by the movement of Celia's fingers. When the song was over, Celia handed the lute to her on sudden impulse; immediately she regretted the action and glanced guiltily at Río, who seemed fast asleep. Suppose the child ruined a string by plucking too hard, or suppose she accidentally dropped the instrument? Where would they get another in this wilderness? But the little girl stroked the lute twice, eliciting a tuneless series of notes, and gravely passed it back.

Shortly afterward, the Gómez family bid Celia goodnight and disappeared up the stairs to their bedrooms. The sun had retired shortly before, leaving the dying hearthfire as the room's only illumination. Celia lay on her back, watching the flickering play of light on the rough-hewn beams of the ceiling. Another night was passing, and tomorrow would make three weeks that she had been marooned in this Spanish world. Her command of the language had improved by a number of obscenities; her innate aversion to filth had faded away; and her feeling of despair had intensified till it was as much a part of her life as her heartbeat. With a slight shiver, although the evening air was warmer than usual, she turned over to go to sleep.

When she awoke, Río was sitting in a chair at the table, eating a boiled egg and a slab of corn bread while talking to Gómez.

"There's a cooked egg for you still, *chiquita,*" he said, tossing something small and white toward her.

She caught it left-handed, while her right hand still rubbed at sleep-laden eyes, and Río laughed.

"How do you feel?" she asked.

"Very bored with that question. Come, have your breakfast and we'll go to the river. Gómez tells me a certain boat owner could be persuaded to take us downriver."

"Persuaded to take you to Cebolla Dulce, where perhaps you will find another boat . . ." He paused, as if expecting Río or Celia to finish his sentence for him.

"We will do that, *chiquita* . . . as soon as you eat that egg."

She started on some corn bread, too, but Río made her finish it on the way to the dock. The sun was warm, and Río walked slowly. The pack and bedroll felt much lighter than she remembered, and today they did not remain on her back long enough to become ponderous. The river was less than half a mile from the smithy; a couple of rafts, a canoe, and a somewhat larger cargo boat were moored at the small dock. The large craft was twenty-five or thirty feet long and pointed at bow and stern; atop the small cabin in the middle of the deck was an oblong sail. The owner was aboard. He was short, brown, and wiry; the whites of his eyes showed yellow, possibly a result of imbibing too much from the earthenware jug that hung like a bloated appendage on his left hand.

"Yes, I'm Jorge Restrepo y Vega. What do you want?"

"How much to go downriver?" asked Río.

Restrepo squinted at them, sizing them up with hard eyes. "How far?"

"How far do you go?"

"Maybe to Cebolla Dulce, maybe farther. You want to go?"

"To Cebolla Dulce," said Río.

"Both of you?"

"Yes."

"One *peso duro*."

"That's too much. When are you leaving?"

"For a *duro*, I'll leave now."

"And for a *real* . . . ?"

"Maybe next week. I'm waiting for a few things before I leave. Right now I have only half a load."

"Nonsense," said Río. "You have nothing to wait for that you will not *still* be waiting for after your return."

Restrepo turned away, fingering his lower lip. "Six *reales* and I leave this afternoon," he suggested.

"Two *reales* and leave now."

"Four, and I'll leave as soon as I can get more provisions." The jug gurgled significantly.

"Three."

"For three, one of you will have to help me pole," he said ominously.

"Well, three and a half."

As it turned out, Restrepo was captain and crew all by himself, and Celia had to pole anyway. Fleecy clouds ran ahead, but the sail lay slack on its yard; the river current was as brisk as an old man's hobble. Restrepo steered lazily, sitting in the stern with his feet propped on a barrel and a jug near his hand, while Celia tramped up and down the deck along the gunwales, driving her pole deep into the mud of the river bottom.

"Why are we paying *him* to let *me* work?" Celia demanded at last.

"Do you know how to steer?" Río inquired.

"No."

"Then keep on. The wind will come up later."

"This is worse than walking."

"No, *chiquita*. You carry nothing but a wooden pole. Have you lost the habit of work so soon, my little floor-washer?"

Celia scowled and moved away from him, resolutely planting her pole in the bow of the ship. She stood there like a figurehead, looking south, the brim of her hat pulled low on her forehead. The muggy air was dead; and their leisurely motion on the river created no breeze. As the sun rose higher in the sky, the planks became scorching to the merest touch and unbearable to sit on. Celia could feel the sullen heat of a bad sunburn spreading across her forehead, nose, and cheeks.

A low conversation began in the rear of the boat, but Celia refused to turn and take part.

"Enough, enough!" Restrepo shouted.

Celia glanced over her shoulder and saw Restrepo gesticulating wildly, nearly smashing his jug on the back wall of the cabin in his animation. Then Río took the tiller from him, and the boat owner stalked forward and unlimbered a pole that lay in an inconspicuous groove against the cabin. Sullenly, he plunged it into the water on the starboard side. Río removed his shirt, dipped it in the water, and made a seat of the wet cloth for himself; he draped an arm over the tiller and stretched out in much the same way Restrepo had. The boat owner cursed but continued to pole, and Celia, somewhat mollified, copied him perfunctorily on the port side.

Evening fell and still there was no wind. They tied up by a cottonwood tree, and the men took turns on watch. Celia slept soundly.

At dawn, they set off again. This time a light breeze helped, and after passing a few small villages, they arrived at Cebolla Dulce. Here, the walls of the town came down to the river, sheltering a dozen boats in dry dock. Three wharfs jutted from the shore, and myriad small craft were moored to them, as well as several boats similar to Restrepo's, but much larger. Back of the harbor lay a row of buildings that might have been warehouses, and beyond them the tall spire of a church was clearly visible. As they tied the boat to a pier, a church bell began to ring.

Celia soon guessed that the bell was a signal to the

townspeople that a boat had come down the river, for a considerable crowd had gathered at the land end of the wharf by the time she, Río, and Restrepo stepped ashore. The men of the town stood in front, their flintlocks trained on the newcomers, and many children peeked from behind their father's legs, though their mothers and sisters attempted to restrain them.

Río pushed Celia ahead. "Spread your arms wide. They think we may be river pirates."

Celia did as she was told and smiled and nodded in addition, though her heart was in her throat at the sight of all those weapons aimed in her direction.

"Restrepo y Vega from San Esteban!" shouted someone in the crowd, and immediately the guns disappeared and the townspeople streamed forward to surround Restrepo and his passengers. The women squeezed ahead of their men now, chattering rapidly, asking Restrepo about his goods and for news of people upriver. The crowd moved him backwards toward the boat in its eagerness to reach his wares, but Celia and Río were able to bull their way through the tumult.

"I think the wharf will collapse," Celia muttered as she glanced over her shoulder at the crush of bodies. Then, seeing Río's pallor and the way he held his side as he walked, she reached out to support him.

"A moment, *chica*," he wheezed. "I am one enormous bruise, and that tunneling through the mob has done me no good." He leaned against a nearby wall for several minutes, and gradually his breathing eased. "There is an inn not far from here. To the right, at the end of the street."

Like Verdura and San Esteban, Cebolla Dulce's streets were narrow and crooked, made of hard-packed yellow earth. Houses were jammed together on both sides of the street, their second-floor balconies shading the traffic below. Once, through a narrow alleyway, Celia caught a glimpse of a tidy backyard vegetable garden. Most of the buildings wore a fresh coat of whitewash, and the few that possessed first-floor windows also had ornamental grilles installed—a feature common in the Latin America Celia knew, but one which looked incongruous here, where the houses had gabled roofs and wooden shingles.

The inn was set back from the street. In front of it, separated from the thoroughfare by a wooden fence, was a patio of inlaid bricks. Two large honey locusts shaded the patio, with clusters of flowers growing between the roots; a trellis over the gate bore a hardy growth of ivy and a small sign that proclaimed "LA POSADA DEL DESCANSO."

Río opened the gate and limped up the path to the front door. He raised his fist and pounded loudly.

"*Momentito! Momentito!*" came a muffled voice from deep within the building. Hasty footsteps approached the door, and then the loud snick of a bolt heralded the appearance of the landlord.

"Río! Río, my friend!" exclaimed the hunchbacked ancient who opened the door. He was a shriveled-up twig of a man with long white hair and a drooping white mustache that completely covered his lips.

"Let us in, Sandoval," said Río. "I am . . . in great need of rest."

The innkeeper reached out to Río with gnarled, palsied hands. "My house is yours, *amigo*, for as long as you wish to stay. Come in, sit down; my grandson will bring you wine. The day is warm, and a little wine will refresh, yes?"

"A soft seat is all I ask. You still have one, don't you?"

"But of course. The *softest*. Anibal, *ven acá!*"

Inside was a small parlor furnished with several high-backed chairs, a low table, and one lumpy settee toward which the old man steered the ailing *trovador*. It was a quaint and oddly cheery room; its windows were trimmed with red burlap curtains, and the gray floorboards were almost hidden under a large braided rug of brown and green. The horns and ears and pelts of various beasts crowded two walls, and a vast, rough fireplace entirely filled another.

"Ah, just as uncomfortable as I remember it," Río murmured. "Thank you, old friend. And while I rest here, you may ready a room for us."

"Quicker than a cock's crow," cried Sandoval, bobbing his head and scuttling off through a side doorway.

Almost immediately, a young man appeared from one of the other doorways. He was good-looking, in an impish way, and thin almost to emaciation, with delicate arms and hands. He carried a ceramic carafe under one arm, and this he offered to Río, along with a cup.

"Welcome to our house," he said, showing brilliant white teeth in a wide grin. One curling lock of shiny dark hair fell forward as he bent over to fill the cup.

"You've grown since I last saw you, Anibal," said Río. "You're almost a man now."

"Seventeen years old soon enough, *señor,*" replied the youth. "Old enough to take over the inn when grandfather dies." He leaned forward to deliver a conspiratorial whisper. "His coffin is in the back room— a *cuartillo* to see it. Two *cuartillos* to see him touch it like a woman. . . ."

Río shook his head.

Anibal glanced at Celia. "Will the lady want a separate room?"

Celia had dropped into a straight-backed chair, wiping the sweat from her face with a dirty sleeve. She grimaced wryly when the boy referred to her as a "lady." She hadn't seen a mirror in some time, but, judging from her scratched and blistered arms, she knew that her face must look wretched.

"No," Río replied. He took a hearty swig of the wine and leaned back with his eyes closed.

Anibal offered Celia a cup of wine next. When she had finished her drink, he retrieved the cup with both hands, pressing her fingers lightly as he did so. She pulled away from his grasp, frowning, not sure that he was merely expressing his friendship. She glanced sharply at Río, but his eyes were closed, and the gentle rise and fall of his chest indicated that he was sound asleep.

"He must be tired," Anibal whispered. "Come into the back with me and I will show you something interesting."

"I'll bet," Celia muttered in English. "If you don't mind, I'd rather rest here." Of course, he might only wish to show her his grandfather's coffin, but she had no desire to see that, either.

The boy shrugged and walked out of the room.

Celia almost fell asleep herself before the elder Sandoval returned to announce that the room was ready. Río opened an eye at the innkeeper's first quiet step on the carpet, which made Celia wonder if he had been asleep at all.

Their cubicle for the night was small and snug and surprisingly cool, considering the heat outside. It had a real bed—a wide affair stuffed with straw—covered by worn linen sheets of a faded hue that might once have been blue. There were even two feather pillows. On the floor was a brown rug of the same kind as in the sitting room, but the wooden walls were bare except for a large crucifix over the bed.

"Sandoval's grandson will fix us something to eat around sundown," Río said, yawning. He took off his blood-stained, sweat-soaked shirt and tossed it toward Celia. "Give this to him when he knocks at the door; maybe he can do something with it." He stretched out on the bed. "Take my boots off, *chica*."

Celia tugged at them. "You were awake, weren't you?"

"Do you think so?"

"Why didn't you say something?"

"Why should I? He's growing up, that boy."

"Well . . . don't you care?" She ripped the second boot off and flung it down.

He rolled half on his side, propping himself up on one elbow, and the rigid set of his jaw showed what pain that caused him. "I knew he wouldn't force you, so there was no need. You have been too obvious, Celia; if you will not have *me*, I can be sure you will not have a stripling boy. Don't forget about my shirt." He fell back on the pillow with a loud sigh of pleasure and ended the debate by going to sleep.

Celia sat on the far side of the bed, clenching and unclenching her fists. She rubbed her eyes and ran stiff fingers through her tangled hair. She, too, was tired; tired in body and mind. Her brain was still stuffed to overflowing with the past—the dearly remembered past that she cherished like an old Christmas gift. Her body knew the present, knew the soreness of shoulder and back, knew the persistent, fearsome, unwanted ache of desire for the man whose outflung arm lay inches from her thigh. But the future was a blank to both body and mind, and the future preyed on her, drew her into wakefulness in the depths of the night, and tensed the muscles of her calves into agonizing cramps. She looked at him—her guide to the future, so vulnerable in sleep, a tiny frown knitting his dark brows—and wanted to beat her fortune out of him. A tear stole down her cheek as she counted silently: fourteen days with Rodríguez and ten on the trail with Río. Twenty-four days of oblivion; September was almost gone. She wondered what her mother was thinking.

CHAPTER FIVE

The night turned cool, and the coolness lasted beyond dawn this time—Indian summer had evaporated and autumn set in. The town was aflutter with activity; harvest was upon the farmers, and they streamed toward their fields like ants toward spilled sugar. Río and Celia watched the flurry from the patio, where the trees were shedding their leaves in a steady rain and where, in a single night, the ivy on the trellis had turned brittle and begun to crumble away. A brisk wind blew Celia's braids across her face.

"And how do you feel this morning, Río?" asked the old man. He sat in a rocking chair in front of the door and waved and smiled at his fellow townspeople as they passed.

"Better, I think."

Anibal served them milk and bread thickly spread with butter and jam. He hovered too close for Celia's comfort, and she fancied that the oil he wore in his hair was dripping on her shoulder. But a moment later she knew it was rain; a large black cloud blotted out the sun and chased them all indoors.

Sandoval's rocking chair was placed near the cold, clean-swept hearth. "Are you staying with us, my friend?"

Río shook his head. "Only until the rain passes. My services are promised downriver for the beginning of the month, and I shouldn't keep wealthy patrons waiting, should I?"

"Ah, Río, I do not understand why you prefer this nomad's life to a safe, comfortable place at the Marqués's table. If I were a singer, that's where *I* would go."

"A fat life but dull," Río replied. "I go south for the winter and north for the summer and enjoy the best of all places."

"When you're old and crippled like me, you'll be happy for a warm corner in the Castle stable."

"Yes. Yes, I probably will." He glanced toward Celia. "Has the rain stopped yet?"

She went to the door and leaned out to look upward. "No," she reported, "but I can see in the west the sky is beginning to clear."

"We will leave as soon as the rain clouds pass, then."

"Ah, this is too short a visit, my friend," Sandoval sighed. "You have not sung, you have not given Anibal a single lesson on the lute. And I wanted you to see how his archery has improved."

"I am sorry, *abuelito*. Perhaps in the spring . . ."

"In spring I will be dead."

"No. You will outlive me."

"That may be so, but in spring I will be dead. When you leave today, I will never see you again."

Río looked toward the cold hearth. "I have given my word. . . ." His sentence faded into a long silence.

"Then go, my friend," the old man said at last, "for the rain has stopped.

They booked passage on a boat twice as large as Restrepo's; there were no other passengers, but the craft was loaded almost to overflowing with bags and barrels containing grain. The crew consisted of a baker's dozen: five polers worked each side while the captain manned the helm and the last two men stood atop the cabin at either end of the sail, redirecting it at the slightest change in the breeze. Because autumn had brought a good wind with it, their progress was considerably faster than it had been the previous day.

Río and Celia sat on barrels in the crowded cabin, watching the shore drift by through slits cut in the walls. While Río drowsed, Celia strummed his lute awkwardly, improvising chords for a Spanish song she had learned in high school:

> Caballito blanco, reblanco, reblanco,
> Llévame de aquí,
> Llévame al pueblo donde yo nací.

> Little white horse, so white, so white,
> Carry me away,
> Carry me to the town where I was born.

Río laughed at her choice and made her play it again and again until she did it perfectly. Several hours later, the captain came into the cabin to ask her to sing something else—anything else. She complied with the rest of her limited repertoire, repeated until he begged her to be quiet. Her voice had given out by that time, and she obeyed gladly.

During the next three days, Río made her practice as much as her fingers and voice could stand. The crew became visibly hostile—they did not object to the quality of her singing, but only the monotony of nursery rhymes—until several discovered that they could stuff their ears with bits of rag and thus attain some measure of peace.

Río Pato joined the Lodísimo deceptively, cloaking the juncture with islands so large they seemed at first to be peninsulas marking the mouths of several smaller rivers. But the last island that drifted past was a dwarf, and beyond it the river broadened abruptly to three times its former width; the far bank was now almost out of sight. Celia knew then that whatever its name in this world, the river that now ran beneath her feet could only be the Mississippi.

Later that same day they arrived at their destina-

tion. San Felipe Emperador was named, so Río informed her, for that staunch Defender of the Faith,
greatest ruler of Spain, His Catholic Majesty Philip
the Second. Seat of the Marqués Alonso Enrique
Quintero de los Rubios, San Felipe was the capital of
this great lord's far-flung domain, of which tiny Verdura was a remote frontier. Castillo Quintero commanded a low hill well away from the river, and the
city itself surrounded it, sprawling far beyond a stone
wall originally built to protect the urban residents
from Indians.

Here in San Felipe, traditional Spanish architecture
vied with buildings more suited to the climate: stone
walls blended with those of wood, and corrugated
roofs of tile shouldered vaulting gables. The tall stee-
ples of a baroque cathedral towered over the waterfront, utterly dominating the area.

The afternoon was waning as Río and Celia wended
their way through the city. A thousand odors enveloped them—odors of baking bread, roasting meat,
frying grease, and manure. Pigs, dogs, and half-naked
children ran free underfoot, dodging the traffic of ox
and donkey carts, men on horseback, and groups of
women in long, full dresses and dark shawls. Occasionally, a well-dressed gentleman with a spray of snowy
lace at his throat, or an elegant lady veiled by a flowing mantilla, would pass in a carriage drawn by high-
stepping horses, reminding Celia of Old Spain as de-
picted in various novels—novels which had neglected
to mention the stench, the garbage-strewn streets, and
the swarming, buzzing flies.

As they passed the church, she stopped to gaze for a
long moment at its richly carved portals and the life-
size effigy of Saint Philip the Emperor himself in a
niche high above them; suddenly she knew where the
crucial change in history lay. In her world, Philip the
Second had been king, not emperor, and never canon-
ized. Here, garbed in stone armor and a stone coronet,

he looked sternly down on the crowded street, and he
bore two shields before him: on his right, the multi-
plex arms of Spain, familiar to Celia from a dozen history books; and on his left, rendered in high relief and
stark in their simplicity, the three lions of England.
He had conquered it in this world, defeated the last
great enemy of Catholicism. Somehow his ponderous
Armada had proved truly Invincible. Celia wondered
if that alone had been enough to win him sainthood.

Well, it would be something to tell Larry if she ever
saw him again.

She laughed wryly at herself . . . how lightly, now,
she could think of his name.

A few days on the river had allowed Celia's over-
taxed muscles to recuperate from the long trek, yet
San Felipe seemed to stretch on and on and on. They
passed a dozen small market-places where peasant girls
hawked fish and fruit and bread. They passed row
upon row of whitewashed stone-and-wood structures
that faced blank walls to the thoroughfare in the traditional Spanish manner, reserving all windows to the
cloistered patio nested in the center of each house.
They passed stout shopkeepers and toothless beggars,
and even a roughly dressed man with a dancing bear;
finally they reached the western sector of the city,
where they climbed the shallow rise to the crenelated
walls of Castillo Quintero. As they ascended, the
stench of the city faded; the air on the hilltop was
pleasantly fresh.

A broad entranceway, flanked by great-timbered,
iron-banded gates, opened into a vast courtyard. It was
barred by the crossed halberds of four guards, one pair
to each side, who wore crescent-brimmed helmets and
figured breastplates of polished bronze, sleeves and
knee-breeches and cloaks of dark green velour, and
green leather boots. Each man's short halberd butted
against a leather strap on his belt; closer inspection

revealed the weapons to be, in reality, *miquelet* rifles with elaborate ax blades fixed to their long barrels.

"*Hola,* Diego!" Río said.

The leftmost guard turned his head slightly and smiled. "*Bienvenido.*" Then he raised his voice to a shout, saying, "This man is Río, the *trovador,* whom we all know, and may pass through the gate."

At some hidden signal, all four guards ordered their arms and stepped back smartly from the archway. They closed their ranks as soon as the newcomers had passed beyond them.

The first feature of the yard that Celia noticed was its pavement of clean-cut flagstones; in spite of the shallow channel of wear that ran from the gate and round the central fountain, it was the smoothest surface she had trod since leaving Evanston. Not to mention the cleanest: she saw a man in a worn green tunic diligently whisking manure and other litter into a basket he carried over his arm.

The courtyard was a small city, congested with people, animals, and every manner of non-motorized conveyance. Parked near a small wineshop, an oxcart blocked a coach-and-four carved with regal flourishes. Coarse-clad peasants with wheelbarrows scurried almost under the feet of horses bearing fine-liveried gentlemen, whose green berets sported cloth-of-gold cockades. A donkey, heavy-laden with baskets of grain, nudged Celia aside as its owner cursed and fought to restrain it from chomping on a bunch of carrots that poked from an old woman's sack.

Río led Celia to the far end of the yard, where two more armored guards stood in front of a tall stone building with a wide gate no less impressive than the first. Bolted to the wall above their heads was a painted escutcheon, emblazoned with the device of a gilt hawk displayed on a field of viridian. Celia pointed to it as she and Río approached the men.

"His Grace the Marqués's arms. Quiet now." He gave his full name to the guards.

This time they had to wait upon the arrival of a pudgy, balding fellow who maintained the list of people to be admitted without special permission of the Marqués.

"Juan Francisco Manuel Rincón y Carvajal, called Río the *trovador*, arriving sometime in September." His finger ran down the long paper scroll and stopped near the bottom. "Yes; His Grace has provided that you be put in the main hall, with the landless knights." He cleared his throat noisily. "There is no mention of a woman."

"I vouch for her."

"Well enough. Enter the Palace. The Steward will see to you—first door on the left."

A long hallway, dimly lit by wall sconces, stretched beyond the entrance, but Celia got only a glimpse of it before Río steered her to the indicated door, which was slightly ajar. Inside, one high window illuminated a small room in which a desk covered by a thick layer of disheveled papers occupied most of the available space. Behind the desk a man bent over the stack and scratched at the topmost document with a quill pen. A second quill was lodged behind his left ear, and its nib had leaked a large dark blot across his shock of iron-gray hair. He glanced up at the sound of their footsteps on the stone floor.

"Río!" he exclaimed. "We've been expecting you for weeks!" He rose, revealing a physique like a fullback and a knee-length green tunic embroidered on the front with a small golden hawk. He leaned over the desk to clap Río on the shoulder.

Río dodged the gesture, causing the Steward to draw back, more puzzled than affronted. "Sorry, Rafael. If I let you slap me as hard as you normally do, I may faint. A small matter of a bullet wound." He gestured, open-handed, toward his left side.

"A bullet wound? *Dios mio,* let me find you a chair!" He dashed about the room, turning this way and that in the cramped space, belying his rough-hewn physique by moving like a dancer. At last he swept a stack of papers off the top of a low cabinet and insisted that Río sit there. "What do you wish? Doctor Velas, of course. I'll order a cushioned pallet and some fresh clothes. Felipe, *anda!*"

A ten-year-old page in a green doublet responded to the call, bobbing his head as he entered the room.

"Call Don Epifanio Velas to my office. Tell him I insist."

The boy scampered out.

"And what of . . . ?" The Steward glanced toward Celia expectantly.

"I entrust her to your care for a bath and clean clothes. Celia, this is Rafael Terrazas y Aranda, Chief Steward to His Grace."

Celia, who was still wearily unloading her encumbrances, smiled and nodded.

"Entrust her to me for a bath, eh?" Terrazas smiled, showing a gold tooth where one of his canines should have been. "If I had the time, I would keep you to that offer, Río. Carlos! Pepe! Whoever is out there, *anda!*"

A second page, virtually identical to the first, leaped into the room. "Carlos, my lord," he said.

"Take this woman to the maids' quarters and instruct Germaine to give her a bath and clothing and then bring her to Río, who will be in the main hall."

"No," Río said quickly. "Bring her back here. I will be here, too. I want to talk to you, Rafael."

"Very well." Terrazas dismissed the page with a wave of his hand.

The boy bowed and went out, glancing behind himself to make sure Celia followed. He led her down the wide hallway to a cross-corridor and turned left. A series of small, sparsely furnished rooms opened before them, their stone walls almost completely hidden by simply patterned tapestries of various bright colors. The floors were bare and well swept, the hearths cold and ashless. Unlike the Steward's office, there were no windows visible anywhere.

At last they came to the laundry room, where a group of women were scrubbing clothes in two huge cauldrons of water atop a chin-high platform. As Celia entered, one woman opened a spigot at the base of the left-hand cauldron, allowing the dirty, soapy water to flow into a tilted trough and thence out a door in the back of the room. Another woman waited with a bucket to replace the used water with fresh, hot fluid from a large kettle which roiled in a vast fireplace at the near end of the room.

"What do you want?" demanded a stout, red-faced, middle-aged woman. She wiped her dripping hands on the driest part of her damp chemise and climbed down the stairs at the back of the washing platform.

"The Chief Steward orders you to give this person a bath and clean clothing, Germaine," piped the page, and he immediately bounded away, leaving Celia standing in the middle of a crowd of strangers.

"That you need," said the stout woman. "The privy is in the corner; you can get out of those rags after you use it." She gazed pityingly at Celia's bedraggled costume. "Have you nothing else to wear?"

Celia shook her head and walked meekly and gratefully in the indicated direction. The toilet consisted of a wooden seat over a hole in the floor, beneath which a sluggish stream of water passed, sweeping the raw sewage toward some unknown destination. It stank rather less than an outhouse.

Germaine was adamant about Celia's ragged dress. She tugged impatiently at it, lifting the fabric to Celia's armpits. "This is good for nothing. Help me."

Celia raised her arms and let the torn, dirty smock be drawn off her body. She shivered a little, standing there in nothing but her moccasins. Around her, the women scurried back and forth with loads of dripping clothes; they paid her scant attention.

"Pour some cold water in with the hot for the new load," Germaine snapped into the air. Behind her, a thin girl of sixteen or so—the only laundress whose face was unblemished by smallpox—hurried to obey. "We'll throw her in before the clothes. All right, child, up on the platform."

Celia climbed the stairs and looked into the wash-tub, which was slowly being filled by hand with buckets of water, partly from the bubbling pot on the fire and partly from a nearby handpump. Between the two washtubs was an immense wringer, such as her grandmother had used in the days before spin-dry washing machines; the second tub held a full load of soapy clothes, apparently being rinsed. Assisted by the stout woman, Celia climbed into the first tub and scrubbed luxuriously with a cake of yellow laundry soap. She washed her hair, too, lathering it four times in her anxiety to have it clean and itch-free after so many days of filth. Refreshed and relaxed, she clambered out of the tank and rubbed herself down with a rough length of cloth proffered by Germaine. Dead, peeling skin flaked free of her arms and revealed that her sunburn had faded to a pale tan, which still left her much fairer than the laundresses.

"I feel so much better now," Celia exclaimed, toweling her hair vigorously.

Germaine handed her a coarse-toothed comb, then laid out a white, ankle-length dress and a pair of light sandals.

Celia worked on her hair, wincing at the snarls and wishing for a bottle of creme rinse to lessen the labor. The dress was not a bad fit in the shoulders and sleeves, but otherwise it hung loose, straight, and sexless, like a sack.

Arms folded over her sizable bosom, Germaine appraised Celia's new image and nodded slightly in approval. "What am I supposed to do with you now, since that scalawag page has disappeared without telling me?"

"I'm to go back to the Chief Steward's office."

"Can you find it yourself?"

Celia shrugged helplessly. "I don't think so. This is my first day in the Palace."

"Nicolasa, show her the way."

The thin girl, who had been furiously scrubbing clothes since the end of Celia's bath, shook the suds from her arms and scurried to obey. She bobbed a quick curtsey. "Yes, Doña Germaine. Will you come this way, *señorita?*"

The return was a simple repetition of the trip to the laundry room, and this time Celia was sure she would be able to make it by herself if necessary. Nicolasa walked ahead of her, sometimes scampering away like a startled fawn, then stopping to glance around anxiously until Celia caught up.

"I don't come this way often, *señorita,*" she explained. "Only when I have an errand. My clothes aren't fit for anyplace but the laundry." She looked down self-consciously at her damp, stained, and shapeless smock.

At the entrance to the Chief Steward's office, Nicolasa curtseyed and backed away. "Good day to you, *señorita*. You are very pretty." Then she turned and raced away, holding her skirt above her knees to avoid tripping.

Celia knocked at the door. When there was no answer, she knocked again and then turned the handle and pushed.

Inside, Río reclined in a chair that had been found somewhere. He had washed and was freshly dressed in a black shirt and knee-pants, blue stockings, and soft black shoes. A tall, thin man in a long blue coat hovered over him, chattering away in an undertone. At the desk, Terrazas doodled on a blank sheet of paper.

"Come in, Celia," said Río.

As she entered, the thin man looked her over, inspecting her much as the auctioneer Rodríguez had. "Yes," he said. He stepped close, and Celia caught a whiff of perfume emanating from him. A starched white linen ruff about two inches high encircled his neck, and sprays of lace protruded from his long, tight sleeves. He had a black mustache and goatee and dark hair that was beginning to thin in front. He caught a lock of Celia's loose, still-damp hair and rubbed it between his fingers. He peered into her eyes. "Yes," he repeated, more emphatically.

"Yes, what?" Celia demanded.

"Yes, you are blonde and blue-eyed, of course," the man replied, his eyebrows lifting in surprise.

"This is Don Epifanio Velas y Chajon," said Río. "Don Epifanio is a very fine doctor and a good friend."

"We will arrange it, then," said Terrazas. "A little later, I think. Perhaps an hour after sunset." He glanced at the window; the western sky was already red with dusk. He consulted a large brass pocketwatch with an elaborately figured cover. "Yes. Why don't you stay here till then? I'll have supper sent in."

Río nodded and motioned to Celia to take the seat on top of the cabinet that he had occupied before she left the room. As she did so, she noticed that all of their gear except for the lute had been taken away.

Terrazas kindled a small blaze in his fireplace and lit a pair of glass-chimneyed oil lamps with a splint, Don Epifanio left, and one of the pages was dispatched for food. By the time supper arrived, the Chief Steward had cleared a spot on his desk; it was just large enough for the tray that the page returned with. The three of them ate roast chicken in silence and washed it down with dry red wine. Shortly after they finished, a new page arrived with the news that His Grace would see Río and Celia in his private apartments.

"A moment," said Terrazas, and he reached into a drawer of his desk, rummaging about for a moment before finding what he wanted. It was a heavy, silvery chain with a clasp of entwined metal serpents. He fastened it snugly about Celia's waist, letting six or seven links hang down in the front. "That dress really does nothing for you without a belt."

"Make a note of the gift," said Río, smiling.

"More paperwork," muttered Terrazas, and he shut the door firmly behind them.

As they followed the page down the hall, Río hummed lightly to himself and swung the lute with one hand. "You must curtsey when he sees you," he remarked. "And don't speak unless he speaks to you first. Are you nervous?"

"No. Why should I be?"

"Good. This will be a great moment in your life."

Celia shrugged. The prospect of meeting nobility held no glamor for her. She would pretend to be impressed.

"He is a very powerful man. You will call him 'Your Grace.'"

"Yes, Río."

They climbed a flight of stone stairs, and Río stopped halfway up, holding his side.

Celia caught his arm. "Has it opened?"

He shook his head. "Don Epifanio offered me a potion. I'll take it later. Let's go on."

He rested again at the top of the stairs, and then he straightened his shoulders and marched down the hall as if the wound had been a figment of his imagination. Celia hurried after.

Two armored guards stood at attention by a set of double doors that bore the golden bird on a background of green paint. Río gave his name, and one of the guards stepped aside while the other knocked on the door, waited a moment, then opened it.

The room was as opulent as a drafty, hearth-heated stone room could be. The walls were hung with intricately wrought tapestries showing military and religious scenes. The floor was entirely covered by a dark green rug with a thick pile. Velvet-upholstered chairs were scattered here and there. At the fireplace, his back to Río and Celia, stood a powerfully built man of middling height. He wore a green velvet doublet surmounted by a high, starched ruff sewn with silver pinheads that sparkled in the firelight. His stout legs were encased in green silk hose, and on his feet were shoes of green-dyed leather. His fingers glittered with gold and jewels.

His Grace the Marqués Alonso Enrique Quintero de los Rubios turned to face his guests. The firelight made a halo of the pale blond hair that sprang from his scalp and face like a hardy bush.

"*Bienvenido*, Río." His voice was deep and booming.

Río bowed. "Good evening, my lord. May I present the Lady Celia, formerly princess of a tribe far to the north of Your Grace's domain?" He nudged Celia.

She curtseyed awkwardly, suppressing a giggle. No one in her world would have accepted such a bald lie, but the Marqués didn't bat an eye at it.

His Grace gazed on Celia long and hard. His eyes were gray-green, and his eyebrows would have been invisible if they hadn't been so bushy. "Turn around, woman," he said.

Celia glanced at Río, and when he nodded, she turned.

The Marqués caught her arm and scrutinized it. He looked at her eyes. "Is she with child?" he asked.

"No," Río replied.

"And what do *you* say to that, woman?"

Celia flushed angrily, wanting to spit out a mind-your-own-business, but she held her tongue. Being rude to nobility, in a world where nobility held the power of life and death, was hardly a healthy practice. "I am not, Your Grace," she answered.

"Do you swear it by the Mother of God?"

"My lord, her people are not Christians. . . ." Río murmured.

"Then she must be baptized. Very well, I will believe her—*and* you, my faithful Río. You have never lied to me . . . to my knowledge."

"Never, my lord."

"A dark-haired child will destroy the faith I have in you, my *trovador*."

"It will not be my child, Your Grace, and now that we are in your home, the guardianship is yours."

"*Está bien.* Will you take thirty *duros*?"

Río looked the Marqués straight in the eye. "That's a niggardly price for an heir, and a blasphemous one, too. A hundred is little enough, considering her value."

"A hundred? A high price indeed!"

"But consider my expenses and the pains I took. Don Epifanio has no doubt told you of the journey, of my wound, of the cost to my health . . ."

"Enough, enough. Next you will put the tale to music."

"Yes, my lord."

The Marqués stroked his beard thoughtfully. "I will not bargain for my heir like a fishwife. One hundred is yours. Have your comforts been seen to?"

"Yes, my lord."

"Very well. You may leave us."

"Good night, my lord. Good night, Celia." He bowed slightly, backing toward the door.

The Marqués took Celia's arm.

"Wait!" she cried, trying gently and modestly to disengage herself from His Grace's grasp. "What's going on here? What do you mean, 'Good night, Celia'?"

"Quite simple, fair Indian princess," said the Marqués. "I have bought you."

"*What?*" she screamed in English, her distress too sharp for an adopted tongue. "Río, no, you *can't! No puedas hacerlo!*"

"I bought you and I can sell you," the *trovador* replied coolly. He bowed again to her and to the Marqués and slipped out the door.

Her mind in a turmoil, Celia turned to the Marqués. "Your Grace, please understand, I am not accustomed to being bought and sold. If my people knew of the shame that has been heaped upon me . . ." She glanced toward the door, seeing, in her mind's eye, the man who had shared his blanket with her; and now he had turned his back. Was all that she thought had grown up between them merely leading to *this?*

The Marqués put his arm around her shoulders. "The shame is over, Celia. Surely your people would look with pride upon your acceptance into such a noble house as mine."

She licked her lips slowly. "What . . . what do you wish of me, Your Grace?"

"A son." His arm slipped around her waist and drew her to him. She and he were almost exactly the same height. "You are very slim," he said. The softness of his velvet garment and the hard muscles beneath it pressed against her. One of his hands slid downward to cup her buttocks, and the other tangled in her hair. "*Rubia,*" he said—the Spanish word for blonde. His lips descended upon hers, open and wet, and the hairs of his beard and mustache tickled her nose intolerably. She broke away from him to scratch her itching face fiercely, and he laughed deep in his throat.

"Come into the other room," he said, hooking his arm around her waist again and drawing her along beside him as he walked.

The other room was a bedroom, and the snowy sheets and green comforter on the wide bed were turned back, waiting. A single candle burned on the nightstand, casting wild, flickering shadows around the room and lending a semblance of eerie life to the many tapestries that lined the walls.

He began to undress, laying his garments neatly on a maroon boudoir chair.

Loosed from his grasp, Celia backed away slightly. The door behind her was open, but beyond that lay only the other room and its closed door and the two armored guards outside. She doubted that they would let her pass. She could dodge behind a table or a chair and so delay the inevitable for a little while. She could incapacitate the Marqués with a kick, but somehow she suspected that the punishment for such an action would be more than she could bear.

She clasped her hands tightly behind her back, willing their shaking away. This was it. This was what she had dreaded and fought ever since that first time in the backseat of a Plymouth Valiant. This total stranger was going to try his damnedest to make her pregnant. A voice inside her wailed despairingly at the thought. She felt the blood drain out of her face, and tiny beads of sweat broke out on her forehead and neck.

The Marqués was naked now—and uncircumcised, she noted with some calm and curious corner of her mind—and he came toward her to unclasp the heavy chain at her waist. It rustled to the floor. Then he pulled her shift up over her head, and the whole operation reminded her vividly of the similar scene in the laundry room . . . and of the slave auction.

He inspected his property and seemed reasonably satisfied with it. "Thin but strong," he remarked.

He pulled her to the bed and buried his face between her breasts for a moment before mounting her. She was as tight as a virgin, for there was nothing about him that aroused her in the slightest.

She lay there passively, gasping rhythmically as his

heavy body pressed the breath out of her at every
downward thrust. She felt as though she were undergo-
ing endless artificial respiration. Staring past him at a
cobweb on the ceiling, she wondered if this were the
way prostitutes felt. The pain of dry flesh rubbing
against dry flesh increased, as her passionless body still
refused to manufacture moisture for copulation; she
clenched her teeth and her fists against it, and her fingernails dug deep into the pads of her palms, drawing
blood. She began to count backwards slowly from a
hundred, hoping that he would be finished by the
time she reached zero.

Her mind called this rape and screamed silent
hatred of its perpetrator. Rape. Not a violent act at
the point of a knife or after a beating; not a scuffling,
struggling drama in a back alley filled with broken
glass and garbage; but a loveless, lustless coupling in a
wide, comfortable bed inside a prison, where the only
threats hung unspoken in the air.

His Grace's body shuddered in its final spasms, and
then he lay still, a large, dead weight upon Celia's
stomach. After a few minutes, she thought he had
fallen asleep, and she moved a little, searching for
some position less stifling. He rolled away then, and
the sudden cessation of pressure inside her made her
whole body go limp with relief. She lay there, breathing freely and deeply.

Eons passed. The Marqués seemed to be asleep. Celia lay quietly, watching the candle burn low. She saw
numbers in its flame: this was the eighteenth day of
her menstrual cycle; chances were awfully good that
the Marqués's heir would be on its way quite soon.
The candle guttered and went out.

Her eyes became accustomed to the darkness and
perceived that the room had a single tall, glazed window, through which pallid moonlight spilled in narrow lozenges across the floor. Celia rose and walked
over to it. Opening the latticed glass, she looked out

and saw a courtyard—the same one she had crossed earlier that day. To the right was a wall with battlements. She was two or three stories above it and could dimly make out moving figures below. Beneath the window, the wall was astonishingly sheer.

She turned back to the bed. The Marqués lay on his side, half curled into fetal position, hands beneath his cheek. He seemed asleep. She put on her dress and the chain belt, which rattled softly but did not disturb him. She walked barefoot into the next room and then slipped her sandals on.

The door yielded to her touch, but the guards barred her way as she came out into the dim corridor.

"I can't sleep," she explained. "I thought I would walk around for a while."

"Wait here a moment, then," said the left-hand guard, "and I will find someone to walk with you. Those are His Grace's orders." He turned with military precision and marched down the hall into the darkness between wall-sconces. He returned with a sleepy-eyed, middle-aged woman in tow: she wore a long, white nightdress, and a nightcap almost covered gray-shot hair that hung down her back in a single braid.

"I am Ana," the woman yawned. "His Grace the Marqués has instructed me to look after you. Do you wish to be shown your room?"

Celia shook her head. "I want to walk around for a while. Do you mind?"

Ana grimaced. "All right, walk around. I thought you would be tired; I thought you would spend the whole night with His Grace, but if you want to walk around, go ahead. Remember, though, that you may not leave the Palace."

Celia hesitated then, not knowing quite where she wanted to go, and feeling more of a prisoner than ever now that she had a chaperone. She went to the stairs and began the long descent, picking her way carefully with her long skirts lifted. Almost at the bottom, she turned to ask Ana, who was following close behind, where the main hall was.

"No assignations," Ana replied. "His Grace forbids it."

"I just want . . . to talk to someone."

Ana shrugged and pointed to her left.

The vast, high-ceilinged main hall was crowded with sleepers lying on benches and sprawled on the floor; along the walls, beneath each lamp, stood guards with their halberd-rifles upright. Celia despaired of finding Río until she heard the soft sound of a lute being played near one of the two great fireplaces that faced each other at opposite ends of the room. Skirting myriad bodies, she walked toward the sound.

He lay on a low couch, his head and back raised by bolsters and his body covered, from the waist down, by a patchwork quilt. His chest was naked, and the black shirt he had been wearing earlier was neatly folded on the floor beneath the couch, the lute lying on top of it. His left arm dangled over the edge of the couch to touch the lute strings.

"*Buenas noches,* Celia," he said softly. He was away from the other sleepers, but not so far away that he could not have awakened a few by raising his voice.

Celia glanced back: Ana had stopped in the center of the room and settled into a chair from which she could watch her charge. She was out of earshot of a whisper.

Celia sank to the cool stone floor beside Río's couch and folded her hands in her lap. "Why did you do it?" she murmured, looking deep into Río's dark eyes, trying to read what lay behind them.

He reached out and took a lock of Celia's fine blonde hair. He turned it in his fingers, and the firelight caught it and made it sparkle like spun gold. "We have both profited from this," he said.

"I don't understand. He wants an heir, but why me?

There must be dozens, hundreds of women who would be better suited. Women who would *want* to bear his child."

"Many women have borne his children. His oldest bastard is twenty-three or twenty-four. But those women were not *wives*. He is looking for a Marquesa who will bear him a legitimate son."

"But what is so special about *me?* That I'm . . . an Indian princess?"

Río smiled. "No. When he was younger—still a child—His Grace's father betrothed him to a young lady of noble family in faraway México, which is where His Grace's mother, Doña María Antonia, was born. The girl was, in fact, Doña María Antonia's niece and thus His Grace's cousin. She was sixteen when she came north for the wedding, but the journey treated her badly, and she arrived quite ill. She never recovered entirely, and though she bore a son, both she and the child died shortly afterward. When the mourning period was over and His Grace decided to send to México for another bride, a war had broken out and for a long while it was not safe for a woman to travel in those parts. By the time things settled down once more, Doña María Antonia's family had disappeared. That was fifteen years ago, and His Grace has been searching for another bride ever since."

"Aren't there any properly noble women around here?"

"Yes. More than once, the Conde de Pradera has offered his daughter, but His Grace was looking for something in particular, and we have found it for him."

Celia shook her head violently, tearing her hair loose from his grasp. "I don't understand. You haven't told me anything that makes any sense."

"Ah, Celia, I thought you had quicker wits than this. Look around you." He waved an arm at the sleeping multitudes. "In what way are you different from all these others?"

She looked back toward Ana, who appeared to have dozed off. Her eyes returned to Río, to his dark hair, dark eyes, and olive complexion. She held one hand against his shoulder: the contrast in their skin tones was extreme. "I am blonde and all of you are dark."

"Yes, *chica*."

"But His Grace is also blond . . ."

"Exactly. And His Grace's parents and His Grace's brother who died many years ago. He is the last of his line and he wishes to maintain that line pure and unblemished. His bastards sit at his table and bear arms for him, but they are all dark, and he wishes a fair child as his heir—a child he can be certain is his own."

Celia thought about genetics. If the Marqués and his family had been scattering their genes throughout the local population for long enough, a few blonds should have turned up by now. Or maybe not; the fair-skin genes might be so diluted that they were smothered by the others. Human genetics wasn't as clean-cut as pea-plant genetics. Somehow, the Marqués had hit upon the notion of recessive genetic characteristics, and when Celia thought about the blondness that ran so strongly in her own family, she couldn't doubt that he was correct in selecting her to be the mother of his child. It seemed, however, a foolish reason for choosing a bride.

But it hurt bitterly to know that the real choice had been Río's, that he had bought her and shared his blanket with her and protected her at some risk to his own life expressly for the purpose of selling her to someone else. At an enormous profit.

She looked at him reproachfully, tears starting from her eyes.

He reached out and caught one of her tears on the tip of his finger. "*Chiquita*, it is to your profit, too. . . . His Grace is rich and powerful. Present him with an heir and he will give you anything you desire. Gold, jewels, servants . . ."

"I don't like him," she whispered.

"Was it so bad?"

She nodded, and now the tears flowed in earnest, and she bent her head and tried to hide them from him.

"You are doing this to yourself, Celia. If you wish to be happy, you will be happy. You have everything to look forward to. What woman would not trade places with you?"

"I don't want it! I don't want it!" she hissed through clenched teeth. She looked up then, her cheeks streaked by moisture, her eyes red and puffy. She saw him as a blur. *"Dios te maldiga!* How I hate you!"

He laughed softly. "No you don't, and you will thank me someday. But I don't expect it right now. We've been alone long enough, Celia; your *dueña* is fast asleep. You'd better wake her up and go to bed." He leaned back on his cushions and sighed, closing his eyes and thus ending the conversation.

Celia rose and looked down at him. Her hands crept to her belly and clutched the flesh there through the fabric of her dress, as if to tear out something that nested inside. *All right, all right,* she told him silently. *I'll try. I have no choice but to try.*

She faced about, and in the moment that she walked through the dimness toward the sleeping Ana, she felt more alone than ever before in her life.

CHAPTER SIX

Celia was hardly left to herself for a moment in Castillo Quintero. She shared a room in the north tower with Ana, and three maids slept in the antechamber. On her first morning, they helped her dress in a floor-length blue gown which had a starched, scratchy linen ruff at the collar and a long line of ivory buttons down the front. They twisted her hair into a severe knot at the back of her neck and covered it with a dark veil. They tied overlarge velvet slippers on her feet, apologizing for the lack of properly fitting shoes—it hardly mattered since the skirt swept the floor and hid them completely. Ana stepped back and pronounced Celia garbed modestly enough to meet the Dowager Marquesa, who preferred to be addressed in the old-fashioned, grandiloquent manner as *"Excelentisima."*

A guard jerked to attention as Ana and Celia emerged from their rooms and descended a flight to enter the lavender-scented apartments of Doña María Antonia. Here, the tapestries were severe and entirely religious in subject matter: the Virgin looked down upon the room from a dozen angles, and every wall showed at least one Crucifixion scene. In the midst of all this, seated on a plain brown horsehair sofa, veiled and clad wholly in black, was the Dowager Marquesa. Ropy blue veins showed through the transparent skin of her hands, and great jewels sparkled on her bony fingers; she embroidered delicately with a long silver needle, green and gold on a black cloth. Her face was narrow, her pale blue eyes sunk deep into their sockets, her cheeks gaunt and hollow, the skin tight against her skull, showing only a few wrinkles around the mouth and between the brows. Her pure white hair was drawn back tightly and surmounted by a gold comb from which a lacy black mantilla fell. A finely wrought gold crucifix dangled from a thin chain about her neck. She glanced up as Celia curtseyed deeply before her.

"We have been wondering about you," said Doña María Antonia; her voice was strong, with no quaver of old age in it.

Celia wondered who she meant by "we," wondered if that were the plural of majesty, which she had not heard the Marqués himself use.

"We have been wondering from whence you came, what manner of people your parents were, and many other things of which our son has not had the opportunity to inform us. You are from the South?"

"No, *Excelentísima Señora*. From the North, I believe."

"You *believe?* Do you not *know?*"

"I am not certain, *Excelentísima*. I was kidnapped by slave traders and taken far from my native land."

"The *trovador* Rincón calls you a princess. We think this may be an exaggeration. If you were a princess, you would have been ransomed, not sold as a slave. Is this not true?"

Celia fumbled frantically for a tale to fit the Dowager Marquesa's shrewd observation. The Lindbergh law rescued her. "My people are powerful, *Excelentísima*. If the kidnappers had dared to ask for a ransom, they would never have escaped with their lives. My people would have hunted them forever. Among us, the penalty for kidnapping is death."

Doña María Antonia picked up the black lace fan that lay in her lap and snapped it open with a flick of her wrist. Shielding her mouth with it, she spoke to a woman who sat on a stool to her left. The woman shrugged.

"How ambitious are you, child?" asked the old woman.

"I . . . I don't know, *Excelentísima*."

"Normally, we do not doubt the word of the *trovador* Rincón, but we also know that if we were thirty years younger, he would move us far more than he does. He is handsome, is he not? You and he have spent much time together lately. . . . His Grace is very quick to accept you because he desires an heir. Have you been told what happened to His Grace's first wife?"

"Only that she died, *Excelentísima*, and that her child died, too."

"Come, we will allow you to sit at our feet while we tell you the full story, and then you will know what lies in your future."

Celia sat obediently at the hem of the Dowager Marquesa's gown.

"Her name was Rosalía, and she came to us very young and very sick," said Doña María Antonia, her eyes unfocusing as they stared over Celia's head. "A pretty little thing, pale and thin and quickly liked by everyone. Soon enough, her child was born—born with black, black hair. We thought nothing of it, of course, since many fair children begin so, and we informed our son of this, and he was content. But as the weeks passed and the dark hair fell out, the child's birth-blue eyes darkened, and its skin showed a natural dark tint. At last new hair grew in, as black as the first, and His Grace knew this was no child of his . . . and soon Rosalía and the child died. They are buried now in the Castle cemetery." She paused for a long moment, and her eyes refocused on Celia's face. "We tell you this so that when you hear it from a scullery maid or a laundress, you will believe."

"Have no fear, *Excelentísima*," Celia replied softly. "If . . . when I bear a child, it will be His Grace's."

"It is good that you understand. We are also told that you are a heathen. Is this true?"

"My people are far away, *Excelentísima*. Few of them have visited this land, and so we know little of your ways. It is true that I am not of the Faith."

"Then you must be baptized immediately. The thought of our son consorting with a heathen. . . . We pray that it has not endangered his immortal soul. Flora, fetch the priest to the chapel. We will meet him there." She rose from her chair, dropping the embroidery upon the seat, and gestured peremptorily for her ladies to follow.

Celia trailed after the old woman, down the winding staircase. She wondered how much more endangered the Marqués's soul could be than it was by his previous promiscuity, but she knew better than to make any comment. She thought of asking Río about the relative gravity of the two sins, then briskly reminded herself that she intended never to speak to him again. But now, in the light of day, even though her belly ached from the battering it had received in the Marqués's bed, she found it hard to despise the *trovador*. After all, he had never made her any promises.

The chapel was a small but richly appointed room at the far end of a Palace corridor. Its single window showed Christ and the Virgin in stained glass; below, a rack of candles in gilded sconces added their glow to the multicolored sunlight; the altar itself was covered by a cloth that glinted with gold and silver threads. A few young men knelt at the benches, their heads bare and lowered, their eyes closed.

With great dignity—or perhaps with great stiffness because of her age—the Dowager Marquesa knelt in the aisle facing the altar and crossed herself. Her ladies followed suit, and Celia imitated them. For a moment,

Doña María Antonia looked surprised at that, and then she nodded in satisfaction.

Beside the altar waited a short, portly man in black clerical robes. He caught the Dowager Marquesa's eye and gestured toward a side door at the front of the chapel. She followed him through it, and the ladies and Celia followed her, and the priest ducked back to shut the door firmly behind them. They were now in the baptistry; a font of water occupied the center of the small room.

"This is irregular, most irregular, *Excelentísima*," the priest said as soon as he had hurried back to the Dowager Marquesa's side. "Pentecost and Easter—*that* is when adults should be baptized. More than half a year away."

"A tradition is not a law, Padre Juan," said Doña María Antonia. "It is important to His Grace's welfare that the young woman be baptized as soon as possible."

"Yes, yes, I realize that, *Excelentísima*." He bobbed up and down, his steepled fingers almost hidden by the voluminous sleeves of his robe. "Still, I must speak to the Bishop about this, it is so irregular."

At a sign from Doña María Antonia, one of the ladies produced a stool from somewhere, and the old woman seated herself. "When have you ever asked the Bishop's permission for anything done in this chapel? The child has faith and wishes to be baptized today; we will be her sponsor. No elaborate ceremony will be necessary."

"Ah, but the Bishop has baptized the heathen and knows far better than I the ritual—"

"What? Would you cause an old woman to suffer the heat of this windowless room while you send to the Bishop, who is a very busy man and may not be able to come to us for days? Or would you have us climb those endless stairs again without having accomplished our errand?"

"Why no, *Excelentísima*. I wouldn't want to inconvenience you. If only you had given me some warning . . ."

Her hand reached toward him in a gesture of supplication. The pose might have been copied directly from one of the tapestries in her apartments. "This is for our son's soul, *Padre*, that he may not beget a child upon a heathen woman. Surely you understand . . . ?"

The little priest turned to Celia. "Is this your wish, daughter?"

"*Of course* it is!" said the Dowager Marquesa.

"Please, *Excelentísima*. It would be a terrible sin if I baptized an unwilling convert. She must accept Christ as her Savior, she must yield herself to the Church. Can you renounce your heathen beliefs, my child?"

Celia looked down at him from a vantage of five or six inches. He was not precisely her idea of an inquisitor; the vision of him torturing the heresy from her was a ludicrous one. He would be out of breath before the fourth lash. But there was danger in regarding him so lightly, she knew, for Mother Church had always been vastly powerful in Spain. "I am willing to learn, *Padre*. I will do whatever you say."

"We will be her sponsor," the Dowager Marquesa repeated firmly.

"A moment more, *Excelentísima*. My daughter, what do you know of Christianity?"

Celia clasped her hands behind her back and twisted her fingers nervously. "I know of the Trinity—the Father, the Son, and the Holy Spirit. I know of the Virgin Mary, mother of Jesus who died on the Cross for our sins."

"And where did you learn these things?"

"From . . . from Rodríguez, who sold me on the auction block, and from his slaves whom I lived with for two weeks."

"Slaves!" cried the priest.

Doña María Antonia waved impatiently. "She was kidnapped and sold as a slave. The *trovador* bought her somewhere on the northern frontier. She knows quite a bit for a heathen, wouldn't you say, *Padre?*"

"Yes, but she must renounce her false pagan gods, truly renounce them in her heart, and give herself to the Church."

"I do," said Celia. "I swear I do, *Padre*."

"And you must attend Mass and make your Confession and take Communion."

"I will, *Padre*. Just show me how."

"Very well. You will come here every morning for Mass, and afterward I will instruct you in the Faith."

He baptized her then, with a great, windy mass of Latin, and he sprinkled her three times with holy water from the font. Doña María Antonia stood as her godmother and bestowed the baptismal name of Ysabel.

Afterward, Padre Juan patted her cheek in a fatherly way, said he looked forward to seeing her in the morning, and ushered them out of the chapel. Celia was last in line, and she thought his hand lingered on her rump as he scooted her out. A priest? She told herself that she was letting her imagination get the best of her.

The Dowager Marquesa's party wended its way toward the main hall, where the Marqués and his staff were conducting their daily business, and where the main meal of the day was soon to be served.

"My Lady Mother!" said the Marqués, rising from his seat behind a large desk on the dais at one end of the room. He signaled for servants to fetch chairs for the ladies. "What brings you to the hall?"

"The girl has been baptized," Doña María Antonia replied, "and now these old bones must rest before we climb those endless stairs to our bedroom. We have decided to dine with you."

As the Marqués and his mother exchanged further

pleasantries, Celia found her attention wandering. In the light of day, Alonso Enrique Quintero de los Rubios was a stranger, a different person from the blond ogre of last night. She could almost believe it had been a bad dream except for the dull ache in her belly, and the slight soreness between her thighs when she walked. She looked at him and he ignored her. Not pointedly, not rudely. He simply acted as if she were part of the background, with no real individual existence outside of his bed. She experimented with a feeling of hatred for him but found herself unable to sustain it. Even by the standards of her own society, he had been fairly kind to her, and it was no one's fault but her own that she had been unable to react properly. How many other women would be more than willing to profit—to use Río's term—from exchanging places with her?

She noticed Río still on his couch, sitting up now, and beside him bulked the Chief Steward, speaking and gesticulating earnestly. The *trovador* saw her and smiled. She looked down at her hands and found that her fingernails were biting into her palms, opening the half-healed scratches of the night. Inside, she felt empty.

While the meal was being served—beef heavily spiced with cloves and garlic, which made Celia suspect that it was spoiling—Terrazas climbed the steps to the dais and spoke to the Marqués. Celia was close enough to hear his low voice.

"It cannot be duplicated, Your Grace. My best men tried all night. The principle on which it works is obvious enough: concussion causes it to explode violently. But we cannot determine exactly what the substance *is*. We must find the source—a secret formula passed from father to son for generations, no doubt."

"And the powder?"

"An equal puzzle."

"No doubt," growled His Grace. "Dispatch an expedition, then. Send Carril, he's a good man. I will have that secret!"

As Terrazas went out, he bowed to Doña María Antonia and to Celia, which caused the Dowager Marquesa to sniff. "Too soon," she muttered to the nearest lady-in-waiting. "He thinks to please our son by seeming to see the future." She laid aside her knife and fork and rose to indicate that her entourage had finished eating. Her women hastily abandoned half-empty plates and tried to hurry gracefully after their retreating mistress. Celia, who had hardly been able to stomach the pungent food, though she attempted to feign enjoyment, was grateful for the quick exit.

Upstairs once more, she was given a length of dark blue cloth upon which a simple design of a cross and cup and a fish had been traced in chalk. The Marquesa instructed her to embroider it in varicolored threads.

"I've never embroidered anything in my life," she said.

The ladies exchanged startled glances.

"The loom can be set up," said Doña María Antonia. "We are always in need of another tapestry."

Celia shook her head. "I don't know how to weave, either, *Excelentísima*."

"Then you may knit or make lace—"

"I am willing to learn, *Excelentísima*, but I have never done any of these things."

"Then what heathen arts do you know, Celia Ysabel?" demanded the Dowager Marquesa.

"I can sew a little, *Excelentísima*, but mostly I was a . . . a scholar."

"A scholar? What a strange pastime for a woman!"

"It is not considered so among my people, *Excelentísima*."

"You read? You read your heathen tongue? Of what use is that?"

Celia bowed her head in as good an imitation of modesty as she could manage, for her linguistic ability was the one talent of which she was unabashedly proud. "I read and write and speak many languages, *Excelentísima,* and one of them is . . . Castellano." She very carefully used the term that her Argentine boyfriend had preferred as the name of his language. "Spanish," after all, merely referred to its country of origin, where a number of separate languages were spoken, of which one—Castilian—had become the official national tongue and had been brought to America, though not in that order. Celia didn't know whether these people considered themselves "Spanish" in any way. Argentinians considered themselves *Argentine* in her world, but no more than a hundred and fifty years had passed since all Latin Americans had preferred to think of themselves as "Spanish."

The Dowager Marquesa was vibrating her fan with extreme rapidity. "You speak it well, though with a peculiar accent. Bernardina, bring a book from His Grace's library."

One of the ladies-in-waiting curtseyed deeply. "Which book, *Excelentísima?*"

Doña María Antonia waved her fan. "Any book. And find someone who can read, too. We wish to look into this further."

Bernardina lifted her long skirts slightly and hurried away. Everyone around the Dowager Marquesa ran at her slightest command—afraid, perhaps, that if they dawdled she would be dead before they returned.

"We will teach you embroidery and weaving, for these things a Quintero woman should understand. Our own embroidery is well-known here—the altar cloth in the chapel downstairs is the work of our hands."

There was a knock at the door. The Dowager Marquesa motioned for one of her ladies to answer. It was the guard on duty in the corridor outside.

"Your pardon, *Excelentísima*," he said, dropping gracefully to one knee despite his weighty armor. "A servant named Nicolasa says she has a gift to the Lady Celia from the *trovador* Rincón."

"Show her in."

The thin, nervous girl from the laundry entered. Today she was dressed presentably in a clean white smock; her hair was combed, her face washed, and her feet shod. She carried Río's lute cradled like a baby in her arms. She knelt on the floor before the Dowager Marquesa.

Doña María Antonia glanced at Celia. "His lute is the gift? Why?"

"He was teaching me to play it, *Excelentísima*."

"Well, give it to her, don't just crouch there like an idiot!"

Nicolasa stood up hesitantly and held the lute out toward Celia. "He says you must be ready to take his place in the hall when he leaves, *señorita*."

Celia's fingers closed tightly on the neck of the lute. "Leave? He can't leave. He's not well—"

"He says you will need plenty of time for practicing."

Celia grinned wryly. "I suppose I will. Thank him for me, Nicolasa. And tell him . . . tell him I am sorry about what I said yesterday. I owe him a great deal."

"He is a very kind man, *señorita*." She started back toward the door very slowly, glancing from face to face.

"Do you have something else to say?" asked Doña María Antonia. She had begun vibrating her fan again, impatiently.

Nicolasa ducked into a quick curtsey. "*Excelentísima Señora*, Río said that the Lady Celia has a beautiful voice, and . . . I would like very much to hear her sing before I leave. Just a line, *señorita*?"

Celia plucked at the lute. It was in tune. She sang a

nursery rhyme, and by the time she finished, all of the ladies were staring at her.

"That was very good, child," said the Dowager Marquesa. "If only you embroidered as well."

"Thank you, *señorita,* thank you," said Nicolasa. "I see now why Río brought you to us. We had no music when he was gone, but now we shall have it always."

"But surely someone else in the Castle sings . . ."

"A few boys in the chapel at Christmas and Easter," said the Dowager Marquesa. "Singing is a frivolous and useless pastime. You will learn to embroider." She snapped her fan shut and motioned with it for Nicolasa to withdraw.

Celia's fingers tightened on the lute, and one of them slipped off a string, causing a loud twang. She looked at Nicolasa, who was bowing and backing furtively toward the door. Suddenly, Celia fell to her knees before the Dowager Marquesa, bowed her head low and kissed the hem of the old woman's dress—a gesture possibly remembered from some Biblical film. *"Excelentísima Señora,"* she whispered, "may I have your gracious permission to remove this girl from the laundry and make her my maid?"

"What?"

"Excelentísima, there is no one here of my own age. These ladies of rank are far above me in all ways. Please allow me this companion." In truth, she wanted someone to look up to her, since everyone else quite obviously looked down.

"A laundress? A nothing? I forbid it!"

Celia bent her head in acquiescence, and when she lifted it, Nicolasa was gone.

Doña María Antonia directed Celia to begin embroidering the blue cloth she had been given; she hunched over it, stitching laboriously, until Bernardina returned with a puzzled-looking, gray-clad man of middle age in tow.

"This is the man in charge of the library," she said.

"Ronaldo Guerrera de Henares at your command, *Excelentísima*." He was breathing heavily from the long climb.

"The book, the book!" snapped Doña María Antonia.

"I have it here," the man replied, indicating a fat volume under his arm. "Doña Bernardina said you wished someone to read to you . . ."

"Yes, yes, but not you. Give *her* the book."

The librarian handed the volume to Bernardina, who handed it to Celia. It was bound in dark, tooled leather, and gilded letters were pressed into its cover: the Bible. Celia opened it and began to read from the beginning of Genesis. The type face was ornate and difficult at first to decipher, but she managed three or four sentences before being interrupted.

"Anyone could know that by heart, perhaps even a heathen," said the Dowager Marquesa. "Give it to me for a moment." She lowered the tome to her lap and opened it at random. Pointing to a particular line in the middle of a page, she said, "Read this."

" 'Nevertheless, the people refused to obey the voice of Samuel, and they said, No, we will have a king over us.' "

Doña María Antonia glanced sharply at the librarian. "Has she read this correctly?"

The man bent over Celia's shoulder, found the passage with his finger, and nodded.

"Very well. This Bible is yours, Celia Ysabel; may it guide you well." She nodded at the librarian. "You may go."

For the rest of the afternoon, Celia sat quietly in Doña María Antonia's apartments, the Bible on her lap, the embroidery on top of it, the lute propped against her stool. Her embroidery was abysmally sloppy, and the Dowager Marquesa made her rip it out every few minutes. Her fingers grew stiff and began to tremble; she dropped the needle often and once had to crawl around on the floor to find it. Her back began to ache, but every time she unconsciously leaned back to alleviate the strain, her shoulders met empty air and she almost pitched over. The ladies observed her discomfiture in sour silence; their fingers flew, creating marvels of design on cloth not dissimilar to that which she was slowly destroying. Evening fell, and two large oil lamps were brought in so that the ladies could continue to work.

At last, the Dowager Marquesa put her sewing aside and dismissed the group. Ana took charge of Celia and led her away to her own rooms.

"You will go to His Grace again tonight," the middle-aged woman said.

Celia nodded glumly.

"Why do you frown? He is a great and kind man, and you are honored to share his bed." She sighed wistfully. "When I was much younger . . . I was very handsome in my youth."

"He's had many women, hasn't he?"

"I hope to God that now he has found what he has been searching for." A touch of bitterness colored her tone. "He would not acknowledge *my* son." She helped Celia out of the blue gown and into a low-cut, high-waisted white lace nightdress.

"A lovely gown," Celia murmured.

"His Grace ordered it as a gift for you."

"Yes, I suppose he *is* trying to be kind. . . . They don't like me, do they?"

"It is too soon," Ana replied, tightening the red ribbons beneath Celia's breasts. "When you become pregnant, everything will change. They remember Rosalía too well, and she was shy and skilled at woman's work, while you are neither. But when the child is on its way, they will accept you for its sake." She slipped a heavy, wine-colored cloak over Celia's shoulders. "If you want that girl Nicolasa . . . ask His Grace for her. Come along now."

Ana left her at the door to the Marqués's chambers. The guards opened it for her and shut it softly behind.

He was signing some papers, but as soon as he heard her footsteps he rose and came toward her, his long, casual robe rustling. His bejeweled hands brushed the cloak away from her shoulders and let it slide to the floor. He kissed the bare skin at the base of her neck. "Lace becomes you," he whispered, drawing her tense body against his. "Still nervous?" He laughed quietly. "Like a new bride."

Again, the animal mating was distasteful and painful to her. She let him use her body while she tried to think of other things. Would tomorrow be as tedious as today, or would she find something to occupy her mind as the stupid embroidery occupied her fingers? She had to convince the Dowager Marquesa that she really had no facility for such things. The library was a possibility, if it contained more than the Bible. There was the second part of *Don Quixote*, which she had never read—if it existed in this world. It had been written shortly after the period of the Armada, if she recalled correctly. And there were the Twelfth Century romances like *Amadis de Gaula*, which she had never had an opportunity to look at. They were epic poems, probably set to music, and Río might know them and teach her, especially if he were serious about her taking his place when he left.

Río. For a moment, she tried to imagine it was Río who labored, sweating, atop her unresisting body. But it was too difficult a fantasy to maintain; those loose, full lips and that heavy, husky body were all wrong.

He finished and withdrew, leaving her drenched in his sweat and plastered with fine blond hairs from his chest.

"Your Grace?" she whispered, wondering if he were asleep already.

"Mmm?"

"Your Grace, may I ask a small favor of you?"

He got up on one elbow and looked down at her. "What is it?"

She licked her lips, tasted the salt of his perspiration on them. "I am . . . a stranger here, Your Grace. I would feel much more at home if someone my own age were with me."

"Ah, my mother and her old women. Well, there must be someone young around. I've sired a few myself."

"There is a girl who works in the laundry; her name is Nicolasa."

"Nicolasa? I don't know of her. Ask Terrazas—he keeps track of who does what." He turned away and curled up for sleep.

"May I have her as my maid? And get rid of the others who are assigned to me?"

He yawned. "All but your *dueña,* if you like. Ask Terrazas; he'll arrange it. You may leave now."

It was a matter of moments till Celia was in her own room once more.

In the morning, when she went to see the Chief Steward, she wore a green-sleeved, black gown belted by the snake-clasp chain he had given her—was it only two days before? There was a mound of papers and parcels on his desk; somewhere behind them, Celia could hear the scratch of his quill pen.

"Don Rafael?" she called, craning her neck to see the top of his head as he bent low over his work.

"Ah, yes, the Lady Celia," he said, looking up with a smile. "Your rooms are adequate? The food agrees with you? There is the small problem of the shoes, I know, but the cobbler promised to deliver them today or tomorrow."

"I'm surprised you can remember it, Don Rafael."

"Requirement of the job, my lady. How may I serve you?"

"There is a girl who works in the laundry. Nicolasa."

"Nicolasa Gonzales," supplied Ana, who stood by the door.

"Yes, Nicolasa Gonzales. I would like her as my personal maid in place of the three girls who sleep in my antechamber now. If she doesn't mind."

"This can be arranged easily enough, if His Grace approves."

"He does," Celia replied.

"Then is there something else?"

"The library. I'd like to read some books. And pen and ink and paper; there isn't any in my rooms."

Terrazas's eyebrows raised. "I had heard that you read. Do you also write?"

"Yes. I want . . . I want to keep a journal. And perhaps to draw. I'd like a better light than the candles that are in my room, too—a lamp such as you use here in your office, if possible."

He shrugged. "A page will deliver the necessary materials. Choose what you like from the library, but treat those books kindly. Many of them are old and falling apart."

"Thank you, Don Rafael."

"You are quite welcome, my lady. I look forward to serving you in any way possible." He smiled again, and it was a smile with a promise behind it.

Celia left with a prickly feeling crawling up the back of her neck. There was more to Palace life than the straightforward, virtuous path the Dowager Marquesa planned for her. She thought about Rosalía and wondered how it could be possible. Was it all just a vast game, never meant to develop into anything more than flirtation: a look, an unobtrusive touch, perhaps even a few love poems here and there, as some of Río's songs hinted? How was she expected to react? With haughty indifference, flattered blushes, or angry denials? *Rosalía, Rosalía, were you caught in this, too?*

Upstairs, Doña María Antonia was ready to attend Mass. She handed Celia a rosary of green and black beads with a gold crucifix and told her to cover her hair. Ana produced a veil from somewhere and fixed it on Celia's head in the proper fashion. The Dowager Marquesa then led the party down the long staircase to the main floor.

In the chapel, Celia had to kneel on a hard wooden bench that grew harder as the minutes passed and the priest in his white vestments droned the endless Latin ritual. Beside her, Doña María Antonia knelt on a flat little pillow, her eyes closed, her withered body motionless except for her thumbs, which ticked off the beads of her rosary like clockwork, and her lips, which moved in silent devotion.

Celia shifted uncomfortably, searching for some position that would treat her knees more kindly. Behind and before her, the chapel was crowded; she thought she recognized one of Don Rafael's little pages in the back, near the aisle. How could such a young child kneel so still for so long? Celia found herself desperately whiling away the minutes by conjugating irregular verbs.

At last it was over. The priest had vanished through that side door in the front of the chapel, but before the room had cleared of whispering, milling people, he returned, dressed in the more familiar black cassock he had worn the previous day. He headed straight for Celia.

"My daughter, it is time for your lessons."

Somehow, she didn't want to be left alone with him, but she needn't have worried, for Ana remained as chaperone. The three of them passed through the baptistry into another small, tapestry-lined room which must have served Padre Juan as a combination bedroom and study. Here, Celia was able to sit on a chair with a back and drink a leisurely glass of red wine while Ana occupied herself with needlework.

"Saint Philip himself authorized a catechism for the heathen many centuries ago, and the Bishop has advised me to begin with that. Please repeat after me: *Pater noster qui est in caelis . . ."*

Celia echoed the Lord's Prayer in Latin and then in Spanish, and when he commended her excellent pronunciation of the Latin, she said, *"Padre,* if you will let me write down the words, I will be able to memorize them more quickly."

He gaped for a moment, and then he went to a sideboard for a quill, bottle of ink, and heavy paper.

Her first few strokes with the quill blotched and spattered, but she soon got the hang of dipping just the nib into the ink and of pressing very lightly on the paper, and she was immediately intrigued by the variations of line width that a quill pen produced. After a little experimentation, she settled on a lettering style that resembled printing more than writing, but which was clear and legible, if not elegant. She wrote so well and so quickly that Padre Juan dictated the *Ave Maria* to her also. She indicated the differences in pronunciation from the classical Latin she was more familiar with by parenthetical phonetic symbols, which the *padre* understood to be letters of her native Indian tongue.

"I would like to give you a Bible, my daughter, so that we might discuss the earthly life and works of Our Lord . . ."

"I have one already, *Padre*—a gift from Doña María Antonia."

"Ah, then since you know how to read, study the Gospel according to St. Mark."

"Yes, *Padre.*"

"There is more . . . but perhaps I am allowing my zeal to carry me away. The mind can only hold so much at one time. Learn what I have given you, daughter."

"I will, *Padre.*"

The priest leaned back in his chair and sipped at his second glass of wine. "It is often thus, so the Bishop has told me upon occasion. He was a missionary in the North for many years, and he found that Indian con- verts were often the best Christians. I wonder why it should be so?" Rummaging in his desk, he found a pipe, packed it with tobacco from a small pouch in the top drawer, and lit up. Aromatic fumes drifted about his head like a halo as he mused, looking off into space beyond Celia's right shoulder.

After a long silence, she asked, "May I be excused, *Padre?*"

"Of course, my child. I didn't mean for you to try and answer my question. It is enough that you be a good Christian and leave the answers to God."

Out in the chapel, she remembered to kneel and cross herself before the altar. As she passed into the corridor, she felt a great invisible weight lifting from her, and she breathed deeply, flooding her lungs with cool, slightly musty air. She leaned against the wall and found the stone faintly damp.

"I wish to go to the library, Ana."

Ana led the way.

Ronaldo Guerrera de Henares was there, dusting the books lovingly, and he helped Celia search through the modest number of shelves. No *Don Quixote* was to be found, nor any other book that Celia recognized, so she selected a volume that appeared to be a chivalric romance. It had been published in 1923 in Nueva Cádiz; the prose was flowery and had a pleasant archaic flavor absent from the everyday language of San Felipe. Later, after another abortive attempt at embroidery, she suggested reading aloud to the Dowa- ger Marquesa and her ladies. Doña María Antonia ac- quiesced reluctantly but was soon caught up in the narrative and keenly disappointed when Celia's voice gave out. She was so pleased by the new entertainment that she made no remark except an exaggerated "Hush!" when timid Nicolasa came in with a page who announced her as Celia's new servant.

That evening, Celia bathed in the laundry room again, astonishing the washerwomen, who assured her that no one but the ultra-fastidious Marqués immersed his entire body in water more than once a month. It was unhealthy, they declared. One result of this circumstance was that the whole Palace smelled faintly of sweat; another, more disquieting, was the possibility of lice. Every time Celia saw someone scratch, she fancied that the itch was an insect bite; she lathered herself vigorously, hoping that whatever vermin might infest the onlookers would stay away from her. The soap she used this time was pleasantly scented, a gift from the Marqués; she was grateful that, of everyone in the Palace, at least he had some notion of cleanliness.

After the bath, she played the lute until he called for her. In his bed, she was bored, restless, and uncomfortable, but the pain was not as great as before—her body, like her mind, was beginning to adapt to necessity. Back in her room, she found the lamp and the writing utensils sent up by Terrazas. After Ana had shown her how to ignite and adjust the light, she scrawled a few lines diary-style—in pig Latin, just in case English had not entirely become a dead language. What she said of the Marqués was not at all complimentary.

The days passed. Nicolasa, freed from the drudgery of laundering and possessed of a vast new wardrobe suitable to her station, idolized her mistress and jumped to run the smallest errand for her. Padre Juan, impressed by Celia's reading speed and by her ability to memorize long prayers in a short period of time, praised her to the Dowager Marquesa. Doña María Antonia smiled occasionally and finally gave up trying to force Celia to embroider on that square of dark blue cloth.

Celia immersed herself in the library, in the lute, and in theology. One night, while pondering the concept of Confession, in preparation for a discussion of it in the morning, she found herself tempted to confess to the sin that the Marqués and his mother and even Padre Juan were condoning—fornication. She wondered how the priest would defend his doublethink. But she sighed and decided not to yield to the urge to score such a trivial and meaningless point. He would hem and haw and change the subject, surely. Instead, she scratched at a piece of paper with her quill, scribbled out a calendar, and counted days. Then she counted again, as a cold hand clutched at her entrails. She told herself she was not surprised, but she lied. "Why am I so goddam fertile?" she screamed in English to no one in particular. Part of her was still saying, at that very instant, *no, it can't happen to me*.

Her menstrual period was two weeks overdue.

CHAPTER SEVEN

Everyone in the Castle was talking about the mysterious death of the peddler Diaz in the middle of the courtyard—he was standing in a crowd of people, hawking his trinkets, when two bullets came out of nowhere and blew away the back of his head. Rumor had it that a madman with a double-barreled pistol had been hiding in a haywagon near the peddler and had murdered him for reasons known only to the lunatic brain. Another rumor said that a nameless nobleman had commissioned the killing over a bit of silver jewelry that turned out to be pewter. At any rate, the Marqués's guards had swarmed out into the courtyard seconds after the event and cleared the area, and no one could say exactly what, if anything, had been discovered.

But Celia had heard two shots in quick succession and formulated her own theory.

"You're looking well," she said.

Río looked down at her as she sat in one of the easy chairs that had recently been delivered to her chamber. He wore traveling clothes—dark shirt and pants, his own brown leather boots, a long gray woolen cloak, and a low-crowned sombrero. "The doctor pronounced me healed, and now I must go north on an errand for His Grace."

"To buy guns."

He smiled slightly. They were alone in Celia's room,

except for Nicolasa, who sat on the floor at her mistress's feet. Ana was in the anteroom, undoubtedly listening at the door.

"I'm curious about the shooting, Río, and I think you can explain it."

He said nothing, made no motion.

"Will the Marqués punish you if you tell me?"

"Still asking questions, Celia? I shouldn't have expected you to change in one short month."

She stood up and paced the length of the chamber. "I've learned that the Conde de Pradera, who so gallantly offers his only legitimate child as a match for the Marqués, has been trying for years to encroach on His Grace's borders. Patrolling the rivers is a hard enough job without having to man garrisons along a land border. A few thousand rifles with mechanisms like that pistol you brought from the North would mean the difference between victory and defeat—or at least stalemate—in the coming war."

Río watched her narrowly. "How do you know there will be a war?"

She stood at the east window and looked down at the courtyard. "There will be a war as soon as Pradera realizes that his daughter will have to find a different husband."

He studied her, and then he rubbed his cheek with an index finger. "Yes, you walk like a pregnant woman. Have you told His Grace?"

She shook her head. "There's always the possibility that I'm wrong."

"And you've only been there a month. Too soon for the Palace laundresses to know, though they'll realize soon enough. Are you sick?"

"Not yet. I don't know much about it, but Nicolasa says her mother never got sick before the third month."

"I am very happy for you, Celia."

"I'm sure you are; you and your hundred *duros*."

She turned and looked across the room at him. "I haven't seen much of you since we've been here."

"Don Epifanio forbade me to climb the stairs, and you aren't often in the main hall. Have you been practicing the lute?"

"Yes. Do you want it back?"

"No. Keep it for me. I'll be back before winter sets in."

"You *are* going to Verdura, aren't you?"

"Yes. Capitán Carril was not very successful."

"But he brought back at least one rifle, didn't he? And the Marqués stood at the window of his bedchamber, which overlooks the courtyard. Like so . . ." She leaned toward the half-open casement, lifting her arms to aim an imaginary rifle. "Did he kill the peddler on purpose or by accident?"

"He is an excellent shot. The peddler was a Pradera spy—no loss. But His Grace said afterward that if he had missed and killed some innocent, loyal subject, both Carril and I would have . . . suffered. Fortunately, it was a very accurate rifle."

"Why are *you* going?"

"Because I am acquainted with a few people there. Carril was the wrong man to send—a good fellow but unknown. I, however, was in no condition to travel, and His Grace was in a hurry."

"You're sure you're all right now?"

"Yes."

She looked at the floor, at the finely woven green carpet. "I have missed you the last month. They keep me sheltered. And my lessons . . . Be careful, Río; watch out for river pirates."

"I came to say good-bye and to give you some extra lute strings." He dug into the pouch at his waist and produced a small packet. "Will you play for me before I leave?"

Listlessly, she picked up the lute, strummed a chord and sang,

Cabillito blanco, reblanco, reblanco . . .

Río listened and nodded, but whether in remembrance or approval, Celia could not tell. When she put down the lute, he took her hand and, bending over it, kissed the knuckles softly.

"I trust I will return to find you Marquesa."

Then he was gone, and a few minutes later, as she sat by the east window, she saw him cross the courtyard on horseback and pass through the imposing Castle gate into the city beyond. She wondered if he would return to report that the unknown source of guns had dried up. A few rifles here and there might be left over from before, but if Larry were dead, the Marqués was doomed to disappointment.

And if Larry were alive, the Marqués was certain to contact him sooner or later. Of course! It was inevitable. Celia clutched the chair arms and forced her excitement down. She wasn't worlds away from Larry; she was in one of the few places that might communicate with him. If he were still alive. She thumped her fist on the windowsill until Nicolasa reminded her that she must soon read for the Dowager Marquesa.

The pattern of days and nights lacked something for Celia. She had read through the entire Palace library by this time, and there were no other titles to be had in San Felipe Emperador. The publishing houses of America lay farther south, and it took years for their meager production to trickle north—and even then it was the older books that were being reprinted over and over again. Literary creativity seemed uncommon in the New World, and widespread illiteracy might be both cause and effect of that situation.

She asked the librarian about getting books from Europe, but he only shook his head.

"A European book is a rarity indeed. Europe sends us very little these days. And takes little from us, now that all the gold is gone. Even the tax collectors have

SHADOW OF EARTH 137

abandoned us, though His Grace still sends the yearly
gift to Emperor Fernán by way of Nueva Cádiz. Or is
it Emperor Carlos? Well, one of the two."

"Surely there is something . . . some news, at
least."

Ronaldo shrugged. "Spanish ships still land at
Nueva Cádiz—that's at the mouth of the Lodísimo—
but the news is quite stale by the time it comes to San
Felipe. And often distorted. The only certainty is that
there is a war. There is always a war . . . with the
Turks, with the French; with the Swedes, I think,
most recently. Or perhaps the Russians. A northern
land, anyway. But that is nothing to us; we have our
own wars."

When she had discreetly asked around, she found
that no one knew any more about what was going on
in Europe, and no one cared. It was all too far away;
talking about Spain or France was like talking about
Mars. Even speculation was considered absurd. Nicolasa, however, confided to Celia that her grandmother
had told her that at least one race of Europeans had
two heads and four arms. "And they breathe fire, but
those can't cross the ocean because the water puts their
fire out and then they die."

A large, yellowed globe that occupied a corner of
the library showed fabulous monsters cavorting in
mid-ocean and on the fancied continent of Terra Incognita Australis, which appeared far larger than the
real, undiscovered Antarctica. Australia was missing,
and the contours of North and South America—
labeled "Nueva España" and "Peru," respectively—
were highly distorted at their extremities. The area Celia knew as Canada merged with a ragged and partly
imaginary north-polar land mass that included Green-
land. An atlas containing newer maps turned out to be
no less inaccurate, and when questioned, Ronaldo
could only shrug and wonder why anyone would be
interested in so much ice, snow, and hardship.

A map of North America—dated 1880—unfolded from the atlas with a crackling sound that caused the librarian to inspect the aging paper anxiously. He warned Celia to be more careful—these were the Marqués's own maps, which very few people were allowed to look at, and His Grace would be angry if they were damaged.

"By the look of it, this book hasn't been opened in years," said Celia.

"I am responsible for it, Lady Celia; it will be ready when and if His Grace requires it," the librarian replied stiffly. He took a white handkerchief from his pocket and gently dusted the top of the volume that rested beside the atlas's empty place.

Celia handled the map with greater delicacy, bending close to read the fine print. She saw that Nueva España was divided into large areas separated by such natural boundaries as rivers and mountain ranges and bearing names like "Audiencia de México" and "Presidencia de Guadalajara." She recognized the southernmost names: they had been the same in her own world until the early Nineteenth Century, when a wave of republican revolution swept away the Spanish colonial governments. Here, the old names had obviously hung on, and new ones in the same pattern had been added: "Presidencia de California," for example, was a densely populated strip running up the western coast almost to the Alaskan peninsula. Towns with Spanish names crowded the map nearly to illegibility in some localities, becoming sparser to the north; the area east of Verdura, which Celia had known as the eastern industrial heart of the United States, was marked "Territorio de los Indios"—Indian Territory. In her world, the British had colonized the continent from the Atlantic seaboard, pushing the Indians westward ahead of them; here, the Spanish had colonized from the south and driven the Indians north and east.

Straddling the Mississippi River (Río Lodísimo)

and extending well to the east and west to include the areas Celia knew as Indiana, Illinois, Iowa, and Missouri was "Presidencia de San Felipe Emperador," with its capital city "La Ciudad de San Felipe Emperador" near its geographical center. Celia recalled that when the Spanish colonial system had reached its ultimate elaboration, each subdivision of Nueva España had possessed its own judicial body, the *audiencia*; in those subdivisions known as *"presidencias,"* which were usually on the frontier, the president of the *audiencia* was also governor of the area and directly responsible to the Viceroy of Nueva España, who represented the King of Spain and resided in Mexico City. Celia asked Ronaldo how the system worked now that contact with Europe was so tenuous.

"The old names," he said, shrugging. "They hang on. His Grace is *presidente,* yes, and the *audiencia* advises him, but there is no Viceroy. It's been a long time since the last Viceroy left. The Empire was very big, perhaps too big, and so the Emperor loosened his hold on us."

"Then the Marqués has no superior and this is really a kingdom. Why doesn't he call himself a king?"

Ronaldo straightened indignantly, his bearing suddenly almost military. "His Grace's ancestor was a Marqués in Europe two hundred and fifty years ago, before Emperor Carlos the Seventh appointed him to the Presidencia de San Felipe Emperador! Other men have assumed titles they have no right to, but His Grace would never do so."

"What other men?"

"The Conde de Pradera, for one. His great-great-grandfather was a low-born adventurer who gathered a group of fellow-paupers and set himself up as a self-styled *conde.*"

Well, that's how it all started in Europe, Celia thought, but she didn't antagonize Ronaldo, who obviously had firm convictions, by voicing her opinion.

"I don't see Pradera on this map," she said, squinting at the tiny, ornate lettering.

Ronaldo pulled a rolled map from a high shelf and spread it out beside the atlas. This rendering showed the Presidencia, with its northern boundary at Verdura, and a few surrounding territories. Outlined in red was a smaller region, partly within the Marqués's realm and partially enclosing more northerly lands that had been labeled Indian Territory on the previous map. Red letters proclaimed it "Pradera" and indicated its few, scattered towns and the capital, "La Ciudadela del Conde."

Celia indicated the portion of Pradera which seemed to overlap the Presidencia. "This is the disputed land?"

"This," he said, brushing his forefinger lightly against the map, "*this* is His Grace's land, given to his family by Emperor Carlos the Seventh. About that there can be no dispute. This upstart, this *conde*, so he calls himself—how does he dare to encroach on Quintero land?" His face grew red as he spoke of the quarrel and of others like it. The catalogue of petty squabbles between the Marqués and his neighbors was a catechism the librarian had committed to his soul as well as his memory. Castillo Quintero was the center of the universe, and the first Marqués Alonso Enrique Quintero de los Rubios—after whom most of his descendants were named, and in whose honor they omitted the matronym that was a traditional part of the Spanish surname—was Adam. It was a dreary inventory, devoid of great men and great accomplishments; since the earliest days of the Presidencia, its borders had undergone constant minor fluctuations as one neighbor or another decided he was willing to fight for a few square miles of land. If men with more grandiose schemes and abilities ever existed, Ronaldo and the Presidencia de San Felipe Emperador knew nothing of them.

Missing, too, from the register of history was any mention of the great inventions that had made bigger and better wars possible after the Industrial Revolution. San Felipe had no power beyond draft animals and water wheels. Without steam engines, electricity, and mass-production factories, not only was advanced weaponry nonexistent, but widespread conveniences of Celia's world were available only at a premium; some that were common in Evanston, Illinois, were unobtainable even by the Marqués himself.

For example, there was no plumbing above the first floor in Castillo Quintero. In the dead of night, rising to relieve the pressures of elimination, the Marqués and everyone else in the Palace had the choice of descending to the latrines on the ground floor or using a chamber pot. On the coldest winter days, when the spring which fed the latrines froze solid, there was no choice at all. In milder weather, the flowing water washed waste away, but so slowly that it left a lingering odor behind. The pipe which carried the used water emptied into a gully just outside the Castle walls, and when the wind was wrong and the rear gate ajar— as it was during daylight hours—the stench circulated throughout the Palace.

The same spring supplied drinking, washing, and cooking water, which was drawn off before it reached the latrines. Between these two points was an open sluice. Celia suspected that the supposedly pure water was being contaminated by the waste and causing the attacks of dysentery which were not uncommon in the Palace. She ordered her own drinking water boiled, but, not satisfied with this half-measure, she laboriously drew up plans for a flush toilet and a new sewer system that would efficiently separate pure water from waste. Proudly she presented them to Don Rafael Terrazas.

"Very ingenious," he said, after inspecting the diagrams. "But I see no need for this. We would have to tear down and rebuild the back of the Palace to accommodate these pipes, and to lay perhaps a mile more . . ."

"It would be best to drain the waste beyond the city."

"Impossible! The cost of the pipe alone . . .! Just to get rid of a little smell. . . . Lady Celia, I assure you that you will soon become accustomed to it. Even for the mother of his heir, I don't think the Marqués would approve of this."

She tried to explain, but she could not show him bacteria nor make him understand the germ theory of disease. He was satisfied with the status quo and did not see that her suggested alterations were a vast improvement. The Palace had efficient enough drains, and installation of the new system in other parts of the city, where there were no natural springs to aid sanitation, would require tearing up streets and buildings. The more Terrazas thought about it, the more appalled he was by the magnitude of the operation. In deference to her status-to-be, he did not call her a lunatic, but he politely and firmly advised her to forget about plumbing.

Upstairs, Celia wadded up the diagrams and tossed them into the chamber pot. As a Connecticut Yankee in King Arthur's Court, she was a failure. Without a fortuitous eclipse, without the pocket lighter that invariably overwhelmed scores of ignorant natives in as many adventure novels, and—more important—without the basic knowledge to construct tools with which to build better tools, she was helpless. She realized how empty her mind was, how ineffectual she was without the technology she had always taken for granted. She knew how to wire an electrical plug—what an utterly useless skill in a world without electricity! Yet, she had no idea how to introduce electricity into this culture. To begin at the beginning, to reconstruct an industrial technology single-handedly as the Yankee did, was impossibly far beyond her powers. The usual liberal-arts curriculum offered by American colleges did not include a course in the construction of steam engines and dynamos.

If only she had known what would be necessary—books, tools, and knowledge of how to use them. If only she had known she would be marooned in this unfamiliar world . . . she could have set herself up as a queen instead of a lowly pawn.

Celia shook her head, drove the thought from her mind. That was Larry, not her. Larry was the one who wanted to profit from this decadent empire. If Celia had known about the kidnapping, known even that she would emerge unharmed and the wife of a great nobleman, known what that life would really be, she would have stifled her curiosity and never stepped into that target circle in Larry's back room. She struck her fist against the wall, remembering once more that she had vowed to try and fit the role Río had given her; thinking about what might have been would never help her do so.

Although occasionally allowed to entertain in the main hall, more often Celia was compelled to sing or read to Doña María Antonia and her ladies—a stony audience at best, and a highly critical one now that they were accustomed to the innovation. One day, when Celia had pleaded illness and been excused from the Dowager Marquesa's presence, she sat in her room, doodling on a page of her diary. She was translating folk songs from English, pleased at how easily she could rhyme the lines, even if the words had to be juggled a bit to maintain some semblance of the original meter. A couplet came to her:

> *Cuando nos reuniremos otra vez—*
> *En trueno, relámpago o lluvia, nosotras tres?*

> When shall we three meet again—
> In thunder, lightning, or in rain?

She read it aloud to Nicolasa, who sat in the corner, embroidering. It scanned better in English, but it wasn't too horrible as translated. She fancied rendering all of *Macbeth* into Spanish, or at least as much as she could remember; she had played one of the witches in a high school production. It seemed a futile effort, though, since so few people in the Palace—and in San Felipe—could read.

And then the idea of performing *Macbeth* crept upon her. It was, of course, hardly feasible, even if she could make an adequate translation from memory. Who would act in it? And how would they learn their lines without knowing how to read?

The translation took her four days. It was true to the plot of the original, and as true to the actual dialogue as her excellent recall could make it. Her talent for poetry, even in Spanish, turned out to be less than the Bard's, but she didn't worry about disgracing his reputation. The plays had all been written after the defeat of the Armada; with Spain victorious, God alone knew what had happened to Protestant Will Shakespeare during the confusion that must have followed. That he had never written a thing was highly probable, which would make Celia the sole source of *Macbeth* and whatever other Shakespearean plays she chose to recreate.

I might become famous. At least as famous as those bad Roman copies of lost Greek statues.

But that was not her primary consideration.

After Mass one morning she went to Don Rafael Terrazas's office with the finished translation under her arm. She found him at his usual pursuit.

"How may I serve you, Lady Celia?" he said, laying his pen down for a moment.

"I wish to put on an entertainment, Don Rafael. I

have written a play, and I want to ask your help in presenting it."

He shrugged. "A troupe of traveling actors comes through San Felipe on occasion, performing *comedias*. That is during the summer. I don't know if they could be persuaded to try your play."

"No, I wasn't thinking of that. Some people from the Palace. I see a lot of landless knights in the hall—surely they have time to spare."

"I doubt if many of them can read."

"Then I will teach them the parts as Padre Juan teaches the *Pater Noster*. A little time each afternoon. Can it be done?"

He leaned back in his chair. "What does Doña María Antonia say to this?"

"I haven't asked her. Must I?"

"No, I suppose not. Is that the play there, under your arm?"

She nodded.

"Let me see it."

She handed him the manuscript and watched anxiously as he scanned the first few pages. When he showed no sign of laying the sheaf down after four pages, she cleared a place for herself on top of a cabinet and sat down to wait. Nicolasa knelt on the floor at her feet.

A long time later, he turned the last page. "What do you call it?"

"El Conde Glamis."

Terrazas rubbed absently at the ink stain on his temple and leaned back in his chair. "I look forward to seeing it performed." He smiled. "Now I suggest for Glamis himself, me; for Condesa Glamis, his wife, yourself, and to hell with the idea that women ought not to be actors. My three pages can be the witches—we'll dress them as old women, and with their high-pitched voices no one will know. If Río were here, I would suggest him for this Duff person, but since he is gone, Ronaldo the librarian will do. That leaves only a few small parts that you will have to teach by rote; the rest of us can read well enough for ourselves."

"I didn't think you would be so enthusiastic, Don Rafael."

"When you are my age and have heard the same epics and seen the same *comedias* a dozen dozen times, you will understand how welcome a diversion like this is. Before whom do you intend to perform this entertainment?"

"I thought . . . for Doña María Antonia and the ladies—"

He shook his head emphatically. "For everyone. Poor Río, that he should miss it!" He called the pages in and dispatched them with messages for various people around the Palace. "We must have more copies of the manuscript. Three more will do. Take this note"—he scribbled a few lines on a scrap of paper— "to Ronaldo and give him the manuscript. He knows a scholar or two who can copy it. It's not for printing, though—we'll want to keep it a secret for a while yet, eh?"

"You overwhelm me, Don Rafael," Celia said, taking the note.

"This is not for your sake alone, Lady Celia. Are you well these days?"

"Well enough."

"Good. Good. Let us all meet in the library the day after tomorrow, after Mass. I look forward to being in your play."

Don Rafael threw himself into the play as if he had limitless time and energy. He learned his lines quickly and helped his three pages, who were not quite as proficient as he had assumed, to learn theirs. But he disappeared promptly as soon as rehearsal was over, and word circulated in the Palace that he had begun to work late into the night on his papers and reports.

"He thinks he's Saint Philip the Accountant," Ana

said. At Celia's puzzled look she crossed herself quickly. "No blasphemy meant, Lady Celia, but he likes it well known that he works as hard as did the Holy Emperor himself."

As director of the play, Celia enjoyed herself immensely. At last she could give orders instead of taking them. True, she had to cope with the conflicting opinions of her actors—none of them was *entirely* willing to let her make the final decisions—and she virtually had to teach them how to act, but considering the material she had to work with, everything progressed quite smoothly. The pages stumbled over their lines, but at least they understood the concept of speaking in chorus—they were choir boys in the chapel at Christmas and Easter. Don Rafael was larger than life, and his booming lines could be heard through the solid oak doors of the library, where they rehearsed. Ronaldo was timid and had to be urged to assert himself, especially in the fencing scene with Don Rafael: he couldn't get used to pretending to be the Chief Steward's social equal. The man who played Duncan so fancied the pewter crown that Terrazas ordered for him that he couldn't keep his fingers off it—he readjusted it half a dozen times every minute it sat on his head. Celia coaxed and pleaded and invoked Terrazas's authority, and as the weeks flew by, the Comedia Quintera, as she had christened the group, smoothed itself out and became nearly professional.

"I can almost understand the delight of being a traveling actor, the satisfaction of learning one's part and playing it well," Don Rafael said just before the performance. He looked out at the audience from behind a tapestry-covered doorway. The long, drooping feather in his red cap tickled Celia's nose as she tried to look over his shoulder and count the house. She had not argued for costumes, but everyone in the cast was wearing brightly colored clothes. Even Nicolasa, who had been drafted as part of Condesa Glamis's retinue,

was bedecked with ribbons. She and the other lesser
female players had also chosen to wear powder, rouge,
and mascara for the special occasion, a practice that
was usually frowned upon by the Dowager Marquesa.

Their stage was the dais at one end of the main hall.
Entrances would be made though the audience, as in
theater-in-the-round. Courtiers sprawled in chairs and
on the floor, and the Marqués and his mother sat on
comfortably upholstered couches in the front. Padre
Juan occupied a stool beside them.

"I am . . . nervous," said Terrazas.

"I don't feel well myself," Celia remarked, touching
her belly with the flat of one hand. A queasy feeling
was growing in the pit of her stomach.

"Perhaps you should lie down." He touched her elbow, but she shook him off.

"It's almost time for your entrance."

On the stage, a gangling youth had introduced the
play and set the scene: night, a windy hilltop—the
best substitute for a heath that Celia could imagine in
America.

> Cuando nos reuniremos otra vez—
> En trueno, relámpago, o lluvia, nosotras tres?

The sound of the three pages chanting was more for-
lorn than foreboding, and even Terrazas seemed
lonely and frightened up on the dais in front of his
friends and associates. He played Glamis curious but
fearful, and it was all right: it fit the mood of the
scene. He was stronger afterward, having acquired his
stage legs, and his calmness communicated itself to the
others. Miraculously, no one forgot his lines.

Celia herself had no trouble beyond a few butter-
flies. She let herself go, weeping and wailing the mad
hand-washing scene, and soon enough she was offstage
permanently and could sit in the back of the audience
and watch the finish of the play. Nicolasa was with

her, watching her mistress instead of the actors, and when Celia suddenly blanched and reached out for support, Nicolasa's thin hands were there, amazingly strong and steady.

They crept away from the main hall just before Duff killed Glamis, so they never knew whether Ronaldo had summoned enough bravado to carry it off. Nicolasa produced a bucket from some invisible storage place in the corridor, and Celia bent double to vomit wretchedly, over and over, until there was nothing left in her stomach, and then again, until the dry spasms shook her body like a terrier shaking a rat. At length, when only tiny quivers remained and Celia's ragged breathing had begun to settle down, Nicolasa wiped her mistress's face with the hem of her skirt and smoothed back the sweat-sopped tendrils of fair hair.

"I thought it was supposed to be *morning* sickness," Celia slurred. "What a horrible taste. I'm so dry now I can't even spit."

Ana, having lost sight of her charge, had come out into the corridor and found the two young women standing over a bucket of stinking and easily identified fluid. She took Celia's right arm, leaving the left to Nicolasa. "Come, my lady, you must go to your room and lie down."

"The play. Is it over? What do they think of it?"

"They like it. Come along now, my lady."

Her legs shook, but she was able to climb the stairs with her maids' help. Tucked into bed, she felt incredibly weak, and only with difficulty could she raise her head for a sip of wine. The liquid burned her throat, which was raw from stomach acid, but at least it cleansed her mouth of the bitterness of vomit.

Don Epifanio came up to look at her—she knew him with her eyes closed, by the scent of his perfume.

"Any pains?" he said as he pulled a chair close to her bed and sat down.

She nodded faintly. "I've had mild cramps occasionally for the last week or two."

"And your time is . . . ah . . . overdue?"

"Eight weeks."

"Ah," on a high note. He tugged at his goatee. "I think we can safely tell His Grace that the heir is on its way."

Celia closed her eyes. "How long will this sickness last?"

"Not long, not long. A week or two. Eat plenty of bread but no butter. Stay away from grease. You are strong and healthy—I foresee no trouble."

"Is there something you can give me? My stomach is very bad."

"Don't eat or drink anything till morning. Take some dry bread before you get up. You'll be fine." He patted her hand and rose to leave.

"Don Epifanio, did you see the play?"

"The play? Oh, yes."

"What did you think of it?"

"Very amusing. A folktale of your own people, wasn't it?"

Celia was surprised he had guessed so near the truth and stung that he hadn't given her any credit for originality. "Yes, it was."

"Rest well, my lady." And he was gone.

"Nicolasa?"

The girl looked up from her embroidery. "Yes, my lady?"

"Go back downstairs and find out what the audience thought of my play."

"Yes, my lady." As she went out, Ana came in to take her place and make sure that Celia was comfortable.

Staring at the ceiling, feeling a bleakness overcome her, Celia realized that she suffered from morning-after depression. It was all over, the writing, the rehearsing, the premiere. Nothing was left. There would be no second performance because everyone had seen the first. What did she expect Nicolasa to bring back—critical praise? They would all react like Don Epifanio; they'd like it or not and say so in a word or two, and that would be it. The letdown was greater, of course, because Celia hadn't been there to hear the applause and take a bow.

She sat upright suddenly. "Ana, did they applaud?"

Ana turned a puzzled face toward her mistress. "Applaud?"

"Clap their hands, you know?"

"Clap?" Ana shrugged. "Why should they do that? There was no music."

God! What did they do to show their approval? Snap their fingers? Stamp their feet? "Well, did they shout *olé!* or what?"

"Surely not! The Dowager Marquesa would never approve."

Celia sighed; she found herself wishing someone would send her flowers. And then her stomach began to roil, and she only wished for Dramamine.

Nicolasa returned with the expected news—the court had enjoyed the presentation, and His Grace sent his thanks to the author/director/leading lady. He had also heard that she was sick, and so there would be no summons to his bedchamber that night.

"Leonora will be glad to hear that," Ana muttered to Nicolasa.

"Who is Leonora?" asked Celia.

Ana shut her mouth firmly and looked away, but Nicolasa came to her mistress's bedside and whispered, "His current lady-love."

Celia shrugged, uncaring, relieved that she was free for a night. If only her stomach would settle, she could enjoy that freedom. She slid into a restless sleep that was periodically interrupted by bouts of nausea.

In the days that followed, Celia's morning sickness did not restrict itself to the hours before noon. She ate when the sight of food did not entirely revolt her, which was rarely, and she slept fragmentarily at various times of day and night. She lost weight, till her elbows and collarbone emerged in sharp relief. Doña María Antonia allowed her to skip Mass, and Padre Juan made the long journey upstairs to give her Communion, which made Celia think that everyone expected her to die. She felt rotten enough to die; she hadn't felt so bad since her childhood bouts with mumps and influenza.

"How much longer, Nico?" she asked when the nausea has lasted two weeks.

"I don't know, my lady. Why don't you try to eat something?"

Celia turned to Ana, her face gray at the thought of food. "How was it with you, Ana?"

"I don't remember, my lady."

"You remember!" Celia cried, and her voice sounded hollow in her own ears. She sat up and pointed a thin index finger at the middle-aged *dueña*. "You remember everything, but you won't tell. You think you'll scare me, don't you? You're keeping the truth from me!"

"Lady Celia, you are raving!" Ana said, startled. She pressed her mistress back against the pillows. "You haven't eaten enough to keep a bird alive. Hunger is making you say these things!"

Celia struggled against Ana's restraining arms. "He won't give me anything to stop the sickness. Don't you understand, he *has* to, or I *will* die, and I'll take the baby with me. I'll jump out the window, I'll fall down the stairs. He must *do* something!"

"Get Doctor Velas," Ana told Nicolasa.

"Can you hold her?"

"Yes. She's very weak. Hurry!"

Don Epifanio was puffing from the long run up the stairs. "What's this?" he said when he saw Ana holding Celia down on the bed.

"Don Epifanio!" Celia cried, reaching out toward him.

He took her hands and helped her sit up.

"Don Epifanio, you must help me. I can't stand it much longer." She clenched her teeth and fists against a sudden wave of nausea; sweat sprang out on her forehead. "You must have some kind of medicine. Even opium—"

He held her hands tightly. "Impossible. Opium would harm the child."

She shook her head wildly. "I don't care about the child. Do something for *me!*"

He touched her forehead, then poked at her stomach. "Is there any pain?"

"No, just this horrible nausea."

"There is no fever. You must bear it, my lady."

"I can't." She laughed brokenly. "I can't keep food down. I'm starving to death. The child is killing me."

"It is this way for all women. Ana has borne a child, and she is alive and well. You must stay calm and have faith, and soon the sickness will go away. And then you will be so hungry you will get fat."

"How soon, Don Epifanio?"

"Soon. Rest now."

After he had gone, Celia adopted a control so iron that it made her teeth ache. She would starve to death with dignity. She asked for the lute, and when it was brought, she played it for the first time in many days.

She plucked at it endlessly, aimlessly, making up words and melody as she went along and forgetting them as soon as they were sung. She walked around her bedchamber barefoot, never straying too far from the bucket that sat beside the bed, but she didn't need it often now since there was seldom anything in her stomach. She imagined the baby resting in her womb and kicking up at her stomach every once in a while, just to make sure it stayed empty. She thought to detect the first gentle bulge of the expanding uterus, though Ana insisted the time was still too early.

Eventually, she was too weak to walk around. *Dehydration,* she thought. *Some liquid must be getting into my system or I'd be dead already. How long does it take a person to die of thirst?*

"If I were home, they'd give it to me intravenously," she mumbled one day while Ana tried to urge some water past her lips. But she said it in English, and Ana just shook her head. "You think I'm raving now, me and Lady Macbeth." A tear started from each of her eyes, proving that there was water somewhere in her body. "Shouldn't waste the stuff like this," and she wiped the moisture away with the sleeve of her nightgown. "Oh, Ana, I don't want to die. *No quiero morir,"* she said miserably.

She was afraid to look in the hand mirror that lay face-down on her dresser. It would surely show her as a skeleton, perhaps not too dissimilar to Doña María Antonia, with her gaunt cheeks and parchmentlike skin. The Dowager Marquesa hadn't been in to see Celia recently, in spite of the fact that her rooms were only on the next lower floor. No one had been in to see her but Don Epifanio, Nicolasa, Ana, and the priest.

They're walling me up, forgetting me provisionally. They're not sure yet. She struck her belly with one weak fist. *Miscarry, damn you, you lousy parasite.* "This wasn't in the deal. This wasn't in the deal at all."

In her dreams, she saw Larry. He was running to her across a wide meadow, his arms out, but no matter how fast he ran, he couldn't get near her. And all the time he was shouting her name, *Celia, Celia, Celia . . .*

"Celia, wake up."

A cool, hard hand on her forehead. She opened her eyes and looked up, focusing with difficulty on an olive-toned face softly limned by candlelight. Aquiline nose. Dark eyes.

"Río?" she murmured.

He sat on the bed beside her and put an arm around her shoulders to help her sit up. "I have some bread and blackberry jam for you, Celia, and you are going to eat it all."

She shook her head, dimly noticing two other forms—both in long white nightgowns—standing at the foot of the bed. "I'll only throw it up." She spoke in English, but he seemed to understand.

"You will eat if I have to shove it down your throat."

She ate, tiny bite by tiny bite, leaning against his arm. There was hot *camomilla* tea to drink, heavily sweetened and laced with mint.

"Breathe deeply through your mouth," he said.

She obeyed, and for long minutes, the food kept going down. She tasted the sweetness of it and felt it hit the bottom of her stomach like a series of small rocks.

It stayed down for almost an hour, and when she vomited, Río held her head over the bucket.

"I can't, I can't," she gasped.

"This is a good start," he said. "You'll eat again in a little while and again after that and all day and all night if you must."

"We've tried, we've tried," said the woman shapes at the foot of the bed.

"She'll do it now; won't you, Celia?"

By and by, when she felt better, having regained some of the strength and weight she had lost, she couldn't decide whether the nausea had simply run its course or Río had actually forced her to overcome it. Patiently, he had fed her the same food she had rejected from the hands of Ana and Nicolasa. The only physical difference was in the tea: they had served it plain, but he loaded it with fragrant spearmint leaves

and costly sugar filched from the Marqués's storerooms with the complicity of the Chief Steward. The
sugar was really all that sustained her until the morning sickness became *truly* a sickness of the morning,
leaving her afternoons and nights relatively free of
misery.

Able to get out of bed at last, she wobbled around
the room on his arm, ignoring the soreness that developed in her calves from the unaccustomed use. At the
window, she leaned out to breathe the cold, crisp air of
the New Year and to watch men in green shoveling
snow from the courtyard. She had missed Christmas,
but Padre Juan had climbed the stairs to give her
Communion again and to tell her about the celebra-
tions in the Palace and in the city.

Ana came up behind her as she stood at the window.
"His Grace wishes to know when you will be well
enough for the wedding."

Celia bent her head and looked at the windowsill.
"Tell him . . . a week or so if I don't have to stand
up for a very long time."

Ana curtseyed and disappeared, leaving Nicolasa to
chaperone the pair.

"You stand quite well now, Celia," said Río.

"I'll have to rest in a few minutes."

"Perhaps you should sit down before you get tired."
He guided her toward the bed.

"You haven't told me what became of your errand."

"It was not successful. I was supposed to find the
source, but the man from whom my . . . acquaintances
received their goods has disappeared entirely."

Poor Larry, thought Celia. *He never guessed he'd
discovered this world just to die in it.* She bit her lip.
It's all over. It's all over.

"I'll return in the spring with an army large enough
to search for the source until it is found. It can't be
too far from Verdura, else why choose such a small,
backwater town as an outlet?"

"Has the Conde de Pradera learned of the new guns yet?"

"Oh, undoubtedly; but winter will stop him, too."

"I see. I'm sorry that your journey was so . . . fruitless." *More sorry than you can imagine.*

He shrugged. "Not entirely fruitless. I brought back three more guns, and an interesting Christmas present for Her Grace the Dowager Marquesa."

"What would that be?"

He smiled. "I knew your curiosity would rise at that. If you feel up to walking to her apartments, you can see for yourself."

Nicolasa slipped a woolen mantle over her mistress's shoulders, and with the maid on one side and Río on the other, Celia was able to negotiate the flight of steps between her own door and the Dowager Marquesa's. The gift had been unpacked and set up just inside the doorway to the sitting room.

"How nice that you are feeling well, my dear," said Doña María Antonia, looking up from her inevitable embroidery.

Celia made no reply, for she was fascinated by the gift, an odd contrivance of metal and wood which bore a familiar name, ornately figured in gold:

SINGER

CHAPTER EIGHT

Larry was alive. Celia felt dizzy with relief and leaned more heavily on her escorts. Alarmed, they lowered her into the Dowager Marquesa's own chair and chafed her wrists, as if they expected her to faint.

Larry was still alive. He *had* to be, for Celia herself had given him the idea of selling sewing machines in this backward world the day before the kidnapping. He couldn't possibly have had time, that last morning, to locate an old treadle machine and transport it to the alternate world. Larry was still alive, and that meant she had a chance to go home. She'd had enough of chamber pots and half-spoiled meat and pregnancy without modern medication. To hell with what her parents might say about an illegimate child, and to hell with being Marquesa. The smoggy streets of Evanston—now a dim memory—seemed infinitely more desirable than the vastest domain in Spanish America.

Río lifted her lightly in his arms and carried her back to her own room, while Ana and Nicolasa trailed behind. "Enough is enough," he said. "A little walking each day and you'll be fit for the wedding soon enough."

Celia tried not to think about the wedding; it was a formality and would not bind her to the Marqués and Castillo Quintero any more tightly than she was already bound.

With Río's support, encouragement, and moderate bullying, she was fit, by the week's end, to endure a long, exhausting ceremony in the town's cathedral; she was pleasantly surprised to discover that the Marqués had ordered a simple, brief ritual in the Palace chapel, attended only by a dozen members of the court. Arrayed in her beige lace bridal gown and matching mantilla, a costume which had been the Dowager Marquesa's own, she stepped sedately down the aisle, leaning lightly on Don Rafael Terrazas's arm. His three little pages carried her train, muttering garbled lines from the play and giggling from nervousness, as if the wedding were theirs instead of Celia's.

Alonso Enrique Quintero de los Rubios, splendid in a green doublet upon which every feather of the golden bird had been separately embroidered in glinting metallic thread, waited patiently at the altar. He seemed taller than ever before, seemed to look down at Celia from a great height as she approached him. He smiled a cool, public smile and took her hand. Together, they knelt before Padre Juan. Again, Celia was surprised: she had assumed the Bishop would perform the all-important ceremony.

In the silent chapel, close from the heat and breath of many bodies, where plump Padre Juan perspired in the layer upon layer of cloth that tradition demanded he wear, Celia and the Marqués were forevermore joined together—for richer or poorer, in sickness and in health, or in whatever manner prescribed by the incomprehensible Latin ritual. Celia lost track of the progress of the ceremony, although she had been briefed and knew a smattering of the classical tongue, and not until the priest signaled her impatiently did she remember to speak her line.

"Volo."

The Marqués slipped a gold band, fashioned as a ring of feathers and studded with emeralds, on to her left hand, and Padre Juan lifted his arms in benediction. It was over.

The Marqués rose from his knees, pulling Celia up

with him, steadying her as if uncertain she had regained her full strength. He presented his arm, and together they turned and marched down the aisle toward the main hall, where a wedding supper awaited them.

The noise that had been notably absent from the chapel commenced with the supper. All who had been at the ceremony sat down at three tables arranged in a T in the center of the polished floor. Stewards ran hither and yon with steaming dishes and flagons of wine. The Marqués toasted his bride, and Terrazas toasted them both, and someone else toasted the heir-to-be, and by the time the toasts were finished, everyone was laughing and shouting. Landless knights, travelers who had been given hospitality, and servants not normally allowed among the courtiers, but who had put on their best clothes for the occasion, materialized to swell the crowd and the din. The Dowager Marquesa ate sparingly and retired early with her ladies. Río, who had been assigned to entertain the crowd, could not be heard above the tumult and walked out.

Celia found herself virtually alone at the head of the table. The Marqués was leaning toward a small knot of men to his left, telling unlikely off-color stories. A number of people had begun to dance to their own singing and clapping—a wild, gypsy circle dance which led up onto the benches and across the very table in the midst of food scraps and overturned cups. Celia drank a glass or two of wine and picked at her meal, but as the drunkenness and clamor increased, her head began to pound. At last, she tugged at His Grace's sleeve.

"My lord, I am very weary. May I retire?"

He turned toward her, his eyes unfocused. He bent close to her mouth as she repeated her request more loudly. "Go on, if you want," he said when he finally made out her meaning.

She motioned to Ana and Nicolasa, who sat demurely at the foot of the T and the trio rose and wended its way upstairs, the new Marquesa leading the way and her maids carrying the long train of her gown.

In her own room, Celia slumped across the bed.

Ana rushed to her side and lifted free the long mantilla. "Tired, my lady?"

"I don't know. My head was hurting, but it's better now."

Nicolasa began to unbutton the back of the gown. "*Cha,* Ana, we must call her 'Your Grace' from now on."

"There are too many titles in this Palace already," Ana replied.

"But she is the Marquesa and due far more respect now than when she was his . . . concubine."

"Ana is right. Titles are not so important among ourselves. Other people will show me proper respect, but I need a few friends who will always tell me the truth and who will not worry about trying to flatter me." The gown slid to her waist as she sat up; listlessly, she stood and let it slither all the way down.

"Then, my lady, I will call bread, bread; and wine, wine," said Ana. "You do not seem a happy bride."

Naked for a moment, Celia shivered. Her room, high in the tower, was cooler than the rest of the Palace during chilly weather. She slipped quickly into a long nightdress and a woolen mantle.

"In my place, you would be happy, I'm sure," she said.

"I, too, my lady," said Nicolasa.

Celia sighed heavily. "I treated you both very badly while I was ill. I'm sorry. Please forgive me."

"Padre Juan says it is a miracle that you are alive," said Nicolasa.

"You prayed for me, didn't you? Both of you?"

The *dueña* and the maid nodded.

Celia gripped their hands firmly. "Ana, you are my mother, and Nico my sister—all the family I have in the world."

Ana glanced toward the door; it was closed. "I understand you and I do not understand you, my lady, but if I were in your place, I would keep my own counsel. Come now, it is time to go to your lord."

"What, tonight?"

"Tonight of all nights."

Celia's head bowed. "Of course."

His Grace's bedchamber was empty when the guard let Celia inside. A small fire had been laid in the hearth, but the room was cold. She sat on the bed and drew her feet up, curling them under the covers. She leaned back on the heaped-up pillows and waited. And waited. Her eyelids drooped.

A hand on her shoulder woke her. The Marqués.

"What are you doing here?" His words were slurred, and the candle in his left hand was tipped precariously.

"My lord," Celia gasped, shaking sleep off with a toss of her head, "this is our wedding night."

"Out, out; I've done my duty by you," he said, and the sentence was punctuated by a drop of hot wax splashing onto Celia's arm. "Out, I say!" He swept her from the bed as if she were a bit of rubbish he had found on the sheet, and when she stumbled over her own tangled legs, he caught her shoulder in a bruising grip. "Don't hurt yourself. Go to bed early, get plenty of rest for my son." He gave her a gentle shove toward the door.

Relieved, Celia hurried out of the room. As one of the guards escorted her to her own apartments, she happened to look back to see a cloaked and hooded figure admitted to His Grace's rooms—no doubt that was Leonora, whom Celia had never seen. She laughed grimly to herself and reflected that it was just as well that the Marqués did not love her. He would not miss her when she left. And she *would* leave; and she would find Larry, if it took her ten years.

Ana and Nicolasa were asleep in the bedchamber, assuming, no doubt, that Celia would be gone for the rest of the night. Celia gently closed the door between bedchamber and anteroom. Pulling the cloak tightly about herself, she settled onto a low couch beside the anteroom's single candle. The oil lamp sat nearby, cold and dark, but she made no attempt to light it. The lute was on the floor, within reach of her limp arm; she plucked its strings, found them sadly out of tune, and lifted the instrument to correct the situation.

"*Caballito blanco, reblanco, reblanco* . . ." Very softly she sang, and the melancholy tune made her skin prickle.

"You sing best when you are unhappy," came a low voice from behind her.

Celia whirled at the first sound, holding the lute aloft in her left hand, as if it were a talisman to ward off evil.

He came out of the shadows in a far corner of the room and knelt on the floor beside her couch; the candle cast the sharp line of his aquiline nose across his face.

"Mother of God, Río, you startled me."

"I am sorry, Your Grace. I didn't mean to."

" 'Your Grace.' " She set the lute down and covered her face with one hand. " 'Your Grace.' "

"Your Grace, the Marquesa Celia Ysabel de Quintero de los Rubios. Did you ever dream, when you were living in Rodríguez's slave pens, that it would ever come to this? The Palace, the Castle, the vast domain of His Grace, are all yours."

"And the Marqués himself belongs to Leonora."

Río shook his head. "Leonora will pass, as the others have passed, but *you* are the Marquesa."

"So was Rosalía."

Río waved that away with one hand. "A different matter entirely. The child, after all, was not His Grace's." At this, she cast him a quizzical look. "Rosalía was pregnant when she arrived, or hasn't your *dueña* told you that yet?"

"Doña María Antonia told me; but in some respects her tale was not very clear." She paused. "Clear enough in others."

"Come, *chiquita*," he said, taking her hands between his own, "you know whose child you carry. These are rootless fears."

"You are right, Río. If His Grace had any doubts, he surely would not have married me."

"Of course not."

She looked into his eyes suddenly. "Help me escape. Now. Tonight."

There was no surprise on his face, only a steady, bland, unreadable expression as he said, "No."

She leaned forward urgently, her nails digging into his fingers in anguish. "You're the only person I can turn to."

"These are strange thoughts for a new bride."

"I can't stay. I can't spend the rest of my life this way!"

He pulled one hand free of her rigid grasp and touched her mouth with three fingers. "You will wake people who are sleeping peacefully. Calm yourself."

She fell back on the bolsters and stared angrily at the dark ceiling.

Río looked down into her face. "I could give you many reasons why I cannot and will not help you leave. I could say that I don't wish to return His Grace's silver, or that I value my head quite highly, or that I consider it a matter of honor. But I know you will find some way around each reason I give—some way that will satisfy *you*. You've suffered, and I can't blame you for wishing none of it had happened, but the worst is over, Celia. You're well now, and you're

Marquesa, with all the privileges and respect and wealth that go with that title. Do you wish to have gone through all this for nothing?"

"It's already nothing," she whispered. "A woman, though she be a Marquesa, has no real privilege here; in my country, the lowest scrubwoman is freer than I am. I can't even leave my room without my *dueña* or some other guard, and I can't leave the Palace at all. So much for my great privilege! I'm a prisoner; no more, no less."

Río's expression was puzzled. "Why would you want to leave? Where would you go? Everything you could want is here."

"I can't believe you said that! You, Río, who spends his summer wandering, who said he might settle down when he was old and crippled. You of all people should understand how I feel!"

He shrugged. "I am a man and you are a woman. You can't wander as I would. Where would you bear your children? In a hollow tree?" She was about to retort angrily, but he stopped her. "Yes, I remember what you once said about your people having children only when they wanted them, but you're not among your people now, so you must live as *we* do, and among *us* a woman's place is at home, taking care of her man."

She closed her eyes in despair. "I never realized how sweet my life was until I left it. I have nothing here. I've been here months, yet I'm still a stranger."

"The child will change that."

"Ah, yes, the child. The child. His Grace has given me clothes and jewels and a child." She held up her left hand and gazed at the heavy ring. "Beautiful, isn't it? I always liked rings. Did Rosalía wear it?"

"It's been in the family a long time."

"Tell me, Río—was her lover here, or did she leave him behind in México?"

"He was captain of her escort, and he stayed until she died."

"And afterward?"

"I wasn't here, of course, but the story says he disappeared."

"Never to be heard of again."

"Yes."

"His Grace had him murdered."

Río shrugged. "Who knows?"

"He did, didn't he?"

"After all, it would have been more proper to let His Grace be first . . ."

"And he killed Rosalía and her child, too!"

"Celia, that has nothing to do with you."

"Oh, Río, what kind of man is this you've given me to? Why couldn't you have bought me for yourself? I could have loved a minstrel's life. Give him back the money and take me away from here!" She twisted the wedding ring from her finger and pulled back her arm to fling it across the room.

Río caught her wrist, then pried the band out of her grasp. "Such a beautiful ring," he said, slipping it back onto her finger. "Think of it as a gift from me. It is, you know. This whole life . . . A better gift than a minstrel's wanderings. See how I stay, how I cling to it through the whole winter? Something in me knows how good it is." He stroked her shoulder gently. "You shiver. Think how cold it would be in the forest at this time of year."

"It's cold enough here."

He put his arm around her, warming her with his body heat. "You should go to bed."

She shook her head.

"Then I know a warmer place than this." He lifted her in his arms and carried her to the dark corner in which he had hidden while listening to her song. There, a mound of cushions and quilts made a cozy nest on the floor. He set her down gently and took her mantle to add to the coverlets.

She clung to him, savoring the strength of his body. "Don't leave."

His hands moved to her back then, firm and warm. "Of course not," he whispered. "I've waited long enough, don't you think?"

His mouth was hungry, but hers was hungrier, and her flesh was moist for him as it had never been for her husband.

She slept nestled against him, his breath light on her neck, and she dreamed they were still in the North on their long journey to San Felipe Emperador.

At dawn, Nicolasa woke her mistress with a touch on the forehead.

Celia jerked awake, flooded with fear, clutching Río's shoulder, but he yawned and stretched and smiled. He drew her into his arms once more and kissed her long and tenderly, then stood up to dress without haste.

Nicolasa wrapped her mistress in a long cloak and tried to coax her toward the warmth of the inner chamber. But Celia glanced back at Río, who was lacing up his tunic.

"*Te amo*," she said. "I love you."

He reached out and touched her tousled hair, sweeping a strand away from her eyes. "You see—there is something to stay here for."

"Is there danger, Río?"

He shook his head. "When you go to Confession . . . confess something else. We wouldn't want Padre Juan to have a mortal sin on his conscience."

"And His Grace?"

"Is quite happy with Leonora. Don't you think so, Nico?"

"He would never harm you, Señor Río," said the girl. There was hero worship in her eyes as she gazed at him.

The *trovador* laughed softly. "I'm not so sure of that, but don't worry, Celia." He slipped an arm around her waist and patted her belly with his free hand. "We will take good care of his fair-haired son." He kissed her forehead. "I will see you later today, *chiquita,* and next time we will make love more comfortably, on your bed."

Yawning, Celia allowed herself to be led into the other room, where Ana sat on a boudoir chair, sewing.

"Good morning, my lady," said the gray-haired *dueña.* "Do you feel well?"

Celia searched for a trace of sarcasm in Ana's voice, but there was none. "I didn't want to disturb you last night," she said, "so I slept out there." She glanced at Nicolasa for some sign, but the thin girl was busy laying out clothes for the day.

"You have no secrets from us, my lady," Ana told her. "If you wish privacy, we will move our beds to the anteroom."

"Ah, well . . ." Nicolasa drew off Celia's cloak and started to slip a chemise over her mistress's head.

"You are beginning to show," Ana remarked, pointing toward Celia's middle.

Celia did not perceive the swelling herself until Nicolasa tried to fasten the waist of a form-fitting blue velvet dress—it was very tight and closed only with a struggle.

"It is time for other clothing," Ana said. "Nicolasa and I have been working on some."

Today, in place of her plain woolen cloak, there was a new mantle of plush-lined black wool trimmed with mink—a gift from His Grace. It was very heavy, but as snug and warm as a quilt. Celia pulled it over her shoulders and slipped her feet into soft, knee-high, fur-lined boots for a walk on the balcony. On her way out, she tore a chunk of bread from the loaf that sat on the table beside her bed; she nibbled on it as she strolled, to quiet the mild turbulence of her stomach.

January was cool and crisp. Below the tower, covered by a blanket of snow and looking like a picture postcard, lay San Felipe Emperador. Though it was still quite early and the winter sun had barely cleared the horizon, the clean-swept courtyard was already bustling, and in the city beyond, moving carts and people packed the new-fallen snow into a thin, hard layer of ice. Beside the gray ribbon of the river rose the church spires, misted in smoke from innumerable chimneys atop nearby buildings. They were almost as tall as the tower upon which Celia stood, and she fancied that some lonely bell ringer lurking among them could see her. Sometimes, during the last few weeks, she had thought about throwing herself from her Rapunzel's prison; her body would fall within the courtyard and undoubtedly be buried in the Castle cemetery, but *she*, Celia, would have made her escape. Her ultimate escape.

But this morning the air was crisp and cool, and such morbid thoughts were far from her mind. Río had wiped away the ugliness of this existence and made the boredom that was left more bearable. A kind of serenity had overcome Celia as she drifted to sleep in Río's arms, and it was with her again now. She felt she could at last think clearly. If nothing could be done at this moment, at least she could plan for the future. Larry was alive, and the Marqués was extremely interested in Larry's armaments. Very well; when the next expedition was sent in spring, she would find a way of sending Larry a message, of telling him that she was alive and in need of rescue.

Larry. Río. Parents, school, home. Río.

Before last night, she had been certain, but now her certainty was shaken. She would have one winter in which to make her choice.

Later that day, Ana and Nicolasa moved their beds into the antechamber.

When Río returned that afternoon, he had a new

lute with him. He tuned it to match his old one, which was now Celia's, and they were able to sing duets. During the following days and weeks, he procured a carved wooden chess set and taught Celia the Spanish version, *Axedrez de la dama*. He also showed her a game with a seventy-eight-card tarot deck, and he read a fortune of happiness and prosperity the first time he laid out the cards. Together, they began a version of *Romeo and Juliet,* she translating from English and he casting the lines into poetry accompanied by appropriate music. They made no plans for performing it, though, for Celia's strength had waned too far for her to essay the roles of director and actress—the further her pregnancy advanced, the more rest she required. Too, there was less enthusiasm for a second play. Discreetly queried, Don Rafael demurred: he had let his work pile up dangerously during the rehearsals for *El Conde Glamis* and had not yet caught up. The librarian had never completely recovered from having to "murder" his superior, and the other players balked at once again memorizing so many lines. *El Conde Glamis* had capitalized on novelty, but now the novelty had worn off, and the erstwhile participants understood that beneath the polished, final performance lay a great deal of hard work.

"Perhaps it is just as well," Río remarked.

"Why do you say that?"

"Because only you could play Juliet, *chiquita*. Who would be Romeo?"

"You, of course."

He shook his head. "We can do whatever we like, you and I, as long as His Grace does not see it. But if we embrace in front of his eyes, and in front of the whole court, even in a play, then it becomes a matter of honor."

She grimaced. "I should have known. The game. The unwritten code."

He waited for her to explain, but she didn't, preferring to leave it hang in the air, remaining as enigmatic now as he once had been to her. She dipped her quill and continued the writing for its own sake. Each evening they would read the day's production to each other, with Nicolasa and Ana as an audience. Nicolasa would always applaud—she understood that Celia considered it a high form of praise.

As the winter grew colder, the fire in Celia's bedchamber was kept blazing brightly all night, and Río would lie in bed with her for warmth as well as for love. When her back began to ache, he rubbed it, and when her head pounded, he stroked her temples and eyelids as if he had spent his life doing nothing else.

By mid-February, four and a half months into her pregnancy, she knew something was wrong with her diet. Her skin was sallow and pale, and she could hardly drag herself around the room. She drank milk twice a day and forced herself to eat liver—which she loathed—for its iron content. Vegetables had disappeared from the table soon after the New Year, for the winter was a harsh one, even in the southernmost of His Grace's territories. However, there was a store of apples in the depths of the Palace, and Celia was alotted several a day. In fact, Nicolasa reported that on the whole, Celia ate more varied meals than anyone else in the Castle. Ash Wednesday had passed with prayers and smudged foreheads, and Lent was well-begun, but only the Dowager Marquesa fasted. Everyone else, even Padre Juan, had some excuse for ignoring the traditional dietary restrictions. Celia, of course, was never consulted about her own desires because of her pregnancy. In addition to food, she daily consumed a number of potions concocted by Don Epifanio, intended to restore her lost vitality. Neither the apples nor the potions could raise her energy above a minimal level, however: dressing in the morning exhausted her, and often she was too tired to attend Mass.

Under Río's supervision, she exercised.

"You will need to be strong for the birth," he insisted. "Lying in bed all day makes you weak."

The exercises were simple enough and carefully gauged not to tire her greatly, but Don Epifanio disapproved of them.

"She must rest," he said. "Except for a walk on the balcony for fresh air, she must not overtax herself."

"I won't overtax myself," Celia assured him.

After Don Epifanio had left, Río snorted. "I've seen women living in the wilderness, chopping wood, drawing water, and pulling a plow until they gave birth."

"I'm sure he means well."

"God deliver you from doctors, Celia. My mother, who bore ten children, could give you better advice. Don Epifanio wishes to make an invalid of you, and you are *not* an invalid."

"I thought you and Don Epifanio were friends."

"He is a friend of a friend, and so we tolerate each other courteously. The man has not seen a birth in ten years. He hangs on here at court because Doña María Antonia thinks his potions help her. His Grace has hardly been sick a day in his life."

"You mean he isn't a good doctor?"

Río shrugged. "A doctor can set a bone or saw off a leg. He can dispense potions that may or may not work. But he is a man, and a woman knows more about pregnancy and birth than he. True, Ana?"

"True enough," the *dueña* replied. "Women were bearing children long before there were doctors."

"Well, he might be useful if I should need a Caesarean . . ." Suddenly, her mouth went dry; she had commented, forgetting for a moment the state of the medical art in San Felipe.

"*Madre de Dios!*" Ana exclaimed, crossing herself. "Do not even think such a thing!"

Celia glanced at Río, her throat tight. "It can't be done."

He looked away. "It *can* be done, but the mother does not usually . . ."

Celia's right hand went to her belly, then curled into a fist. She forced a dry laugh. "What a silly thing to worry about. It happens so seldom. There has never been one in my family. The Marqués is not a very large man, and I am not a very small woman, even if I am too thin. No, I won't worry about it."

But later in the evening, strumming on the lute, she thought about delivery. How little she knew of it! Four and a half months from now, her uterus would begin to contract rhythmically; the sacs enclosing the fetus would burst; the child would be ejected. It sounded simple. How long the process lasted or how much pain it entailed were mysteries. She had never given a thought to pregnancy as long as her bottle of Pills had been handy, but now she regretted not having taken advantage of a modern university library when it was available.

Ana professed not to remember her own confinement. Nicolasa insisted that her mother, who had borne twelve or thirteen children, had experienced only minor discomfort. Río assured her that proper exercise would minimize both the time and the pain. But Celia knew that they were hiding the truth from her. What they said might be valid enough, but there was more that she couldn't guess, more that they knew would frighten her; she could read it in their eyes. The very fact that they had to hide something frightened her.

Later that day, her head began to ache, and she sent Nicolasa downstairs for a bag of ice to put on her forehead. This, like her other occasional headaches, was at least partly due to inflamed sinuses, which sometimes forced her to sleep sitting up in order to breathe. The Palace, of course, was cold and dry; any water that found its way into the air from an open container set near the fire condensed and froze around the shuttered windows. Back in Evanston, Celia had relied on anti-histamines during the worst part of the winter, and she had even become addicted to nasal spray for a couple of years in high school. Here, she had to suffer and breathe through her mouth.

Nicolasa returned with the ice bag, but this time it was ineffective. Río was called, and he stroked her eyebrows gently, but the touch of his fingertips was like the crash of sledgehammers, and she had to ask him to stop almost immediately. Her temples felt as if they were about to burst. Río and the servants left her alone then, with a single candle glowing in the far corner of the room, hoping that the darkness and the silence would cure her naturally, but when they returned a little later, thinking to find her peacefully asleep, she lay awake, tossing and turning exhaustedly.

"Brain fever?" wondered Nicolasa.

Río shook his head. "Get some more ice."

Again, the ice was useless, and they were standing around, shrugging helplessly, when a knock sounded at the door of the antechamber.

"Perhaps some hot tea would be of assistance," said Don Epifanio. He held a tray upon which sat a large mug of aromatic brew. "I heard of the Lady Celia's unfortunate headache, and I thought I would bring her a soothing drink." He sat down on a chair beside the bed and offered the mug.

The minty smell—different from spearmint and partly drowned by Don Epifanio's perfume—was hauntingly familiar, and the hot liquid was sharply astringent as she swallowed it. She fell back against the pillows, one arm across her eyes, and tried again to will the pain away.

"An old wives' remedy," said Río, after sniffing the empty cup. "I'm surprised you know it, Don Epifanio."

"I know a great number of things," the doctor replied stiffly. It was obvious that he had heard of Río's remarks concerning him—it was nearly impossible to keep anything a secret in Castillo Quintero.

Ana hushed the two men and drew them out into the antechamber, where they exchanged a few polite nothings and Don Epifanio rocked from leg to leg—at the far end of each rock, he was able to see into the bedroom, where Celia still lay with one arm over her eyes. He kept looking at her expectantly, but she didn't move.

She was caught up in the miracle of fading pain. Whatever had been in the brew was muffling the hammer that pounded at her skull. As her head cleared and her body relaxed, she recognized the aroma at last: oil of wintergreen. She had concocted the synthetic version of the oil herself in high school chemistry. Methyl alcohol and salicylic acid, yielding methyl salicylate. Like its city cousin, plain aspirin, oil of wintergreen was a painkiller.

She waved and smiled at Don Epifanio. "You're a very good doctor."

He was barely able to disguise his satisfaction. "If the pains should come back, please send for me and I shall bring more tea. *Buenas noches.*" He swept out of the room, carrying the tray under one arm.

Nicolasa looked pointedly at Río, her eyebrows raised.

He tossed it off with a wave. "I knew the remedy, but not where to find the plant near the Castle in the middle of winter."

"You have insulted him," said Ana. "Don Epifanio went to school in México."

Río shrugged. "So he says. Well, he is a better doctor than I thought, which is good. Still, he'll have a midwife or two helping him when the time comes."

Celia looked up at the ceiling and grimaced. She

had a premonition that aspirin would not be nearly enough when the time came.

"You'll stay with me, won't you?" she whispered to Río.

"If you wish it, of course."

"When the baby comes. I think I'll need a strong hand to hold."

He twined his fingers in hers and smiled. "Don't worry, Your Grace."

"I won't. I won't." She gripped his fingers very hard.

Behind him, Ana and Nicolasa backed out of the bedchamber and closed the door softly behind themselves.

CHAPTER NINE

In early March, while the weather was still stormy and gray, Río and Capitán Carril took a detachment of troops north toward Verdura. Their objective was, of course, to locate and capture, if necessary, the source of the new weapons that were issuing from that area. The squadron went on horseback, trailing a few wagon-loads of supplies, but the Marqués planned on sending a galleass upriver to meet them and return with the booty when the weather cleared.

Before he left, Celia had wracked her brain for some kind of innocent-seeming message she could send Larry via Río. The only ruse that came to her seemed transparent, but she tried it anyway. She wrote her Chicago address, 2427 Touhy, on a small piece of paper and gave it to Río.

"Doña María Antonia requests more needles for her sewing machine, if you can get them while you are north. These numbers and letters are engraved on the ones we already have."

He pocketed the paper without a word and kissed her good-bye.

Celia learned to run the sewing machine, which took no talent at all, in order to make baby clothes. Ana would lay the patterns out on wool or velvet or cotton, and Celia pinned the pieces together and sewed straight seams into them.

The ladies of the Palace still marveled at the tiny, precise stitches that the machine made so swiftly—far tinier and more uniform than any of them, even the Dowager Marquesa, could produce. Many of them wanted copies of it, for although Doña María Antonia let almost anyone run it for long hours, there was still too much sewing in the Palace for a single machine. She would not allow the most skillful artisans in San Felipe to take it apart or tamper with it in any way, however, for fear they would ruin it. Every day she oiled it with the purest, clearest oil available in the city, and every day she sewed with it herself for a little while before allowing anyone else to touch it. For the rest of the day, except during Mass, she would sit in her chair across the room from the machine—for she still kept it in the antechamber of her apartments—and listened to the steady beat of the treadle. Anyone who tried to pump it too fast received a glare and an imperious summons to leave off sewing for a few days. When a needle broke, the Dowager Marquesa clutched her heart as if she had been stabbed and hastened to examine the sewing area for damage, elbowing aside all the women who bent assiduously over it.

Celia learned to knit at last, leaving the embroidery of the other clothing to the grandmother-to-be and her maids. She found knitting dull and tedious, and she kept dropping stitches and having to rip out large segments of finished work and do them over. But little by little, she mastered the art and made a very plain little sweater with a cross worked into the front. As a reward for her diligence, Doña María Antonia gave her a fine scissors with steel blades and elaborate handles of silver inlaid with turquoise—an elegant gift imported from the South and, as the Dowager Marquesa pointed out, practical as well. Celia tried to appear grateful for this fresh symbol of her imprisonment.

Spring arrived, bringing clear, calm weather, and the galleass went upriver. Celia watched it from the tower parapet: it resembled a caterpillar on the distant water as it rowed slowly upstream, sails unfurled to

catch the light morning breeze. Celia paced restlessly
till it was out of sight, then paced again, wondering
where Río was and where Larry was. Her bed was dismally cold and lonely that night.

Immediately after Mass on Palm Sunday, Don Rafael, who had been absent from devotions, took the
Marqués aside—as Celia followed Doña María Antonia out of the chapel, she saw them conferring together at a bend in the corridor. She passed close
enough to hear a few key words that assured her the
expedition to Verdura had returned, and instead of
climbing the stairs behind her mother-in-law, she
begged to be excused because of lingering breathless-
ness. With Ana and Nicolasa trailing her closely, she
went to the main hall and ensconced herself in a large
chair near one of the twin fireplaces. Ana produced
enough knitting to keep the three of them busy for a
week or two, and they plunged into it, heads bent
modestly, their mantillas veiling their faces. But every
once in a while, Celia would glance toward the doorway that led to the main corridor. Several times she
saw Terrazas's little pages run across the room, and once
the man himself strode by. At last His Grace entered
and took his place on the dais, flanked by his usual
lieutenants. The room cleared out; the noisy hangers-
on who ordinarily spent most of their waking hours
there were firmly guided away by armored guards,
and the few travelers who had been given the hospitality of the Palace were ushered to other quarters by
polite, green-liveried servants. Celia asked for and received offhand permission to stay if she remained quiet
and out of the way—the hall was being cleared for open
space, not for secrecy, which was impossible to attain
within the Castle. Occupied by only a dozen people—
His Grace and his advisers, the three women, and a
few guards—the hall seemed overwhelmingly large, its
ceiling as high as a church's and its polished floor a
vast, bright plain. Some of winter's tapestries had been

removed, revealing walls faced in part with striated gray and white stone. An empty ballroom waiting for the dancers to arrive.

When they entered, they tracked in mud. Don Rafael came first, walking backward, guiding a double row of forty brown-clad men carrying crates. They heaved the boxes onto the dais and levered them open with chisels, revealing stack after stack of oilcloth-wrapped Enfield rifles. The Marqués lifted one, turning it over and over and running his hands along the slippery smoothness of its barrel and stock.

Last to arrive were Capitán Carril and Río; between them walked a dirty, bearded man whose arms were manacled behind his back. Larry.

Celia's hands froze, and one of her knitting needles hit the floor with a tiny clack. The sound startled her out of her mesmerized state, and she bent quickly to retrieve the stick, letting her mantilla fall forward and hide her features. If Larry noticed and recognized her at this moment, it would do neither of them any good.

The trio passed a few yards from Celia's place and stopped at the foot of the dais. Río and Carril saluted the Marqués. Larry bowed, then slumped to his knees, his head hanging in obvious exhaustion. His clothes were torn and stained, his hair and beard matted and disheveled.

"This is the man," said Carril. "The guns came from him. We searched the whole area and made a set of detailed maps, but we could not find the place where they were made. He admits that he sold them, but he insists that he does not know where they came from."

"Where did he get them?" asked the Marqués.

"At first he would not say, but his tongue loosened a bit after a while, and he told us he got them from a peddler from the North."

"I don't want a middle-man," said His Grace, turning away from the three men. "I told you to find the *source*."

"Your Grace," said Río, mounting the first two steps, "no one in Verdura has ever seen a trace of this other peddler. The man himself is not a native of the area and does not live in the town, but he has no horse, no wagon, no camp. In the middle of the winter he had guns to sell, and no one knew where he had gotten them."

"Well, what does it mean? If the man is not a Verduran, what is he? Where do these guns come from?"

"He refuses to tell," said Carril. "We did not dare torture him too much, so we brought him here. Perhaps a prison cell will further loosen his tongue."

"You!" said the Marqués. He grabbed a handful of Larry's hair and pulled his head up. "I must have those guns."

"I will bring you all the guns you desire if you set me free," Larry croaked.

"I desire the source. I will bring the men and their tools to San Felipe Emperador, where they will make guns for me and me only. Where are they?"

"I am only a middle-man, Your Grace. I do not know where they are."

"Why did you not lead my men to your peddler?"

"He meets me in the woods every few weeks."

The Marqués glanced questioningly at Río and Carril.

"There was no peddler during the three weeks we searched the woods," said Carril. "This man came with guns at odd times . . . once a week, once a month, sometimes every other day."

"He took payment almost entirely in jewelry," added Río. "At Cebolla Dulce, a friend told me that there seemed to be a great many weddings taking place in the North, for the trade in rings along the Río Pato had increased a hundredfold. The man could spend our coins in Verdura, but if he is from far away . . . perhaps our money is worthless in his homeland."

"Gold and silver worthless?" exclaimed the Marqués.

"Perhaps there would be too many questions asked about the strange coins. And about the raw gold, if he melted them down. His people may have a law against selling such weapons in other lands. I know if *I* were their king, I would have such a law for my own protection."

"So would I. You bought every gun you could find?"

"Yes, Your Grace."

"You seem to think his native land is very far away. California, perhaps? I have heard of many wonders there—sometimes the earth moves, and giant waterspouts spring hundreds of feet high from solid ground." His Grace tugged thoughtfully at his beard. "It is too far away to send an army, even if we knew the route . . . yet it cannot be so far if he brings guns every week. Surely he has some cache, perhaps in a cave. . . ."

"Believe me, Your Grace, we searched thoroughly," said Carril. He nudged the prisoner with one booted foot. "Tell us where you're from and it will go easy with you, fellow."

Larry shook his head. "I need sleep," he muttered.

The Marqués turned his back. "Take him downstairs. We'll see what a day or two without food will do for him."

Two men who had carried in crates came forward to drag Larry away. With a shock, Celia realized that one of them was wearing Larry's belt. She nudged Nicolasa and pointed him out, telling the girl to remember his face and his belt.

The Marqués continued to talk to Río and Carril in low tones and to examine the firearms and ammunition for some minutes, while Celia's trembling hands fumbled with her knitting. Nicolasa, noticing her mistress's agitation, leaned forward to ask if she was all right.

"It's nothing, nothing," Celia replied. She pushed herself out of her chair, one hand firmly gripping the left armrest. Her mind was in a turmoil. Plans had to be made, Larry set free and flight north accomplished swiftly. She had already felt the child moving within her—a disquieting sensation—and soon she would be too unwieldly for the trip.

Río, finished with the Marqués's business, came over to Celia and offered his arm. "May I help Your Grace upstairs?"

She nodded and leaned lightly on him, wishing she could ask him for advice. She wanted to throw the whole thing at his feet—two worlds and all—and beg for his help, but she knew it would be useless. Even if he understood, he had already made his position with regard to her escape very, very clear, and Larry's arrival would not change his mind.

"A very strange man," he said. "This captive who calls himself Lorenzo. Some of the people of Verdura think him a demon and his guns gifts from the devil. They were quite happy to see him leave in chains."

"So your mission was unsuccessful again?"

"Not completely. We found *him* after all, even if we didn't find the source. No one in Verdura knows more about the guns than *he* does."

"What will happen to him if he doesn't really know where the source is?"

"He knows."

"And if he won't tell?"

"He will tell. Why so curious, my lady? Or have I just answered my own question?"

"Did you offer him money?"

"Of course. A princely bribe, and he refused. I can't blame him for that. There's no limit to the amount he could make by selling the guns freely. But, of course, he is no longer free."

"He'll be tortured?"

"Yes. Do you wish to watch?"

She recoiled from him. *"Dios mío,* no! But *torture* . . . the poor man looked so pitiful. . . ."

"He has only to tell us where he gets the guns. He can't possibly think more of his profit than of his skin. Now, let us speak of other things: Sandoval, for instance, was still alive when I passed through Cebolla Dulce, in spite of what he said last fall. He is thinner, though, and Anibal is taller . . ."

But Celia was too restless to pay much attention to Río's tale, and after a while she pleaded exhaustion and retired, alone—for he had further business with the Marqués—to her bed. She stared at the ceiling for a while, tired but unable to sleep. The memory of Larry's haggard face kept returning, making her hurt deep inside. Her stomach quaked at the thought of the torture he must have endured already. And yet, why hadn't he led them directly to the spot in the forest and disappeared to safety before their very eyes?

Unless this was part of a plan to rescue *her!*

She turned that over in her mind: Larry acting the decoy while the police or the FBI or *somebody* trailed him to San Felipe, waiting for the right moment to grab her. If he received the note, he knew that Río was the key to her whereabouts. Perhaps he had a radio transmitter hidden on his body, or *in* his body; even now the authorities might be encircling the Castle, waiting for his signal.

It all smacked too much of James Bond, but Celia decided she had to find out immediately. An hour or two before dawn she rose and dressed swiftly and with astonishing energy. Knowing she would not be allowed out of her room unaccompanied, she laid a firm hand across Nicolasa's lips to wake her and keep her silent. Ana appeared to be sleeping soundly. After swearing her companion to secrecy upon Christ's holy blood, Celia led the way to the corridor. The two of them sauntered out of their rooms as if predawn strolls were part of their normal routine. The guard passed them as he always did—though she was not allowed to leave the building, Celia could roam the Palace as she liked.

The entrance to the dungeon was close to the laundry room. Nicolasa found it easily.

Instead of forbidding them to descend, as Celia had feared, one of the guards offered to light their way with a lantern. Expecting to find the depths of the Castle eerie and forbidding, full of vermin and mold and bones of long-dead prisoners, Celia was pleasantly surprised. The stone steps were scrubbed clean, though well worn, and there was not a single cobweb overhead. Only a slight mustiness and the absence of windows indicated that they were underground.

"You won't find any ghosts down here, Your Grace," said the guard. "Nor a single rat." At that, something dark and furry skittered across their path: a gray cat. The guard bent over to stroke its glossy coat. "If your Grace wants a pet, this one will have kittens soon."

Celia smiled but said nothing.

They passed the room used as a storehouse for apples—now almost empty—and a wine cellar, and came at last to the prison.

"We have only one inmate now, Your Grace—in the last cell."

The narrow passage opened into a large room where a small fire in a central brazier augmented the dim glow of a wall sconce. To the right was a display of chains, manacles, and instruments of torture, many of which Celia could not name. To the left was a row of stout wooden doors, each with its own tiny, shuttered window. One of these windows—the last in the line—was swung back, displaying a barred opening.

"Here he is, Your Grace." The guard held the lantern high so that its bulging glass lens directed a thin shaft of light into the gloomy cell. "You can see he's well-cared-for. I'm not allowed to give him any food, but he's got a whole bucket of water for cleaning and drinking."

Larry lay upon a pallet of straw on the far side of his cubicle; he was shackled to the wall by short lengths of chain at wrists and ankles. Their approach must have awakened him, for he turned his head toward the visitors and blinked at the new, strong source of light.

"Open the door," said Celia. "I wish to speak to him."

"Ah, I can't do that, Your Grace, not without His Grace's or Capitán Carril's orders."

Celia tilted her head and regarded him balefully. "I said open the door. I can't speak to him this way."

The guard cleared his throat. "If Your Grace will wait a little while, I'll send someone to ask the Capitán—"

"Come now, this is your Marquesa who gives you this order."

He looked down, unable to meet her gaze. "I'm sorry, Your Grace; I cannot take the responsibility."

"Listen to me." She took him aside, away from the door, and spoke in an undertone. "This man is from Indian country and speaks a language I know. The Marqués wishes certain information from him, and perhaps if he thinks he is speaking to someone sympathetic, someone who will help him . . . Do you see what I mean?"

The guard's brow furrowed. "If Your Grace will just come back later—"

"Now is the best possible time, when he thinks I come secretly." She smiled conspiratorially. "I will tell His Grace that you were of invaluable assistance. Think! If the wretch confesses at last, it will be to

your benefit, and if not . . . I'll tell no one you unlocked the door."

The guard chewed his lip, frowning. "I would like
to help you, Your Grace . . . but if he harms you, it
will mean my head."

"He's in chains, isn't he?"

"Yes."

"Then there's no danger. Don't worry, I'll stay out
of his reach."

"Well . . . all right, but Your Grace, please, you
must not step beyond the threshold."

Celia nodded. "Open the door. And move away so
that I can seem to be speaking freely."

With a great show of reluctance, he unlocked the
door and then backed off until the glow of the lantern
he held was as feeble as that of the brazier. Celia signaled Nicolasa to go with him.

"Larry," she whispered.

He squinted up at her. "Celia?" he muttered, half to
himself.

She raised a finger to her lips. "Try not to show
emotion. The guard may not understand English, but
he can read a face or a voice well enough, I'm sure."

Larry sat up slowly and leaned forward, manacled
hands resting on his knees. "What are you doing here?
They told me a blonde girl was drowned trying to escape from slave traders. The description sounded like
you, and I couldn't find you in town; I searched and
searched. I had to assume you were dead. What happened?"

"Too much, but let it go for now. I was sold as a
slave and wound up here. Did you get the message I
sent with the men who captured you?"

He shook his head. "I didn't get any message."

"Then you didn't bring anyone with you?"

"No."

"Can you send for help?"

"No." His head sank into his hands. "I never looked ahead. I never dreamed this could happen."

"You've got to get out of here."

"They took my belt. The big fellow with the scar on his cheek took a liking to it. No use going anywhere without it."

"I'll get it back, don't worry. Why didn't you trick them into walking through the target area with you? You could have gotten away easily."

"At first I didn't want to disappear into thin air—they'd think I was a devil, and I'd never be able to come back. Later, when I realized they weren't going to take no for an answer, it was too late. My hands were chained behind my back and I couldn't reach the stud. Then the big fellow decided he wanted a souvenir, and that was it. God, if only I'd realized how determined they were!" His hands curled into fists. "Christ, if he's cut a new notch in it, we're dead! Celia baby, we've got to get out of here!"

"Yes. And soon. Tell them you'll show them the place."

"They don't trust me. They want me to draw a map and they'll go search for the place while I stay here as hostage." He laughed, a bit hysterically. "I know they won't believe the truth." He struck his forehead with one fist. "I've *got* to get out." He raised his head, and his red-rimmed eyes found Celia's face. "What was that he called you: Your Grace?"

"I'm married to the guy who wants you to talk. It wasn't my idea."

"You have influence over him? You can get me out!"

She shook her head. "Not that much influence. He's too single-minded. If he ever guessed that I knew where the guns came from . . ." She shivered and pulled her cloak more tightly around her shoulders. "I'd be down here, too, in spite of the baby."

"Baby?" His eyes fell to the level of her belly.

She twitched the cloak open a bit to expose the roundness of her abdomen. "He doesn't waste much time. That's why I'm here—a blonde breeding machine."

"How far . . . how long to go?"

"Maybe three months. That's why we've got to move soon. That and the torture they're planning for you."

"I saw the stuff. Straight out of a grade Z horror film."

"Have they hurt you so far?"

"Just a little police brutality where it doesn't show. I can take more, though I'd like to give a little of it back."

"You'll have to tell the truth sooner or later. . . . But no, they'll never believe you. Or if they do, they might . . . they might burn you as a witch. Some of them are very superstitious." Her fingers curved into fists. "We've got to think of something."

His eyes roamed the cell, as if searching for an answer in its stone walls. "Vouch for me. Tell him you know me. Tell him the truth—that we're from the same place. Say you want to have your baby at home where your mother is, and I'm the only one who knows how to get there. It doesn't have to hold any farther than Verdura."

She shook her head sadly. "You don't know him," she said.

"Bribes! Surely you have jewelry you can bribe the guards with. You got here to see me. Sneak me out disguised as your maid!"

Tears were starting from her eyes. "You don't understand. No one goes in or out without the Marqués's orders. I'm not allowed to leave the Palace. I'm too valuable as a brood mare. I'll have to be disguised. Both of us. Oh, damn it, let me think! There must be some way!" She raised a fist to her lips and bit the knuckle savagely. "I've got to leave. They'll miss me soon upstairs. Hold on for a day or two; I'll think of something." She gazed at him compassionately. "I'll tell him I can't bear the thought of you being tortured. I don't think I can do any better for now, but maybe it'll help."

"Thanks, Celia. Whatever you can do. And . . . if we get out of this, I'll make it up to you, I promise. I'll shut down the machine. I was wrong to try to use it for my own ends."

"Let's talk about it later, when we're safely away. Larry . . ." She gazed at him silently for a long moment, remembering things that had happened a long time before.

He tried to step toward her, forgetting that his chains were so short. He rattled them angrily. "When I thought you were dead . . . I wanted to kill myself. It was my fault. I should never have let you come. I didn't take enough precautions. Oh, Celia, I've missed you so much. . . . Your parents called and I couldn't tell them. I was still searching and hoping. . . . I should have called the police, I should have gotten help, but I wanted to keep the secret. . . . Can you ever forgive me?"

"Of course, of course. I could forgive you anything."

"I love you, Celia."

"And I love you. Oh, Larry . . . hold on, sweetheart. It won't be long. I'll manage something. I wish . . . I wish I could kiss you." She backed away, making no motion of farewell.

He bowed awkwardly, unsmiling, and said in Spanish, "*Adiós*, Your Grace."

Celia backed away, signaling to the guard that he might relock the door. To his inquiring glance, she replied a shrug and a shake of the head, silently admitting her failure at the supposed interrogation. His apprehensive frown and the speed with which he conveyed Nico and herself upstairs convinced Celia that the matter would not be reported to his superiors.

And now she had a bit of blackmail that might be useful in freeing Larry.

Hungry, Celia directed her footsteps and Nicolasa's to the kitchen where sleepy cooks were just beginning to gather the raw materials for breakfast—silver trays for His Grace and for the Dowager Marquesa had already been assembled, the Quintero-crested flatware gleaming in the mellow hearthlight, the engraved crystal waiting to be filled with the morning's beverages. When Celia appeared in the doorway, three apprentices ran to help her to a chair, and the head cook himself approached humbly to ask if he could be of service. At her direction, he had a small table laid with two meals, which he served piping hot—far hotter than they ever reached the room in the tower.

As she chewed without tasting, Celia turned the situation over in her mind. The decision she had dreaded making was made, not by careful deliberation during a long winter, but in the instant she had seen Larry dragged into the main hall in chains. She loved Río, leaned on him, clung to him. His presence had made this life bearable, and leaving him would tear her apart, but Larry was home and security and the world she understood, where she could expect more from life than knitting, sewing, pregnancy, and purdah until she shriveled up and died. She had loved Larry first, still loved him, and the choice was obvious.

The two young women went to the chapel, which was deserted at this hour, and knelt on a bench far from the door and equally far from the altar. Celia had tucked her rosary into the waistband of her dress, intending to say she was going to chapel in case anyone questioned her on the way to the dungeon. Now she drew it out and fingered the green and black beads, murmuring the *Pater Nosters* and *Ave Marias* absently.

When at last she looked up, her mind still blank,

she found Padre Juan beside her. His face was set in its most concerned expression.

"Is something wrong, my daughter? You are here so early."

"I couldn't sleep, *Padre*. The child was moving, so I came downstairs to pray for it." The lie was prompted by the very real fluttering, tickling sensation in her belly.

"Ah, well, I am told that is quite normal—it shows the child is well and strong. A boy, surely."

"I hope so, *Padre*."

He touched her shoulder. "Your eyes are red, my daughter. Have you been weeping?"

She smiled. "Just sleeplessness."

"It will be a little while before Mass; do you wish to lie down and rest? There is a cot in my room . . ." His fingers moved down her arm and circled it just below the biceps. The heel of his hand brushed her breast, seemingly by accident, then brushed it again.

Does he think I came downstairs for him? She twisted slightly and rose to her feet, disengaging his grip with the motion. "I think I will return to my room and miss Mass this morning."

His eyebrows lifted. "This is Holy Week, my daughter."

"I am not well, *Padre*. I must rest as much as possible for the child's sake."

"Yes, yes. Well, God will forgive you, and I shall tell Her *Excelentísima* that I saw you at prayer early this morning."

"Thank you, *Padre*. Come, Nico."

Nicolasa, her shadow, followed silently.

Upstairs, in the privacy of her bedchamber, where only Ana—who had awakened at last—could overhear, Celia asked, "Nico, is there anyone in the Palace who is what he ought to be?"

The maid looked confused. "What are you asking me, my lady?"

Celia sat in the center of her bed, her legs crossed tailor fashion beneath her voluminous skirt. "Padre Juan is a priest, yet the way he touched me . . . Don Rafael, Río, the Marqués . . . Even I, the faithful wife, am false. Only Doña María Antonia is real." Glancing up, she saw that Nicolasa was still puzzled. "No, it's not your fault. I've been suffering from cultural shock, and I think I'm finally beginning to recover. Life is never as simple as it appears, and the rack can be much nastier than the hydrogen bomb." She chewed on her lower lip. "Ana, will you go to the kitchen and get me some tea?"

When she was certain that the *dueña* was gone, she said, "Nico, do you remember the man I pointed out to you yesterday?"

"Yes. His name is Jaime Fernandez and he has a post on the west side of the Castle wall."

"Excellent, Nico."

"He's champion wrestler of His Grace's troops."

"You saw the belt he was wearing?"

"You pointed it out, my lady: a wide belt with a square brass buckle."

"Good. I want you to take the cobbler round to Fernandez's post and have him look at that belt so he can make an exact copy of it. But don't let Fernandez know what you're doing. Do you understand?"

"A gift, my lady?"

"A surprise. Don't tell *anyone* about it."

"It's for Señor Río, then."

Celia smiled. "You won't tell him, will you?"

"Such a plain belt, Your Grace. Surely a silver buckle, or an engraved one . . ."

"No. I want something he can wear freely at all times, something he won't have to lie about. An *exact* duplicate, Nico."

"As you wish, my lady. I will go as soon as Mass is over."

"Don Rafael will give you the money; just tell him

you're buying some things for me. Order a pair of shoes while you're there. Can't you go now?"

"I can't leave you alone, my lady."

"Ana will be back in a little while . . . Oh, all right. His Grace's orders, I know. They can be bent but not broken."

Nicolasa looked down at the rug. "If something happened to you, it would be my fault."

Celia reached out to pet the girl's hair. "I know, I know. Another hour won't matter." She wondered if Holy Week would make the Marqués more lenient with torture than he would be otherwise.

There was a knock at the door of the outer chamber. Nicolasa answered it and stepped aside to let Río enter.

"Stay out here, Nico," he said. "I want to talk to your mistress alone."

When he was inside the bedroom, he shut its door firmly. "What did you think you were doing this morning, Celia?"

She looked up into his eyes and pretended to be puzzled. "I went to the chapel."

"I followed you all the way downstairs. All the way."

"Oh." Celia seated herself in a chair by the fire and put her feet up on a velvet ottoman. "I was curious to see how the prisoner was being treated. I was surprised at how clean the prison was. No rats, no spiders—"

"You spoke together in a strange language. About what?"

She tried to keep her voice low and casual. "Where were you? I didn't see you."

He stood beside her, his hand on her shoulder. "What did you speak about? Don't shield this man, Celia. You know him, don't you? He's from your homeland, isn't he?"

"When I heard him speak in the main hall—his accent—I knew he was from my country," she replied smoothly. "I had to ask him if he knew of my parents, if anyone was looking for me. Surely you understand, Río." She gazed up at him pleadingly.

His hand moved to her throat and cupped her chin. "Don't lie to me, *chiquita*. No lies between us."

"I felt sorry for him. I told him to tell His Grace whatever he wanted to know."

Río sighed. "A long time ago you said a man named Larry Meyers knew the way to your homeland. You had been told he was dead, but you didn't believe it. He was too strong to kill, you said. Do you remember Tomás and José, who kidnapped you from him? Do you remember that you smashed José's own pistol over his head?"

The blood drained from her face.

"My memory is good, my lady, and I was busy in Verdura. This Lorenzo is your Larry Meyers. You were down there planning an escape, weren't you?" He frowned, and his lips set in a hard line.

She trembled, her eyes growing wide. "You frighten me when you look like that, Río." She raised her arms to circle his waist, but his rigid body was out of reach. "What do you want me to tell you?"

"I thought of it long ago, but since you always insisted you couldn't find your own way back, there was no reason to tell His Grace. Your people, who can control the bearing of children, who look upon women as equal to men—they make the guns, don't they?"

"I don't know the way, Río. I swear to you that only Larry knows the route!"

He let go of her chin and leaned forward so that she could rest against him. His arms went around her and pressed her head against his stomach. "I thought you had really changed this time," he said quietly. "I thought I could keep you here. What is it about this man that makes you want to run away with him?"

She hugged him tightly, snuffling back incipient tears. "I don't want him to be tortured. The Marqués would never be able to conquer my people. Why won't he just let Larry keep on trading as before?"

"Because he doesn't want his enemies to get the new weapons, too. If he controls the source, or at least learns the secret of manufacture, his borders will be secure." He paused. "Do you happen to know why those metal cartridges fire upon concussion?"

Eyes closed, she shook her head.

"And the powder inside that is not true gunpowder . . . ?"

"It's called smokeless powder, I think, but I don't know how it is made."

"There are far too many gaps in your knowledge, *chiquita*."

"I never needed to know things like that!" she exclaimed, jerking away from him angrily. "The average person doesn't carry a gun or skin a rabbit or build a fire in my country!"

"And you do none of those things here, so why leave?"

Her head bowed. "You wouldn't understand."

"I understand that this Larry Meyers has a strong hold on you, Celia. What is it? Do you love him?"

She folded her hands in her lap and said nothing.

He went to his knees in front of her in order to look into her face. "You spoke to him as if you cared for him. Was he your lover?"

His tone was gentle, and she couldn't help taking his hand between her own. "Yes. Yes, we were lovers. I want to go away with him."

"And he promises to take you to your homeland if you help him escape?"

"Yes."

He stroked her cheek with his free hand. "Let him rot, Celia. He paid Tomás and José to kill you."

Stunned, she shrank back.

"You were lucky they wanted to make a little extra silver by selling you as a slave. They handed you over to Rodríguez and told Larry Meyers you were dead."

"No! It isn't true!"

"It *is* true."

She searched his face and found nothing to bely the conviction in his voice. "But he loved me," she said in a stricken tone. She recalled that last day as if it were only moments gone—his kiss, his touch, the close warmth of his flesh. But the trapdoor, the guns, and the locked room were part of the kaleidoscope memory, too. She had badgered him for weeks about that room; for a long time he had been annoyed at her persistence, changing the subject or falling silent when she brought the matter up, but finally he relented. Relented and made her wait a day before he took her into the Spanish world. He'd had a long morning in which to prepare . . . for anything.

She hugged herself with crossed arms and rocked slowly to and fro. "I thought . . . I thought he loved me. I thought that sharing our secrets was a sign of the strength of that feeling. I never dreamed he'd want to kill me . . . for my curiosity." Her voice broke on the last word.

Río scooped her up into his arms and carried her to the bed, where she could weep in comfort.

CHAPTER TEN

Celia lay awake in the darkness, listening to Río's placid breathing. She was calm now, tearless and rational. Her deep feeling for Larry had evaporated; he was a pitiful creature—selfish, greedy, and hopelessly shortsighted. From the beginning, he had treated the world of Spanish dominion as a plaything; he acted the role of a demiurge, supremely confident in his strength, cunning, and ultimate immunity. He never fully realized that this world could be crueler and more relentless than his own. He unconsciously dismissed the threat posed by a society without H-bombs and global calamities—one which also lacked the veneer of restraint engendered by Geneva Conventions and nuclear stalemate. And now he was paying the price of his arrogance.

His duplicity no longer seemed inconceivable; she now accepted it as an ugly fact of life. But did he actually purchase her *death*? Perhaps Río exaggerated his crimes for effect.

She recalled Marmaduke, the mouse that Larry had used in his early experiments. Marmaduke, a laboratory animal raised in a germ-free cage, fed and cared for all its short life, had been set free when its usefulness ended. Set free, to survive in a world of predators and disease . . . if it could.

Or had it been disposed of in some other fashion? If so, Celia was indeed the luckier.

Larry was still the key to returning home. She

doubted now that he had ever loved her; his avid caresses and easy endearments seemed in retrospect a convenient ploy for securing a devoted tutor. Yet her body, if not her *persona,* surely pleased him well enough once; she hoped the distortion of pregnancy did not utterly repel him, for she meant to let him believe their old relationship persisted. A trusting, even passionate façade would smooth the trip northward.

She wondered if he had changed at all. Was he no longer quite the man who had ordered her abduction? How honest had he been down in the dungeon, half-starved, hobbled, and aching from torture? Had any real remorse tinged his attitude toward her—a remorse held back because she showed no sign of suspicion? Or were his professions of relief and affection merely a continued sham, cloaking an amoral disregard for her own safety and desires? If they somehow won free of the Castle, acquired weapons, supplies, and perhaps a guide for the upriver journey, would he be tempted somewhere along the way to rid himself once more of an old encumbrance?

At the end, she would have to trust him. She could not possibly watch him every instant of the homeward trek, especially pregnant; when she needed her sleep more than ever before. A bodyguard would only arouse *his* suspicions; without money (but for the few coins she had won at cards) she could not hire one anyway, and she knew of no one she could trust in such a capacity . . . except Río, whom she dared not ask. Perhaps Larry's gratitude at being freed would be great enough that he would not consider murder. Perhaps.

His face—it loomed before her eyes yet. He'd tried valiantly to render his features free of stress, but a shadow of fear lurked in his eyes. She had never seen him like that, never seen any human being so except on a movie or television screen. At the time, her heart had melted, but now she felt an acid triumph rise within her—a vengeance fulfilled for those moments on the auction block, for the many nights in a loveless bed with her Lord-and-Master, and for all her other miseries. She would work speedily for Larry's release—but not too speedily, that he might relish his captivity as she had relished hers.

An ultimate escape was beyond her for the moment anyway. She feared it would always be beyond her, but she put that fear aside and concentrated on a more immediate matter: without the belt, the most foolproof plan would be useless. In the first instant of recognition, down in the main hall, she had thought of buying it from Fernandez, but she forced herself to reject that idea immediately. It was a plain belt, as Nicolasa had said; well made, of good leather, but no better than any dozen such a journeyman cobbler could finish in an afternoon. An offer to purchase would surely be viewed with rightful suspicion: Fernandez would examine the belt closely, searching for the hidden value. In his place, Celia would certainly pry at the laminated leather with a knife, probing for jewels or a secret message. One heedless slash of a sharp blade might render the tiny electronic components unstable or totally inert, and here Larry could never make repairs.

Theft remained as the only viable means of procuring the belt. Who to trust to accomplish it? Nicolasa?

Trust. If her experience of the last few months had taught her anything, it had taught her to trust no one.

She raised herself on an elbow and looked down on Río's sleeping form. One arm was flung over his head, and his face was bent into the crook of his elbow so that only his cheek and ear were touched by the dim ember-glow from the hearth. The only proof of Larry's crime lay in Río's word, yet she had accepted that, at least partly. Emotionally, she trusted Río completely; intellectually, she realized that she could never be sure of him. He had his own motives—motives she barely understood—and his own standards by which to judge his behavior. To the best of her knowledge, he had never lied to her, but too often he had avoided telling the truth—behavior disturbingly reminiscent of Larry. Both men seemed to have used her for their own ends. Who was she to believe: the old love or the new?

Tormented, she rose and spent the rest of the night at the east window, wishing everything were different, wishing that she would wake up in her apricot bedroom in Chicago, this whole life a bad dream. The first light of dawn streaked the eastern sky when she heard the bed groan; a moment later, Río's hand touched her shoulder. She turned and clung to him silently, not caring why he was there, only glad that he was.

At breakfast, after the *trovador* had left on one of his myriad mysterious errands, Nicolasa became very chatty. Yesterday, after seeing the cobbler, she spent the afternoon out in the courtyard, picking up the latest gossip, which naturally involved the new prisoner.

"If you ask one of the guards, he knows nothing, but every merchant in the yard has a different notion of who the man Lorenzo is and why he is here. Partido the butcher says he is not a prisoner at all, but really a dealer in black arts who is setting up some kind of magical engine that will make His Grace invincible in war. Well, I told *him* that what I saw in the main hall two days since was enough to convince me that black magic or no, the man is a *prisoner*, and His Grace seems to be certain that chains will hold him fast. What kind of sorcery is it that cannot break loose from a prison cell?"

"The man's a smuggler and a spy, with no more magic in him than my little finger," said Ana.

"Then there are several who believe him to be one of His Grace's illegitimate sons, who trafficked with

Pradera about exchanging some northern territories for an alliance against the Marqués."

"*Cha!*" said Ana. "None of His Grace's sons could be so stupid. Besides, this man has nothing of Quintero about him, not the walk, nor the look, nor the voice; he's a foreigner, most likely a savage from the North or East. His dialect is peculiar." She glanced at Celia with a quizzical expression. "It reminds me somewhat of your former accent, my lady."

Celia had gradually abandoned her Argentine lilt as she became accustomed to the clipped, almost nervous speech pattern of her companions. She shrugged. "*Castellano* was not my native tongue; perhaps it was not his, either." She feigned a deep interest in her delicately carved fan.

"The wine vendors have heard that Lorenzo is given no food, and they have begun to accept wagers on the number of days it will continue so. Partido has bet three *reales* on six more days," said Nicolasa.

"How does he explain that, if he thinks Lorenzo is not a prisoner?" Celia inquired.

"He says the magician is purifying himself for some mystic rite, perhaps even a Black Mass."

"Never!" cried Ana. "His Grace would never permit such a thing, and Partido is a blasphemer to suggest it!"

"He might, if it would win the war with Pradera," Nicolasa replied.

"If Padre Juan could hear you say that!"

"There's only one place in the Palace a Black Mass could be held, so Padre Juan must already know."

"Nicolasa!"

"I only repeat what Partido told me and is telling everyone else."

"He must be joking," Celia interposed, for the sake of peace.

"Well, everyone knows by now that Padre Juan spoke with the prisoner and discovered that he was never baptized and did not *want* to be baptized. He does not believe in God." She crossed herself, Ana did likewise, and Celia followed suit.

He hasn't much to lose, Celia thought. *He's already in the pit as deep as he can sink and still be alive.* Who was the greater fool—him for being honest and escaping the endless ministrations of religion, or her for living a tedious lie? She said aloud, "I can't see how that means he will be holding a Black Mass in the Palace chapel, Nico."

"A heathen," said Ana, shaking her head. "An atheist!"

"I wish I could watch it," sighed Nicolasa. She had taken to being an audience with great enthusiasm.

Ana frowned stormily, as if about to launch into a holy tirade, and Celia decided to put an immediate halt to the conversation. "Ana, will you go to Doña María Antonia and ask if I may have permission to visit in her apartments later today? I feel a desire to watch skillful, silent women engaged in womanly tasks."

Ana withdrew in a huff, clearly miffed at being cut off in mid-lecture, but too aware of her position to remonstrate. Since she had become Marquesa, Celia had noticed that people did her bidding much more readily than before.

When the *dueña* was gone, Celia turned to the younger maid. "And what of the belt, Nico?"

"He promises to have it finished by tomorrow afternoon. We had no difficulty in finding Fernandez and observing him without his knowledge."

Celia clacked her fan against the oak armrest. "Good." She rose and reached for a light cloak. "Let's go for a walk."

Outside, the guard stationed on the balcony inclined his head stiffly and raised his halberd-rifle in a salute appropriate to Celia's rank. Then he resumed the stony stare and rigid posture that always made him seem more a fixture of the building than a human being. Celia nodded wordlessly, accustomed by this time to the deportment expected of his guardsmen by the Marqués. Early in her captivity she had attempted in vain to engage this very man in conversation; she soon discovered that the guards of the Palace were chosen for, among other things, their taciturn natures.

Celia raised her fan before her lips. "Is Fernandez at his post now?" she asked in a voice that she hoped would be inaudible to the guard.

"Yes," replied the maid in like manner. She squinted, frowning, toward the far end of the west wall, which was separated from their tower by a series of small courtyards. "From this distance, I don't think I can say which he is, but I know his duties end at sundown."

Celia glanced speculatively at Nicolasa. "Do you think him handsome, Nico?"

She shrugged. "Señor Río is more handsome."

"I know how much you admire him, but let us leave Señor Río out of the conversation for a moment; we speak of Jaime Fernandez."

"Well, he is not ugly, but there are better-looking men in the guard. There's one behind you, for example."

Leaning into an embrasure, Celia gazed at the doll-like figures in the yards below. "Nico, you've been very good to me. You've borne with my whims and my illnesses cheerfully and without complaint; I couldn't have found a better companion anywhere. You're like a sister to me."

"It is *my* privilege, my lady. What was I as a laundress? Nothing. Now I serve the Marquesa; I know that may not mean a great deal to you, but it is a fine new life for me."

"What if . . . what if something should happen to me? What would you do then, Nico?"

Nicolasa grimaced. "Go back to the laundry. What else?"

"You wouldn't want to do that, would you?"

"No; my new work is much more pleasant."

Celia contemplated Nicolasa's plain but well-cut gown. It was a simpler version of her own attire, made of cheaper fabric, without the lace and embroidery that lately festooned all of her apparel—Ana and Nicolasa lavished their sartorial skills on her voluminous, high-waisted gowns, utilizing materials they would not dare expend on their own adornment. Yet the young maid's clothing was infinitely finer than the ragged, sweat-stained chemise she had worn in the laundry—a chemise that had been one half of her entire wardrobe.

"So, you are grateful for the opportunity to enjoy this new work? And you would be grateful for my continued favor, would you not?"

"Of course, my lady." Nicolasa looked worried and confused. "Have I done something wrong?"

"No, not at all." Celia paused a long moment, carefully considering her next words. "Nico, what would you do for me?"

"Why . . . anything, my lady. Is there something you need?"

"Would you steal for me?"

Nicolasa laughed. "Why should you need to steal? The Marquesa, heavy with His Grace's child, can have anything she wants."

"No, not *anything*."

"Anything worth having, unless it be the moon and the stars, which no mortal can give."

"You have not answered my question."

"Well . . . is there danger involved?"

"A kind of danger."

"What do you mean?"

"Are you a virgin, Nico?"

The maid's face flushed. "Ah, that kind of danger."

Celia waited for an answer to her question.

"Well, my lady . . . no, I am not a virgin any-more."

"Then, Nico, I must have something stolen, something important, and it must be kept completely secret. The person from whom it must be stolen may have to be seduced. Perhaps not, but I don't really know how else the thing can be accomplished."

Nicolasa bit her lip. "My lady, this is a large favor you ask of me."

"I know. Well?"

"Who is the man?"

"Will you swear to do it?"

"My lady, how *can* I if I don't even know who he is?"

Celia glanced toward the guard, wondering if he had heard Nicolasa's last remark, which had seemed inordinately loud for a whisper. "Jaime Fernandez," she murmured.

Nicolasa glanced across to the west wall. "I have never met him," she said flatly.

"But you know something about him."

"I know something about the Bishop of San Felipe, too, but I do not *know* the man. To lie with a stranger, to take the chance of bearing a stranger's child . . . My lady, I have no faithful lover to care for me, and after I have stolen from this man, he surely would not want me for his *amante*." She gazed at Celia appealingly. "Is there *no* other way to do this?"

Celia sighed. "Well, I won't insist, Nico. All I ask is that you swear to me that you will tell no one what we have discussed today."

"No, of course not."

"Swear on your immortal soul."

"I swear on my immortal soul—dear Mother of God, what oaths you ask of me!"

"I must be sure, Nico, that you won't tell anyone, not even Señor Río. This is very important to me."

Nicolasa straightened. "My lady! I would never betray your confidence!"

"Very good. I have something simpler for you, then. I want to meet Jaime Fernandez. Do you think it can be arranged?"

Nicolasa pursed her lips. "He is allowed in the Palace, of course, as one of Carril's picked men."

A movement at the corner of her eye warned Celia that Ana had stepped onto the balcony and was rapidly approaching. "I want to see him tomorrow night, Nico, and no one must know, not even *him*," she whispered swiftly, and then Ana was with them.

"Doña María Antonia pleases to have you wait on her this afternoon at whatever time is convenient to you, and she desires you to bring your lute, if you are not too tired for such diversion," said Ana.

"Very good," Celia replied. "Come, I've had enough air; let us go inside for a game of tarot." With a surreptitious glance at the west wall, she swept by them and on through the portal.

Río had taught her a bridge-like game played by either three or four people using all seventy-eight cards of the tarot deck; the ladies whiled away a great deal of time with it. Cards had never held much interest for Celia; she had never become even a novice bridge-player, though the game was perennially popular among the students on the Northwestern campus. Nevertheless, she frequently indulged this pastime now as a way of escaping for a little while from the pressure of her dilemma. She won often and had collected a sizable hoard of small change from Doña María Antonia's ladies. The Dowager Marquesa herself had lately deigned to take a hand or two; she was a shrewd player, and Celia didn't have to try very hard to lose to her. Secretly, Celia was pleased that the imperious and ascetic Doña María Antonia was not, after all, completely immune to vice.

Río came that night, and in the privacy of the bed

Celia did not try to hide her curiosity concerning Larry.

"He has said a number of things, but none of them has any bearing on the information we want. He is strong, this old love of yours, but the Marqués will break him. I can hardly believe that personal greed would carry him so far; a man values life more than money, does he not, or are there men of your homeland so different from the men I have known?"

"It was greed, I think, for a long time," Celia replied, "but not anymore."

"What then? Can he fear war between the Marqués and his overlord? *His* side, with those weapons, would have the advantage unless it is extremely weak in numbers."

"No, not weak in numbers. Much stronger than you could conceive, and farther away, too, than you can ever know. You'll never find it without him, believe me, Río. You must tell the Marqués so."

"Tell me about your trip to Verdura, before the slave-dealers took you. Was it forest or plain? Was the sun to your left, to your right, or what?"

"I can't tell you, Río. Truly, I *cannot* tell you how I came to Verdura. Through the forest—that's all I know. *He* knows the way; if you kill him, you'll never find it."

"Ah, the Marqués is a great believer in maps. And I, too. If Larry Meyers can find the way himself, he can draw a map of it, or I and Carril could draw a map from his description. Why does he delay; why does he allow himself to be tortured?"

"Free him and follow him."

"No. After all, he gave his *amante* over to slavers—how can a man like that be trusted?"

Celia sighed. "You will never find it without him."

He caught her hair and turned her face toward him. "Why are you so certain?"

"I know it."

"But *why* do you know it?"

"If you had been with me when I left my homeland and came to the Marqués's domain, you would understand how I know. I can't explain any better than that."

Río made an exasperated noise. "I wish I could make sense out of that."

"I am sorry I'm so stupid."

"Is it really stupidity?"

"Do you think I'm lying? No, Río! As I love you, I swear I can't describe the route to my country."

His fingers touched her mouth. "Don't swear by love—that's no oath at all. Love is a pretty dream, but nothing a person can lean on."

"Do you love me, Río?"

"Would I have kept your secret from His Grace if I did not?"

"For the sake of the child, and the wealth, honor, and position you will derive from your hand in its existence—of course you would."

"Well, you have learned something during this winter."

"I have learned only that everything I thought I knew was false."

"That is more than most people learn in their whole lives."

"Río, what will happen to Larry if he doesn't yield?"

"I don't know. But I would guess that moment is a long way off yet."

"What have they done to him?"

"Not much. They tried the whip again today; the Marqués wants to leave the bone-crushing implements till last. Perhaps you would care to watch tomorrow, knowing what you know about the man?"

She grimaced. "No, I don't think I could bear it."

"Not bear the pleasant taste of vengeance?"

She turned that over in her mind, prodded it, found

the very notion barbaric, yet appealing. She could veil herself heavily and watch from a distant gloom, where Larry could not see her; no longer would she merely imagine his torment. The way her pulse quickened at the thought surprised her. "I'll do it."

After lunch the following day, she donned a dark, bulky mantle with a large cowl; under the hood she wore a closely woven veil. No one would have recognized that muffled figure as Celia; it could have been man, woman, or infernal minion as it stepped carefully down the stairs. It trailed behind Ana, Nicolasa, and several other curious Palace ladies, all of whom were preceded by Río, who held a lantern for the descent. The dungeon was dark, but a dim glow ahead beckoned, guiding them to the interrogation chamber. There, Carril and a few of his men had Larry tied by wrists and ankles to a vertical iron grate.

Celia stood well back, in shadow, though there was no real need to do so; Larry faced away from her, and lashed tightly as he was, he could not turn his head in her direction. The pale bare skin of his back was crosshatched by oozing red welts.

Río left the women in darkness while he spoke in low tones with Carril.

Celia was less shocked by Larry's wounds than she expected to be. In fact, she felt a mild thrill of satisfaction that he had been well beaten. The whip wielder was seated at the moment, smoking a pipe of fragrant tobacco; the lash dangled casually from his loosely clenched fist, trailing in a circle that framed his foot. Now and then he would glance at Carril expectantly. At a nod from that officer, he rose, kneading the muscles of his working arm with his left hand.

"Nothing has changed," Río told Celia, "except that he is beginning to tell outrageous lies. Well, perhaps this is progress of a sort; previously, he refused to say anything."

"What kind of lies?" Celia asked.

"You'll hear some of them, perhaps. Watch."

The whipman raised his arm and brought it down again in one fluid motion, and the sound of the blow echoed through the halls of the dungeon. Larry's body jerked, then shivered as if a sudden draft had chilled it. He moaned, panting, then cried out sharply as a second stroke fell almost exactly atop the first.

"Please believe me!" he sobbed. He twisted his head to one side, and Celia could see the whitish streaks where tears had washed the accumulated grime from his cheeks. "Oh, please, God, believe me!" The braided leather snake struck again, slicing like a razor through his flesh, licking up blood as it went and scattering red droplets on the straw underfoot. He subsided into a low, bubbling wail, in which mangled fragments of English and Spanish occasionally surfaced.

Carril dipped a tin cup into a bucket of water at his feet and offered Larry a drink. "How many times must I assure you that when you tell the truth, all of this will stop? The Marqués will give you food; he might even clothe you in velvet and silk. Why do you insist upon misleading us with fancies of other worlds and other histories, or whatever this is that you talk about?"

Larry gulped at the water, choking himself in his eagerness. "No fancy," he coughed out afterward. "Science."

A bad word-choice, thought Celia. *Science means alchemy and astrology to these people.*

Carril shook his head. "I don't want to do this, I never wanted to do any of this. If only you had told us everything at the very beginning, how much easier it would have been for all of us!"

"A world in which Julius Caesar became king of Rome," Larry said. "A world in which Jesus was killed as a baby—"

Carril glanced at the whipman and nodded his head.

"No more!" shouted Larry, catching the movement in the corner of his eye.

"Then the truth."

"I told you the truth."

"Well, I don't believe in magic, so you'll have to think of something more reasonable than those fairy tales you've been telling us. Give him three more lashes."

This time Larry screamed. Loudly. The skin on his back was beginning to hang in tatters.

Celia closed her eyes and turned away, feeling queasy. Vengeance was suddenly a sour taste in her mouth. "Inform Río that I wish to leave," she said to Ana.

Dutifully, he lit their way upstairs. In the sanctum of her room, alone, he said, "He's been saying things like that all day, telling of 'alternate probabilities' and 'parallel worlds.' It does sound like sorcery, or perhaps the word-play of philosophy. You know him—does it *mean* anything?"

For an instant she was tempted to say yes, she knew exactly what it meant, and it meant exactly what it seemed to mean. But she quashed the impulse. "No," she said. "Perhaps he's gone mad from the pain."

"A man can take more pain than that."

She shuddered. "I wish I hadn't gone to watch it. I don't feel well now. Río, I think I'll lie down. I don't think . . . *querido,* don't come to me tonight. I have to rest. Please, I would prefer it so."

"So? You saw him and felt . . . pity, yes?"

"I don't know."

"You think with your heart instead of your head, Celia. Well, nurse your pity, and while you sleep alone tonight, remember that *he* preferred to sleep alone, too."

She sighed. "I thought I would enjoy watching him suffer, but it sickened me. I only wish he had never existed. Please, for your part in his suffering, leave me for tonight; I'll feel better disposed to you in the morning." She tossed aside the heavy veil, which she had been clutching in both hands since they entered the room.

Río reached out the arm's length that separated them, touched her yellow hair with the tips of his fingers. "Believe me, I would prefer it, too, if you were simply an Indian princess who had never heard of this man. Good night, *querida*. If you want me, Nico will know where I am."

When he was gone, she realized that she really hadn't wanted him to leave. He was a good person to have around when the world was falling apart, and she could have used a few hours of the furnace-heat of his body. She sat on the bed, and it was cold as ice.

Sometime later, Nicolasa ducked in and closed the door snugly behind her. "It's ready," she said. "He was waiting at the doorway of the hall when we went downstairs, so I hung back and picked it up, I think without being seen." She drew a well-wrapped bundle from beneath her ample skirts.

Celia restrained herself from snatching the package out of Nicolasa's hands and clawing the cloth wrapper off with her fingernails. They undid the knots one by one and gently rolled the contents out onto the bed.

The belt. And, as far as Celia could tell, a perfect copy.

"And Jaime Fernandez?" Celia asked.

"He'll be here late tonight; he thinks I'll be waiting for him in the antechamber." She smiled roguishly. "I was shameless. I made him believe that I had been watching him for months, waiting for my chance to make an assignation. He was eager enough."

"Well, you're a pretty girl, and you've gained weight in the right places since you left the laundry."

"*Cha!*"—he just liked the thought of an easy woman. He'd have taken me then if I hadn't pleaded important duties for Your Grace."

Celia threw an arm around the maid and hugged her. "Good, Nico."

The girl frowned. "My lady, I can't help thinking . . . of Señor Río."

Celia touched the smooth leather of the belt, the cold metal of the buckle. "Oh?" she murmured.

Nicolasa ducked into a curtsey. "It is nothing, my lady. It is not my place to ask you any questions."

"Señor Río . . . will be away this evening." She was relieved now that she had not been forced to manufacture some flimsy excuse to get rid of him.

"Ah."

"And now we will choose a proper dress for my greeting of Jaime Fernandez. A comfortable dress. A loose dress. And I will tell you the other small thing I wish you to do."

"My lady, please . . . please be careful. For the child's sake."

"Ah, yes," Celia replied without any inflection at all in her voice. "For the child's sake."

It was deep night when Fernandez arrived. One of the two guards knocked gently at the door, prepared to turn the newcomer away if no one answered his summons. But the panel swung open, and Ana relayed her mistress's instructions that the man be allowed in.

The anteroom was dimly lit by a single candle; Ana guided him through it and opened the connecting door to allow him to pass into the bedchamber. Then, without entering herself, she closed the door behind him.

This room, too, was dim, because the only source of light was a low fire in the hearth. But he could see well enough to recognize that a woman in a long, pale dress sat motionless in a boudoir chair in the darkest shadows.

"Nicolasa?" he whispered.

"No, not Nicolasa," Celia said, rising from her chair.

She stepped forward, and the firelight gleamed in her hair.

Fernandez gazed at her quizzically, his face showing plainly that he strove to identify her. Suddenly, he bowed. "Your Grace," he said, "please forgive this intrusion. A young girl told me she was your maid, told me to come here tonight and meet her. I beg you accept my apologies—"

"No apology is necessary. *I* wanted you to come here tonight, not my maid."

He straightened slowly. "How . . . how can I be of service to Your Grace?"

"I saw you in the hall a few days since," Celia said casually, "and I thought that I would like to . . . talk to you." She lowered her voice a bit at the end of the sentence, made it throaty, hoped it might be sexier that way. Larry had once said that her normal tone was a bit strident, and for a time she had trained herself to a lower pitch; she'd neglected it these last few months, but it was still available now that she needed it. She smiled, staring directly into Fernandez's eyes. One searching glance as he entered the room had shown her that he wore the belt, and now she concentrated her whole attention on a disarming demeanor.

He was obviously uncertain and uncomfortable, shifting from foot to foot and glancing around the room to avoid her steady gaze.

"Sit down," she said softly. "Here." She indicated the velvet chair that had been placed beside her boudoir chair for this evening.

"I can't presume so, Your Grace."

"Of course you can," she said, resuming her own seat. "Please." And when he still hesitated: "I would consider it a favor."

Gingerly, he sat down.

Celia turned to a low table at her elbow. A flagon of wine—prescribed by Doctor Velas for medicinal purposes—and a pair of cups stood there; she poured drafts for both of them, his a bit heartier than her own. "I saw you, and I thought to myself that you were quite a well-built man." She would have said handsome, but she suspected he knew himself too well to believe that; he was no beauty, too rugged, too uneven of feature, and his lank, limp hair trailed over his collar in greasy, untidy clumps. But his chest was broad, his shoulders wide, and his waist slim enough to set off the first two.

He accepted the cup and drained it at one gulp. Celia refilled it, smiling, wishing the flagon were twice as large. She sipped at her own drink, gazing at him over the rim.

After the third cup, he relaxed and returned her smile, and when she bid him come closer, he was no longer timid. His lips were flavored by the wine, and he was a gentle and careful lover, mindful of his own strength and of her swollen belly. Anxious to find favor in her eyes, he performed assiduously whatever task she set him, and he never noticed Nicolasa stealing into the room to exchange his belt for another exactly like it.

But Celia noticed.

He was gone, after thanking her awkwardly, with a promise to come again whenever she liked. She knew he would brag to his friends, that shortly the whole Palace—and Río, too—would know who had slept with her this night. She ignored those thoughts. The belt was in her hands, and that was all that mattered. She turned it over, inspecting it by the light of the oil lamp. The stud, a barely noticeable lump on the buckle, was in its proper place; the leather appeared to be undamaged.

"Thank you, Nico," she said, and silently: *You will never know how grateful I am.*

She fell asleep clutching the belt like a rag doll.

The next day, Holy Thursday, was one of religious observance; the Palace was readying itself with Masses and Communion for the celebration of Easter. Celia spent most of her day in the chapel with the Dowager Marquesa, her mind occupied with constructing a plan of escape. She toyed with various ideas and sundry disguises, but none of them seemed feasible, and the large question mark—how to free Larry from the dungeon—presented an unassailable barrier. She was willing to seduce a guard but chary of using Nicolasa as a confederate again; this time, the reason for her actions would be only too clear. Still baffled, she wished she could pray for assistance, wished that she believed someone would hear her prayer and send aid.

Late in the day, Río joined her unobtrusively, elbowing Ana aside to kneel within whisper-distance.

"Come into the corridor."

Outside, he led her to a bench in an alcove and sat down beside her. "If you have any favors to ask of His Grace during the Easter season, forget them. Stay away from him, away from his table and away from the main hall."

"Why?"

"His Grace is in ill-temper, and at such times rather unpredictable. Go up to your room and stay there."

"Río, I don't understand."

"Celia, he *will* hear about Fernandez—I don't know why you were foolish enough to see him."

Celia stiffened. "That is my affair and does not concern you."

"Well, it will concern the Marqués."

"How? He has said nothing about *our* relationship."

"Do you think I speak of your lying with him? *Mierda! I* know there was no lust behind your summons."

"I saw him in the hall a few days ago and thought him attractive. Everyone else in the Palace seems to live so—why not me?"

Río gripped her arm tightly. "I see that you do not care to speak of this matter, so I won't press you. But it may seem suspicious to some that you trysted with a man who so recently returned from a trip north with a *particular* prisoner, a man you never met before last night and who has no visible qualities which might make him specially desirable to a woman. Do you understand what I say?"

Celia went white. "Coincidence," she murmured.

"In your position, my Indian princess, you can little afford coincidence. The thought of seeing your pale flesh stretched on the rack is not a pleasant one, yet I think that His Grace wants those guns even more than he wants an heir." Río released his almost unbearable pressure on her arm and apologetically stroked the place he had hurt. "Ah, Celia, why couldn't you forget the poor bastard?"

"So he's a poor bastard now, is he? You pity him," she said bitterly. "Yet the torture continues."

Río shook his head. "No more; he's dead."

For a moment, Celia thought her heart would stop.

"And at the worst possible time—as of today, we're at war with Pradera."

CHAPTER ELEVEN

As Río predicted, the Marqués's fury was intense. Carril was demoted and sent north into battle as a foot soldier. The whipman was whipped himself and thrown into the very chains and cell that the prisoner had occupied, there to rot on little bread and less water for an unspecified length of time. The Marqués could no longer be spoken to except in the mildest of tones, and the most innocuous of subject matters could bring out the hurricane of his wrath. The ladies avoided his table and his company, and only the most discreet and faithful of his retainers dared to look at him while they ate—he took every glance as a personal affront and would, likely as not, order the viewer out of the room, or even the Palace, immediately. He berated *himself*, Río related, for not having applied the lash with the delicacy of his own hands.

Reports from the field of battle indicated that the Conde de Pradera possessed a sizable number of the new rifles.

"Has he found the source?" Río paced the length of Celia's bedchamber, gazing out the north window at the end of each lap. He could see the river and the boats that were bringing the bodies of the dead home to San Felipe for burial. "His Grace is driving me mad, questioning me over and over again about our findings in the North. Yet we found nothing, *nothing*. The man might have flown down from Heaven for all we could discover of him! Yet the Conde de Pradera has guns. He *must* have found the source!"

"I doubt it," muttered Celia. She stared steadily out the east window and listened to the mournful tolling of the cathedral bells and thought of all the men whose lives had terminated because of Larry's greed. Perhaps they would have died anyway, killed by flint-lock rifles, but it seemed to Celia that they died more easily, more quickly, more cheaply, because of the Enfields.

"I wish I could believe that. Yet, San Felipe loses and loses, and the war comes closer to the city. Peasants are streaming southward, their villages burnt, their relatives slaughtered. What are pitchforks and *miquelets* against those guns?"

"Be glad he didn't sell them nuclear weapons." But she said that in English.

"His Grace now suspects that the source was inside Pradera all the time, that Larry Meyers was a traitor to his Conde, peddling them to us."

"No."

"Of course, *you* know. What secrets are locked in your brain, Celia? Where is your country?"

"My country is right here, under our feet, all around us, from sea to shining sea." She laughed mirthlessly, her fingers tracing the dovetailed stonework around the window. "From the Atlantic to the Pacific, from the Great Lakes to the Gulf of México, and, of course, I cannot omit Alaska and Hawaii. My country, the United States of America. My city, Chicago, Illinois. Would you believe there are buildings over one hundred stories tall in my city?"

"No."

"I didn't think you would. I hardly believe it myself anymore. But when you find the city and the buildings, you will find the source of the guns. Right here, yet farther away than you can imagine, Río. Much farther."

"Don't speak in riddles."

"I'm not. Truly, I'm not. But Larry couldn't make you understand, either."

Río pulled another chair to her window, sat down opposite Celia, and took her hands in his own. "There is something to understand, is there not? Something *you* understand and think I cannot. Try, Celia. Try to make me understand. Is it Europe, even Spain itself? Or an unknown land far to the north? Or deep in caves under our feet? Is that what you meant? Try to explain, Celia. Every day the battle creeps closer as our men retreat; it may mean our lives."

She glanced toward the wooden wardrobe that held her clothing. Inside, the belt hung on an inconspicuous hook behind her wedding gown. All that scheming for nothing. "There's no cause to worry, Río; they must run out of ammunition eventually, and now that Larry is dead, they'll get no more."

"How can you be so sure?"

She smiled slightly. "And His Grace, who was strong enough to defeat the Conde before the new guns appeared, will again be strong enough when they are useless." The doorway had to stay open, armaments had to flow smoothly and continuously from one world to the other, or else the balance of power would shift ponderously back to its original configuration. The Conde could not defeat the Marqués without massive outside aid, and when that aid was withdrawn, the Conde was left high and dry. *Such a tenuous link,* she thought; *one man's life.*

Congestion of the lungs, they called it. One lash too many had cracked a rib; starvation and further torture had done the rest. Pneumonia. Not fatal in Evanston, Illinois, not even always fatal in San Felipe, given tireless nursing by some devoted person; but down in the dungeon of Castillo Quintero—inevitable death.

She had fallen into a daze of despair at the news. Without Larry to lead the way, home was lost in the trackless forest of the North—a mirage, a dream. Only the guns themselves remained to attest to its existence; soon they would be useless, and those that were not melted down for horseshoes would rust and rot to nothing. Larry himself would be forgotten completely.

How could a single man accomplish anything in the face of cultural inertia? *She* had tried, with her plays and her plumbing, and had failed totally to effect any change; instead, this world had fit her into *its* scheme, had stripped from her every vestige of her previous life and molded her anew in its own image. It was a regal image now, better than that of a slave, but it was not one she would have chosen willingly. After months of practice, she still found it oppressive. And now, as never before, she was forced to accept it as the role she would fulfill for the rest of her life.

"You want the truth, you say. Well, I'll give you what I know of the truth, but it won't help you in any way." She leaned her head against the tapestry-covered wall and looked at the ceiling, away from Río's face. But she kept a tight grip on his hand. She deliberated awhile, searching for an appropriate example. "Think of His Grace's ancestor, who came to San Felipe from Europe. Think if he had been killed in battle before he ever came to the New World. What would have happened then?"

She felt his hand twitch as Río shrugged. "Well, someone else would have been sent in his place, I imagine. Someone had to govern the territory."

"But not the Marqués Alonso Enrique Quintero de los Rubios. Someone else. Perhaps someone with dark hair. Perhaps."

"Yes. Perhaps."

"Then, where would we be today if that had happened?"

Silence as Río considered that. At last: "I would not have bought you on the auction block at Verdura."

"I would still be a slave, perhaps scrubbing floors in

some frontier hut, perhaps something worse. But you and I would not be here together. Perhaps even this Palace would not be here."

"Yes, many things would be different."

"*That*, you see, is what Larry Meyers would call an 'alternate probability.' One probability is that the Marqués's forebear came to the New World, and the alternate is that he did not. Think of them as two forks in a road. All of history is like a long road with many forks, every branch leading to a different possible world. Do you follow this?"

"Yes, but it seems a meaningless play of words, akin to the puzzle of how many angels can stand on the head of a pin."

"Please, accept what I say for a little while. Now, think of the Invincible Armada."

"San Felipe's conquest of England?"

"Yes. What if the Armada had been unsuccessful?"

Río pondered that awhile, then said, "I cannot imagine how the world would be different. One conquest more or less . . ."

"But it might be different somehow, just as it would be different if someone else had been sent here in the first Marqués's place."

"Well, yes, it might be different somehow."

"England might have been free to settle this land instead of Spain. We might be speaking the language of England instead of the language of Spain."

"Would the Emperor allow such a thing when the Pope gave *him* the New World?" Río laughed briefly. "I think not."

"Perhaps he would have been too busy in the southern part while England settled in the North. Perhaps by the time he or his descendants were ready, England would have been too strong to be forced out."

Río sighed impatiently. "I will accept that for now, but this conversation contains far too many 'perhapses.' "

"Just a little longer, Río." She watched his face for the first signs of utter disbelief. "Now you must imagine that the defeat of the Invincible Armada actually happened somewhere. Not here, not where we can see or touch or sense it in any way, but in some other world—a world which took the alternate branch at that particular fork in the road. The inhabitants of such a world would not believe that *this* world existed; they would think their own the only world. Suppose then, that a man of this world found some way to travel to a world arising from that other course. Suppose he found that the people spoke a different language, and had customs that differed from his own; suppose they wanted to know of the strange, far-off country from which he came. Would he be able to explain to them? Would they not think him mad, or a fool and a liar?"

Río's face bore the same steady, bland expression she had seen before; he withheld comment, knowing there was more to come.

"The world in which the Invincible Armada could not conquer England, in which England settled the northern New World—that is Larry's world . . . and *mine*."

His grip on her hand tightened momentarily; he rose and moved close beside her, touching her hair, then pressing her face against his hip. "No, *chiquita*, it will not pass."

She choked on her own laugh. "Didn't I say no one would believe? Me and Cassandra." She rubbed her cheek against the rough fabric of his breeches. "Larry Meyers was the only person who knew how to travel between worlds; now that he is dead, there won't be any more guns or ammunition. They came from my world, you see, and my world is gone. All gone." She sobbed painfully, her throat constricted. "You stupid fools, killing the goose that laid your golden eggs."

"Yes," he murmured. "We were fools not to realize

the limit of his endurance . . . and of his devotion. Men have died before for what they believe in, for their land and their families. They are dying at this moment in the North for those reasons."

"You're wrong, you're wrong!" she sobbed. "He believed in nothing but himself and he died for *money*." She looked up, her face reddened by tears. "I've told you the truth, Río, I swear it by anything you like."

"No," he said. "Don't swear." He bent and kissed her tenderly. "Tell no one what you have told me. I know you find the life of the Marquesa . . . restricting, but you would be far more restricted if you were locked in this room forever." He kissed her again. "Oh, *querida mia*, why have you fashioned this tale?"

Gazing into his face, she saw deep concern there, and confusion. She slumped back in her chair. "Go away, please. Leave me alone. I want to listen to the bells."

He went, but she heard him later, singing a love-ballad on the stairway outside her chambers.

She picked up her lute and sang . . . in English.

The Castle prepared itself for a long siege and for the tremendous influx of townspeople that would occur when the enemy army came over the horizon. Provisions streamed in from the surrounding countryside; every available room was transformed into storage space. Attendance at Mass was larger than ever, and Padre Juan was the only person who was happy about it. Every hand was busy, even those that normally did nothing but look decorative. Only Doña María Antonia refused to become involved, sequestering herself in her rooms and lamenting the absence of her ladies, who were commandeered to oversee the sorting of vegetables in the dungeon storerooms.

Ana and Nicolasa alternated caring for their mistress so that each could be useful on lower floors for part of the day. Celia herself sang and strummed the lute; in her condition, she was not expected to work and would, in fact, probably be forbidden to take any part if she attempted to offer her services.

She had no intention of volunteering. She alone was confident that there would be no siege—with his supply of guns and ammunition cut off, the Conde would never dare to attempt such an inroad into his enemy's domain. She sang and whistled and laughed easily at Nicolasa's tales of labor in the storerooms. She sang in English, gliding across the parapet or through the halls, even down to the ground floor, where people hurried by her with time for only a curious glance at the pale, blonde woman in the voluminous mantle.

She was perpetually pale now with anemia, in spite of the wine Don Epifanio prescribed to build her blood, and her feet dragged, but her voice, sometimes dismally off-key, rang out with every English song she had ever heard. She no longer cared whether the lute harmonized; often she played discords just for the pleasure of making noise. Her favorite song became "Buckle Down Winsocki," which she crooned with slow monotony, interspersed with giggles. If someone asked her what the words meant, she concocted a wild tale of love and death, a different one for each questioner. Río heard reports of these and asked her which was the actual translation. "None," she replied truthfully, and broke into raucous laughter.

She banished Río from her bed and took to walking the upper stairways at night with a lighted taper while Ana or Nicolasa trailed behind, yawning. She slept at odd hours, usually during the day, and demanded her meals at random, even when she was not hungry. She summoned Padre Juan in the middle of the night, demanding Communion; when he arrived, she enticed and spurned him by turns. Clothed in a gauzy negligee, she would sit upright in bed to deliver her whispered Confession of fanciful, indelicate cravings. Ever closer to him she would lean, till her lips nearly brushed the large, hairy lobe of his ear, and her breasts swayed outward, barely restrained by the low neckline of her gown. When his fingers crept forward for a sly caress, she would elbow his hand aside and laugh in his face. Once she almost had him in bed, could feel the stiff prod beneath his cassock as he bent over her . . . but she yawned and abruptly ordered him out. Yet he returned every time she called, either because of her rank or because he had hopes the "lascivious Marquesa"—as all the Palace now referred to her—would eventually spread her legs for him.

The Marquesa talked to herself—raved—in a strange language. At times she appeared to speak to an impalpable companion; at other times she was obviously reciting poetry. And still other times, she would sit by a window and stare at the sky for hours.

At last, even Río could not reach her.

"What do you hope to accomplish by feigning madness?" he demanded.

She stared out the window without moving.

He came up behind her chair and encircled her with his arms. *"Querida."* When she made no reply, he swept her hair aside and kissed her neck. "You are poor company when you sit like this. Come, play the lute and sing with me, as we did during the winter."

She continued to ignore him.

"Don't you love me anymore?" he whispered.

For answer, she turned to stare at him dully, scanning his features as if he were some anonymous page. "You may leave now," she said coldly.

As her belly swelled, stretching her skin painfully taut, the creature within sapped more and more of Celia's energy. Day by day, it surged more restlessly, as if trying to beat its way out of her womb; often, when she lay deep in sleep, lost in endless, aimless dreams of another life, it would wake her with a shocking kick to the bladder or stomach. She longed to strike it then, to lift it by the heels and slap it till it wailed for mercy, and more than one purple bruise on her abdomen attested to her angry, futile attempts to still its activity.

On a certain morning, she woke thinking that once again she had been kicked awake. Groaning, she tried to roll over and discovered for the hundredth time that she could not do so, that she was trapped in one position by the lopsided girth of her pregnancy. She glanced at the darkened windows and sighed, knowing that she had not slept enough and that almost no one else was likely to be up at this chill, dim hour before dawn. She wept a groggy tear or two and damned the mindless entity that had brought her back too soon to the actuality of her existence.

Abruptly, she realized that the cause of her waking was not some interior disturbance but a noise—a brief, resonant noise, somewhat muffled by the bulk of the Castle, that she vaguely recognized as the report of a distant skyrocket.

The north window flickered with the light of two fresh blasts, and intermittent gunfire echoed in reply.

"The siege, the siege!" screamed Ana, rushing into the room, her gray braids in wild disarray. "We must hurry to the storerooms!"

Celia allowed the *dueña* to help her rise, to slip shoes on her feet, and to throw a cloak about her shoulders; then she moved toward the north window.

Ana caught her arm in a frenzied grip. "They'll see you, they'll shoot you!"

As if to confirm her fears, the window shattered, showering the room with fragments of glass.

"Oh, come away, my lady, come away!" Ana babbled. She was near tears, and her hands were shaking.

Celia touched a stinging spot on her cheek, then stared in wonder at her blood-daubed fingers.

"Come, my lady," said Nicolasa, catching Celia's free arm.

They had only stepped into the antechamber when the outside door burst open and Río entered, shirtless and panting. "I've come to take you to safety," he said. The thin trail of blood on Celia's face caught his eye. *"Dios!* Are you hurt?"

"They can't have any ammunition left," said Celia. Outside, explosions were frequent and gunfire almost continuous.

"Apparently, you were wrong," he replied. "Shall I carry you, or can you walk?"

"But I *can't* be wrong!"

He swung her into his arms. "We've no time to argue." He passed through the corridor and descended the long stairway with sure, steady strides. The lower floors of the Palace were full of rushing men, armed and armored, laden with bags and boxes of ammunition; their hubbub was deafening, almost drowning out the sounds of battle beyond the walls. Río threaded his way through the crowd, narrowly avoiding collisions, interposing his own body whenever he sensed that Celia might be jostled. He shouted, *"Make way; make way for the Marquesa,"* but he could not be heard above the din and abandoned the effort. Eventually, he managed to join a stream of bodies—mostly women and children—flowing toward the entrance to the subterranean chambers of the Palace.

Below, the empty prison cells had been thrown open and were now crowded with those who could be of no use in the fighting. Río located the Dowager Marquesa and her entourage and deposited Celia there. "You'll be safe now," he said.

Celia glanced around at the milling crowd. There was panic in the air, in spite of the careful siege preparations that had been so long under way. No one had believed that this day would really come. "What happened, Río? I *couldn't* have been wrong!"

"The Conde was a better general than you, Your Grace; he held back some for the *real* fight." He made a small, public bow and disappeared in the throng.

"Where are you going?" Celia shouted. But either

he did not hear or his answer was lost in the noise of the mob.

"So nice to see you, my dear," said Doña María Antonia. She sat upon a large silk bolster on the stone floor and was dealing cards for a round of tarot. Three white-faced ladies sat quite near her on a cloak and watched her nimble fingers shuffle the deck. "Will you take a hand?"

Celia glanced uncertainly at the flipping cards; they seemed to blur and slide before her eyes. She must have seemed unsteady, for Nicolasa ran to her side to support her and urge her to sit on a stool that the maid had somehow acquired during their downward trek.

"Don't be frightened, daughter-in-law. Castillo Quintero has never been taken, and if my son is half the soldier his father was, it never will be." She dealt the cards as coolly as if she had been upstairs in her somber bedroom. "It would appear that the upstart Conde was only distracting us in the North, while a company of grenadiers rode through the mountains to attack San Felipe from the west. He thought to find Castillo Quintero undefended, the fool. There ought to be more light down here; we can hardly see the pips." She opened the play and glanced expectantly at Celia. Suddenly her eyes narrowed. "Child, what is that upon your cheek?"

Nicolasa dabbed with a handkerchief at the drying smears of blood. *"Excelentísima Señora,* pardon me for speaking, but Her Grace was struck by glass from a broken window." When Celia winced at a gentle touch, Nicolasa peered closely at the wound, then carefully plucked out a small shard which still had been embedded in Celia's skin. A fresh gout of blood flowed forth and dripped down Celia's neck, staining the collar of her nightdress.

One of the pallid ladies turned away.

"Where is yesterday's strength?" murmured the

SHADOW OF EARTH 231

Dowager Marquesa, casting a reproving glance at the squeamish woman. "How can you live through each month if blood sickens you so?"

"I'm thinking of the wounded," the woman said faintly.

"Well, think no more; they have arrived."

A sudden hush fell on the crowd as every face turned toward the stairway, every neck craned for a view of the procession that descended. Padre Juan led, pausing frequently to look back over his shoulder. Behind him, litter-bearing soldiers trod a careful cadence; for all their gentle precision, almost every step drew a moan from somewhere along the line, from a man whose limbs trailed limply, or from one whose lower legs had been blown off. Others of the injured were mercifully unconscious; the gore that ran from ragged gashes in their chests and bellies soon coated the stairway and floor with a thin, slippery film.

Doctor Velas brought up the rear of the procession, and the litters were settled in a corner of the main hall which in other times had been used for torture. He chose a few anxious-looking women from among those who pressed close to the victims and directed them to perform the various tasks necessary for treatment. Some of these women wailed as they worked, for the men they nursed were their own men, and many of them would never rise from the pallets upon which they now lay. With warm but unboiled water, the women bathed the injured parts; with poultices of sweet-smelling but sadly ineffective herbs, they packed the raw, macerated flesh; with lengths of gray rag they bound the gaping rents through which bright blood steadily drained away. The cloth was quickly soaked, the water brown in many buckets; the women wept unashamed, and if their tears mingled with the discolored water, no one cared. Padre Juan passed among the sufferers, solemnly administering extreme unction to all.

Celia drew near them by degrees, fascinated by the horrible scene. One of the soldiers she recognized as the guard who had been stationed on the balcony where she had strolled innumerable times. His chest and throat were bloody, and large red bubbles formed at his nostrils with every breath, but his eyes were open, and they swiveled toward Celia as she approached.

She had never heard him utter a sound, and he did not now, but his left hand lifted a bit and somehow she knew that he wished her to touch it. His skin was cold and clammy, but his grip was strong, as if he were grasping life by holding her hand.

The plump woman who tended him did not weep but worked methodically with sure, impersonal movements; she had tended another before him and would move on to a third after. Among all the throng, there was no woman to grieve for him, unless she was hidden out of sight in some far corner. There was only Celia, who did not even know his name.

Padre Juan approached, bearing his vial of holy oil. He glanced inquiringly at the young Marquesa, who ignored him, then proceeded with a rapid version of the sacrament.

To Celia, the rest of the room blurred and faded; above the tumult of shrieks and sobs, she could hear one sound: *his* labored breathing. A horrid rattle began in his throat, as if he were choking on phlegm. His eyes, which had been following the priest's gestures, became glazed, unfocused, staring toward—but not at—the stone ceiling. His hand twitched, its convulsive grip loosening spasmodically. He coughed violently, spewing up a froth of red mixed with black clots, and when the seizure ended, the sound of his breathing did not return.

Celia stared full at his face, which death had dreadfully contorted. She had not really known him; they had bowed solemnly to each other once a day for many months, and he had never seemed more animate than the crenelations of the parapet. Yet he had been human, his flesh and breath warm, and now that life had deserted him, Celia felt as if a part of her had died, too. And deep inside, she was reminded of other times, other wounds, and other suffering endured stoically. Still clutching his motionless hand, she wept, and she would not allow herself to be led away from the corpse for a long, long time.

That night was quiet, and morning did not bring a renewed attack. Guards waited, alert, by their cannon on the walls, but they saw nothing to fire at, not a single grenade-bearing horseman, not even a rooftop rifle pointing in their direction. A cautious party dispatched to flush out the enemy found only frightened citizens hiding in their cellars. The Marqués strutted like a rooster, certain that the superior skill of his elite corps had turned the tide—and not at all deflated when his officers reported that the strange new guns had been found by the dozen, abandoned empty along the roads leading out of the city.

Damage to the Castle, which had been built to withstand attacks by Indians who had never learned to make bombs or cannon, was nevertheless slight, for the enemy had come without heavy, horse-drawn artillery. Damage to Castle personnel was considerable, and the Castle cemetery, a large plot beyond the postern gate, was the scene of substantial activity during the following days; the sound of wailing hardly ceased from dawn to dusk, and the woman who wore brightly colored garments was rare indeed.

Celia noticed little of these consequences of war; a cushioned litter, carried between two burly guardsmen, transported her from the dungeon to her tower room while she writhed in labor, a full month premature.

Doctor Velas, Terrazas, Ana, Nicolasa, and two strange women stood around the bed, speaking to each other in subdued tones. Celia tossed her head from side to side on the pillow; her belly was knotted in a single, agonizing, unending cramp.

"It is too early," said Don Epifanio. "Is this, then, the Marqués's child?"

Celia heaped every Spanish, French, and English obscenity she could think of on Don Epifanio's head.

"Not *exceptionally* early," offered Terrazas.

Celia moaned, "Can't you do something for the pain?"

"No, not *exceptionally* early, if we can trust the *trovador.*"

"Relax; *relax*," said Ana.

"I can't. The pain is too much. I can't, I can't. Where is Río?"

"He'll come soon." She wiped the sweat from Celia's brow.

"Has the tea arrived?" said Don Epifanio.

"Yes, here it is." Terrazas poured a cup for himself, one for Doctor Velas.

"Medicine?" Celia asked hopefully.

"No, just tea."

"Give me some of the pain-killing herb tea."

Don Epifanio shrugged. "It will make no difference."

"Oh, please, please."

The herb tea came, and it made no difference at all.

The cramp was like a menstrual cramp, or like constipation magnified a hundredfold. She curled into a fetal ball, clutching her swollen belly, teeth clenched against the moans that were building in her throat.

Someone began rubbing her back; it was Río.

"Forgive me," she whispered, "for sending you away."

"Hush, *chiquita,* and think about the son you are bearing His Grace."

The pain faded abruptly, and Celia lay back, panting. "It's gone."

"Gone?" echoed Don Epifanio, and immediately he and the two strange women converged on Celia, patting and prodding her belly.

"It will return," said one of the women, and she settled into a chair and pulled some knitting from her apron pocket.

"Must all these people be here?" Celia asked.

"It is customary," Río replied. "They will make certain that no other child is exchanged for yours."

"Has that ever happened?"

"No."

The pain returned, redoubled; it lasted a moment or two and faded, marking the initiation of real labor—rhythmic uterine contractions spaced a few minutes apart. Celia had known about the contractions, but she had not been prepared for their reality: they were a fist clenching, twisting, tearing at her entrails. The pain was unbearable, yet she bore it because she had no choice. She begged for opium and was denied. She moaned, thrashed, tore at the bedclothes, clawed at the hands that held her firmly to the bed, screamed in English for God, her mother, and Río.

Between contractions, she wept breathlessly and leaned against Río's strong arm. Her eyesight was hazy now and shot with golden sparks. She saw the Marqués at the foot of the bed, looking on with unconcern. "You bastard!" she screamed in English. Then the pain rose again, and her shrieks were inarticulate.

Hours passed. The night waned, and morning sunlight crept through the window. The knitting woman put aside her completed handiwork. Terrazas called for breakfast, and everyone but Río and Celia ate.

"I'm going to die," she said between pains.

"No," said Río, and his hands tightened on her. "You will *not* die."

"I can't bear any more."

"Soon, *chiquita. Soon.*"

"No more. No more. *No more!*"

Hands pushed her thighs up and apart. "Now you must push," said someone at the foot of the bed.

"Now you must push."

"You must push."

"Push."

"*Push!*"

Celia's scream pierced even her own ears this time, as it ricocheted off the walls. A giant scrabbled at her innards, trying to rip her body apart from crotch to throat. A tremendous pressure threatened to explode the back of her skull. She clutched the arm that encircled her shoulders, bit hard into the corded flesh; the rusty tang of blood seeped down her throat. A subway train roared through her head, and the whole visible world spun slowly, sickeningly, while the pain mounted and mounted to an impossible crescendo . . . then subsided, pulsing, to nothing more than a deep ache.

Above the sound of her own hoarse whimpering was another—the offended cry of a newborn infant.

"A boy," said Doctor Velas. A long silence. "A beautiful blond boy."

"Congratulations," Río whispered. Blood still welled in the tooth-marks on his arm, but he ignored it and supported Celia so that she could see the child.

The Marqués held his son, a red-faced wailing blob of flesh wrapped in a white cloth. He smiled a fatuous smile at Celia. "Here is your son, Lady Celia," he said. "The first, I pray, of many."

Celia turned her face to Río's shoulder and wept.

CHAPTER TWELVE

The child was given to a wet-nurse because Celia was not strong enough to feed it herself. Soon after delivery she developed a fever, diarrhea, and a malodorous vaginal discharge; weak from loss of blood and dehydration, she could hardly lift a hand, yet insomnia plagued her. She lay awake night after night, propped upright on a mound of pillows, tossing feebly, eating little of the delicate morsels sent up by the solicitous head cook. Doctor Velas dosed her with herbals, but they did nothing for her appetite or exhaustion; he offered the opiate he had withheld for the child's sake while she was pregnant, but she awakened from its stupor no better than she had been before.

"The wine vendors are taking wagers on your recovery," Río told her in a lull between songs. He spent his days at her bedside, trying to recapture the personal magic that had brought her out of decline once before.

"I hope you have made a profitable wager," she whispered.

"I will lose a great deal of money if you fail me."

"Sorry, Río. I realized when Larry died that the people of my world are not strong enough to survive here." She lacked the energy to elaborate, aloud, on a subject he could not comprehend, but the argument was clear in her mind. Modern medicine, taken for granted by the inhabitants of the United States, had made natural immunity redundant. The diabetic, the asthmatic, the anemic, the too-susceptible were kept alive to transmit their defective traits to the next generation; in a more primitive environment, like the world of the conquering Armada, they succumbed early. Just as she was succumbing now. Any Evanston doctor could have cured her, but Evanston was a world away, and penicillin a figment of her imagination.

In early America, frontier wives had often died young.

And even for the robust males, who never faced the strains of childbearing, death lurked in every village and rode the wind and water: anthrax, cholera, diptheria, typhoid fever, plague—all the diseases that had ravaged and limited human population for millennia. They were all here, hidden within the deceptive beauty of forests and prairies and lakes unsullied by the Industrial Revolution.

And then there was the war. Indochina, at least, had never been on her doorstep.

To be Marquesa and die—what kind of choice had Río given her so many months ago?

Padre Juan came to offer Communion, and she hated him for it.

"Listen to me, Celia," Río said when they were alone once more, save for Ana. "Ignore him when he comes to cluck over you. He knows nothing. You *will* live. This illness is common, and some die of it— many, I will not lie to you—but some do recover. You must fight!"

"I have no strength to fight with," she murmured. "The child took all my strength."

"Shall I have the little one brought to you, to give you back some of that strength?"

"No!" Her shout was weak and robbed her of breath for a few moments. "I won't see it!" she gasped. "A child of rape, not my child at all! I won't have it near me!"

He put a reassuring hand on her shoulder. "No one will ever force the child on you if you do not wish to see it. Its burden upon you is ended."

His sleeve, rolled up to the elbow, exposed the marks of her teeth on his flesh. "I'm sorry I hurt you, Río," she whispered.

He bent to kiss her. "You may bite me any time you wish." His lips brushed her cheek. "I want so much to lie with you, *querida*. You must get well soon."

She wept quietly against his shoulder. "I've been so vile to you this past month."

"The first pregnancy is the most difficult; it does strange things to the heart as well as the belly. The next will be easier, I promise you. And we can be together again, as before."

She closed her eyes and turned her face from him. "It's all quite calculated, isn't it? You're a wonderful servant to your master, Río, and a marvelous psychologist—keep the Marquesa happy in any way you can: wait on her, sing to her, even fuck her if necessary. The blond babies must arrive on schedule every year. I'll wager you've made a greater profit from me than a few pieces of silver."

"*Querida*—"

"No, don't call me that. I loved you so much, Río, but you never loved *me* at all. You had a mission to perform, for a fat reward, and you never loved me at all."

"*Querida*, you are—"

"No, please. I was a fool. It seems I've often been a fool." She sighed deeply. "Don't leave me, Río. I don't want to die alone."

"You didn't leave me," he said softly.

"You've paid that debt already."

"Not yet. Not till you're well again." He kissed her fingers. "And you *will* be well again."

As the days passed and she sank no further, she began to share his certainty, and a new resolution budded within her. Her fever subsided gradually, her appetite returned, and she slept more easily, yet she feigned the same weakness and insomnia; the vials of laudanum prescribed by Doctor Velas she secreted deep in the stuffing of one of her pillows. When no one was watching, she would do isometric exercises under the covers to build up her strength; it was a slow and tedious process, but she persevered, hoping it would be effective. A month and a half after delivery, she still seemed unable to stand without the support of another person under each arm, though in reality she could walk with ease. Don Epifanio declared that the major symptoms of her illness had definitely abated, yet he admitted, with some consternation, that she might remain an invalid the rest of her life.

She had a plan now, a rather wild plan that she never would have considered in the days when Larry was alive, a plan devised at the prod of desperation. And though she was indeed desperate, she felt confident and clear of mind. She gave no thought to failure now; that was a luxury she could no longer afford. Only boldness would carry her through to freedom.

She knew now that she had experienced a nervous breakdown during those last weeks of pregnancy—a breakdown triggered in part by Larry's death, but also by Río's rejection of her true story. For a while, she had been the only person in this world aware of the truth; when she sought to share that knowledge, she realized she was the only one capable of believing it. Alienation, as much as despair, had pushed her over the edge.

Shock had brought her back: the cold, clammy hand clutching hers, the imminence of death, the fear and grief that had permeated the underground level of the Castle, and the violent reply of her own body to that emotion. Part of her died beside that nameless guardsman and in the long hours of torment and days of despair that followed. Río's attempt at consolation reminded her forcibly that she was not to be released from the baby mill; all she had suffered to date was truly but a prelude. If mania still possessed her, at least now she would wring some method from it.

She developed cravings. A handful of strawberries, she insisted, would put her to sleep far better than any of Don Epifanio's brews. In the hours before dawn, Nicolasa or some other maid had to dress and run to the stalls of the earliest-rising vendors, just outside the Castle walls, to choose the plumpest strawberries, the most luscious peaches from the East, or the juiciest oranges from the South. Or watermelon, radishes, tomatoes, plums—every night the craving changed, and no one could guess what would be desired next. But it would always be some luxury that had not been stored against the siege.

While she munched, Río would sit up with her, watching the sun rise and talking of the future. "His Grace plans to send another expedition in search of your homeland—or perhaps two, in different directions. The Conde, also, so our spies tell us, has such plans."

Celia laughed. "As well search for the fountain of youth."

Later: "The expeditions have left for Indian lands to the North and East. The East especially is very dangerous territory, but His Grace feels he has no choice."

"You're not going with them?"

"I have not had a great deal of success in the past. Capitán Fernandez is leading them this time."

"The same . . . ?"

"The same. He was promoted. A good man, but I think His Grace had other motives, as well, for this choice."

"I suppose I must allow my husband to approve my lovers, though he does not offer me the same privilege." She pretended to struggle with her pillows, pushing herself into a more upright position. Río made no attempt to help her, ostensibly because the minimal exercise would do her good; Celia wondered, sometimes, if he did not suspect her malingering. "You are a better lover than Fernandez."

"After all, I know you better."

"Yes, you do know me well."

"Better than anyone in Castillo Quintero."

She lowered her eyes and plucked with exaggerated feebleness at the bedclothes. "Do you think me mad?"

He gazed at her for a long moment. "I do not *wish* to think you mad."

"That is not an answer."

But he gave no other.

Blazing summer, almost exactly a year after that fateful morning . . . Don Epifanio declared Celia would very soon be fit to return to her lord's bed. She protested that she was hardly strong enough to stand alone, and he replied that there was no need for her to stand at all. A litter would be provided to transport her to the Marqués's apartments. The Marqués himself desired it so, five days hence—when (so Nicolasa explained) Leonora planned to leave the Castle for a short visit with a pregnant sister in a town to the south.

Suddenly, a zenith of desperation had been reached.

Ana busied herself with the last-minute sewing of flounces and ribbons and lace to Celia's nightdresses, while Nicolasa sat enthralled with the soft new fur robe His Grace had bestowed on Celia in gratitude for their son. She could not resist the smoothness of ermine-trimmed mink, nor the cool luxury of the fine blue satin lining. She swirled it about her shoulders, inside out, right side out, stroking the pile as if it were a living creature, a cat, instead of an inanimate article of apparel.

"Ah, this for the first son," she crooned. "Think of what the others will bring."

"Less," said Ana, her eyes upon her needlework. "It is the first that is most important."

"Oh, but a second to insure the line; this one, God save him, might not be as healthy as he seems."

"True," said Ana. "There is always the chance that he will die young."

Celia lay on her mound of pillows, eating purple grapes and pretending to be calm. It was early evening, just sunset, and she had several hours to wait before her plan could be implemented. "Tell me, Ana, what would have happened if the Marqués had never married? Who would have been his heir?"

Ana shrugged. "No one knows."

"But there are other sons; not legitimate, but *sons*."

"Yes. Some by high-born ladies, too, but none he wished to recognize. Perhaps he would have changed his mind someday."

"Where are they, these sons? No one has ever pointed one out to me. Were they banished at birth to remote parts of the country?"

"Not banished, no. They are with their mothers, or the older ones are in the army. One of Don Rafael's pages is His Grace's child."

"And your son, Ana? You mentioned him, but I have never seen him."

"My son?" Her fingers trembled, dropped the embroidery needle into the jumble of threads and scraps in her lap. She searched for it with unusual awkwardness. "My son is dead."

"Oh, Ana, I'm sorry." She checked an impulse to rush over and comfort the *dueña*.

"It was while you were ill. He was only twenty years old."

"In the army?"

"Yes, the army. How else does a man die these days?"

"And have you no one else? No husband or family?"
She found the needle and began to stitch again.

"No, no husband. I never cared for another man but His Grace. My family . . ." She smiled, a bit too brightly. "There is you, my lady, and the child, and the others you will bear. I must confess that before you arrived at Castillo Quintero, I thought my Diego might become His Grace's heir. He was the oldest left alive, the strongest, the handsomest. He was fair, too, almost as fair as you." She lowered her gaze to the needlework. "Well, perhaps not *quite* so fair . . ."

"Ana . . . you don't hate me because of *him* . . . ?"

She sighed. "The blame does not lie with *you*, my lady; what can a woman do when a man commands?"

"Yes," murmured Celia. "What *can* a woman do?"

"A woman can do a great many things," said Nicolasa, "if she is clever. If her child, for example, becomes Marqués. Do you not think that Doña María Antonia has everything she desires? When she speaks, this Palace obeys, even to the Marqués himself."

"To have the same privilege," said Celia, "I must wait twenty or thirty years."

"Doña María Antonia waited."

"She had nothing else to do."

"A soft way to spend the years," said Nicolasa.

"A tedious way to spend the years."

"Not with Señor Río at your side."

"Even so."

"*I* would not be bored."

"You are not I, Nico. I always wanted more from life than a lover."

"You have your child. Your future children."

"*More* than children."

"What else is there for a woman than a man and children?"

"There is more. Not here." She touched the ornately carved headboard of her bed with a fingernail, lightly at first, and then with greater pressure, drawing a long, thin scratch on its polished surface. "Not here, but somewhere, there is more."

Nicolasa made a noncommittal sound, as if she did not wish to be insolent by contradicting her mistress's statement but could not quite bring herself to agree.

Celia watched the oil lamp on the mantel, gauging time by the level of fuel in its glass base. It would burn dry before her moment came. She thought of Río, could almost see his face in the steady flame; since her confinement, he had slept downstairs, visiting her by day and in the early evening, and never without a chaperone. Downstairs—a world away. If all went well, she would never see him again, never kiss his lips, never feel his arms around her, never know his comfort and his passion. She choked back a sob and turned her face to the wall as tears overflowed her lids. Whatever he was, she loved him as she had never loved another human being. Almost, she wished her plan would fail. But only almost.

A single fresh candle was lit, to burn all night, as Celia preferred. Ana and Nicolasa began to prepare themselves for sleep.

Celia, who had feigned drowsiness, yawned. "Nico, before you go to bed, will you go down to the kitchen and bring me a cup of tea and a biscuit?"

Nicolasa, who had run similar errands almost every night for many weeks, nodded without comment, relaced her bodice, and departed.

Through the open connecting door, Celia could see Ana slipping into her own bed in the anteroom—since moving their beds out of the inner chamber the previous year, Ana and Nicolasa had never bothered to move them back in. This had given Celia a large measure of nighttime privacy, and she had used that privacy to the utmost.

She had torn a small hole in one of her bolsters and hidden three vials of Don Epifanio's sleeping potion deep in the stuffing. Now feathers flew as she probed for the flaskets; her fingers touched their smooth surfaces, drew them into the light. Made of pale green

glass, stoppered with aromatic corks. each held perhaps an ounce of a fluid that was cloyingly sweet, yet
with a bitter undertone of paregoric.

Celia swung her feet over the edge of the bed and
stood up. It was not the first time she had stood since
her confinement, though if Ana saw her, she would
think so; Celia had early realized that the *dueña*'s bed
was placed at such an angle that, reclining, the woman
could view nothing of the inner chamber but a tapes-
tried wall. Nor was Nicolasa's pallet in a less circum-
spect position. Celia had taken full advantage of this
situation in her nocturnal endeavors, always mindful
of the shadow cast by the candle and of the tiny noises
her feet made on the thick carpet. When her keepers
thought her fast asleep from the effects of the potion
and had themselves gone peacefully to sleep, she had
risen and gained strength.

This time was not like the first; then, she had tee-
tered and nearly fallen, nearly cried out for the supporting arm of her *dueña*. This time, though she felt
some strain in her calves, she crossed swiftly and surely
to the wardrobe and groped for the belt. Lifting up
her nightgown, she drew the length of leather about
her newly narrow waist, buckling it at the tightest
notch and letting it slide downward to rest securely on
her hips. Reasonably stout shoes, which she formerly
wore for walks on the parapet in fair weather, were
hidden behind the lighter buskins and embroidered
slippers meant for indoor use. She pulled out the former and slipped them on. Concealed beneath more
sumptuous wraps was the old, wine-colored cloak she
had worn when only the Marqués's concubine; during
one nocturnal span she had fashioned an inside pocket
in that cloak so that she could carry a few coins, Ana's
tinderbox, a candle, and other suchlike small items.
The pocket was empty now, and its contents-to-be scattered about the two chambers.

She draped the cloak around her shoulders and

stowed two of the green vials in its pocket; the third she tucked into the temporary repository of her puffy sleeve. At the mantelpiece, she took down the silver candlestick which was twin to the one still holding a lighted taper. As she had discovered some nights earlier, its base was solid, of reassuring weight; she gripped it by the narrow neck, clubwise. So armed, she worked her way to the side of the open doorway and peeked into the antechamber. A single candle burned there, too, awaiting Nicolasa's return. Ana appeared to have fallen asleep already, her mouth half open, one arm thrown over her eyes.

Celia approached the bed. Gingerly, she sat upon its edge and, at the same instant, clapped her free hand over the dueña's mouth.

Ana's arm slid aside, revealing bleary, blinking eyes. She made a muffled sound and plucked at her mistress's fingers.

"Silence," said Celia.

Ana's eyebrows lifted in puzzlement.

"If you make a single sound, I will kill you." She brandished the candlestick.

Ana's eyes tracked from the improvised club to Celia's face and back again.

"I have something for you to drink," said Celia, and as she lifted her hand from the dueña's lips, she let the vial slide into her palm. A flick of her thumbnail uncorked it. "Drink," she commanded.

Ana sniffed the bitter brew and wrinkled her nose. She opened her mouth to say something, and Celia dumped the potion in. Ana coughed and struggled to rise, but Celia held her down by one shoulder and calmly and purposefully raised the candlestick. "I do not *wish* to hurt you, Ana, but I will smash your skull if you disobey me."

The dueña lay still, breathing heavily and staring at the makeshift bludgeon.

Celia calculated silently, weighing the speed with

which the potion usually acted against the length of
time Nicolasa had been gone. At this hour, all the pots
and pans had long since been scoured and put away,
and the cook was asleep. The maid would have to fill
a kettle with fresh, cold water, add wood to the
kitchen embers to make a useful blaze, wait for the pot
to boil, prepare the infusion, find the biscuits. . . .

Ana slept, snoring lightly. Celia poked her several
times to make sure.

Free to prowl both chambers now, Celia swiftly ap-
propriated candle stubs, tinderbox, a cake of soap, scissors, a mirror, a comb, and the small change she and
Ana had won at cards. She retrieved also, from a corner
of Nicolasa's clothes chest, the three diminutive ceramic pots of oily makeup that the girl had treasured
from her performance in *El Conde Glamis*—rouge,
green eyeshadow, and black mascara. There had been
no other opportunity to wear them, for Doña María
Antonia considered a painted face garish and abomi-
nable in the sight of God, but Nicolasa had kept them,
showing them to Celia before she buried them among
her few belongings. Often and often, during her nocturnal exercise, Celia had dug for these containers,
merely to verify and reverify their existence, never daring to remove them to some more secure hiding place
for fear their absence might generate unfortunate in-
quiries. Now, with a sensation of mounting hope, she
wrapped them in a handkerchief and tucked them
among the other tidbits in her pocket. She then ensconced herself in the boudoir chair to await Nicolasa's return.

The outer door opened, and although Celia could
not see it from her vantage point, the rustle of skirts
and the light, quick footsteps identified the entrant as
Nicolasa. Pausing a moment at the *dueña*'s bedside,
the maid whispered, "Ana?" Answered only with
snores, she resumed her progress toward the inner
room.

"The cook was gone," she said, addressing her mistress's bed. The mounded pillows fooled her careless glance, and it was not until she had placed her tray on the small nighttable that she perceived the sheets covered no human form. Only then did she gaze beyond, to the chair. "My lady!" she gasped. "You are out of bed!"

"Yes," said Celia.

Nicolasa hurried to her mistress's side. "Do you feel faint? Do you wish to lie down again?"

"No and no," Celia replied. "Bring the refreshments here, Nico." She munched the hard anise-flavored biscuits quickly, scarcely tasting them, and downed the tea in a gulp. "I am feeling quite well this night, and quite restless. Truly, a short stroll would please me."

"A stroll?" echoed Nicolasa. "Wait, let me wake Ana, and we will help you—"

"No, that is not necessary. I feel strong, strong enough to walk alone. Let it be just the two of us, as in days past."

"My lady, if something should happen in your weak condition . . ."

"If I begin to feel weak, we will return. But I must regain my old strength; Doctor Velas has said so, has he not?"

Nicolasa nodded doubtfully.

"See, I have my cloak already; getting it has not tired me. I am stronger than you think." She rose, feigning the slight wobble she had completely lost a week before. Slowly, she walked toward the door. "Come along."

"My lady . . ."

"Come along," Celia said, letting a bit of exasperation creep into her voice.

Nicolasa caught up the small lantern from her tray and came along. The guard passed the two women wordlessly and did not betray any amazement to see the invalid Marquesa emerge from her chambers on her own two feet. Much later, when they went off duty, the news would begin its brushfire flight through the Castle. Later.

Celia ambled toward the stairway.

"Oh, no, Your Grace, not the stairs," said Nicolasa.

"Why not? What else is there to do up here but listen to Ana's snores?"

"If you should become dizzy—"

"If I should become dizzy, I am sure one of these strong guardsmen could be persuaded to carry me back to my room." Carefully, for she had not negotiated stairs for many weeks, she began the descent.

"I am afraid, my lady; cannot this stroll wait until the daylight hours, when Doctor Velas can—"

"Nonsense, Nico. Come along." She reached back, grasped the girl's wrist firmly, and pulled her along.

In the middle of the night and lit only by Nicolasa's tiny lantern and by wall sconces placed at wide intervals, the stairway seemed steeper and longer than ever before. Twice, Celia paused, not tired but uncertain as to how far away the ground floor remained. Nicolasa whispered anxiously, continuously trying to persuade her mistress to return to the upper stories, continuously offering to run for assistance, but Celia kept a tight grip on her arm and plunged onward. She seemed to be descending miles, into a nether region; she expected flames to begin licking at her ankles any second. Yet it was only cold stone steps after all, step after step, down, down, until, suddenly, the last one merged into the broad stone floor of the main Palace corridor.

Celia felt exhilarated, but she succeeded in preventing the emotion from reaching her face. She turned to Nicolasa, tried to look sheepish, and said, "I think we should go to the privy."

Nicolasa laughed nervously. "What a reason for getting out of bed!"

"Well, let's go." She did not relinquish her hold on the maid's arm.

The laundry-latrine room was empty and dark; the tubs on their platforms were shadowy, ogrelike shapes.

"I don't like this place," said Nicolasa.

"Too many unpleasant memories?"

The maid nodded.

"Well, there are a few unpleasant memories here for me, too, but I don't care. Give me the lantern, Nico."

Nicolasa obeyed.

Still clinging to Nicolasa's wrist, Celia set the light on the floor. Shielded by her cloak, she dipped into the pocket with her free hand and palmed the scissors and the second vial. When she rose, she loosed her grip on the maid's arm, circling her shoulders instead and drawing the girl very near. "My friend," she said, raising the scissors point toward Nicolasa's eyes, "do not cry out."

Nicolasa's mouth gaped in astonishment.

"Not a word." She moved a finger, and the vial peeked out from her fist. "Drink this."

Nicolasa stared, fascinated, at the scissors.

"Nico, if you do not drink this, I will have to kill you. There is no third choice."

Nicolasa's mouth formed a word: mercy.

"Drink, and all will be well."

Nicolasa grimaced at the taste, but she downed the bitter draft.

Celia pocketed the empty flasket, then dragged the girl over to the nearest bundle of laundry, which she ripped apart with the aid of the scissors. She chose the handiest piece of cloth—a petticoat—and, stepping on one end of it, tore off two irregular strips. These she used as a gag, stuffing one into Nicolasa's mouth and winding the other about her head, all one-handed, for she was afraid to let the girl go for an instant, lest she try to run. The gagging completed, Celia ripped another garment to shreds for wrist and ankle bonds.

When she was satisfied with the lashings, she hooked her hands under the maid's armpits, dragged her up the steps to the washing platform and levered her into an empty tub.

"I'll be nearby. If I hear a sound from you, even if it brings the guards as swift as lightning, I'll reach you first, and no one will ever hear a word from you again. I swear it, Nico, on Christ's blood."

The bottom of the washtub was in black shadow, but Celia thought she saw the sparkle of Nicolasa's wide eyes.

Celia ransacked the Palace laundry until she found a plain gray garment like any worn by the ordinary washerwomen. It was large in the waist, fitted for a woman of considerable girth; Celia slipped it on over her nightdress, and it effectively camouflaged her slimness. It had not yet been washed and stank of human sweat. Then to the crucial part of the disguise: Celia uncapped the three pots of color and began to mix. She had tried it only once before, by candlelight, with a tiny dab each of red and green on the inside of her wrist—so little that it could not possibly be missed if the owner of the tints decided to inspect her belongings. By laborious blending and smoothing, she had achieved a translucent brownish hue on an area not much larger than a silver dollar; this time she would have to cover both hands, her face, and her neck. Her mirror informed her that the process was a slow one. The pigment was suspended in a viscous medium that spread thinly only after a maximum of rubbing; soon her face was sore, but it was also swarthy. Next, she dipped two fingers into the mascara pot and proceeded to daub her eyebrows, lashes, and hair. The teeth of her comb blackened as she smoothed newly raven locks over her ears and fastened them with a fillet. The total effect was startling; it would take a good many washings to restore her Nordic paleness, and until then, she would look more a proper inhabitant of this world than ever before.

She wiped her dirty fingers on the ragged scraps of petticoat, resumed her wrap, picked up the lantern, and straightened stiffly. Her back, unused to all this descending of stairs and lifting of bodies, ached abominably. She kneaded it with her knuckles for a minute, then pulled up her hood. Certain by this time that Nicolasa slept as soundly as Ana upstairs, she directed her footsteps toward the main gate of the Palace.

But before she left the laundry room, she ripped the hated symbol of bondage from her finger. Her heart told her to throw it as hard and far as her arm could manage, but her head remembered that it was made of gold and precious gems; the brief battle between them ended with the ring joining the other items in her pocket.

She turned a corner into the familiar corridor, where the door to Terrazas's office was shut tight; at this hour even he, the tireless worker, was asleep. At the end of the hall, the single guard who barred passage to the front gate lounged against the wall, his halberd-rifle propped beside his right leg. When he saw Celia's lantern, he snapped to attention, raising his weapon to order-arms.

Celia twitched at the hood of her mantle. Even in deep summer, the night air would be chill, would give her an excuse for muffling herself. She did not recognize the guard's face, and that gave her hope that he would not penetrate her disguise; that and the fact that he would not be expecting the ailing Marquesa to be wandering the Palace corridors alone in the middle of the night.

"*Buenas noches,*" she said softly. "Her Grace desires me to go into the city on an errand."

"What, again?" said the guard. He relaxed his rigid

stance and reached for the iron ring set into the gate. "Why can she never wait for daylight?" he muttered, bracing himself to overcome the inertia of the massive panel. It swung slowly open, just wide enough for Celia to slip through, which she did with alacrity. The two exterior guards eyed her as she passed; she smiled at each of them and walked steadily and briskly away. To them she was just another maid sent out on a midnight errand by the whim of the Marquesa. They had grown used to such in recent weeks—a factor that Celia had counted in her favor.

The courtyard was deserted. Even the sweepers, having concluded their tasks for a few hours, had retired. She was alone with the full moon and the smooth paving stones. It would be some time before the morning crowd arrived to fill the court with bustle and noise. She thought of pausing for a moment to look back at the building that had been her prison for so many months. She thought of it, but she never broke her stride, never turned her head, and finally she came to the great outer gate, gave the same story to its guards, and was passed. The gate closed behind her, and she descended the easy slope into the city, welcoming the stench of garbage that greeted her, for it meant freedom.

She steered her course by the moonlit spires of the cathedral. No more the Marquesa. The Marquesa had done her duty and died in the service of her lord. The woman with the lantern was someone else, someone whose path, though long and lonely, was her own. Her fingers tightened on the scissors. *Let anyone try to stop me now,* she vowed fiercely, *and I will rip him apart.*

Far behind her, there was the sound of footsteps.

CHAPTER THIRTEEN

Adrenaline surged through her veins, not in response to fear, but to ferocious indignation—and underneath that, a long pent-up rage. A low criminal, she thought, daring to follow her, daring to think of violent pleasure and perhaps a few coins in the bargain. The scissors rested hard and familiar in her fist; she only wished it were a weapon at once more lethal and bloody, a weapon that could better sate her lust for vengeance.

Ducking into the nearest side street, she doused the lamp and merged with the shadows between two buildings. She could not hear him now—he stepped too softly or not at all, waiting perhaps for the echo of her own light step or the rustle of her skirts to cloak his movements. Celia strained her eyes but could perceive no skulking figure from the niche where she hid. Had he abandoned the chase, assuming that she entered a house on this street?

Far away, a watchman tolled the hour and the all's-well. A cat in heat yowled, was answered half a dozen times, and drew a scrambling, galloping band of toms across the roadway. Under cover of this noise, Celia moved on to a darkened, recessed doorway, then to another, then to a niche beneath an overhanging upper story. If her hunter still followed, he had quickly learned greater stealth; when the cat-sounds died away, the night was silent. Celia was tempted for a moment to double back and hunt *him*, but rationality prevailed over her stewing emotions.

Holding her skirts bunched in one hand, a maneuver that kept them reasonably quiet, Celia skipped from shadow to shadow, heading east toward the river, guided by the Big Dipper when the spires of the cathedral were obscured by near buildings. The smell of the river became ever stronger. Before first light, traffic appeared on the street—an oxcart, a wheelbarrow, a peasant with a bundle on his shoulder. She heard many footsteps as she neared the waterfront, but she could not tell if any of them were following her.

She dragged her feet now, near exhaustion. Her legs trembled; she continued toward the wharves only with a great effort of will. Thoughts of her pursuer no longer concerned her—if he were the Marqués's man, he would not have been so furtive and retiring; if he were a common cutpurse, he would hardly dare follow her into so populous an area.

She had spotted the inn back when she and Río first arrived in the city. It was a rough, ramshackle place set among the docks, built of whitewashed planks and variegated stones. A number of shingles were missing from its steeply gabled roof. On that day, it had been bustling and noisy with drunken sailors—one of them had cocked a red-rimmed eye at Celia and crept behind her for a pinch before Río could cuff him aside. No one would think to look for her in such a place.

Before dawn, the inn was quiet. Inside, a diminutive old man was sweeping the filthy floor with a broom of switches; in one corner, a drunk slept sprawling across a long wooden table; across the way, three men played cards by the fitful glow of a tallow lamp. The whole room was thick with the odor of sour ale and rancid fat.

Celia approached the sweeper. "Have you a room with a good door-lock that I can take for the day?"

He squinted up at her, his face a mass of sagging wrinkles. "A room?" he muttered. Then his gaze shifted over her shoulder, fastening on something behind her.

Before she could turn, a firm hand had closed over her arm just above the elbow. "What are you doing here?" said a too-familiar voice.

Río.

He pulled her around to face him, and her hood fell back, revealing her dark skin and hair. A look of incredulity crossed his face, and he was speechless for the moment.

Celia yanked her arm out of his grip and backed away.

He recovered himself then and lunged for her, but she skipped aside and hurried out the door. He followed at a run.

Spent as she was, Celia nevertheless found a reserve of energy to sustain her. A glow on the eastern horizon signaled dawn; she paralleled it and soon found herself in a small market area, where she had to dodge vendors busy with their baskets and barrows of merchandise.

"Rape! Rape!" she screamed. When heads turned in her direction, she pointed at Río, a scant ten feet behind her, and shouted again.

"Stop her!" Río yelled. "She is my wife!"

A low murmur arose, but no one made a move to attend to anything but his own affairs.

"He is not my husband!" Celia gasped. "Rape! Rape! Murder and rape!" She stumbled on rocks and sliding pebbles; the cool morning air burned her throat and lungs. She knew she could not outrun him. She swung around a wooden fruit stand, putting it between herself and Río. "Stay away from me!" she shrieked, plucking an apple from the vendor's bin and hurling it hard at Río's chest. He ducked late, and it bounced off his shoulder.

"Momentito!" said the vendor, who suddenly found himself the hub of a merry-go-round. "You owe me a bit of silver for that apple, *señorita!"*

"Keep him away from me! He's trying to kill me!"

"Grab her," said Río, dodging back and forth in his vain attempts to head her off. "She's my runaway wife!"

"Señor, your marital difficulties are not my problem; you owe me half a *cuartillo* for that apple."

Celia kept the cart between them and tossed another apple at her adversary.

"A whole *cuartillo!"*

"Stop her and you'll have that money and more!"

"If you try to stop me, I'll kill you!" shouted Celia, brandishing the gleaming scissors. She threw a third apple, then scooped up a large clod from the roadway and shot that at him, too. He stooped, and the missile smacked a horse behind him.

"Querida, stop this!"

"Leave me alone!"

"Let's sit down and discuss the matter like civilized human beings."

"We've discussed it before, and I am tired of discussion. Go away!"

"Querida, come back with me."

"Never."

"Where will you go?"

"Don't worry about me."

"Please . . . I love you."

"If you touch me, I'll kill you. I swear it!"

"You don't mean that."

"I swear it by Christ's holy blood."

The vendor interrupted. *"Señorita, señor,* please carry on your conversation somewhere else; you are destroying my trade."

Celia snatched a series of peaches and oranges from his stand and volleyed them wildly; one orange clipped Río on the side of the head, but the rest of the fruit whipped by harmlessly. "Leave me! Leave me! Damn you, go away!" Her voice cracked on the last word, and she clenched her teeth to hold back hysterical tears that threatened to ruin her disguise.

"Wait! Stop! Enough!"

Celia halted, panting.

"Please, let me speak to you. I promise not to force you to do anything."

"I don't believe you."

"I swear by Our Lady."

"I still don't believe you. For your own advantage, you'd foreswear on your mother's head."

"Soon the market will be filled with peddlers, shoppers, even His Grace's men-at-arms. Do you wish so many people to see us quarreling?"

For the first time, she noticed that a small crowd had gathered around them, and it was steadily growing. The thought of the Marqués's men appearing on the scene almost panicked her, but then she realized that Río had intended exactly that. Yet it was true that by daylight, some of the Marqués's men might penetrate her disguise.

"*Chiquita,*" Río said, sensing her indecision, "come aside and talk with me. What danger can there be in talking?" When she still hesitated, he added, "You are armed, remember."

She glanced down at the scissors clenched in her left hand. "Yes, I am armed. I was disarmed once." She lifted her eyes defiantly. "But never again."

"Never again," he agreed. "Come."

She pulled up her hood and edged around the fruit stand, still leaving an ample ten feet between them. "Where do you want to talk?"

"Down by the river. We can sit on one of the deserted wharves."

"Then, in order to escape you, I would have to swim."

"You won't have any need for escape."

"I *will* do my best to kill you. There won't be any hesitation this time."

"I believe you."

"You never believed me before."

"Nevertheless . . . I believe you."

She sighed. "Walk ahead."

"*Señor, señora*, my fruit!" said the vendor.

Río asked, "How much do we owe you?"

"A full *real, señor*."

"Here." Río flipped him a coin and turned without waiting to see if he caught it.

A deserted jetty was close at hand. He walked halfway to the end and waited for Celia to catch up.

She stopped at a mooring post, well out of his reach, and leaned heavily against its weathered surface. She held the scissors ready, in her right hand. "How did you know I was leaving?"

"I sleep lightly, and in the right place—at the foot of the stairs. I recognized your walk."

"Why didn't you stop me sooner?"

"I wanted to see what you were doing. Your disguise is very effective; until I saw your face, I could not understand why the guards let you pass."

"And now?"

"Come back to the Palace."

"Never."

"Where will you go? Where *can* you go?"

"I will search."

"But you've said so often that only Larry Meyers—"

"I will search if it takes the rest of my life. I will *not* stay here."

"Celia—"

"No! Nothing will persuade me to return to that life. *Nothing*."

"Any woman in the Castle would gladly trade places with you. Any woman in the *world* who is below your station!"

"Any woman in *this* world, perhaps."

"Celia, the Marqués intends to conquer the Conde, destroy him as a rival and annex his lands . . . and the Indian lands beyond. By the time your son is old enough to rule, he'll have a *real* kingdom."

"The future expanse of San Felipe does not impress me."

"But the power, the riches of a greater country."

"What do I care for power and riches? Will they save me from the fever? No, Río, you cannot convince me to stay."

"Please, Celia, stay for me. Because I love you."

"No. Not even because *I* love *you.* Love is not enough."

"What *is* enough?"

"I'm not sure. Managing my own life, pursuing my own future. Being *something,* not just a mother or a wife, even if I'm called a Marquesa. And living without fear of the fever—the doctors of my world can cure it quite easily, along with much other illness that is deadly here."

"Then send for one of them."

"You speak as though you heard only my talk of the fever," she exclaimed angrily. "Are you so rudely inattentive to your Marquesa?"

"I heard, but I do not understand how a woman can be greater than a queen."

"I don't want to be a queen! There are other things, Río—things you can't imagine—that I would rather be!"

He gazed at her doubtfully. "Is His Grace so very repulsive?"

"I don't love him. In fact, I hate him, but that has little to do with my decision. I don't want to be a prisoner for the rest of my life, not even for you. I want to go to my own country, and I *will* go there. I've talked to you now, and there is your answer. Good-bye, Río.

I . . . I will miss you; truly I will." She swallowed painfully, a hard lump knotting her throat. "Goodbye." She trudged toward the road.

"No, wait!" cried Río.

She shook her head, blinking back tears. She held the scissors ready, but he made no attempt to approach.

"Wait, you must be tired. You've walked all night."

"I'll keep walking if I must."

"Celia . . ."

"Stay away."

"Celia . . . let me go with you."

She squinted at him. Her eyes were dry and itchy from lack of sleep. "You'll try to take me back."

"No. No one else knows yet that you are gone." He glanced at the sun, which was now well clear of the horizon. "But they will soon. We must get off the street."

"I'm disguised."

"I am not."

Celia closed her aching eyes for a moment. "No. You're not."

"Come. I know an inn." He walked toward her with his arms half-raised.

She moved a single step back, swaying. "No."

"Trust me."

"I trust no one."

"Trust me. Please." Slowly, he came closer.

With a wavering hand, she kept the point of the scissors in line with his throat. When he continued to advance with smooth, unhurried movements, she thought to run, but her legs were like gelatin—before her mental command could be translated to action, his outstretched hands held her shoulders, steadying her.

"If you try to take me back, I'll poke out your eyes; they can't beat me for it—I'm the Marquesa."

"I hope to keep my sight for a long while yet," he replied.

She dropped her arm and sagged against him, her head falling to his shoulder. For a full minute, he waited motionless, then lifted her limp form in his arms; she was fast asleep.

CHAPTER FOURTEEN

The ache of a swollen bladder woke her. Hazily, she perceived that something was missing, something important: she no longer felt the comforting weight of the scissors in her hand. Sitting up, she found herself alone on a wide bed in a dark and unfamiliar room. Her outer dress and cloak had been removed and laid over a stool, leaving her clad only in a cotton nightgown. The belt, however, still embraced her reassuringly.

A thin line of daylight peeked through the bottom of the closely shuttered window. By this meager illumination she searched for the chamber pot, finding it at last in a low cabinet opposite the bed. Atop the same cabinet sat a ewer of water, a bowl, and a towel; she poured some water to rinse her face, then suddenly remembered her makeup and refrained.

Barefoot, Celia crossed to the window and cautiously unlatched the shutter. In the distance she could see the towers of the Castle and, behind them, the setting sun—a scene of unquestioned romantic splendor, yet it left her cold. She scanned the deserted street below and, leaning out the window, scrutinized the fifteen-foot wall separating her from the ground. An ornamental grillework shielding the first-floor window appeared to offer the only possible foothold.

She bolted the door, then checked the pocket of her cloak; all her small possessions were still there, including the scissors. In silent haste, she dressed.

A rope of torn sheets would have been a great aid, but Celia decided she could not afford the necessary delay. Gripping the woodwork with tense fingers, she swung her legs over the sill and gradually lowered herself full length from the window. Her left foot grazed the top of the grille and soon found a toehold amid the wrought-iron flourishes; the metal vibrated ominously under her weight but held.

Celia rested, breathing heavily.

There was no other purchase on the blank wall—no outcropping of brick, no chinks, nothing but gritty, featureless stucco. Hard-packed earth lay eight feet below, and no way to reach it except by dropping off.

She leaped away from the wall and fell—and fell, and fell. . . . She tried to relax and roll with the impact, but the ground smashed upward crushingly, knocking her breath out and jarring her senses. She struggled to her hands and knees, weeping and biting her lips with the fierce pain that shot through her chest; her lungs felt empty and, for some moments, as if they would never fill again. At last, she drew a ragged breath and, moaning a little, crawled to the wall and shakily hauled herself upright. Her forearms were badly skinned, and her side was numb, but she seemed to have no major injuries. She rested for a time, then straightened resolutely and headed north into the twilight.

Río fell into step beside her before she reached the main thoroughfare.

"You didn't have to leave the hard way," he said. "The door was unlocked."

Furiously, she threw a punch at his belly, but he caught her fist before it connected.

"Let's not begin our trip on bad terms, *chiquita*."

She squinted at him in the waning light. He was dressed for travel, not for the social life of the Palace; an undistinguished cloak half-obscured the *miquelet* and dagger slung on his hip. His dusty old boots appeared to have gone unpolished for months.

"How did you know I would use the window?"

"A foolish question."

She took a deep, calming breath. "What happens now?"

"Your face is streaky; perhaps you should repair it."

"You mean, you were serious about going north with me? Or is it that you want your master to see my clever disguise?"

"My *patrón* . . . my *former patrón* . . . thinks his yellow-haired Marquesa may be hiding somewhere in the Palace, since no one saw her leave the building and she is much too weak to go farther anyway."

"Does he not think it extraordinary that his faithful Río left the Castle the same night as the Marquesa?"

"Since the Marquesa's confinement, Río has been busy with a number of pretty young girls of careless virtue, both in and out of the Castle. That night was no different from many others."

Celia stiffened. "Is that true? Have you really been . . . fooling around with other women?"

"His Grace thinks so. Here, let us stand in this shadow while you apply more color to your face. *Dios!* What a mess Mendoza's sheets must be!"

She juggled pots of makeup and, while Río shielded her from the view of passersby, blended the pigments once more. "When do you think he'll realize I'm not in the Palace?"

"He believes you are mad, you know; there has been ample evidence of that these past months. Madness explains why you have no desire to be Marquesa; His Grace has never met a sane woman who *didn't* want to be Marquesa." Río's eyes flicked back and forth, studying each person who passed along the narrow street. "One never knows what a lunatic will do; she might creep from place to place, always one step ahead of her pursuers, and so be lost for days, till hunger or thirst made her careless. Or so I suggested to His Grace."

"You've been back to the Castle, then. While I slept."

"Of course. How else could I find out what sort of search is going on?"

"Did they question you?"

"Yes, but Ana and Nicolasa both swore that I had not seen you the whole day, which was true enough. I said I had been at the Inn of Three Horses, with a friend."

"And he believed you?"

"His Grace trusts me. I have done his bidding well; he has no cause to think I would betray him."

Celia smoothed her cheeks one last time, then gazed at him speculatively, her head cocked to one side. "And would you betray him?"

He gripped her shoulder through many thicknesses of cloth, and he bent to brush her lips with his own. "Yes."

"And in this particular case," she persisted, "are you betraying him, or are you merely pretending to betray him?"

He breathed an exasperated sigh. "Our transportation is around the corner. Let's go."

A large brown horse and a smaller dappled one were hitched at the rail behind the inn. The brown—the same that Celia had seen Río ride before—lifted its head in recognition as the *trovador* approached, and it shifted restlessly and snorted when he passed it up to caress and cajole its smaller companion.

"Can you ride?" Río asked Celia.

She grimaced. "I rode a pony once, when I was ten."

"Well, Mariposa is a gentle beast; you'll have no trouble with her. Pull back on the reins when you want to stop, loose them—and perhaps give her a little kick—when you want to go; tug gently to the right or left to turn one way or the other. Mostly, she'll follow my Trigueño. Now, into the saddle; we must clear the city by dawn and cross the river with the farmers bound for their fields." He reached for Celia's elbow, to give her a boost, but she eluded him, ducking under the rail to put a barrier between their bodies.

"Río, go back. They will know you're helping me."

He shrugged. "Eventually, yes, they'll know. But not too soon, I hope. I spent the day at the Palace, lounging and acting quite normal. His Grace wanted me to help in the search; I suggested a number of likely hiding places, but pleaded boredom and begged his leave to visit someone in town. I told him he could reach me at the Inn of Three Horses—an establishment a considerable distance from our present location.

"When I left, I was wearing my fine Palace clothing, not the kind a man would wear who planned a long journey. No one followed me. I had money, of course, and purchased our traveling gear and Mariposa at a small shop I know far from the main markets. I hope I have purchased a full day's start as well."

"You truly think you've fooled him?"

He made some tiny adjustment of the dappled horse's bridle. "I left my lute at the Palace. His Grace believes I love my lute more than any woman." He sighed. "I left *both* lutes at the Palace. Yes, I think that will give us the time we need. Will you come now, Celia?"

The stirrups were low enough that she required only a slight assist.

"If you're hungry, you will find bread and cheese and jerky in the saddlebags." Río mounted with graceful ease and twitched the reins; his horse turned obediently toward an alley that seemed a mere crevice between two buildings.

Mariposa lurched forward, swaying from side to side as she walked, making Celia cling with terrified fingers to the saddle horn and wonder if the saddle itself would not soon fall off and her with it. Yet there was a soothing regularity to that rolling gait; soon Celia found herself adapting to the monotony of it, and her convulsive grip on the pommel relaxed. It began to feel natural to be riding a horse, much more pleasant than walking, and she marveled that, in her previous life, she had never taken it up as a hobby.

Río's route twisted and turned through the narrowest of streets, where overhanging roofs provided utter darkness and Celia's feet scraped the walls of flanking buildings. She had lost all sense of direction by the time the houses of San Felipe began to thin and fall away.

A small party of farmers, who talked to each other in subdued voices, waited at the bank of the river while the ferry was readied for crossing. With them were draft animals—horses, donkeys, a couple of oxen—hitched to carts bristling with rakes and hoes. Men and animals alike wore wide-brimmed sombreros against the heat of the day, which had just begun to dispel the mists of dawn.

Río and Celia dismounted.

"If their fields are on the other side of the river," Celia whispered, "why don't they live *there* instead of living on this side and crossing every day?"

"Formerly, they *did* live there, but the Conde burned their homes, and now they are afraid to rebuild in the same place, in case he returns. They feel safer on this side."

Celia strained her eyes for a glimpse of ruins, but the river was so wide and misty yet that she could barely see the opposite bank.

The ferry—a flat wooden raft with waist-high fencing of half-rotten, horizontal rails—accepted all passengers for a small toll. Four polers pushed off from the shore and steered the craft on a diagonal course across the river, whose current was too swift to allow a more perpendicular route. Water-borne traffic was still light at that early hour; few of the boats which had tied up for the night at San Felipe had begun to move out of the harbor on their southward journeys. A lone patrol vessel, its sail bearing the Marqués's crest, bobbed at anchor in midstream.

The crossing was accomplished without mishap; Río and Celia did not hesitate at the wharf while the farmers dispersed but immediately entered on the rough road that paralleled the river. On the opposite side of the road was a scorched cornfield. Though most of the ruined stalks had been plowed under, a fringe of charred stubble still bordered the new furrows—pathetic shreds of blackened straw with powdered ash clinging here and there.

"Wait!" cried Celia, staring at the sun. "We're going *south*. Why?"

"South to México," said Río.

She reined in her horse. "*No!* I don't want to go to México. North to my homeland!"

"Your homeland is lost. You told me that a dozen times."

"I will find it."

"Celia, we cannot go north. The Conde is still powerful in the North."

"The Marqués defeated him, I thought."

"In San Felipe, but not in the northern territories. The war is not over."

"But lately I've heard of no great battles, seen no boatloads of dead—"

"Not yet. But I know, His Grace knows, that the Conde is far from finished. He's in the North, waiting, planning. . . . His Grace's spies think perhaps the real siege has not yet come. So we can't go north, you see. The South will be safe; His Grace will never search for you there, not with a war to keep him busy. We can lose ourselves in the vast cities . . . maybe Nueva Cádiz, or even La Ciudad de México itself."

Celia's lips narrowed to a firm, thin line. "There is

no need for you to come with me. Go back to your master. The former Marquesa will take care of herself." She swung her horse around, nudged it with one heel, and was rewarded with a leisurely trot in the appropriate direction.

Río matched her pace, caught Mariposa's bridle with one hand, and brought the horse up short, nearly tumbling Celia from the saddle in the process. *"Idiota!* Would you ride into the middle of a war? How will you take care of yourself when the Conde's men tear off your clothes and cast dice to see who will be the first to mount? Nor are the Marqués's men more polite. You think what you have seen in the Castle is everything? You think every man in the army stands at silent attention his whole day, bowing respectfully when a woman passes? *Santa María,* you *are* mad!"

Before he could catch her, Celia slipped her feet out of the stirrups and slid out of the saddle. "I am going north," she said, backing off warily. "You may go wherever you like."

"I cannot allow it." He urged his horse forward and bent nearly double reaching for her.

Celia drew the scissors from the pocket of her cloak; it shimmered in the early-morning sunlight. "The decision is not yours. I am not the same woman you brought to San Felipe, Río. You cannot stop me from going north."

He stared at the scissors for a long moment, then straightened slowly to lean back in the saddle and rest his hands on the pommel. "The danger, Celia—"

"I don't care about the danger. I can kill a stranger as easily as a friend."

"And lose your own life in the bargain."

"I think if you came with me, I would have a better chance, but I cannot force you. I wouldn't want to force you. How often must I say good-bye, Río?"

"No more," he said. "I have no desire to say good-bye at all."

She gazed up at him pleadingly. "Come to my country with me, Río. We'll be safe there, from the Marqués, the Conde, even the Indians. Come with me."

"The Marqués's arm is long, his fury intense, and the North lacking in crowds to hide us. When the war is over, he'll search for us; he knows you're from the North."

"By the time the war is over, we'll be safe. He'll never find us, believe me. No more than he found the source of the guns."

"You are so certain, now, that you can find your way."

"Yes, I am certain." She knew the machine in Larry's back room was switched on, as he had left it many months ago, before his death. If no one had broken into his home and meddled with the apparatus, the enabling field would be waiting, and the belt would lead her to it. She intended to quarter the forest around Verdura until telltale resonance in the belt signaled the proximity of the target area. But she feared revealing any of this to Río, who might attempt to exorcise her demon by depriving her of the belt—or even by destroying it. She thought better of him, but she could not risk such a consequence, no matter how small the likelihood. "Quite certain," she said, gazing straight into his eyes.

He stared down at her, his face unreadable. "*Are* you mad?" he said at last.

"What answer will satisfy you?"

He shrugged. "North, then. Perhaps His Grace won't think us fools enough to go there."

She remounted the docile Mariposa, and they rode north, with the rising sun to their right and the scent of the river in their nostrils. The miles fell away, and when they stopped to sup from the well-stocked saddlebags, the pall of dark smoke from thousands of chimneys in San Felipe was a mere smudge on the sunset sky. They camped well away from the river, where a screen of trees would hide their fire from any nocturnal boatmen.

"How long do you think it will take to reach Verdura?" Celia asked, gnawing at a hunk of cheese the size of her fist.

"Perhaps not so long as it took us to reach San Felipe last year. What do you propose to do when we arrive?"

She gazed up at the darkening sky and pulled her cloak more closely about her shoulders—a cool night wind was rising. "It would help to know exactly where the slave-traders captured me."

Río chewed meditatively on a blade of coarse grass. "Perhaps Tomás or José could be persuaded to show us, if they are still in town."

"They might be gone?"

"Life changes quickly on the frontier."

"Well, it is not absolutely necessary. Just easier."

"And if we do not find them?"

"You'll see."

"I hope you have a plan, *chiquita*. I hope all this is not merely a delusion."

"Remember, then, that madwomen are unpredictable."

"So I told the Marqués. I said, 'Ask Don Epifanio if you doubt it.' "

"Ha. The expert. The expert who almost lost his prime patient."

"Really, he did very little. The midwives delivered the child."

"I know. I knew when I first smelled his perfume that he would never dirty his hands with birth blood. But he was in charge. I'm surprised that anyone in the Palace is still alive, with such an expert as a doctor."

"He is a doctor like any other doctor; he knows how to saw off a leg." Río spat out his grass blade and busied himself with the bedrolls. He spread a single pallet large enough for two.

"Río . . ."

He looked up.

"I can't sleep with you," Celia said very softly. "Give me one of the blankets, and I'll sleep over here by the tree."

"I want you, *querida.*"

"I might get pregnant."

"True. There is always that possibility."

"I do not wish to become pregnant again. Not here; not now. Perhaps never."

"Well, you had a hard pregnancy and a hard birthing; it will take time to forget."

She turned her face away from him. "I will never forget," she whispered.

He laughed. "All women forget. My own mother forgot nine times."

Celia clenched her teeth. "I pity your mother."

He rose and circled the fire to stand in front of her, his wavering shadow engulfing her. He touched her shoulder, then gently tugged her arm, but she sat immobile and cold as a glacier. *"Querida,"* he said, "don't make me sleep alone tonight."

She shook her head. "In my own land, I wouldn't worry. Remember, I told you my people have ways of preventing conception. But here the chance is too great."

He knelt and pulled her rigid body into his arms, enveloped her firmly set mouth with his lips. Celia yielded for a moment, returning his embrace with unrestrained ardor, but when he tilted her back in the grass, she wrenched herself free of his warmth.

"I promise you," she said, panting and trembling, her throat tight, "when we reach my homeland, I will lie with you. I promise."

"And if we never reach your homeland?"

"Don't say that!"

He sighed. "I know you desire me now, *querida.* Why torture yourself with this foolish self-restraint?"

"Because my fear is stronger than my desire."

Río looked into the fire. "There are those methods condemned by the Church . . ."

Celia went over and snatched a blanket from the couch he had been preparing. "There are dangers in them, too, and the greatest danger is that I will forget my fear for a moment and be a thousand times more frightened thereafter. No. I sleep alone until we achieve our goal."

"There's no need to sleep alone. Only lie beside me; I won't rape you."

"Don't tempt me, Río; I'd hate you for it afterward. We have more than one blanket this time—I won't be cold."

He took the remaining cover for himself and rolled up in it close to the fire. "Very well, we will play this game for a while. Go to sleep now and we'll get an early start in the morning."

Celia curled up in her blanket and closed her eyes, but sleep would not come, though she was tired and comfortably warm. She opened her eyes and gazed across the dancing flames at her companion. "Río," she whispered.

"Yes?"

"I love you. Truly, I do."

"Go to sleep, *querida*."

She wondered how long he would continue to humor her "lunacy."

The next day was very much a repetition of the first. They saw more evidence of the enemy's passage through the land—a burnt-out farmhouse this time. Twice they passed toiling farmers who watched them with suspicion, apparently afraid any strangers might be the vanguard of a fresh sortie. Some fields were totally abandoned, their tillers dead or too fearful to return; weeds had claimed the furrows, choking and dwarfing the grain.

Río Pato branched off from the Lodísimo, meandering northeasterly. Río and Celia followed its eastern shore, using the path that had been beaten by generations of northbound travelers, occasionally dipping into the forest to avoid being sighted from the many towns that hugged the far shore or from the few boats heading south. The east bank, far less populous than the west even at San Felipe, quickly lapsed into wilderness, and the road faded to no more than a rutted cart track, then a game trail; sometimes it disappeared entirely, and the horses had to pick their careful way through the brambles and nettles and thorny wild roses that covered the ground.

As the vestiges of civilization fell farther and farther behind, chipmunks, rabbits, squirrels, and deer became commonplace. Some evenings, Río would kill a small animal with a toss of his knife, to supplement the ample but monotonous store of bread, cheese, and jerky in their bags. Celia found herself enjoying the process of cleaning and cooking game; she felt as if she were living her life backwards, as if this were a reversal of the southward trek of the previous year. She could almost see home, a finite distance in the future.

As if consciously participating in this reversal of events, Río announced on the sixth day that on the morrow they would ford the river at Cebolla Dulce and stop at the Posada del Descanso. Sandoval, he thought, would have news of conditions in the North.

The river flowed to their left, ten or twelve feet lower than the brush-covered, near-invisible track they followed. Late-afternoon sunlight touched the water with red gold. A sultry breeze stirred small waves and ruffled the treetops and Celia's hair. Río scanned the outskirts of the forest for a likely campsite.

Down the river, with big square sails unfurled to catch every whisper of wind and oars slapping water in smooth rhythm, came a fleet of galleasses.

Río wheeled his horse about, crowding Celia's mount toward the gloomy shelter of the forest, but not before she glimpsed two lines of cavalry flanking the river.

And not before they had glimpsed her.

"The Conde's men," said Río. "Stay close to me!" He bent low in the saddle to avoid overhanging branches and headed southeast, diagonally away from the river and the oncoming troops.

The failing light, the omnipresent brambles, the gnarled, jutting roots of countless trees—all conspired to slow their flight. Celia thought she could hear hoofbeats following them, but when she dared to glance back, she saw nothing but timber. Still, Río kept their pace as fast as possible—faster, indeed, for Celia's horse stumbled twice, and only by clutching its neck was she able to keep her seat.

Río gazed back over their trail, saw no visible pursuers, and ducked into the shadow of an enormous oak. With saddlebags draped across his shoulders, he stood up on the horse and stretched for the lowest bough, a limb as big around as a powder keg. He hoisted himself onto the limb, locked his knees about it, then reached down for Celia with his strong right arm.

She glanced up uncertainly. Río's hand dangled at least three feet above her head.

"*Now, chiquita,*" he whispered.

Clutching the pommel with one hand and the cantle with the other, Celia worked one knee into the saddle. Mariposa moved uneasily beneath her as the reins fell loose, but Celia fought the urge to cling tight to the saddle; she lunged upward, grabbing wildly for his extended arm. He caught her left elbow, and she dug both hands into his shoulder as he jerked her up and over the sturdy bough.

They were both in the tree now, heads together, feet pointing opposite ways. Río rummaged in the saddlebag, finding a couple of lead minié balls; he threw them, singly, at each horse's rump. Trigueño started at the sudden blow, snorted, and bolted away to disappear in the gloomy forest; Mariposa whinnied forlornly and followed him out of sight.

Río edged back toward the bole of the oak, motioning for Celia to follow; shortly they were settled deep among the leaves, her cloak wrapped about both of them. He laid his hand against her lips when human voices—cursing human voices—passed very near, and her trembling arms tightened around him. From their leafy hideaway they were unable to see the owners of the voices, which faded slowly into the distance. By then, nightfall was full upon them, and the crickets and katydids had long since begun their nocturnal chorus. Río and Celia remained in the tree, dozing fitfully, till the sun was well risen. Then they climbed stiffly down from their perch and returned cautiously to the river, where the well-beaten brambles attested to the passing of the army. On the river and in the woods there was no other vestige of man or horse.

"Well, without mounts, our journey will become a bit longer than I had hoped," said Río.

"They were on their way to San Felipe, weren't they?"

He nodded. "Where else? An army of that size . . . thousands of men. The Conde thinks His Grace doesn't expect an attack from the northeast." He looked up into the sky. "Do you smell smoke?"

Celia nodded. "All night."

"So did I. I thought it was their campfires—they must have camped soon after we saw them—but now I'm not sure. It smells . . . larger."

Celia gripped his arm. "A forest fire? One of their campfires may have—"

"I do not think so. I think . . . I have an idea we'll find out soon enough."

Where the army had trampled brambles and bushes to a flat green mat, walking was not difficult, and the miles slipped by rapidly. The scent of smoke became

ever stronger, and it was not long before Río and Celia were able to discern a gray cloud rising above the
forest on the western bank of Río Pato. When forest
gave way to cultivated fields, they discovered the
source of the smoke.

"They burned Cebolla Dulce," said Río.

No flames were visible from this distance, but the
ruins smoked like a small volcano; the light breeze
barely disturbed the columns of airborne soot and ash.

A band of ragged people stood at the east rim of the
river—shirtless men, shoeless women, naked children
clinging to their mothers' shifts—and gazed across the
water in melancholy fascination. They hardly spoke,
and some wept, not least of those a few of the men.
Río's and Celia's approach startled them, and their
first reaction was to back away, to scatter and flee toward the forest. But an old man with a lined, smoke-
blackened face limped forward, his arms outstretched
to the newcomers. It was Sandoval.

"Ah, Río," he said, and his lips half-curved into a
heavy-hearted smile. "Where have you come from? Did
you see the soldiers?"

Río embraced his friend. "I saw, and I spent the
night in a tree to avoid being shot. How did you escape the burning of your town, *abuelito?*"

Sandoval shrugged. "I am a useless old man, and the
soldiers were more interested in other things. . . .
Come, let us sit in the shade, my friend. Cebolla Dulce
is destroyed and will not rebuild itself no matter how
long we stand by the river and yearn." This last comment was aimed at his fellow survivors, but none of
them heeded. He and Río and Celia found a comfortable spot beneath a hickory tree.

"Poor Cebolla Dulce was quickly overrun," the old
man said. "Who would have thought that Pradera
would strike so far east?"

Río surveyed the battered refugees again. "I don't
see Anibal," he said softly.

"Ah, Anibal." Sandoval's wrinkled hand went to his forehead and, trembling slightly, wiped away a drop of sweat. "No, you will not see Anibal again. His Grace's soldiers came some months ago and spoke of the glory and loot and women to be won in the service of His Grace; he went with them, and not long afterward, they sent his body back to me. I have seen my grandson die and my town die, yet here I am, unafraid of death, and I live. How strange is fate!"

"Indeed," murmured Río. "What will you do now?"

Sandoval shrugged. "My neighbors and I—tomorrow we will all think more clearly. Perhaps we will begin to rebuild Cebolla Dulce. And yourself, Río? You chose a bad time for traveling. Where are you bound?"

"North."

"North? On His Grace's business again?"

"No." He glanced sidewise at Celia. "On my own."

Sandoval turned curiously to Celia, squinting, but if his aged eyes penetrated her disguise and recognized her as the blonde woman Río had brought south the previous year, he showed no sign of it. He waited a moment, as if for some elaboration, then said, "I wish I had a clean bed to offer you, my friend."

"I wish I had a bed to offer *you, abuelito*. Will money be of any assistance . . . ?"

Sandoval shook his head. "Keep your money, Río; you may need it. Silver won't rebuild Cebolla Dulce. But we have strong hands here—perhaps more than these few if, as I hope, others escaped into the forest. Every extra back, however, would be useful . . ." He looked hopefully at Río.

"No, I cannot stay. I've given my word."

The old man shrugged. "Well, I have no hold on you. But will you not share our dinner? Two of them went after a deer some hours ago—"

"I think not. You have enough mouths to feed already. We'll continue on our way." He rose, dusting

dry grass from his pants and shouldering the saddlebags, which had slipped to the ground beside him.

"You travel light," said Sandoval.

Río grimaced. "Formerly, we had horses, but now
we'll be walking."

"A long walk?"

Río shrugged. "In the hot sun, any walk is a long
walk."

"Take care of yourself. Río."

"Of course."

Sandoval got up creakily, embraced Río and kissed
his cheeks. "I feel I won't see you again, my friend."

Río smiled gently. "You say that every time we
part."

"No, this time I feel it is true."

Río looked at the ground and then, for a brief instant, at Celia, who gazed back silently. "Well . . .
perhaps this time you are right." He clasped the old
man's right hand in both of his. "Be with God, *abuelito*."

"Go with God, *amigo*."

Río grasped Celia's forearm just above the wrist
and fairly dragged her away. Not once did he look
back.

Celia looked back, and she saw Sandoval standing in
the shadow of the hickory tree, shading his eyes to
watch the two travelers go their way.

When they were out of sight and out of earshot, Celia said, "I release you from any promise you've made
me, Río. If you want to stay and help these people—"

"Quiet, *chiquita*. I know my own mind."

"He loves you, Río."

"He is a great-hearted man and loves many people,
but I have no desire to stay in Cebolla Dulce." He
smiled at her and laid his arm across her shoulders.
"You would not stay there with me, true?"

"True."

"Then let us say no more about it. This is war, and

many towns have been burnt and will be burnt in the future. You and I must care for our own lives."

North. Walking stretched and limbered the muscles that horseback riding had made sore, but it left a particular ache of its own in calves and thighs. They camped early that day, in deference to Celia's exhaustion. They made a cold meal from their provisions and, blanketless, they curled up together with Celia's cloak as a ground cloth. Río kissed the nape of her neck and fell asleep with one arm coiled around her waist; Celia lay stiff and unyielding for a long time, her mind and body in a turmoil from his nearness, from the warmth of his flesh, from her own conflicting desires. Finally she slept, dreaming that their naked bodies were locked together; but she woke in sweaty anticipation of his climax.

North, and the burning days, hotter by far on foot than on horseback, stretched on endlessly. The path of the invading army disappeared, presumably where they had forded the Pato. The forest thinned, yielding at last to prairie and then to a marsh that smelled strongly of skunk and onions. Río knew a route that skirted the worst bogs, yet it was not precisely dry land; the load of muck that their shoes picked up made every step a herculean effort, and periodic scraping afforded small relief.

"I don't remember any place like this," Celia said, lifting her skirts, which had accumulated a border of yellow-brown sludge.

"We were on the west side of the river then. If the Conde left a garrison anywhere in the North, this is the least likely place for it."

"Indeed. For anyone," Celia muttered. She could not imagine why Chicago had been built on such an unpleasant site.

Late that day, they entered Verdura from the south. The town seemed unchanged. The deeply rutted streets were still narrow and crooked, the clapboard cabins as weatherbeaten as ever, the auction block yet centered in the dusty square. A few plainly dressed people went about their business: all men—not a woman in sight.

"I think we might find a room behind the tavern," said Río, and he turned their path toward the ramshackle structure whose only identifying mark was a gray wooden sign swinging from a chain over the front door: the sign bore the crude but recognizable outline of a jug burnt into its surface.

The establishment's proprietor was surprised to see travelers and made much of Río and Celia, turning down the bed for them, helping them with their gear, and lighting a candle in the small, dark room he rented for an exorbitant price.

"Now, you must know, *chiquita*, that I have no real friends in Verdura," Río said. "No one to ask for help in case of trouble, no one to leave you with for safekeeping. And the last time I was here, I came with His Grace's troops, who are not loved in these parts, though they are hated slightly less than the Conde's, I think. Therefore, while I look for Tomás and José, you will stay here, with the door locked, and if anyone tries to enter, you are free to use the scissors upon him."

"Why can't I go with you?"

"Well, first, I'm sure you are tired, and second, someone has to stay here and watch our baggage. I have little desire to walk about Verdura all evening with saddlebags over my shoulder."

"Very well. Be careful."

"Of course."

While he was gone, Celia paced the room, in spite of her sore legs and feet. She tugged at the shutter of the one tiny window, but it was nailed shut. She brushed dried mud from her dress and shoes, then dug in the saddlebags for food, finding only a few scraps of jerky. She had almost acquired a taste for jerky in these last few days, and she munched some now, washing it down with the last drops from Río's canteen. She paced again, periodically throwing herself down on the bed in an attempt to get some sleep, but tired as she was, her mind was wide awake and whirling with excitement.

The candle guttered, and just before it went out, Celia lit the other that the landlord had left for their convenience. This second was half burnt when Río returned.

"I found Tomás working at the smithy and gave him a *cuartillo* to meet us here tomorrow. We'll get an early start."

"What did you tell him?"

"Nothing."

"And José?"

Río kicked off his boots and stretched out on the lumpy bed. "José, it seems, is no longer on this earth. He engaged in a small dispute at this very tavern, the last time the Conde's men passed this way, and one of them killed him."

Celia could not suppress a smile of satisfaction. "Was this small dispute over a woman?"

"Tomás did not say. His death amuses you?"

"I had no love for him. He tried to rape me."

"Well, I can at least understand his motives. Come, lie down; we need some rest."

Fully clothed, Celia positioned herself on the very edge of the mattress, as far away from Río as possible, as if the few inches that separated their bodies could somehow be a tangible barrier between them.

Río laughed softly and rolled over to kiss her shoulder. "The bed is quite large enough for both of us," he said.

"Sleep well," she replied.

He yawned and turned onto his stomach. His outflung hand rested on her hair, trapping it, reminding her of his presence all night.

Celia awoke before Río and quietly rose from the bed without—she thought—disturbing him. Lifting her bedraggled skirts, she unbuckled the hidden belt and replaced it over her several layers of clothing, where she could reach the stud in a moment. Her body itched from the salt of accumulated sweat, and she yearned for a cool bath, but she dared not wet her skin; the dark makeup had all been used up, and she was not ready to resume her former appearance—not until she was home.

The landlord provided breakfast, which included ham and fresh eggs, a welcome treat after the monotony of cheese and jerky. Río and Celia ate in their room, and they had just cleaned up the last remnants of their meal when Tomás knocked at the door.

Río flicked the bolt aside. "Enter."

Tomás was thinner and more wiry than Celia remembered; below the ragged sleeves of his cotton shirt, the cords of his arms stood out in sharp relief. He smiled hesitantly in greeting, and a gap showed where he was now missing one of his large, yellow incisors.

"How may I serve you, *señor?*"

Río glanced expectantly toward Celia.

"Do you recognize me, Tomás?" she inquired.

Tomás squinted at her, frowning. He shook his head.

"I used to have yellow hair, Tomás."

His eyes widened. "The woman with Señor Lorenzo!"

"Truly. I know, now, what really happened. I know that Lorenzo paid you to kill me."

Tomás held up his hands, palm outward. "But we didn't kill you! Surely you are grateful for that!"

"Let us not discuss my capacity for gratitude. I want something from you, Tomás, a very small thing. I want you to lead us to the place where you and José found me."

"You mean, out in the forest?"

"Exactly."

Tomás licked his lips. "The *señorita* truly wishes to go into the forest?"

"Yes. Do you wish payment? I can offer a few coins."

Tomás rocked nervously from foot to foot. "One never knows what is in the forest, *señorita*."

"You are afraid," said Río.

Tomás smiled sheepishly. "That is true."

Celia asked why.

"The soldiers of Pradera. One can never predict where they'll be. They have a special interest in Verdura that brings them back again and again; each time they make trouble—take a few women, kill a few men. That is how my friend José died: he insulted one of their officers. Some people have gone south, including Rodríguez, the slave dealer; he said the soldiers were bad for business."

"And the special interest in Verdura . . . ?" inquired Río.

"Guns. They think someone here in the town makes great numbers of new guns. And when they find no one so employed, they become angry. Recently I have begun to think of moving south myself."

"But they're gone now," said Celia.

"And they may return any day," Tomás added.

"We will pay you four *reales* to lead us to the place where you kidnapped me."

Tomás shook his head.

"Six," said Celia.

"I might do it for twenty."

"We can afford no more than six *reales*," said Río, "so you will have to settle for that."

"Then you will have to find the place without my help."

"Very well," said Celia. "You may leave."

"What?" exclaimed Tomás, his eyes opening very wide.

"I said you may go," Celia replied. "The price is too high; therefore we cannot engage your services. *Adiós*."

Tomás raised one hand in supplication. "*Momentito, señorita*. I did not realize that your purse was so empty. Please, I will lead you for, oh, twelve *reales*, to be sure." He looked from one to the other hopefully. A stony silence ensued. "Ten?"

Celia glanced at Río for confirmation.

"Lead on then," said Río.

They picked up the saddlebags and settled the bill with the landlord. Tomás coaxed them into stopping at the smithy so that he could strap on a loaded *miquelet*. "In case we should meet a cat, or something." He would not leave the town without it. While they were there, Celia traded her finely wrought scissors for a small hatchet on a leather loop.

Río stayed close to Tomás, one hand casually hooked near his hunting knife, which he could draw much faster than a *miquelet* could be unlimbered, cocked, aimed, and fired.

It was a long walk. Celia remembered it as a protracted horseback ride, though she discounted much of the subjective length as a function of her discomfort and terror at the time.

"Here we are," said Tomás.

Celia thought she recognized the small clearing and the tall, strawlike grass within it, but in all directions the surrounding forest looked unfamiliar. She tried to remember how long she and Larry had strolled hand in hand before arriving here. Quite a while, as she recalled. He once told her the belt would vibrate a hundred yards from the target area, and now she had to depend on that assertion.

"You can leave now, Tomás. Give him his ten *reales*."

Río tossed a small jingling bundle to their guide.

She circled the clearing once while Río watched in

puzzlement and Tomás made no move to depart. She circled the clearing again, at a greater distance.

"*Chiquita?*" said Río.

"I know what I'm doing," Celia replied. She pulled the hatchet from its loop on her belt and blazed every third tree trunk she passed.

"Can I help you?"

From Celia's viewpoint, the clearing was almost lost in the foliage. "Yes; keep me centered on the clearing. I am walking circles about it, wider and wider until . . . until I recognize something from the path Larry and I traveled from our homeland. So far, the landscape is strange to me."

Río turned to Tomás. "Are you sure this is the right place?"

Tomás's head bobbed quickly. "Absolutely certain, *señor.*"

"Let us follow, then. You should know best how to locate the clearing from inside the forest."

They spiraled outward. Celia kept one hand on the belt at all times, waiting for the slightest tremor. The spiral enlarged. Celia tried to calculate how far they would have to walk to circle the clearing at hundred-yard intervals for a mile radius, but without paper and pencil, she could not trust the appalling approximate answer that came to her—fifty miles! She fervently hoped that what had seemed a rather long jaunt through the woods was really no more extensive than a few city blocks.

The palm of her left hand began to itch; automatically, she rubbed it on her thigh, then placed it back on her hip. Once more, it itched. Abruptly realizing the nature of the sensation, Celia checked her stride. She slid her hand along the belt and isolated the center of vibration several inches to the left of the buckle. When she pivoted in that direction, the resonating spot shifted to the front of the belt, right under the brass buckle. A few steps forward and the vibration seemed to gain in strength. She moved again, and now she was sure. Her blood seethed with adrenalin, yet she forced herself to walk with a slow and measured pace toward the target area. She knew she was at its apex when the resonance became a crescendo throughout the fabric of the belt.

"Río," she said, turning toward the men who followed her in some confusion. She beckoned excitedly, her composure lost. "Río, this is the place!"

He caught up with her in long strides which left Tomás a dozen yards behind. "This is what place?"

Celia was smiling and biting her lower lip. "Come close to me, *querido,* and I'll show you."

"What will you show him, *señorita?*" called Tomás, hurrying toward them. "Show me, too."

They glanced back at their erstwhile guide. His double-barreled pistol was drawn and cocked and pointing straight at Celia.

CHAPTER FIFTEEN

"Mierda!" muttered Río, his fists clenching.

"Tomás, what are you doing?" asked Celia.

"I am waiting for you to show us whatever is here."

"What . . . what do you think is here?"

Tomás smiled. "Let us not play games, *señorita.* I am not stupid. Now, if you will point out the exact spot where they are buried . . ."

"Where *what* are buried?"

"The *guns, señorita. The guns!*"

"What guns?"

Tomás waved his *miquelet* restlessly. "Lorenzo's guns! What else would anyone be searching for in this forest?" His eyes flickered to the weapons on Río's hip. "No sudden motions, either of you. Rincón, put your hands up high." Río placed his hands behind his head. *"Señorita,* drop the ax." She complied. "Now, with three fingers only, remove the pistol and dagger from Señor Rincón's belt and toss them—carefully!—to the side."

She did as she was told, feeling Tomás's eyes track her every movement. "Really, Tomás, there are no guns," she insisted.

"Please!" he cried, almost in anguish. "I am not the utter fool you think me. Hurry up, now; point out the exact spot, or I will shoot you and search for myself."

Celia took a deep breath and slipped an arm around Río's waist, urging him close.

"A very tender scene, *señorita,* but I wait most impatiently," said Tomás. His fingers tightened on the pistol, shaking a little.

Celia's free hand found the stud, pressed it.

The dappled afternoon light winked out.

"What's this? What happened?" cried Río, grasping her arms too hard.

Celia sagged against his chest, her heart racing, and only his convulsive embrace kept her on her feet. "Wait. Wait till your eyes adjust to the dark. We're safe." As her pupils dilated, she began to discern the outlines of Larry's back room, illuminated by the hazy light that filtered through the single grimy, frosted window. The consoles, the filing cabinet, the filigreed pole were all there: the naked red bulb on the pole had burned out after months of continuous service.

"Where . . . are we?" Río hissed.

"This is the other world of which I told you," Celia replied. "The world in which the Invincible Armada failed to conquer England. *My* world." Wincing, she tried to peel his tense fingers away from her flesh. "Río, you're hurting me."

He let her go abruptly, and his hands remained open, half-raised in mid-air, as he scanned his surroundings. "Mother of God, my head is spinning," he muttered. "I have never believed in sorcery . . . but . . . how did we get here?"

"With this belt." She unbuckled it and tossed it onto the table, where a duplicate belt lay neatly coiled. "It belonged to Larry Meyers; Fernandez took it from him, and I obtained it from Fernandez. By standing within this circle and pressing a stud on the buckle, the wearer can travel from one world to the other. And even take another person with him." She clambered out of the pit of the target area, found the light switch near the door, and flicked it on. The overhead fixture remained dark, and Celia surmised that the electric company had shut off the house current for nonpayment of the bill. Fortunately, the doorway between worlds had an independent power source. "This is Larry's house," she explained, "and it occupies the same space as the spot in the forest where we were standing a few moments ago."

"And the forest . . . ?"

"In this world there is no forest. Instead there is a city called Evanston. A city of eighty thousand people."

"Eighty thousand!"

"And not far away is another city of many millions."

"There are no such cities!"

"Not in your world, perhaps. My world is a bit more crowded. Come." She held her hand out to him. "I'll show it to you."

The dining room was less gloomy, lit by sunlight diffusing ochre-yellow through old window shades. Unwashed dishes lay on the rickety wooden table, and wrinkled clothing hung on the folding chairs. Over all was a thick layer of dust, and a musty, attic smell. Each footstep stirred up clumps of fuzz and left a clear imprint on the floor.

As she suspected, none of the marvels she wished to demonstrate were in working order. The pilot lights on the stove were out, and there was not the slightest hiss of gas when she turned the knobs. The hot water was cool. The refrigerator, the appliance most alien to Río's experience, was warm and full of mold.

"Well, soon we'll go outside," Celia said. "But first I must wash myself. I won't be too long."

Leaving Río in the kitchen, she scampered into the bathroom, closing and locking the door behind her. With great pleasure, she stripped off her filthy, reeking clothes and tossed them into the corner behind the toilet. The shower was chilling, but she reveled in the penetrating spray, soaping and rinsing her hair half a dozen times. Rivulets of dark, greasy mascara flowed down her body and swirled about her feet. The bathroom walls were sprinkled with suds by the time she finished.

While drying herself on a mildewed towel, she peeked into the medicine chest; tucked behind a bottle of cough syrup was a small vial with a well-remembered label: "FOR POST-COITAL CONTRACEPTION—AVOID EXCESSIVE USE."

She found Río gazing out the living-room window, holding the tattered old shade aside with one hand. He did not seem to notice the soft sound of her barefoot tread.

She stood in the living-room doorway, pink and naked but for the faded terrycloth tied loosely at her hips. "*Querido.*"

He turned slowly, letting the shade fall back against the glass. His brow was creased.

"Love me," she said.

He embraced her ferociously, squeezed and kissed her with too much force, but she didn't mind. She wanted the pressure of his body around her, upon her, within her. She clutched his hips, grinding her crotch against his thighs and felt, in turn, his hands kneading her flanks. Suddenly he lifted her, carried her swiftly down the hall into the bedroom.

The coverlet, she noticed, was already turned back.

Later, she lay in the crook of his arm, glad to be alive and with him and home. She nuzzled his shoulder and rubbed her leg against his with casual affection. She felt free at last—free of anxiety and the Armada world, its dirt and sweat and blood and terror. The only worthwhile part of San Felipe had come with her; she kissed him with lingering passion. Then she stretched joyously and rolled off the bed.

"I think there will be something here to fit me," she said, padding to the closet for a look at the available wardrobe. While Río donned his own clothes again, she selected a pair of orange shorts and a cocoa shirt.

"Is that . . . properly modest?" Río wondered.

Celia glanced at her reflection in the mirror and grinned. "It's proper and comfortable," she replied. "My people would consider yours terribly overdressed, at least in the summer."

"And drab."

"We have dyes and fabrics your merchants never dreamed of." She found Larry's keys on the dresser. "Ready?"

He draped the saddlebags over one shoulder. "I hope so."

She took his hand, squeezed it hard, and led him toward the front door. A mound of mail from the drop slot was spilled across their path; she kicked it aside.

The afternoon was hot and bright, the air tangy with light smog—an odor nostalgic as never before. At the corner where the residential street crossed a major thoroughfare, traffic was at an average, pre-rush-hour density. As they waited for the light to change, a jet droned overhead, descending for a landing at O'Hare Field.

Río looked everywhere with large, questing eyes—at the traffic lights and the traffic, at the bungalows and three-story apartment dwellings, at the asphalt streets, cement sidewalks, and grassy lawns; but when Celia indicated the source of the sound, he stared and stared upward, uncomprehending.

"That's an airplane," said Celia. "A ship that flies. Thousands of them travel all over the world every day."

"Thousands?"

"And each one is large enough to hold a hundred people or more."

"A hundred people," he murmured, squinting into the west. "How . . . how does it stay up?"

Celia hesitated, then shook her head. "I don't really

know. I've never thought about it; I just accept it as part of my world. It's only one of many marvels, Río. You'll see more, much more."

"Yes," he said, transferring his gaze to the somewhat-less-marvelous auto traffic.

"Come on. We'll catch a ride into Chicago."

"What?"

"My city. It isn't far, but I don't really feel like walking the whole distance."

On the next green light, she headed for the gas station on the opposite corner.

While Celia moved from driver to driver inquiring for transportation into the city, Río watched an attendant open the hood of a car, check the oil, fill the radiator, and adjust the carburetor. He jumped back when the engine revved suddenly under the man's knowledgeable fingers, and he had to turn away, coughing and weeping, from the unexpected and alien irritation of the exhaust. He noticed the pumps then, and stared as they ticked off gallon after gallon, dollar after dollar, and stopped automatically.

The attendant racked the hose and asked Río a question in English: "What can I do for you, friend?"

Río smiled and shook his head uncertainly, but before anything else happened, Celia glided up and caught his arm.

"If anyone tries to talk to you, say, 'I don't speak English.' "

"What does that mean?"

"*No hablo* . . . and 'English' is the name of our language. You'll have to learn it one of these days."

" 'I . . . don't . . . speak . . . English.' " His mimicry of her was fairly accurate.

"I found someone who will take us near my parents' home."

Behind the wheel of a sporty chartreuse convertible sat a long-haired young man, who was an instructor at Northwestern University according to the parking

sticker on his rear windshield. He smiled from behind
an enormous pair of bubble-lens sunglasses as Celia
and Río climbed into the front seat beside him. One
hand on the wheel, the other hanging out the window,
he waited not a second after the door slammed before
flooring the gas to take advantage of a break in
traffic.

Celia felt Río's arm tighten convulsively about her
shoulders at the sudden acceleration. She rubbed his
thigh reassuringly, then snapped the single passenger
seat belt about both of them. She laid her head on his
shoulder and looked at the world sideways for a while,
enjoying the furious rush of wind that whipped the
last traces of moisture from her hair.

A few minutes brought them to the heart of Evanston and a long series of ill-timed stoplights that slowed
traffic to a crawl. Río goggled at the tall buildings
and the broad glass windows with their eye-catching
displays of merchandise and odd props. Celia noted
that a new bank has risen while she was gone.

"First time in Evanston?" asked the driver.

"*His* first time," Celia replied.

"Have you told him they turn it off at nine
o'clock?"

Celia chuckled. "That's why we're going to Chicago." English felt strange and wonderful in her
mouth, like a new ice cream flavor. *Ice cream?* She realized with a sudden intense yearning that she hadn't
tasted ice cream in a year. . . .

Over the border between the cities, Clark Street was
a madhouse. Traffic moved at a pace determined by
jaywalking pedestrians and double-parked trucks. A
stalled car, its hood raised and its female passenger
looking very embarrassed, occupied the center of the
intersection at Touhy; their driver stopped behind a
frozen line of traffic and began to curse.

"We can get out here," Celia said, extricating herself
and Río from the seat belt. She reached across his

body to manipulate the door handle, which was momentarily baffling him. "Thanks so very much for the lift."

They walked west, passing under the Chicago and Northwestern commuter tracks.

"It isn't far now," said Celia. "*Dios*, I'm hungry."

"There's jerky," Río replied, indicating the saddlebag slung over his shoulder.

"Ugh. I'd prefer my mother's tuna salad."

"What's that?"

Celia grinned, her step quickening. "Strange exotic food not available in San Felipe." She wiped her sweaty face with a tail of her shirt. "What a hellishly hot day." She prayed the air conditioning was working. "It isn't far now, not far at all. I hope my parents are home; I don't have my keys anymore."

"They will be glad to see you."

"I'm sure."

"What will you tell them?"

"I don't know." Back in San Felipe, she had thought about them occasionally, thought about their probable reaction to her disappearance: frantic phone calls to all her friends, then to the police; disappointment leading at last to resigned acceptance of her death. Yet, in the escape, she'd had no regard for anything but the ever-present now and the next footstep. She'd made no plans beyond Verdura, afraid to think of the alternatives. Now that she was on a familiar street, about to reenter her life, to attempt to pick it up where she had left it, there was the small matter of a year's absence. Not to mention Río.

Whether or not to expose Larry's invention—ultimately the whole matter boiled down to that. Her parents could not be trusted to keep the secret. If they believed her, it would not be long before newsmen and federal agents were knocking at their door. And the Government would use Larry's discovery for its own purposes, as he had predicted.

Or would it? Larry had emphasized the offensive potential of the portal. Yet, as long as missile-launching submarines roved the oceans, the device could only be one more element in the U.S. arsenal. Merely as a weapon, it was not the solution to nuclear stalemate. However, as a defensive measure, it held much more promise: whole cities might be instantly shunted to the alternate world in case of atomic attack. Of course, whatever was in the way in the other world would have to be removed first . . . a difficult task in the case of, for example, San Felipe, which occupied the approximate site of St. Louis. Certainly the Marqués and his people would never go packing at the behest of the Secret Service, and all-out destruction of San Felipe was probably out of the question: somewhere in the echelons, someone would balk at this ruthless operation—hopefully the President. In any case, a news leak could be deadly to the Administration involved: public opinion would surely roast any group that was known to have condoned such an iron-clad atrocity.

As a strategic device, then, the portal was fairly useless to a government as vulnerable, in its way, as the United States.

Totalitarian regimes, however, might have little regard for such second thoughts.

She began to concoct a fabulous tale that would account for her long absence and for her Latin companion.

Her heart was pounding frantically when the long, stepped walkway of her home came into view. She paused to drink in the familiar setting—the gabled, red brick edifice, the tall hedgerow, the cement porch with its cracks and wrought-iron railing. The tuck-pointing her father had been talking about for years had finally been accomplished, and the wooden trim of the roof had been repainted a muddy brown. The white drapes were drawn snugly across the big picture window, shielding the living room from the heat and glare of the afternoon sun.

Celia glanced at Río once before stabbing the door-bell, and she felt a vast sense of relief that he did not speak English.

The door opened.

CHAPTER SIXTEEN

Celia relaxed in her bedroom, which her parents had kept exactly as she had left it. She was exhausted, surfeited with kisses and hugs and glad tears of reunion. Her tale of months-long amnesia and abrupt awakening in Arizona had been accepted with astonished exclamations.

"Amnesia? Amnesia?" Mrs. Ward kept repeating incredulously. It was clear to Celia that her mother could barely bring herself to accept such an explanation, but when her entreaties elicited no alternative, she subsided into murmurs of "you're so *thin*, Celia!"

Indeed, the bathroom scale showed that Celia had lost fifteen pounds, and her clothes of former seasons were quite loose at waist and hip.

"Why didn't you call when you regained your memory?" her father demanded. Irritation was beginning to show through his relief. "We thought you were dead!"

"I couldn't, Poppa. There weren't any telephones where I was."

"No telephones? Is there a town in America that doesn't have at least *one* telephone?"

Celia nodded.

To the insistent queries concerning her recent activities, she replied only: "I don't want to talk about it; I just want to collapse. I came home as soon as I could, believe me, and now I'm tired and hungry."

Mrs. Ward rushed into the kitchen to throw two extra steaks in the broiler for dinner.

Río baffled Celia's parents. During the meal, when they were all seated around the kitchen table, he ate slowly, subjecting his surroundings to a scrutiny more intense than was warranted by idle curiosity. The stove, the refrigerator, and the dishwasher were major targets of his inquiring gaze; also the Brussels sprouts, which he treated with great suspicion. He had introduced himself by his full name, rolling the sonorous syllables from his tongue so rapidly that only a native speaker of Spanish would have known where given names ended and surnames began. He punctuated the presentation with a formal bow.

"This is Río," said Celia. "I love him, and I hope . . . I hope you'll come to love him, too."

"You're married?" asked Celia's mother.

"No."

Her parents exchanged glances, then smiled somewhat stiffly. They addressed a few meaningless niceties to Río, but when he replied with the only English sentence he knew, they said, almost in unison, "For heaven's sake, *why* doesn't he speak English?"

"He'll learn," replied Celia.

After dinner, Celia excused Río and herself, went to her room, and closed the door firmly. Beyond, she could hear her parents talking to each other in excited voices and then spreading the good news, via telephone, to every relative and friend they could think of. Soon the procession of visitors would begin, and Celia wanted to be well rested for the ordeal. Briefly, she wished she were as ignorant of English as Río.

"Outdoors, the air is hot and still, yet inside your house, though it is not built of stone, the air is cool," said Río. He had opened the bedroom window and now sat on the sill, leaning out.

"It's called 'air conditioning,' " said Celia. "We use it in the summer as we use heat in the winter. We like to be comfortable. Close the window, *querido*, you're letting in the warm air."

A few moments later, he was examining a table lamp, turning it on and off, unscrewing the bulb, tracing the wire to an electrical outlet. Gently, Celia prevented him from probing the live socket.

"Don't touch anything strange without asking me first if it's safe." *He's like a child*, she thought. *A child has to be instructed in coping with the dangers of his environment.* The thought of her tall, strong Río as a child made her smile and stroke his cheek. "Now that we're in my world, *I* am the teacher. You won't need to know how to skin a rabbit here."

"I guessed as much." He returned her affectionate gesture absently, his mind distracted by the view through the lace curtain of the bedroom window: the Wards' next-door neighbor was clipping his hedges with power shears, and his son was mowing the lawn with a power mower.

Celia glanced out the window, too. "I never realized how little I know about the things I've always considered commonplace. We'll get some books tomorrow, Río. We'll find out how it all works."

"Yes, this force electricity . . . I would like to know how it works."

They slept together that night, ignoring her parents' gentle hint that he bed down on the living-room sofa. Celia had never shared the bed in her frilly, ultra-feminine bedroom with anyone—she had never dared to broach the subject to her folks. But this night, she didn't ask for their opinion, and they were still so glad to have their daughter home again that they said nothing beyond the single mild suggestion.

The next morning, Celia borrowed her mother's car and drove with Río to the library. There, while he watched the library copying machine reproduce book pages with a flash of light, Celia discovered that electricity was far more complex than she had ever imagined. The problem was to convey to him an elementary knowledge of a branch of physics for which his cultural background was hopelessly inadequate, using an extensive technical vocabulary that his language did not possess. A monumental task! Nevertheless, Celia selected Blackwood and Kelly's *General Physics,* a text which Larry had once recommended to her, and hoped for the best. Galvani, after all, had started with a frog's leg. *If nothing else,* she told herself, *he will learn not to stick his fingers in a light socket.*

"Electricity," Celia began, after reading earnestly for some minutes, "is the power of lightning harnessed to the service of Man."

Río's eyebrows raised. "How do you get it down from the sky?"

"We don't. We make our own. You know what a lodestone is, don't you?"

"A rock that attracts objects made of iron? Don Epifanio had one once; he ground it to a powder, mixed it with wine, and gave it to Doña María Antonia as a tonic."

"Ugh," said Celia.

"You make electricity from a lodestone?"

"In a way." She referred to a diagram in the book. "Look here, Río: this is a lodestone shaped like the letter 'U.' Its two ends are called 'poles.' Radiating from each pole to the other, through the empty space between them, are invisible lines of force."

"Invisible lines of force?"

"Yes. These invisible lines of force pull iron to the poles of the lodestone. They are created by invisibly small things called 'domains,' each of which is a tiny lodestone with two poles, one at either end. Now, if you place a coil of wire between the poles of the 'U' and rotate the coil . . ." Here she referred to another diagram: ". . . you cut across the lines of force. That produces electricity."

Río stared at the book, puzzling out the perspective

of the illustration. "Each of these things, then—the lamps, the refrigerator, the air conditioner—has a lodestone inside . . ."

"No, no. The electricity for thousands of homes is all made in one central place, where the force of water or steam turns large coils between the poles of giant magnets. It is brought here by long wires, very much like water is brought from one place to another in pipes." She unplugged the nearest lamp, took it apart, traced the internal wires for him; she showed him how plugging it in and closing the switch made a complete circuit.

"I'm amazed that holes can be made through wires so fine," Río said.

"There aren't any holes in the wires."

"Then how does the electricity flow through them?"

"It doesn't flow *through* them. It flows *in* them." And then she had to explain electrons, atoms, charge, conduction, resistance, electromagnetism, and a host of other concepts. Each explanation required a dozen others, until her head began to swim. It was rough going for a Romance languages student who had taken the university's course in History of Science rather than physics or chemistry. Some of the material she could hardly grasp herself; she was sure that most of her explanations sounded like magic.

"It isn't simple," she told Río. "It took people hundreds of years to make all the discoveries that led to radio and television. But everyone in my country accepts them as part of everyday life; we grew up with them, so they don't seem extraordinary to us."

Río stared at the television screen. Celia had tuned in the Spanish-language UHF station, but the announcer was talking about the crosstown expressway, the space shuttle, and other matters totally incomprehensible to a person from San Felipe.

"The longer you're here, the more normal everything will seem," she promised him. "Eventually, none of these things will be strange to you. But I cannot explain it all in a moment; there's just too much. Perhaps now, though, you begin to understand why I didn't feel comfortable in *your* world?"

"It's time for my program, dear," said Celia's mother, coming in from the kitchen.

"Go ahead, Mom. We're not watching this anymore."

Mrs. Ward settled into her chair with a cigarette and a cup of coffee. She touched the remote-control channel selector, then the color adjustment. The skin tones of the soap opera characters moved from green through ochre to purple before assuming a semblance of natural hue.

"Yes," said Río. "I think I begin to understand."

Celia took his hands. "I want to show you my city, *querido*. There's so much to see; we could wander for years and never see it all."

Río shrugged. "Whatever you wish."

"Mom, can I have the car again? We want to go downtown."

"Won't you see the doctor first, dear, just to make sure you're completely recovered?"

"I told you I'm all right, Mom; don't worry."

"You've had amnesia once, you know; you can never tell—"

"You can never tell when I'll be hit by a truck, either. Don't worry about me; I'm fine. And I have a chaperone; if I keel over on the street, he'll be able to tell the police my name and address."

"I worried about you so these past months. . . . I hate to let you out the door for an instant."

Celia kissed her mother's cheek. "I know, Mom, but really, I'm okay now. We'll be back for a late supper."

Mrs. Ward sighed. "The keys are in my purse."

Just past noon, traffic on the Outer Drive was light. The day had turned overcast and windy, though rain was some hours away yet; out on the gray and choppy lake, two sailboats were gliding into Belmont harbor. The neat parkland on either side of the Drive seemed skimpy to Celia since her travels through the forests of San Felipe, but the high-rise apartment buildings beyond appeared imposingly tall—monuments to the Industrial Age. At one time Celia had been proud of her city's lakeside parks, but now she was as proud of the skyscrapers as if she owned them; the Anglo-American Twentieth Century had its faults, its wars, slums, pollution, and prejudice, but it also had a special magnificence.

She parked in the underground garage, and they rode the escalator up to Michigan Avenue. Celia knew it was silly, but the sight of the Prudential and Standard Oil Buildings brought tears to her eyes. Home was beautiful.

Hand in hand, they walked to the State Street Mall. There, the theater marquees glowed red, orange, and yellow even though it was daytime, and the Magikist sign poured forth continuous news in moving lights. Buses rumbled by; cars, taxis, and newspaper trucks contended for space on the cross-streets, beeping at each other raucously. Policemen whistled and waved, directing traffic. Chanting converts to a rising Eastern cult squatted under the Marshall Field clock, peddling incense and glossy booklets on interplanetary travel by transcendental meditation and astral projection. Shoppers by the thousands tramped the pavement in search of bargains and glitter.

Río and Celia window-shopped. They walked by the Civic Center, viewed the fountains and the arcane Picasso sculpture, made more so by large rust-holes. Skirting the demolition of the Lake Street El, they crossed the river via a massive, gray-girdered bridge from the Big Bill Thompson era, pausing in the middle to inspect a huge barge that lay at anchor below. They circled the solid, steel-and-glass cubism of the

IBM Building to join the better-heeled shoppers on north Michigan. Celia bought a new belt at Saks.

On the way back, a Western epic at the Roosevelt Theatre caught her eye. "It's like TV, only larger," she told Río on the way in. For two hours their senses were assaulted with wrap-around Technicolor deserts full of avalanching cattle and blazing gunfire. The popcorn was very good, but overpriced.

"The size!" Río exclaimed after the show. "I felt like an ant, and yet I also felt as if I were there, with the actors. You say the bullets and blood were not real . . . ?"

"The people who make movies are very clever at simulating injury and death."

They emerged from the theater late in the evening, and as they stepped away from the marquee, Río gasped.

High above, the sky was a black dome, but the streets of downtown Chicago were lit bright as day by arc lights and the neon fluorescence of restaurants, shops, theaters, and ads. Everywhere, lights moved, flickered, changed color; arrows leaped and dove, headlights slid past like a river of glowing coals.

Celia smiled. "Quite a sight, isn't it?"

Río stood in the middle of the sidewalk, oblivious to the pedestrians who detoured around him. He gaped, his eyes tracking from the spiral-lit twin towers of Marina City in the north, to the giant Sears sign that seemed to float in space above Van Buren Street.

Slowly but firmly she guided him to Michigan Avenue and the garage. A light mist was in the air, precursing rain, and a strong breeze off the lake occasionally stopped them in their tracks and tore away their breath. The garage was cool and damp, as usual.

The downpour began when they were halfway home. On Sheridan Road, the high-rises were beaded curtains of light, the rest of the world muffled in wet crepe. In the short dash from the curb to Celia's front door, they were both drenched.

Celia's mother hugged her, crying. "I was getting so worried. Oh, you're safe, thank God, that's all that matters."

Celia patted Mrs. Ward's shoulder. "Take it easy! There was never anything to worry about." A sudden chill prickled her skin. "But I could use a hot shower right now." She glanced back over her shoulder. "And Río, too, I bet."

They shared the shower, soaping each other's backs, and wound up making love in the tub. But Río's face was wan; he hardly smiled, even when Celia playfully licked his nose.

"Río, is something wrong?"

He blinked at his image in the mirror. She was showing him how to shave with an electric razor.

"This is a marvelous world," he said. "A world full of marvels."

"I told you it was. And there are more; you've just begun to see them. Tomorrow we'll go to the Museum of Science and Industry, and you'll *really* see some marvels." She gave him a robe and slippers borrowed from her father, donned her own wrapper, and they went out to the dinner table.

Over cherry pie, Mr. Ward asked, "Ah . . . Celia, what kind of plans do you and . . . Río . . . have?"

"Plans? Tomorrow we go to the Museum of Science—"

"For the future, I mean."

"Oh. Well, I don't know. I thought we'd consider that when he learns some English."

"What I mean is . . . what kind of work does he do?"

"He's a singer. He plays guitar."

Mr. and Mrs. Ward relaxed visibly. "Well," said Celia's father. "At least he isn't a migrant worker."

Celia's mother cast Río a sidelong glance. "Honey, are you two going to get married soon?"

"We haven't discussed it yet."

Celia's father cleared his throat. "It doesn't look good, both of you here in the house and not married. I don't like it. The neighbors will talk."

Celia pushed her unfinished dessert aside. "We'll find an apartment, then. Do you want me to start looking tonight?"

"Wait! Celia dear," said her mother, "no one is asking you to leave!"

"Río stays with me, here or someplace else."

"Well then, perhaps it *would* be best if you moved out," said her father.

"No!" cried Mrs. Ward. "Frank, she just came home! I won't let her leave again!"

"This is my house, Doris, and I don't want my daughter living with some . . . some itinerant musician under my own roof."

Celia stood up. "All right, Father," she returned coldly. "Is my bank account intact?"

"Yes, but—"

"Then, to shorten this melodrama, Río and I will leave in the morning."

"Celia!" wailed her mother. "What will you do? You've never had a real job; you don't know any kind of work. What about school?"

"I'll manage, Mother. School, too, even without your help."

Her father exploded. "Well, I'll be damned if I'll pay for it under these circumstances!"

"Somehow that doesn't worry me. Good night." She turned to Río. "I think we should leave the table now," she said in Spanish. "Before my parents shoot us."

He gulped the last bit of pie, stood up, bowed formally to the Wards, and followed Celia to the bedroom.

She locked the door, and without turning on the lights, she went to the window and pressed against the glass, gazing at the light on the telephone pole in the alley.

"They were quite angry, weren't they?" said Río.

"Moderately angry. I expected something like this eventually. They don't like the idea of you and me together and not married. So tomorrow we leave."

"For where?"

"I have friends from the university we can stay with temporarily. I know a few who will probably still be living where they were when I left. As soon as possible, we'll find a place of our own. I have some money for immediate needs, but we'll have to get jobs. Maybe singing, at least for you. You'll have to start working on your English—"

"Celia?"

"Yes?"

He came up behind her, encircled her with his arms, and laid his cheek against her hair. "Let's go back."

"Back?"

"Back to my world."

Celia twisted about sharply. "You can't mean that."

"Yes, I mean it."

She clutched his arms. "No. I can't go back. I won't go back. *This, this* is the better world. How can you deny that?"

He shook his head. "A strange world, full of . . . magic."

"It's not magic!"

"To me, it is."

"You'll get used to it, Río. Everything is new to you now, but soon you'll accept it just as everyone else does, I promise you. Why, you've hardly seen a fraction of it!"

He frowned into her eyes. "I was afraid you would say that."

She stared at him, puzzled. "What do you mean?"

"I have seen . . . wonders . . . and they frightened me. I think I would rather face His Grace's wrath than see more wonders yet."

"Río!"

His gaze moved to the window, fastened on the streetlight, which was blurred by rain. "I don't want to stay here."

Her arms tightened around him. "You'll change your mind."

"You didn't change *yours*."

"That was different."

"I think not."

"Yes, it was; your world is primitive and harsh, and I was a slave in it, always!"

"It is possible to use the belt to return, yes?"

Reluctantly, she admitted it was.

"Then I must go."

"No!"

"*Chiquita,* I brought you to your homeland. Now let me return to mine."

"No, no, no!" She pulled him closer, buried her face in his shoulder. Her stomach churned, and her head felt as if it would burst; she clenched her fists at the pain and nausea, at the tears that smarted in her eyes. "No! I love you! I won't let you leave me!"

He rubbed her shoulders with tense hands. "Come with me."

She trembled. "How can you ask that after all I did to get here?" Her voice cracked on the last word.

He sighed softly. "I didn't think you would say yes."

"Río, I love you."

"And I love you, *querida*. But I cannot remain."

"Another day, Río! A week!" Her fingers curved into claws, dug into his back. "Give yourself a chance to know my world."

"Another week and I shall surely go mad. I don't

know what to touch, where to walk, what to expect when I turn my head. Let me go back to a place I understand!"

"Without me?"

"If you will not go, then without you."

Abruptly, Celia shoved him away. Her eyes were red-rimmed, and her voice shook with stifled sobs. "Coward!" she shouted. "Is this the man who roamed the forests of San Felipe alone? Coward!"

Río gazed calmly into her contorted face. "I am a coward," he said. "And so are you."

"*I?* In what way am I a coward?"

"You would not stay in San Felipe."

"After a year! You have been here scarcely two days!"

"Time enough, for me."

Celia's mouth opened and shut once, and then she wilted; her neck bent and her arms hung limp. She sat down heavily on the bed. Her tears dried, leaving a bleakness inside. "For a while, I thought you were mine. But I was wrong. No one owns you. No one will ever own you."

He touched her cheek with one finger. "Nor you. I knew when you turned us away from México that you would never let anyone else make your decisions again."

"No. Never."

"Would you like to make love again, before . . . ?"

"Do you want me?"

"Yes."

"All right, then."

Morning was bright and sunny. Four people breakfasted in the Ward kitchen without exchanging a word. Celia and Río left immediately after eating.

They hitchhiked to Larry's house, and Celia let them in with the key she had taken from Larry's dresser. Their footprints in the dust greeted them beyond the threshold.

In the back room, she screwed a fresh light bulb into the socket on the filigreed pole. With the last turn, it commenced to glow brightly, indicating that the circuits of the portal between worlds were intact.

Río returned from a trip to the kitchen with a heavy butcher's knife secured at his waist.

Celia cinched the activator belt around Río's waist. "After you step down into the circle, press this stud. That's all you have to do."

"It feels . . . odd."

"That's the resonation. When you stand inside the circle, the whole belt vibrates; outside the perimeter, only the portion facing the circle vibrates. That is to locate the portal area again, in your world."

Río gestured at the worktable. "There is a second belt."

"I noticed it."

"Is there a possibility you might use it sometime?"

Celia swallowed with difficulty. "I have no way of knowing when the device will cease to function. I couldn't risk being stranded in the other world."

"Surely, with all their magic, your people could repair the device?"

"No," said Celia, thinking of the decision she had made when they first set foot in Chicago. She wished it were someone else's. "The secret died with Larry."

"Then . . ." He took her hands between his own. "I will never see you again."

"Not unless you choose to return."

He kissed her softly, deftly, without haste. Then he stepped down into the target area. "I have loved you, Celia; never doubt that."

"You'll love someone else."

His right hand clasped the knife, ready for any danger he might encounter on the other side; his left hand moved to the buckle. "*Adiós, querida.* Take care of yourself."

She photographed him with unblinking eyes, trying to etch in her memory every line of his body.

He vanished, and there came the sound of a hand-clap as air rushed in to fill the void.

CHAPTER SEVENTEEN

Celia stood motionless for a long time. She tried not to think about the past, the year so strange and terrible, and the man just departed. She thought about her plans for the future, her return to an ordinary existence . . . and the responsibility that Larry's death had thrust upon her. She was his heir, in fact if not in law; the doorway between worlds, so near and so fragile, belonged to her. She could smash the consoles with a sledgehammer, fuse their microcircuits with a blowtorch; she could burn the house, too, if she wanted to expunge all traces of Larry's discovery. The important thing was to keep the device out of the hands of the Government. *Any* government.

The naked bulb was a warm orange glow in the center of the room, casting greenish shadows on the walls and floor. Celia touched the switch that would darken the bulb and extinguish the portal between worlds; she hesitated, sapped of strength for a moment, and then she broke the circuit with a brusque motion. The room dimmed and was suddenly cool and blue.

My own decisions, she thought. *My own.*

She remembered Río's world with her body rather than her mind: the taste of half-rotten meat, heavy with spices; the smell of garbage, excrement, and unwashed bodies; the touch of winter-cold stone; the sound of men dying in agony. Her mind knew that all of this had existed in her own world in previous times and still existed in certain areas; but in the other world—stagnant, frozen in a Medieval twilight—it would continue to be the norm for centuries. Perhaps forever.

Delicately, with one fingertip, she traced a section of the pole's intricate pattern. If only nations were less selfish, the portal could bring the benefits of the modern world to the other. It would be a tremendous job, even a dangerous one, encompassing decades, perhaps.

She shook her head sharply and climbed out of the target area. There was a heavy hammer under the kitchen sink, she knew, and many other tools, and matches, too—implements for whichever means of destruction she chose. But she recoiled now from the thought of sparks and smoke and fire, both from fear of personal danger and the dread of possible consequences. Fire was too indiscriminate, and she had no wish to be caught by the police.

On the table lay the duplicate belt; she picked it up, buckled it about her hips. Then she turned to the three drawers of the filing cabinet. The first contained a large manila envelope that chinked when she lifted it. Celia folded back the flap and peered inside at half a dozen gold rings—some of Larry's booty, she surmised. She shut them back in the cabinet. The second drawer yielded a bundle of canvas bags and a few small boxes of electronic components. The third drawer was empty.

Celia leaned against the cabinet, frowning. Larry had been too methodical not to have kept records, but there was no other place in the workshop where they might be stored, no desk, no closet. Were they elsewhere, she wondered, possibly in some unknown bank vault?

Then she thought of the trapdoor in the bedroom closet.

There was a flashlight under the kitchen sink, and its batteries were still full of life. By its glare, she saw that the well beneath the closet was empty—no crates, no guns, nothing but hard-tamped earth. She lay on the floor and, gripping the doorjamb with one hand, leaned into the opening. Her first sweep with the light revealed a board nailed to two of the floor beams—a shelf within easy reach of anyone kneeling in the closet. On the shelf lay a plastic-wrapped package the size of a large, flat book.

By the bedroom window, she removed the dust-coated plastic bag to expose a gray spiral notebook. It bore no name, no title, but the pages were covered with Larry's unmistakable scribbling; the contents were incomprehensible enough, with their circuit diagrams and formulae, that Celia felt safe in assuming they were Larry's records of his project.

With notebook and belt, she went back to her parents' home.

Her mother was at the door almost as Celia opened it. "Where is . . . your friend?" she asked.

"*Río*," said Celia, brushing past her mother and heading for her bedroom.

Mrs. Ward followed closely. "Yes . . . Río."

"He's gone. And he won't be back." She threw the notebook on her bed and went to the closet to stare speculatively at its contents.

"Did you two have some sort of argument?"

"Something like that." On tiptoe, she reached up to the highest shelf, reached for the nested suitcases stored there and pulled them down. "I'd really rather not discuss it, Mother."

Mrs. Ward watched Celia fill the suitcases for a time, and then she said, "You know, you don't have to leave now. Your father will understand . . . that it's all over between you and Río."

Celia shook her head. "That doesn't matter."

"Don't be mad at him, dear. Your reappearance was such a shock. We both went through so much, for so long, it just wore him out. I'll talk to him, Celia; I'll talk to him. Everything will be fine then, I promise."

Celia looked at the clothing she was packing, the soft synthetics: nylon, acetate, acrylic, polyester. She remembered the rough texture of wool next to her skin, the stiff scratchiness of lace at her collar. "I have to leave, Mother," she said. "I've been on my own too long. I can't come back and live by your rules."

"But this is your home!"

"I'm sorry. That's . . . the way it has to be." She shut the largest case and sat on it to snap the locks. "*Please,* Mom."

On the third telephone call, she found a girl friend who still lived in Evanston and was willing to let her sleep on the couch until she could find permanent lodging. She gathered up her bags.

At the door, her mother said, "Do you need money?"

"I have my bank account."

"Here, just in case." She held out a twenty-dollar bill, folded in half.

Celia shook her head. "I'll be all right."

"You might need it for something. Take it." She tucked it into the pocket of Celia's slacks. "Call when you get settled. And don't you disappear again." A wavering smile touched her face, and she gave her daughter's shoulder a tight squeeze. "We do love you, dear, you know that."

"I know," said Celia. She met her mother's eyes. "I'll call."

In the morning she went to campus and tacked signs to several bulletin boards:

Student seeking apartment to share.

The new semester would be starting soon, and there were many such notices posted. She jotted down a few phone numbers of people who were looking for room-mates and called them later that day. Within a week, she made a satisfactory arrangement with two other college women—a three-bedroom flat in Evanston, not exceedingly far from the university. During that week she also visited the Romance Languages Department for advice on scholarships, and she found a part-time job in an ice cream parlor four blocks off campus. She worked all day Saturday, and when she got home that evening she was glad that Anne and Mara were out; she was too tired even for idle conversation. She did not see the message on the chalk board until she went into the kitchen later to make a cup of tea:

> *Phone call from Police. Want you to call back*
> *any day between 3 and 5 P.M. Lt. Keeler.*

And then his phone number.

Anne and Mara were curious when they came home.

"An old traffic ticket," Celia told them. She had no desire to tell her cover story again, not even for the police . . . perhaps especially not for them. At least not soon. She put off calling Lt. Keeler with one excuse after another—she was working, painting her room, registering for class, meeting old friends. Once more he called while she was gone, and then she ran out of excuses and steeled herself for the ordeal.

"We'd like you to come down to the station to answer a few questions," he said.

"Well, I'm pretty busy right now . . ."

"I can stop by your apartment, if that's more convenient."

She thought about her roommates, who both had irregular schedules, and decided she preferred not to talk in front of them. "No, I'll come down. What about Thursday?"

"I'll be here all afternoon."

"How about one o'clock? If you don't think it will take too long. I have to be at work by three-thirty."

"One o'clock is fine."

He was a short man, old enough to be her father, his

hair gray and his suit umber. His desk was one of two behind a glass partition. Celia sat down beside it and waited for his questions.

He wanted to know about Larry.

"When was the last time you saw him?"

Celia frowned. "About a year ago, I guess. Sometime last summer."

"Have you heard from him since then? Phone calls? Letters? Messages passed on by friends?"

She shook her head. "I've been away almost a year."

"And he didn't try to get in touch with you in all that time?"

"He didn't know where I was."

He leaned back in his chair. "You two were pretty close?"

"Fairly close."

"And you left without telling him where you were going?"

"Yes."

"Did you have an argument?"

"No." She cocked her head to one side. "Lieutenant, where is all this leading?"

He spread his hands, palms up. "We just want to know where he is."

"Isn't he in Evanston anymore?"

"Not for the last five months."

Celia hesitated. "Well . . . he has an uncle who might know . . ."

"We've checked out his uncle. And his parents."

She shrugged. "I don't know what to say then. I haven't any idea where he might be. Have you talked to his thesis adviser at Northwestern? Carlson, in the Physics Department."

"He's the one who reported Meyers was missing."

"Oh."

Keeler eased forward to rest his elbows on the desk. "He didn't have a special hideaway, someplace he spent vacations, or someplace he always wanted to go?"

"Not to my knowledge. Honestly, I don't think I can help you, Lieutenant. But if I should think of anything, I'll be sure and call you."

He interlaced his fingers. "We'd like you to call us if you hear from him, too."

"All right."

He stood up, signaling the end of the interview. "Well, thanks for coming down. We appreciate it."

"I'm sorry if I wasn't much help."

He smiled. "Don't worry about that. We'll be in touch if anything comes up." He handed her his office card.

As she left the police station, she could not help feeling sorry for Dr. Carlson, who would never learn the fate of his protégé. She had the nagging suspicion, too, that Keeler somehow knew more than he acknowledged.

On Monday she received the printed confirmation of her enrollment at Northwestern. In the same batch of mail was a request that she see the Assistant Dean of Students at 2 P.M. on Friday—or if that was not convenient, that she call and make another appointment. After consulting her work schedule, she decided the noted time was as good as any. She assumed the meeting would deal with her scholarship application; probably they were going to reject it and offer her a student loan instead. If so, she would have to take it, although she disliked the idea of incurring long-term debt, however reasonable the rates.

When she arrived, she was quickly admitted to the Assistant Dean's inner office, and the Dean—a woman Celia recognized from a Handbook photo—immediately introduced Celia to a thin, middle-aged man who was sitting on a corner of her desk. He had blond wispy hair, pale eyes, and a warm smile that arose unexpectedly from cadaverous cheeks.

"Good afternoon, Celia," he said, standing up and extending his hand to shake hers. "I'm Don Carlson; perhaps Larry Meyers mentioned me to you. I was his research director, and a friend."

Celia stared at him quizzically. "I thought I had an appointment with the Dean."

"I hope you'll forgive that little ruse. I needed a chat with you, and that was the only way I could be sure of getting it."

"What do you want?"

"Any help you can give me. Will you come with me now? Dean Marshall has other uses for her office this afternoon."

"I don't know what I could tell you that I haven't already told the police, Dr. Carlson. I don't know where he is."

"Please," he said. "It's very important."

She sighed. "All right. I have some time."

He opened the door and ushered her out before him. Outside, they walked north, toward the Physics Building.

She said, "How did you know I was back in school?"

"I asked the secretary at Romance Languages to let me know if you reapplied. You were a good student; I thought you might come back eventually."

"A lot of good students drop out."

He shrugged. "Call it grasping at straws, then. Everything else we tried came to a dead end; I had to keep up my hopes somehow."

A certain personal note in his voice awakened her sympathies. "You're really concerned about him, yes? You think . . . something bad happened to him?"

"Larry was one of my best students. Maybe *the* best. About five months ago, he stopped coming into the laboratory. He also stopped answering his telephone and his mail. After a while, I was curious enough to go by his house, but no one answered the door, and I couldn't see any human activity through the windows.

I called his parents then, but they didn't know anything about him. And didn't care to know anything, it seemed."

"I'm aware," said Celia. "They didn't get along at all, not for years."

"And his uncle, too, hadn't heard a thing from him in quite some time. He was willing to go to the house with me and take a look around inside. You understand that by this time I had visions of Larry lying dead in a closet."

Celia started when he said 'closet.' "But he wasn't there."

"No." Carlson glanced sidelong at her. "But we *did* find some fifty thousand dollars' worth of Northwestern University equipment. At that point, I had to call in the police."

"University equipment?" Celia frowned. "Do you mean the gear in the back room?"

He nodded.

"But that was his project. He had permission to requisition those things. *Your* permission."

"That's what he told you?"

"Yes. As I recall."

"Well . . ." He laughed softly, shaking his head. "That didn't include permission to remove them from the lab." The Physics Building loomed before them. "I have a few things to show you, things you really should see. Let's go in this way." He indicated a side door. There was an elevator nearby, and they took it up to the third floor. Carlson unlocked one side of a double door across the corridor. Black-edged lettering on the stationary side read:

MAGNETIC RESONANCE LABORATORY

"Be careful not to bump anything," said Carlson. "It's pretty crowded in here."

The room was long, narrow, lit by tall windows. On

every side were tables and benches loaded with equipment, gray-faced panels and oscilloscopes, bright steel cylinders, plastic pipe assemblies, and snarls of black cords and cables. The clutter looked to Celia like the hasty merger of an air-traffic control room with a plumber's warehouse.

"Over here," said Carlson, edging between two tables. He patted the apparatus that covered one of them—a low bank of switches, dials, and telltales connected to a kind of ringstand with a circular metal grid at the top. "This is Dr. Orlinsky's baby." Squatting, he rummaged through a large cardboard carton beneath the table. "There ought to be some plastic cups in here." He found one and handed it up to Celia. "Would you go out to the fountain and put a small amount of water in this? A couple centimeters will do."

When Celia returned, Carlson took the cup. "Now, watch this," he said, and poured a thin stream onto the grid; with his free hand, he held a cloth wiper beneath the ring, to catch the fluid as it dripped through. Then he carefully blotted the residual moisture from the glittering mesh. "And now . . ." He flicked a series of switches on the bank, and the telltales glowed. He poised the cup over the grid again, and this time he did not employ the towel. He poured out a bit, and the water bounced and sprinkled on the mesh, beading up as if on a highly waxed surface. "Look closely," said Carlson, bending to put his eye on a level with the grid.

Celia followed his example. She saw a fine gap beneath the droplets. They did not touch the mesh at all.

"The field extends three millimeters beyond the mesh," said Carlson. "And it doesn't use a great deal of power. Unfortunately, we haven't been able to expand its effect any farther than that." He thrust the towel below the ring, moved a switch; the water sank through the screen. He shut off the rest of the switches. "We tried various geometries and adjustments, to expand the field, but . . . Well, come over here."

Celia followed him to another part of the room, another table. This time the apparatus was a cage of metal mesh, large enough for a hamster, flanked by two consoles like oversized bookends.

"This is one of the devices that Larry designed." He pushed a single switch, and the telltales lit up. Then he dipped a finger into the cup and flicked a drop of water toward the cage; it passed between the coated wires and wet the tabletop. "It creates a similar electromagnetic field, one with peculiar dynamics, but the Orlinsky effect is not in evidence." He moved the switch back to the *off* position. "Still, something quite odd is going on. There's an unaccountable energy leak in the system. A certain fraction of the input performs no work, generates no heat or light or other detectable radiation. Yet somehow it . . . just disappears. The laws of conservation say it has to go *some*where. We'd like to find out where and how and why." He looked at Celia. "The apparatus in Larry's back room seems to be related to this setup, though on a larger scale. We've measured the field it projects." His gaze was steady on her. "Why do you think he built it at home?"

"Well, it's larger," she said. "Maybe he needed the room."

"That could have been arranged here on campus."

"And the house was more convenient." She didn't like this dialogue; she felt outmaneuvered.

"Oh, no doubt. And secret, too. What did he discover, do you suppose, that made him hide it away from his colleagues?"

She shook her head, feeling somewhat dazed. "I don't know."

Carlson leaned a long arm on one of the consoles.

"Celia, the university isn't interested in taking him to court over this. The equipment appears to be un-damaged and recoverable. We simply want to know what he was doing with it, what his results were. I had everything left as it was in the house—I didn't want to disturb anything until we could talk to him."

And what if they had, thought Celia; *where would I be now?*

"But we've waited quite a while now. The university wants to reclaim its property, and we'd like to see Larry return to his work."

Celia stared at the cage. "He gave me the impression . . . that he wasn't getting anywhere."

"Did he?" His voice was mild. "Dan Orlinsky and I think his large-scale device argues precisely the opposite."

She looked up at him. "You're willing to—as they say—forgive and forget?"

"Under the circumstances, yes."

"But you still have the cops beating the bushes for him."

"We don't know any other way to locate him. Unless *you* can."

A hopeful suspicion crossed her mind. "What you're really saying is that you need him—that you don't know where to go from here."

Carlson seemed taken aback. "No, I don't mean that at all. No question, Larry's cooperation would save us considerable trouble. But we're not working in isolation. Aside from our own data base, there's a group at Cal Tech investigating related phenomena, and another one at Stanford checking our results so far." He paused, folding his arms. "I'd say we should be able to figure out the function of his private setup within the next year, even assuming his office notes are largely spurious. If he's really onto something, though, I think he should be around to share in the credit, don't you?

For what he's done, for what he can do in the future. He was quite a brilliant student, you know."

Celia nodded. "I know."

"Where is he, Celia? You were closer to him than anyone else. You of all people should know where he is."

She frowned. "What makes you so sure?"

He made a sweeping, open-handed gesture. "You disappeared a year ago; according to the police, Larry was the last person to see you. Six months later, *he* disappeared. *Post hoc* reasoning, perhaps, but I have a hunch there's some connection."

"Dr. Carlson . . ."

"Please, Celia; tell me what you know. If you're afraid the university will insist on pressing charges, I can assure you, on my word, that it won't."

Celia turned away from him, gazed around at equipment whose purposes she could not even guess. "This project is so important?"

"Yes."

"And . . . what if Larry never comes back?"

He shrugged. "We'll go on without him, of course."

And I thought the decision was only mine.

The portal loomed in her mind's eye: the glittering pole, the naked bulb, the two consoles flanking the sunken target area. She had thought Larry was working in a vacuum, like some Medieval alchemist in a cellar laboratory. She had considered herself custodian of a mystery, never realizing that few New Worlds had a lone explorer. What had been accomplished once could be repeated. The world of the Invincible Armada existed; therefore, it could be discovered—and rediscovered. Dr. Carlson or his counterparts would see to that. Celia was powerless to stop them all, forever, even if she destroyed the belt, the notes, the house, this university laboratory.

Maybe it was Steam Engine Time. Larry had once told her about that bit of scientific folk-wisdom:

When the steam engine was ready to be invented—or the telephone, or the radio—someone would come along to invent it. Maybe two or three someones. In the world of the conquering Armada, it was never ready, because that world was itself not ready for it, either technically or psychologically. But this Earth of hers was ripe now for Larry's discovery, with or without Larry's participation.

Or hers.

"Dr. Carlson," she said, "Larry is dead."

"What? Dead? You're sure?"

"It's a long story, believe me. But you're right about our disappearances being connected. And I know at least part of the answer you're looking for. There's a belt you'll want to see when you've heard me out. And a notebook."

While she spoke, her mind raced. She had feared government misuse of the portal between worlds. Now she realized she could not prevent that; but she could keep the device from being secluded in some Pentagon laboratory, where only people with security clearances could use it. Carlson would be merely the first to hear her tale. She would be busy these next few days spreading the secret, to newspapers, radio, television, acting before the Government could clamp a lid on the project.

The next few years would be a time of turbulence in the other world. The Twentieth Century would vault in, carried by social scientists investigating a frozen culture, by businessmen seeking profits, by adventurers, sportsmen, ordinary tourists. Governments would vie for markets, resources, and influence; possibly they would realize that more could be gained by peaceful than violent action in the Spanish world. But they would not control the portal—not when universities, corporations, and private individuals alike had access to it. In such widespread availability, Celia hoped, lay San Felipe's chance for independence.

The Twentieth Century would come to the world now ruled by the shade of Philip the Second; it would come with its faults and its virtues, and it would change the face of that world. Celia wondered if this time, on his own ground, Río would be able to accept it. Not that he had much choice.

With all her heart, she wished him luck.

809

Paul Gallico

BEYOND THE POSEIDON ADVENTURE

NOW—ONE STEP BEYOND THE DISASTER
THAT CLAIMED THE POSEIDON!

When the luxury liner Poseidon is capsized by a tidal wave,
only six out of sixteen hundred survive the shipwreck. Rescued by a French naval helicopter, the six are soon returned
at gunpoint to the sinking ship and into a trap of some very
deadly predators.

A Dell Book $2.50

A novel of terror aboard the President's plane, as one desperate man holds the passengers and crew at gun point, high over the skies of America!

"The right ingredients. A top notch yarn." *Pittsburgh Press*

A harrowing flight to the brink of disaster!

AIR FORCE ONE

by Edwin Corley
author of *Sargasso*

A Dell Book $2.50

(10063-1)

DREAM SNAKE

Vonda N. McIntyre

"Rich in character, background and incident—
unusually absorbing and moving."

Publishers Weekly

"This is an exciting future-dream with real
characters, a believable mythos and, what's
more important, an excellent readable story."

Frank Herbert

The *"haunting, rich and tender novel"** of a
unique healer and her strange ordeal.

* Robert Silverberg

A Dell Book $2.25   (11729-1)

The Latest Science Fiction And Fantasy From Dell

815

Cry for the Strangers

John Saul

author of Punish The Sinners

A chilling tale of
psychological terror!

In Clark's Harbor, a beautiful
beach town on the Pacific,
something horrible, violent and
mysteriously evil is happening.
One by one the strangers are dying.
Never the townspeople. Only the
strangers. Has a dark bargain been
struck between the people of
Clark's Harbor and some super-
natural force? Or is the sea
itself calling out for human
sacrifice?